I0522400

# WHISKEY CREEK

FLORIDA CHRONICLES

BOOK 1

CHRISTINE KLING

TELL-TALE PRESS

This book is a work of fiction. Names, places, characters and incidents are the product of the author's imagination, and any resemblance to actual persons, living or dead, events, or locales is entirely coincidental.



Tell-Tale Press
ISBN 978-1-942228-00-4
Visit Christine Kling at
http://www.christinekling.com

Cover Design by 100 Covers

*To Liam*

Those who would give up essential liberty to purchase a little temporary safety deserve neither liberty nor safety.

— BENJAMIN FRANKLIN

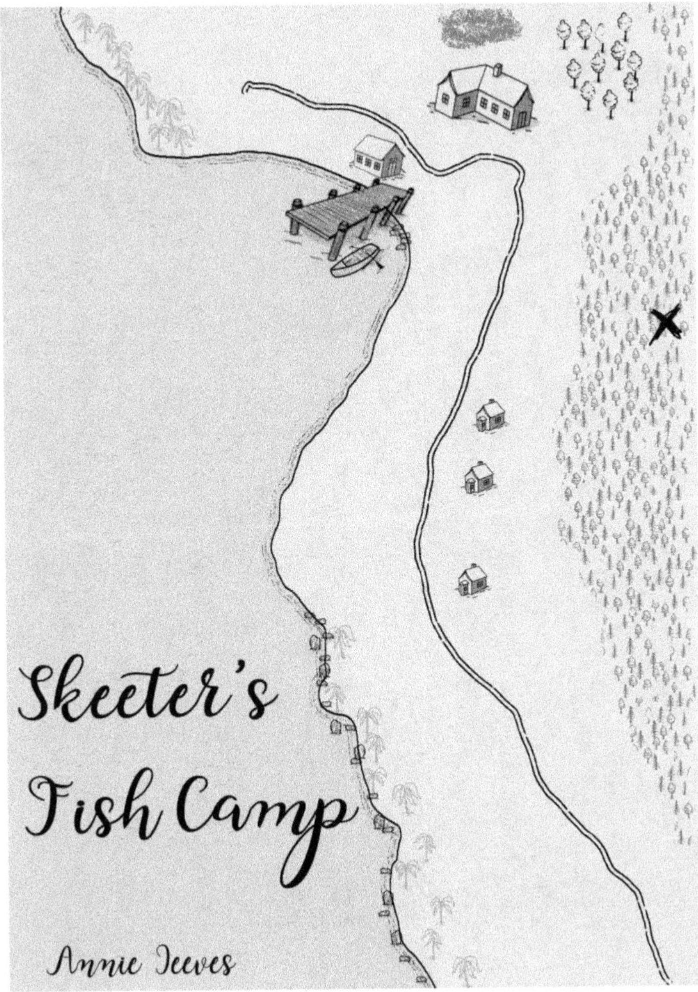
Skeeter's
Fish Camp
Annie Jeeves

# CHAPTER ONE

*Fort Lauderdale*
*December 7, 1941*

Annie Jeeves rested her bare foot on the *Tequesta*'s wheel, steering the wooden sailboat into Port Everglades. Jack and Finn stood on the cabin top furling the mainsail, while their charter guests, a family of three and the son's fiancée, lounged in what little shade the mast offered. The thrum of the diesel engine drowned out their chatter, but Annie guessed it was about the day's catch: two dorado and a hefty wahoo.

Annie returned to the sketchbook balanced on her knee, shading in the figure's shaggy hair. Finn's reddish-brown locks were impossible to capture in pencil. She glanced up at him again and studied the way the strands caught the light. He and her brother were joking as they tied off the last of the sail ties.

Something else in her drawing wasn't quite right. It was the shoulders. She hadn't drawn them broadly enough. Finn was no longer the lanky boy she'd grown up with.

She checked the water ahead, then nudged the helm to starboard to avoid an oncoming fishing boat.

Annie leaned back and sighed. Today had been good; with all the bad news coming from Europe these days, she'd needed a day out on the boat.

"Quite a haul there, folks." Jack adjusted the brim of the white captain's hat he had taken to wearing. He struck a pose, breathing in the fresh air, hands on his hips. "Can't beat December fishing in Florida."

Annie bit her tongue. Since taking over as captain of the *Tequesta*, Jack couldn't resist regaling the customers with his enthusiasm, especially for fishing. Or flying. Or the war brewing overseas.

"Ready to head in, sis?"

"Sure thing."

Finn was strolling down the deck in her direction. She flipped her sketchbook closed, inclined her head towards Jack, then made a gagging face at her brother's theatrics. Finn grinned, stuck out his tongue and made a goofy grimace back at her.

She smiled, feeling her skin flush. But Finn had already turned to coil the mainsheet, leaving her with the unsettling thought that she wanted him to look back.

Jack was still chatting with their guests, pouring on the charm to up their tip.

As she turned the *Tequesta* into the mouth of the New River, the son sidled up next to Jack, eyeing the helm.

"A girl at the wheel, huh? I didn't realize they let women drive ships." His fiancée, her bare shoulders glowing red from the sun, giggled at his side.

Annie flipped her braid back and gripped the wheel. Before she could answer, Jack draped an elbow over her shoulder.

Pointing at her with his thumb, he said, “This isn’t just any girl.”

Good grief, Annie thought. He sounded like a barker at the carnival that came through town last year.

“My sister here is one of the best navigators I’ve ever seen.”

Finn stood on her other side, his arms crossed. “Better than most men I know.”

The charter guests gathered around, including the young man’s father.

“Actually...” Annie couldn’t resist. “I could navigate this river with my eyes closed.”

She remembered the moonless nights helping her father pick up his illicit cargo of Bahamian liquor down at Whiskey Creek. Even as a little girl, she had piloted the *Tequesta* back upriver many times in the pitch-black night.

“Is that so?” The young man turned to his fiancée with a knowing smirk. “You want to make a wager on that?”

Annie narrowed her eyes. “You name it.”

“Five dollars says she can’t do it.”

Jack snorted. “Easiest five bucks I ever made.” He snatched the faded red bandana from his neck and tied it over Annie’s eyes.

“You sure about this?” Finn whispered into her ear. His warm breath on her cheek sent a soft buzz down her neck. She waved him off. No distractions. Five bucks was a week’s worth of groceries. They could not afford to lose this bet.

Easing the throttle forward, she tuned out Finn, the voices of their guests. Just listen to the river. Sense the engine vibrations through the deck and smell the earthy mangrove trees.

“You’re crazy,” Finn said, but she barely heard him.

Annie was busy estimating the boat’s speed based on the engine pitch and calculating the resistance of the outbound tide to determine the probable speed of the *Tequesta*. She mapped the river in her mind, measuring the distance of each stretch of open water, the radius of every curve.

The wind shifted slightly, and she eased the helm. Turning through Tarpon Bend, she felt the pull of the current at the bow pushing her off course any time the *Tequesta* wasn't centered in the channel. She made minute corrections.

Soon, high-pitched voices rang out from starboard, and she knew the Erkins children were running across the lawn at Casa Sonriendo trying to race the boat as it chugged upriver. When the engine noise bounced off the Stranahan house, she cranked the wheel to port. The odor of automobile exhaust meant they were approaching the town.

The tense murmuring among the guests grew, but Annie shut it out, focusing only on the gentle throb of the single-cylinder Lister engine.

When the Andrews bridge traffic rumbled up ahead, she sensed the familiar curve of the riverbank, sketching the old docks in her imagination. With one last turn, the bow swung, and the *Tequesta* slid alongside the wooden pilings to starboard. She slipped her into reverse gear to bring the boat to a stop.

"Unbelievable!" Jack slid the bandana off her head. "Well done, sis!"

The familiar dock was a foot off the beam.

The *Tequesta* bumped against the pilings, and Finn jumped ashore with a dock line in hand.

Jack spun around and faced the young man, palm out. "Pay up!"

With a scowl, the fellow dug a crumpled five-dollar bill from his pocket and thrust it at Jack.

"Keep the fish too." He stomped below, the fiancée in tow.

"You're gonna give me a heart attack one of these days," Finn said.

"Oh hush. When have I ever steered you wrong?"

"Ha! Do you want the list alphabetically or chronologically?"

She laughed and swatted his arm. "You worry too much."

He squinted at her and held off answering a few seconds past comfortable. "Maybe I've got more reason to." When Finn turned away, she took in a deep breath. *What did that mean?*

The father shook Jack's hand. "Mighty impressive." The man nodded to his wife, who handed Jack several bills.

"Captain Jeeves," she said, "you've got quite the navigator here." The wife handed Annie an additional dollar tip.

"Buy yourself something nice, dearie," the father said.

Annie pocketed the bill with a forced smile. "Glad you enjoyed the trip."

After all the guests had disembarked, Jack clapped his sister on the back. "Not bad for a girl, eh?"

She punched his bicep. "Watch it. Anyway, Ma will sure appreciate it. Every dollar counts."

Finn washed down the deck, and Annie put away the fishing poles. Jack gripped the mop handle and leaned against it, the breeze ruffling his hair. "You know, sis, with everything going on in Europe, I wonder if I'm doing right, staying home and all. Plenty of the boys from town have already gone north to enlist in Canada."

"Again with the war talk? Your audience is gone."

"This is important, Annie."

Her airplane-crazy brother had been taking flying lessons lately over at the Merle Fogg airfield any chance he could get—paid for with free fishing trips out on the *Tequesta*.

"Jack, for the hundredth time, I'm not interested in flying and the war's a world away." She tossed a neatly coiled rope into the cockpit locker. "And from what I hear on the radio, America doesn't want to get involved either."

Jack stepped onto the locker and tried to catch her eye. "Look, I know you're sick of hearing about it, but England can't hold out much longer. America's gonna have to step in, and this could change everything for us."

"I don't see how. Fighting some war's gonna get us enough money to get out of this town? All I want is to move back north, reopen Pa's fish camp, and get back to life the way it was before the crash."

"Annie, that's just it," Jack said. "If I join the Navy, I can make a real difference. I can fight for the good guys and protect our way of life here in Florida."

"Or... get yourself killed," Finn said, grabbing the mop. Her brother nearly fell over.

~

When they had finished cleaning the boat, Jack locked up the cabin and the three of them began the walk westward towards Sailboat Bend. Jack was quiet for once, and Annie avoided making eye contact with Finn. It was still early afternoon, and the sidewalks were crowded. Finn carried the fish wrapped in newspaper, leading the way through the housewives, school kids and businessmen who were going in and out of the stores.

At the corner of Coontie Court, Finn handed Annie the fish and peeled off with a wave. "See you tomorrow."

"Hey!" she yelled. Finn turned, and Annie tossed him one of the wrapped fish. "For you and your sister."

Finn gave her a salute.

"Bright and early," Jack yelled. He looked back at Annie. "Charters two days in a row. Busy times with all these soldiers in town."

"I'm working at The Deck tomorrow."

"Finn and I can manage without you."

She pulled back her fist, but her brother skipped ahead, his index finger in the air while singing, *"He's the Boogie Woogie Bugle Boy of Company B!"*

"You're a goofball!" she called out, running after him.

They turned onto the shell drive that led to the family's rented cottage. Their pa, Skeeter Jeeves hunched under the hood of his '34 Chevy Master Deluxe. Tess, the family's Springer Spaniel, lay under the front bumper, thumping her tail on the dirt.

"Hey, Pops." Jack leaned under the hood.

Skeeter looked up from the engine compartment, the brim of his flat cap stained with grease

"How's the ol' Fumblebee?" Jack had nicknamed the car.

Pa shrugged. "Just needs a tune-up."

Jack leaned against the fender. "That's what you've been saying since July, Pops."

"Need any help?" Annie asked, peering over her father's shoulder at the tangle of wires and metal.

"Got it under control, sweetheart." Just after he spoke, a sharp zap filled the air, followed by a pungent odor and a string of curse words. Tess darted out from under the car and stood whining at the kitchen door. Her father pulled his head out from under the hood and raised one eyebrow. "Why don't you go see if your mother needs a hand?"

~

The screen door slammed behind her as Annie followed the dog into the kitchen. Hilda Jeeves, her graying hair pinned up in a bun, stood at the stove. Her lips moved silently as she kept time with the music on the radio. The smell of freshly baked cornbread wafted through the air, mixing with the scent of simmering vegetables and turkey. Annie glanced at the nearly bare carcass, wondering if they'd ever see the end of it.

"Hi, Mama." She leaned in to kiss her mother's cheek. "We brought home some fish."

"I won't say no to that."

Annie smiled at what passed for an affectionate welcome from her mother. After she found room for the wrapped fish in the icebox, she asked, "What can I do to help?"

"Grab that knife and dice those onions." Her mother nodded toward the cutting board. "So how was your charter?"

"Interesting. We made a bet with one of the guests. Won some extra money."

"Really?" Her mother's eyebrows shot up.

Seemed like ever since they came close to losing the family homestead up in Edgewater, money was the only thing her mother cared about.

Annie told the story of the blindfolded challenge as she worked.

"You showed him what girls can do."

"I'm not a girl anymore." Annie moved to the sink to wash her hands.

"You still dress like one in them overalls."

Annie shrugged. "Maybe someday people won't be surprised when a woman knows how to read a chart or handle a boat." She glanced toward the screen door. "Or fix an engine."

"Twenty years old is still a child to me."

"Old enough for young men to go to fight in a war." Annie lopped the ends off a carrot with two loud whacks.

"You're not a man, and the world ain't gonna change overnight."

"Sometimes seems like it's trying to, only not the way I want it to."

The back door banged open, and Jack stumbled in, hair mussed, shirt untucked. He sniffed the air.

"Lord have mercy, are we still eating Thanksgiving leftovers?"

"Quit your bellyaching." Mama swatted him with her dishtowel. "There are children starving in Europe."

"Yes, ma'am," Jack said.

"Pfft. Now you go wash up. Dinner will be ready soon."

"Yes, ma'am." Then he pulled a piece of meat off the carcass and popped it into his mouth.

Annie looked at her brother and mouthed the word, *idiot*.

Soon after, her father came through the screen door and headed back to join Jack in the bathroom. Annie could hear her brother's voice echoing down the hallway, punctuated by their father's rumbling laughter. She shook her head, knowing her brother was probably entertaining their father with his own colorful account of their latest charter.

"Ma," Annie said, "I swear, it's like he can't get enough of talking about the war."

Her mother grunted as she continued setting the dining table. "You know your brother; he's always been passionate about things."

As if on cue, Jack bounded into the kitchen alongside their father. The family moved to take their chairs. Pa hung his cap on the peg above the radio, then took his place at the head of the table. Tess settled under Jack's chair.

Her mother set down the bubbling casserole, followed by a plate of golden squares of cornbread.

The conversation flowed easily. The men discussed the Chevrolet's repairs, while her mother, who worked as a nurse at the local hospital, told a grisly story about a mishap with a severed thumb which Jack and Pa somehow found hilarious.

The radio droned in the background, tuned to a variety

show. But then the music cut out abruptly. The announcer stated:

*"Stand by for a special news flash."*

"Hey, turn that up." Jack waved his fork at the radio.

Pa reached back and fiddled with the knob. The radio announcer's urgent voice filled the room.

*"We interrupt this broadcast for an urgent news bulletin. Japanese forces have launched an aerial attack on the American naval base at Pearl Harbor, Hawaii..."*

# CHAPTER TWO

*Fort Lauderdale*
*December 17, 1941*

Annie hummed along to the tune of Guy Lombardo's *Winter Wonderland* floating from the Philco radio as she strung garland inside the windows of The Deck restaurant. She tugged in irritation at the sailorette uniform she had to wear to work. The hem was riding up every time she lifted her arms. Normally, she loved putting up holiday decorations, but this morning her mood was more annoyed than festive.

Outside, boats bustled up and down the New River ferrying supplies from the port or train station up to the dry dock at Dooley's Basin. In the past week and a half since America had declared war against both Japan and Germany, her town was changing so fast she sometimes felt as lost as Dorothy in the Land of Oz. The papers said the government had already earmarked Fort Lauderdale as a strategic base for both air and sea. Annie sighed and pushed back some loose hair, leaving a smudge of glitter on her cheek.

The kitchen door swung open a crack, and Annie recognized the long dark fingers that wrapped around the door's edge.

"What's up, Emma?"

"Annie, Mama says to remind you that the lunch rush'll be starting soon. Are you about done there?" The fingers tapped impatiently against the wooden panel.

"Just about." Annie climbed down from the chair. "You know there's nobody out here but me. You could just come on out into the dining room."

The fingers disappeared, and the door swung shut. Annie would have to go back into the kitchen to see her best friend's face. Their boss had rules about the kitchen staff entering the dining room, and Emma was a rule follower.

Annie didn't want the war changing things, but nobody was asking her. The signs of upheaval were everywhere she looked, like the garish recruiting poster someone had hung by the front door.

She plugged in the cord, and the colorful bulbs lit up around the window. Annie had to smile when she turned around to inspect the cypress-paneled bar and dining room. The Skipper, as she was required to call her boss, would be happy.

Back in the kitchen, the air was hot and humid. Cora Albury, Emma's mother, stood over the stove, using a fork to lower chicken legs into bubbling Crisco. Dressed in her usual chef's whites, the tall black woman wore her hair wrapped in a colorful cloth while a hint of lipstick highlighted her mouth.

Cora looked up as Annie entered. "This war's got everybody in a tizzy. We're busier than a centipede in a toe-counting contest."

Annie laughed. Wouldn't you know it, Miss Cora could bust her mood. "Seems like the world's turned upside down overnight."

Emma didn't look up from her work. Though she wore an

apron over her dress, Annie thought her friend always looked effortlessly elegant with her long neck and skin the color of maple syrup.

"Town's already changing," Emma said. "Granddad Elzo says the shipyard's fixin' to expand soon. All a sudden, there's more jobs than people to fill them, and they're hiring more black folks."

"Feels like everything's changing," Annie said.

"Change isn't always bad, though." Emma wiped her hands on her apron. "Maybe things'll get better for some of us after this is over."

"Or worse," Annie said, picturing Jack flying through a hail of bullets like she'd seen on the newsreels at the movie theater. "I don't want my family or friends getting caught up in this mess."

"Can't avoid it, sugar," Miss Cora said, shaking her head. "Like my Daddy always says, war's got a way of reaching everyone, one way or another."

Annie was back in the dining room filling the last saltshaker when the front door swung open, and Finn breezed in. Behind him trailed his little sister Bethany, clinging to his hand.

"Annie, am I ever glad to see you," Finn said.

She wanted to tell him she felt the same way, even if it wasn't for the same reason.

"Old lady Dinwiddie's down sick, and I got called in to work. Any chance you can keep an eye on the sprout here for a few hours?"

The girl wrinkled her nose. "I can take care of myself, you know. I'm not a baby."

"I get it, squirt." Finn squatted down to face his sister. "But the shipyard's no place for a kid. Annie here will take good care of you."

"And I'd be happy to, Bean," Annie said, using the girl's

nickname. "We girls will find some fun while the men are off playing war."

Bean's face lit up, while Finn looked relieved.

"Thanks, Annie, you're a lifesaver," he said. "They need all hands on deck to work on this new sub chaser we're building. It's a real monster, 110 feet long. I'll be welding all day."

Annie made a sweeping motion with her fingers. "Then go on, get to work."

"I owe you one," Finn said. He mussed Bean's red hair and dashed for the door.

"And I intend to collect!" Annie called out as the door closed.

She reached a hand out to the girl. "Well, Miss, want me to show you around?"

When they entered through the swing doors, Cora turned from the stove and appraised the newcomer. "What have we got here?"

"Miss Cora, this is Bethany, Finn's sister."

"Call me Bean," the ten-year-old piped up. "Everyone else does."

Cora tapped her lips with a finger while sizing up the scrawny girl in overalls. "You got your brother's hair, all right. He ever feed you? You look like a string bean, Miss Bean."

Annie waited while Miss Cora filled a plate for the girl. Bean stood at her side, peering around the kitchen, taking in the pots bubbling on the stove and the stack of dirty pans in the sink.

"Say, you need any help around here? I'm real good at kitchen stuff."

Annie laughed. "You sound just like your brother. Here sweetie," she set the plate on the counter. "Go on and eat your lunch now."

Bean grabbed an apron off a hook and held it upside down with a puzzled expression on her face. "Just try me. I can peel potatoes, chop vegetables, even pluck a chicken. My mama taught me everything she knew before she died. So put me to work!"

Miss Cora glanced at Annie before taking the apron from the girl. "Sure thing, sweetheart." She tied the apron on Bean, who looked impossibly small in the loose fabric. "Why don't you start by snapping those beans for me?"

Emma set a bowl of green beans on the counter next to the girl's lunch, then slid over a stool. "Climb up here. You can work while you eat."

Annie smiled at Emma as she wrote down the specials on the chalkboard.

"Don't worry about her," Emma said.

"Ha! I think I'm more worried about the two of you. She's a force of nature that one."

Annie pushed backwards through the swing doors carrying the chalkboard.

When she spun around, her boss, Fred Beck was standing at the podium by the front door wearing his jacket complete with shoulder epaulettes and his gold braided captain's hat. After she set the chalkboard down by the waitress station, she grabbed her own round white sailor's cap. She swept her hat onto her head and secured it with a couple of bobby pins.

The clock over the front desk read eleven thirty. Right on time. Let the lunch shift begin.

As Mr. Beck ushered the first customers to a table in the back of the dining room, he caught her eye, and she gave him a little salute. She thought it odd to seat them in the back when there were plenty of window tables, but she pulled her notepad out of her pocket and walked over to their table.

"Afternoon, folks. Welcome to The Deck." The couple looked up from their menus. Annie noticed their clothes were nice quality but rumpled like they'd been sleeping in them. The gentleman stroked his thick beard, while his wife had tears in her eyes. "Ma'am, are you okay?"

The man looked around the dining room before he spoke. "Please excuse my wife. She is very upset."

"I'm sorry. Can I help?"

"I don't think so. It's about our lodging. We just arrived this morning on the train from New York. You see, our son's been stationed here in the Navy. He's working to secure the port."

His wife reached across the table and grasped his hand. "We were so thrilled to come see him," she said, "and to hear of his important work. But..." Her face fell. "The hotel where we booked a room, they claimed no record of our reservation. They had a sign by the door, *'We cater to a restricted clientele'* and, well..."

Annie had seen the sign they referred to, but she hadn't thought much about it. Now she was pretty sure why the couple had been rejected.

From the corner of her eye, Annie saw her boss striding toward her. She could tell from his face that he wasn't pleased with her talking to the couple. She greeted him with a forced smile. "Hello, Skipper."

"Annie, I didn't hire you to chit-chat with the customers," he said. "Take their order and take it to the cook in the galley. These other tables are waiting."

"Of course, Skipper." She flashed him a smile and lifted her notepad and pen.

When she returned with their food, she saw Beck was busy at the front desk talking to Sheriff Clark who had arrived for his usual lunch. Seizing the opportunity, she grabbed one of the paper placemats on the table and flipped it over. She quickly sketched a rough map of the streets of downtown.

Annie leaned in closer to the couple and whispered,

"We're here." She circled a rectangle and wrote 'The Deck' in block letters. "This here is the Temple Emanu-El. I'm pretty sure Rabbi Friedman would be happy to put you up for the night or help you find another place to stay, maybe down in Dania. Everybody in town here's not like my boss and the folks at that hotel."

Annie headed back to the kitchen, weaving between packed tables. The lunch rush was in full swing, with tourists and locals alike piling in. The clatter of dishes and hum of conversation filled the dining room.

She delivered orders in her swift, graceful way, grilled cheese to the fishermen's table, club sandwiches to the well-dressed gals from up north, cheeseburgers to the rowdy boys home on leave.

When she stepped back into the dining room carrying four plates of fried catfish, she saw that Sheriff Clark was seated at his usual table, with the Skipper just across from him.

After she delivered the food, Annie approached their table, pad and pencil in hand. "Afternoon, Sheriff Clark. What would you like for lunch today?"

"Let's see, how's about some of Miss Cora's meatloaf and a cup of Joe." The Sheriff was looking at her as he talked, but not at anything above her neck. He then turned and continued his conversation with Fred Beck as though she were invisible. "Been a hell of a week, what with all these new recruits flooding into town. I tell ya, too many of them Yankees coming down here, stirring up trouble with the locals."

Annie moved to the next table and began stacking the dirty dishes, but their conversation continued.

"Now Walt, it's good for business," Mr. Beck said. "We're happy to serve anyone defending our great country."

She caught a glimpse of the two men as she leaned over

the table to grab the last dirty spoon. Clark was staring at her behind. She straightened and tugged at her skirt before collecting the pile of dishes.

The Sheriff grunted. "Long as they respect how things are done around here. Had to crack some heads down over on Sixth Street the other night. Teach those uppity boys a lesson when they step outta line. Some of our outtatowners didn't approve. I don't need no Yankees telling me how to run my town."

~

Finally, the lunch rush began to subside, allowing Annie a moment to catch her breath. She made her way back into the kitchen and found Emma and her mother cleaning up from the hectic lunch service. Bean was perched on her stool, peeling potatoes with impressive skill for her age.

Annie walked to the screen door that led to the alley out back. She hoped to feel a little cooling breeze. Emma followed her and handed her a glass of water.

"What a difference a war makes," Annie said.

Emma nodded, her dark eyes serious. "It's bringing all sorts of people here. Not all of 'em good, neither."

"We've got enough of our homegrown bad apples. Like that Sheriff Clark." Annie sighed. "I sure don't like the way he looks at some of our customers or you, Emma, when he thinks no one's watching."

"That man's nothing but trouble," Emma waved her hand in the air like she was swatting a fly. "Mama told me he roughed up some fellas on our street the other night. Claiming they were 'out of line.'"

Annie shook her head. "Can't wait for the day someone finally stands up to that man."

"I don't think things are changing *that fast*," Emma said.

Miss Cora walked back and put her hand on her daughter's shoulder. "Day's not over yet, girls. Time to get back to work. That little ball of fire over there is putting you two to shame."

Emma and Annie exchanged a look. *Back to the grind.*

An hour later, Annie pushed through the swing doors into the mercifully cooler kitchen. Miss Cora looked up from the sink where she was washing a big stock pot and smiled.

Annie grabbed a clean apron from a hook and tied it on. "Whew, I thought those last customers would never leave! Skipper just herded them out the door and locked it behind them."

She joined Emma at the prep station and began chopping carrots and potatoes for the evening's soup special. Emma's mother moved to the stove, her voice softly humming what sounded like a hymn. Not that Annie could be sure since her family never went to church.

Little Bean was perched on a stool in the corner, deeply engrossed in a book that looked like it belonged to Emma. Every so often she would pop a slice of apple in her mouth from the snack Emma had given her earlier.

"I am beat!" Annie fanned herself with a dish towel.

Emma didn't glance up from her cutting board. "You say that every day, Annie."

"Well, today I mean it."

Miss Cora clucked her tongue. "It's that war bringing all sorts of riff-raff to town. Mark my words, it's trouble."

Annie and Emma exchanged a look. They both knew trouble had a lot of faces, and not all of them were wearing uniforms.

Trying to shift the mood, Annie said, "You'll never guess what I'm looking forward to? Getting back home to my family's Fish Camp. Jack and I had it great growing up there. Watching the sun rising over the Mosquito Lagoon whilst a flock of pelicans were diving on a school of snapper. Remember when you and your Gramps came up to visit Woody? We gotta go back together one day."

Emma raised an eyebrow but kept chopping. "Travel takes money."

"Everything takes money."

Emma pointed her paring knife at her. "You should study mapmaking. You've got a gift."

Annie gazed up at the ceiling for a moment, then smiled. "Hmmm. Can you imagine making maps of places that never had any?"

Emma tilted her head, a faint smile touching her lips. "You always make it sound like magic. Like drawing's a way into a brand-new world."

"Yeah, well. That's probably all it is." She fluttered her fingers through the air. "Just dreams and magic and make-believe."

Emma frowned. "Don't say that."

"What about you, Emma? What do you want to do after all this?"

"Me?" Emma's hands grew still over the potatoes. She glanced toward her mother, then looked back down. "College," she whispered. "Mathematics, physics. Maybe even astronomy."

She paused, then added, "Annie, I got this ache sometimes, right here." She touched her chest with the flat of her hand. "Feels like I was meant for something more than peeling potatoes in this kitchen."

"Emma, it's a fact. You're scary smart."

"Thanks, Annie." Emma shrugged. "It's just a dream, but maybe someday."

"Hey, imagine us, dreams come true and taking the world by storm!"

Emma laughed. "Or more like a strong breeze." Then she

looked at Annie. “But it’s a good thought.” She looked back down at the pile of potatoes. “How’s Jack? He still talking about joining up?”

Annie pulled the sailor’s hat off her head and slapped it onto the counter. “It’s all he can talk about! I swear that boy has airplanes on the brain. Day and night.” Her expression softened. “He’s alright, though. Worrying me to death, as usual.”

Emma’s lips curved. She didn’t ask more, but Annie caught the shift in her posture.

“So, have you talked to Jack lately?”

“Annie!” Emma turned away, feigning annoyance. “Why would I be talking to your brother?”

“Ah-ha!” Annie laughed.

“Emma!” Miss Cora’s voice sliced through the kitchen clatter. “Stop talkin’ about that boy and finish those potatoes! You got more sense than to waste your time on somethin’ that ain’t never gonna be.”

Annie bit her lip, regretting her teasing.

“Sorry, Mama.”

Emma turned back to her work, but Annie saw the hurt in her eyes.

# CHAPTER THREE

*Berlin, Germany*
*December 18, 1941*

Wilhelm Hersey hurried along the wet cobblestones toward Berlin's government district. The biting wind cut through his threadbare coat. He remembered the year he'd first arrived in Germany as a boy; this same air would have been thick with the Christmas scent of roasting chestnuts and the sharp spice of *Lebkuchen*. Now, it carried only the acrid smell of coal smoke and wet wool.

He passed a queue of women standing outside a bakery, their faces drawn and tired beneath their headscarves, fingers clutching their ration cards. Static-filled martial music blared from a speaker on the corner. A sign on the bakery door announced in bold letters: "No bread until noon." One woman in line muttered under her breath. Will couldn't make out the words, but the fear in her eyes when another woman glared over her shoulder told him enough. Who needs the police when greed can turn citizens into informants.

He detoured around Potsdamer Platz where a November

raid had left two buildings as burned shells, their windows staring blindly at the street. Now, many storefronts displayed large posters of the Führer gazing sternly at passersby. "*Ein Volk, Ein Reich, Ein Führer*" proclaimed the red and black banners that seemed to hang from every available surface.

Will stopped at a cigarette vendor's kiosk. "*Ein päckchen Eckstein, bitte.*"

He was fishing in his pocket for coins when he heard voices shouting harsh German commands. He glanced over and saw them: a family being herded by two military officers down the sidewalk toward him. The yellow stars, hand-sewn to their coats, stood out starkly against the gray morning. The woman clutched her daughter's hand.

"Every day now," the vendor muttered, sliding the cigarette packet across the counter. "Those people. Good riddance, I say. More rations for the rest of us."

Will's jaw tightened. He said nothing, counting out the coins with clumsy fingers.

The little girl—she couldn't have been more than five—stumbled as the SS officer shoved her mother forward. A rag doll slipped from her arms and tumbled across the cobblestones, coming to a stop by Will's feet. The child's pleading eyes found his.

Will bent down, reaching for the doll.

"*Schneller*!" the soldier barked. "Faster! Move!"

Will froze. The child looked back over her shoulder as her mother pulled her forward. The doll lay there on the cold stones, its button eyes staring up at him.

He straightened slowly, turned his back, and swept the cigarettes off the counter. He strode off in the opposite direction, trying to control his breathing and still his pulse.

He'd heard whispers about what happened to those sent East. Labor camps, ghettos, resettlement. The words were vague, but the fear on Jewish faces was clear. Whatever awaited this family, he was certain they would not return to their apartment. Acid climbed up the back of his throat. Thinking led to questions, and questions led to danger. Besides, what could one person do?

A poster on a neighborhood bulletin board caught his eye: "*Melde Feindhörer*!" Report enemy radio listeners, it demanded with an illustration of a sinister ear pressed to a radio. Will unconsciously touched his trouser pocket where he kept the key to his room. Inside that room, in a box under the floorboards, was a small crystal radio set he used at night, his secret lifeline to BBC broadcasts. That tiny act of rebellion was all he allowed himself.

The Reich Ministry of Public Enlightenment and Propaganda occupied a commanding position on Wilhelmplatz, its stone facade unmarked by bombs. The RAF appeared to aim for the factories, not the government quarter. Yet. Will pulled his identification papers from his coat pocket, preparing to show them to the guards, and stepped into line behind the other functionaries who worked in the building.

Another day of crafting lies, he thought. Another day he would avoid being conscripted into the military.

Wilhelm sat at his desk in the cramped office on the third floor. Four metal desks were crammed into a space meant for one, leaving barely enough room for the door to open. He shifted in his chair, the hard wood pressing into his back as he hunched over his typewriter.

He squinted over at the pamphlet resting on his desk. The bold black German script almost mocked him. Another ridiculous propaganda piece he was meant to translate into English for broadcasting across the Atlantic. Will shook his head. One week after Germany declared war on America, and already the propaganda machine was in full gear.

There had been a time when writing was a joy for him. An escape. The stories seemed to flow from his pen to the page as if by magic. The odd boy from America who didn't fit in, who had no friends among the local boys, but rather lived adventures through the pages of his books and stories. The Reich had stolen that joy of writing. Reading remained an escape from the hardships, but it had been years since he had written a word of his own.

He was sick of this job, of peddling lies for Goebbels and his cronies. Did they really think the Brits or the Americans would swallow this blather as the Nazis trumpeted the superiority of the Aryan race and the inevitability of Germany's victory? He longed to crumple up the paper and hurl it out the window, but he knew the consequences for such defiance would be severe.

Better to keep his head down, he reminded himself. Avoid attention. At least here behind a typewriter he wasn't having to dodge bullets. Still, the words tasted bitter as he translated them. "The righteous might of the German army will crush the corrupt democracies of the West," he muttered as he hunted and pecked at the keys. He raked his fingers through his hair. Corrupt? He longed for the West he had known as a child, growing up in Indiana. Fishing with his father at the lake. Playing hide and seek in the cornfields. The boys he had known there had been nothing like the German bullies he'd faced when his mother brought him "home" to Germany.

He rolled the half-finished page out of the typewriter, tossed it into the trash, and grabbed his coat. Will desperately needed to clear the stale taste of propaganda from his mouth. He headed for the stairwell. The wind cut through his clothing as he stepped outside, and the icy air made his throat and lungs ache. He checked his watch in the fading afternoon light. Only 1600 hours, and already the streetlights were on at the end of the narrow alley.

Another long, frigid night alone in his tiny flat awaited after he finished his shift. Some stale bread and sauerkraut for dinner, a bit of reading before falling into his lumpy single bed. It was the same monotonous routine day after dreary day. Yet wasn't this better than being sent to some godforsaken outpost on the Russian front? At least, that was what he kept telling himself.

Once outside, his fingers were numb from the cold as he pulled the pack of cigarettes from his pocket. Fumbling with the lighter, he finally managed to coax a flame. The first drag warmed him from within.

"Got another one of those for a friend?" came a voice behind him. Will turned to see his co-worker Franz stamping his feet on the icy bricks. Will held out the crumpled pack wordlessly. The two young men leaned against the soot-stained wall of the building, smoking in silence as dusk settled over the city.

"Some weather we're having." Franz exhaled a plume into the frigid air.

Will grunted in reply. He and Franz had developed an uneasy camaraderie borne of proximity and circumstance rather than any shared beliefs. Franz parroted the Party's propaganda with gusto while Will questioned how long he could keep doing this. Still, in an odd way, he envied the other man's unwavering conviction. All Will felt these days was doubt gnawing at his conscience.

He drew the last bittersweet fumes from his cigarette before grinding it beneath his heel. "I could certainly use a break from these long days," he said. "Do you think we'll get holiday leave?"

Franz swiveled his head from one side to the other. "Watch what you say, Wilhelm." He spoke in a hushed voice. "We are fortunate to have the jobs we have." Then louder, he said, "I would like to spend Christmas with my sister's family in Dortmund, but that is not for me to say. Our boys out there fighting can't go home, so neither should we."

Will nodded, picturing his own home in Wiesbaden, the rambling cottage behind the big farmhouse, the woods where he had played alone when he had first arrived from America. He wondered if his mother was decorating the family Christmas tree at this very moment, hanging the familiar ornaments as she had done each year no matter where they lived.

"How does an uneducated oaf like you write such perfect English, anyway?" Franz asked.

Will shrugged, taking the crumpled pack back from Franz to shake out another cigarette for himself. "My father was American. I was born there. We lived outside Chicago until I was eleven. I spoke as much English as German growing up."

"An American father?" Franz's eyes widened in surprise. Will wondered if his reaction was genuine or an act.

"Yes, it's no secret. That is why they hired me."

"And here I thought you were German through and through," Franz said.

Will chose to disregard Franz's slight. It was nothing new. He remembered the late-night knock at the door, his mother's anguished cry when she saw the police lieutenant standing there, hat in hand. "My father was an American policeman. Killed in the line of duty."

"*Mein Gott*. I'm sorry, Wilhelm." Franz looked away. "It was good of your mother to bring you back home to the Fatherland after that."

Will lit his cigarette. "Yes, but we were destitute until my grandparents took us in. Even then, I was the foreign boy, the American. Kids can be cruel."

"But you showed them, didn't you? You're German now, a true patriot," Franz said as he clapped Wilhelm on the back.

Will attempted to smile at Franz. *If only it were that simple.* He shivered, ready to seek the warmth of indoors.

The muffled sound of the heavy back door opening gave

him pause. Two men emerged, a flashlight beam playing over the alley walls and patches of dirty snow on the ground. The men wore long wool overcoats much like his own, but Will noticed their boots were not the standard issue. Polished black leather gleamed even in the fading light. His breath quickened as he saw the twin lightning bolts insignia on their collars, the mark of the *Schutzstaffel*. What was the SS doing here?

The taller of the two men swung the flashlight in their direction. "You there. Are either of you Wilhelm Hersey?" he called out.

Will turned to glance at Franz. The man's eyes remained focused on his own feet.

"I'm Wilhelm Hersey," he said, proud his voice didn't quaver. The taller SS officer gave a curt nod for him to come along. With a worried glance back at Franz, Will flicked his unfinished cigarette onto the snow and followed.

The pace was brisk as the imposing officer led him back inside and down a dim rear hallway Will had never explored. The light's beam reflected off polished marble floors, leading him deeper into the cavernous building. Questions swirled. Maybe this was about some mistake in his work? No, the propaganda ministry didn't warrant attention from the SS. Dread settled in his stomach. What had he done to bring the SS to his door?

At the end of a long corridor, the officer halted, opened an unmarked wooden door and motioned Will inside. He blinked in the dim light of a spartan conference room as the burly SS officer shut the door behind him.

A man sat at the far end of the long table beneath the circle of light cast by the sole overhead light fixture. Dressed in a neat gray suit, his spectacles caught the lamp-light. He set down the papers he had been perusing and gestured for Will to take a seat. Up close, he looked to be a man in his mid-fifties, his hair salt-and-pepper, his gaze steely.

"Herr Hersey, please sit. I am Oberst Hoffman of the Abwehr. We have an important matter to discuss."

Will lowered himself onto the hard wooden chair. The Abwehr. Military intelligence. He swallowed as he felt the bile crawling up his throat.

For a long minute, the officer did not speak. The man read through several sheets of paper on the table in front of him.

Will tried to slow his breathing. He didn't know what was expected of him. Should he speak first? He could hear the noise of his own breath flowing hyperfast through his nostrils, and he wondered if the Oberst Hoffman could hear it, too.

"We live in desperate times, Herr Hersey," the man said, looking up at last. "The future of the Reich hangs in the balance."

Wilhelm nodded.

"I understand you are an American citizen, born and raised."

"Yes, sir. My father was American, but my mother is German. I am now a German citizen."

"Are you a loyal German or are your loyalties...divided?" Oberst Hoffman stared at him over the top of his spectacles with an intensity that made Will want to sink below the table.

"My grandfather was one of the first to join the Party in my hometown. He made sure I joined the Hitler Youth as a young boy. *Deutschland über alles*," he said. "Germany, above all others." All the propaganda he'd written these past years ought to be good for something, Will thought as he tried to calm his heart. ""I swear to you, sir, my loyalty is to the Führer alone."

"Good." Oberst Hoffman nodded. "The Abwehr needs men we can trust, men with special skills and connections. Loyal citizens willing to serve their country in her time of need." His stare bored into Wilhelm.

"But Colonel," Will stammered. "I am just a civilian, a low-level translator in the propaganda ministry."

"But you spent your childhood in America. So, you are fluent in English, yes?"

"Well, yes, but—" Will's mouth had gone dry, his palms slick with nervous sweat now.

"Do you still have connections in America? Family, perhaps?"

Will hesitated. "My father had cousins in Chicago," he said finally. "But we haven't corresponded since the war began."

"I don't exaggerate when I say the fate of the Reich rests on men like yourself, Herr Hersey. Men willing to rise when called to serve a greater purpose." He slid an official-looking document across the table along with an elegant fountain pen. "I can't disclose operational details until you sign this oath of loyalty and secrecy. So, what's it to be? Your country is calling. Shall we begin your briefing?"

Will stared down at the document, the colonel's challenge hanging in the air between them. He reached for the pen. He had no choice.

# CHAPTER FOUR

*Fort Lauderdale, Florida*
*December 25, 1941*

Annie scrubbed the large pot, the sudsy water nearly up to her elbows. Her brother reached into the sink and flicked up a handful of soap bubbles, splattering her face and hair.

"Hey!" Annie turned, attempting to wipe her eyes on her sleeve. Jack was hiding behind Finn who held up a dish towel like a flag of surrender. Pressing his lips together to keep from laughing, Finn reached out and wiped the suds off her cheek.

Without a word, Annie handed the pot to him and turned back to the sink.

"Bah humbug to you, too," Jack said.

Ever since Finn's mother had passed, leaving him and his sister orphans, the two of them had been included at Christmas dinner at the Jeeves' house. Starting back when they all still lived up north at Skeeter's Fish Camp in Edgewater and continuing when Finn and Bean had followed the Jeeves family's move to Fort Lauderdale.

Annie felt her brother's hand on her shoulder, then he leaned in between her and Finn.

"Alright then, I've had about enough holiday family time. How do we make a break for it?" Jack whispered.

Finn's eyes narrowed in the way he had that made her insides get all fluttery. "To the beach for the afternoon?" he asked.

Jack nodded. "We really should take the launch out." He took the pot from Finn and crossed the kitchen to place it in the cupboard. "We haven't run the outboard in a while. It needs the exercise."

Tess whined from her spot next to the stove, and Jack reached down and scratched the white fur between her mahogany-colored ears. "Sorry, girl. Not today."

"I want to go!" Bean chimed in, nearly dropping an armful of silverware into the rinse water.

"No room on the boat for you either, runt," Jack said.

Annie pulled the stopper from the sink and dried her hands on a towel. The boat did carry four, but Annie had a pretty good idea who Jack wanted as their fourth.

She squatted to look Bean in the eye. "Hey, don't worry, kiddo. You can stay here and take care of Tess for me. Besides, Mama promised to teach you to knit this afternoon, remember? She's so excited."

Bean nodded. Mama Hilda's undivided attention was hard to turn down.

Jack hung his towel on the front of the stove. "I'll go ask Ma and Pa if we can take the boat. Do you wanna go get..." Jack lifted his eyebrows and inclined his head.

Annie nodded.

"Meet us at the dock in twenty minutes?"

While the boys jogged down the sandy lane toward the town docks, Annie hurried north clutching her straw hat with one hand, a brown paper bag in the other. Once she crossed the boulevard, the houses grew smaller. Emma's little house wasn't much more than a shack, but aside from the big tin tub up on bricks over a fire pit where Miss Cora washed laundry for money, the yard was neat and tidy. Annie rapped her knuckles against the weathered wooden doorframe.

Emma's grampa, Elzo Walker, pulled open the door. Annie knew him well since he had worked as a janitor at the high school she'd attended when her family first moved down from Edgewater. He was dressed in dark slacks and a crisply ironed white shirt. "Merry Christmas, Miss Annie. Come inside."

"Thank you, Mr. Walker. I hope I'm not disturbing you all on Christmas Day."

"You're welcome here anytime, young lady."

Emma's mother was standing at the sink. Her paisley print dress with matching head wrap showcased both her skill at sewing and her stunning figure. The air smelled of fried fish and grits. A small Christmas tree decorated with seashells hanging from strings stood in the corner.

"Merry Christmas, Ma'am," she said as she handed Miss Cora the paper bag. "Mama told me to give you this." Annie knew the bag contained the wax-paper-wrapped ham bone with enough meat to feed Emma's family for a couple of days. "She said with all the extra shifts at the hospital these days, she hasn't got the time or the skill to make soup like you do."

"You give your mama my thanks."

Emma stepped out of the bedroom she shared with her mother. "Merry Christmas, Annie. Is everything alright?"

Annie smiled. Black folks knew surprise visits seldom brought good news. "Sure is. We had a grand Christmas dinner, and now the boys and I are going for a boat ride in the launch. I came by to invite my best friend to come along with us!"

Emma hesitated, glancing at her mother. It wasn't the first time Annie and Emma had spent time together outside work, but they all knew there was a danger to it, more so for Emma than for Annie. Miss Cora pursed her lips, but nodded.

"Don't draw any extra attention if you can help it."

Emma nodded. "We'll keep to ourselves. Don't worry, Mama."

Emma grabbed her faded blue shawl off a hook by the front door. She was wearing a flower print dress with a lace collar that her mother had sewn.

"Y'all be careful now," Mr. Walker warned, his eyes serious. "Remember, you ought not let anyone see you two looking too chummy."

With a final wave goodbye, the girls headed out, maintaining a careful distance as they walked through the near empty streets. While it might look like no one was watching, Annie saw the shift of a curtain here, the angle of a shutter there. Fort Lauderdale had felt like a pretty big town when she'd first arrived from Edgewater, a tiny spot up north on the Mosquito Lagoon, but gossip was still the favorite sport in these parts.

When they reached the waterfront, Annie relaxed. The road that ran along behind the docks was home only to businesses like The Deck restaurant and assorted ice and fish warehouses that were shuttered tight for the Christmas holiday.

She spotted Jack and Finn waiting by the small wooden boat, its white paint peeling away from years of use. The vessel was modest, with two cross benches for seating and a gasoline outboard engine hanging off the stern.

She called out a hello, and Jack waved back enthusiastically. When he caught sight of Emma, his face lit up with a smile that Annie hadn't seen in weeks.

"Happy Christmas!" he shouted. "Let's get this show on the road, or the river as the case may be."

When they got closer, Finn smiled at Emma. "Afternoon, Miss Albury. Glad you could join us."

Annie jumped down into the boat, causing it to rock. She stood with her legs set apart, compensating for the motion, and glanced up at her friend.

Emma was frozen in place, eyes wide, staring at the little boat.

Jack appeared at her side and took Emma's hand. "It's okay," he said.

Without looking at him, Emma said, "I don't know how to swim."

"No problem. I promise I won't let anything happen to you."

Annie reached up to take her friend's other hand while the young woman stepped into the tippy boat and plopped down on the front seat with a muffled shriek.

Jack tossed Annie his black rain jacket with a large hood.

"Put this on," Annie murmured. "It should hide you well enough during the ride downriver."

Emma quickly shed her shawl and pulled on the oversized slicker. The fabric billowed around her, disguising her slender frame. Her hands disappeared inside the sleeves, and the hood masked her features.

"Perfect." Annie pressed her straw hat down tight on her own head.

The boat rocked again as Jack climbed into the boat and settled on the seat in the stern. He yanked on the motor's start cord, and the engine sputtered to life.

Finn untied the dock lines and climbed aboard, pushing the small boat away from the dock. They motored down the

New River, away from the center of town, passing the occasional home facing the water.

As they left the nicer homes close to town and entered the snaking river lined with smaller houses, Annie tensed. "Keep your head down, Emma," she said. "Some of the folks living down here are no friends of ours." The dilapidated house ahead was home to Ernie Finch, a young man who had pestered her when they'd first moved to town. Never did know how to take no for an answer. She'd only found reprieve when Ernie dropped out of school and started running errands for Sheriff Walter Clark and his chief deputy, his brother Bob Clark. The Clark brothers kept Ernie busy.

When the launch neared the point where the river intersected the coastal canal, Annie tipped her head back, one hand atop her straw hat, and took a deep breath. The sky was a flawless watercolor blue after the storm front that had blown through the night before.

"Look there. An osprey." Jack reached over Emma's shoulder and pointed to a large bird of prey passing overhead, a good-sized fish in its talons.

"Beautiful," Emma whispered.

As they entered the bustling maritime district of Port Everglades, Annie relaxed. No one would pay much attention to them there. The few folks at work on Christmas Day wouldn't be worried about a bunch of young folks in a small boat.

Annie sensed Emma's awe at the size of the cargo ships, tugs, and harbor pilot boats that were moored to the commercial docks. Then they passed the harbor entrance where the big ocean swells caught the bow of their little boat, making them all grab the gunwales.

"Hang on!" Jack called back. "It gets rough through here."

Finn hollered like a cowboy at the bucking sensation. Annie snatched her hat off and hugged it to her chest. They bounced over the swells, getting spritzed by salty spray. Once past the inlet, Jack steered them south, running parallel to the low green line of mangroves.

He nudged the boat over closer to the barrier island, and then turned into what looked like a little creek. The air grew quiet when he cut the engine and let the boat drift on the incoming tide. The only noise was the chirping of the tiny birds in the trees that surrounded them. The mangrove branches arched overhead, forming a shadowy tunnel. Using an oar as a pole, Jack pushed the boat through the shallow water towards the sunlight ahead. Annie could see a tiny strip of white sand.

Jack and Finn jumped into the knee-deep water and dragged the boat further into the sheltered cove known as Whiskey Creek.

"Last one to the beach is a rotten egg!" Jack called out.

Finn was right on his heels, bare feet sinking into the mucky sand. "You're going down, Jeeves!"

Annie turned to Emma. "Welcome to our secret beach."

The young women kicked off their shoes and scrambled after Jack and Finn, giggling as their skirts tangled around their legs. As they neared the ocean side of the barrier island, the sounds of Jack and Finn's gleeful shouts reached them, spurring Annie and Emma on. When they broke through the final barrier of seagrass, they caught sight of the vast expanse of the Atlantic Ocean.

Emma's pace slowed. "Sweet Jesus," she said between gasps for air.

Hands on hips, Annie called out, "Wait up!" Then, laughing breathlessly, she tried to catch up.

Their feet were sinking into the soft white sand as they chased after the fellas, until finally, all four friends collapsed onto their backs, chests heaving and faces flushed from their impromptu race.

"Phew," Jack wiped the sweat from his brow. "That was quite the workout."

"Speak for yourself." Annie kicked sand at his bare feet. "I could have run another mile!"

"Sure you could." Finn lay on his side in the sand, his elbow bent, his head resting on his palm.

Annie wanted to come back with a wisecrack, but all she could think of was how much she wished she had brought her sketchbook so she could capture the way he was looking at her in that moment.

Jack got up and rummaged through the picnic basket Mama had packed for them. He pulled out four bottles of Coca-Cola.

"Here." He popped off the bottle caps, then handed one to each of them.

"Cheers," Annie said, raising her bottle in a toast. "To friendship."

"Cheers," the others echoed, clinking their bottles together.

Annie picked up a piece of a broken shell from the sand. "Jack, remember when we were kids, the first time Pa brought us here? You found those pieces of broken blue and white pottery in the sand, and we were certain they must be part of Black Caesar's lost treasure."

Jack chuckled. "You even drew a map trying to mark their exact location, determined to come back and dig up riches beyond our wildest dreams."

"I think I still have that map."

As they reminisced, Finn and Jack sat up and started to peel off their shirts. Annie couldn't help but steal glances at Finn, even as a flush crept up her neck.

Finn jumped up. "Alright, who wants to swim?"

Jack was on his feet in an instant.

Annie shook her head. "You boys go ahead. We'll relax right here."

She looked over at Emma, who was watching Jack strip off his jeans, revealing his swimming shorts underneath.

Nudging her friend, Annie raised an eyebrow.

"Oh stop it," Emma whispered.

Soon the fellas were racing headlong into the chilly December surf, howling with delight. With his windswept brick-red hair and thousand-watt smile, Finn whooped triumphantly after he managed a handstand in chest-high water, before a surprise wave knocked him back under.

"Race you to the buoy?" Jack shouted.

"You're on!"

The boys took off, arms slicing through the water towards the mooring buoy offshore.

"Glad you came?" Annie asked.

"Oh yes," Emma said without taking her eyes off Jack. "Your brother is quite the swimmer."

"They both are. My brother's good at everything he tries."

The girls spread the blanket out on the sand and settled themselves. Annie peeked into the picnic basket and saw that Mama had sent them some cold fried chicken, half a dozen biscuits, and a small crock of strawberry jam.

As the men swam further out, Emma said, "I've seen how you look at Finn. Do you want to talk about that?"

Annie gave her friend an appraising look. Emma just smiled, leaning back on her hands to soak up the sunshine.

"Whatever I might feel doesn't matter. I've known him for as long as I can remember. I'm permanently in the 'little sister' column as far as he's concerned."

"Grampa Elzo once said that young men are so focused on waiting for some grand solar eclipse that they miss the spectacular sunsets happening right before their eyes every single day."

Annie laughed. "That's true enough."

"Finn's smarter than most, Annie. Don't give up on him. He'll figure it out."

"He hasn't had it so easy, Em. His pa walked out on them when Bean was just a baby. Finn was barely ten years old. Then their mama got cancer, and she died."

"Poor Finn."

Annie watched the men playing in the waves. "I was such a tomboy, just one of the boys, always wearing my overalls like Bean does now. I reckon I'll always be that to Finn."

Emma smiled at her. "He's a good man. I've seen the way he takes care of his little sister. Give him time."

Annie turned away from her friend and looked back out to sea. The late afternoon sunlight lit the foaming waves with a golden glow. Finn's laughter carried to the beach on the breeze. She had come to love this place in the southern part of the state, but her heart would always be yearning to go back home.

"Annie?" Emma's voice was barely audible above the sound of the waves. "Do you ever wonder what will happen next? With the war and everything?"

"All the time," Annie admitted, her gaze fixed on the horizon. "I try not to think about it too much, though. It's scary, isn't it? Not knowing what might happen."

Emma nodded. "It is. The way some folks talk. They think the Germans are going to invade us any day now. But somehow, sitting here with you, watching those fellas, it doesn't make me feel quite so frightened anymore."

"Me too." Annie reached over and put her hand on top of Emma's. She watched Jack and Finn emerge from the water, their hair slicked back and their bodies glistening.

The shade from the casuarina trees and palmettos had reached their beach blanket. The young men ran up the beach, hugging their arms to their chests.

"Getting chilly for you ladies?" Jack asked as he reached for a towel.

"Feels like it," Annie agreed, rubbing her arms.

"Maybe we should start a fire," Finn suggested, his teeth chattering slightly. "I brought matches."

"Let's go collect driftwood along the high-water mark," Jack said.

Annie and Emma headed into the woods to collect pine needles and kindling.

Jack returned with a stack of firewood wrapped in his black jacket. After dumping the firewood next to the pit Finn had dug, he draped the jacket over Emma's shoulders. His hands lingered for a moment, fingertips just barely grazing her collarbone.

Emma glanced up, startled. Their eyes met for an instant before Jack turned away. Annie turned away too, embarrassed that she had seen that intimate moment.

Together, the four friends built a small, crackling campfire that cast flickering shadows on their faces.

Annie set out the chicken and biscuits, and the group grew quiet as they ate.

Finally, Jack took a deep breath and looked at Finn with determination in his eyes. "Finn, I've been thinking about this for a long time now." He sat up straighter. "I'm going to enlist in the Navy."

"You're serious?" Finn's eyes searched his friend's face for any hint of a joke.

"Dead serious. It makes sense to do it now before my number gets called. I don't want to be a soldier or a sailor. I want to fly. Besides, I can't just sit by while the world falls apart."

"Jack." Annie reached for his arm. "The family depends on the money you earn on the *Tequesta*."

He shrugged off her hand. "I'll get paid in the military. I can send money home."

Annie crossed her arms, watching her brother, trying to read his thoughts, but his gaze was fixed on Finn. "What about you, buddy? Would you come with me?"

Finn's eyes darted between Jack and the fire. "Jack, you know I'd follow you into hell if I had to," he began, "but I can't leave. I'm Bean's guardian now. I can't just up and abandon her."

"She knows how important this is."

"Bean's just a kid, Jack," Finn said firmly, his voice heavy with regret. "She's lost too many people already. Besides, I promised our ma I'd take care of her." He looked away, and Annie saw the muscles twitch along his jaw.

Emma had gone quiet, her fingers nervously twisting the hem of Jack's jacket. Her expression was unreadable.

"Promise me something, Sis," Jack said, his voice low. "Promise me you won't tell Ma about this. Not 'til I'm gone."

She looked into her brother's eyes and saw the fear and determination. With a sigh, she nodded. "I promise, Jack."

The crackling of dry leaves and the rustling of brush back from the beach made everyone freeze. Wide-eyed, Emma turned to Jack, her voice quavering. "Do you think it might be a gator?"

"No way," Jack said.

Emma exhaled audibly.

"More likely a croc here in the saltwater." Jack strained to listen for any further movement. "But they're pretty rare around these parts."

The brush rustled once more, and Emma scooted closer to Jack. Annie saw her brother smile.

"Maybe we should head back," Annie said, keeping her voice steady. "It's getting late, and I don't want to take any chances."

"Good idea." Emma nodded, eyes wide. "Ya'll know I need to be home soon."

No one said anything for several long seconds. Unlike back home on the banks of the Mosquito Lagoon, where they'd lived a more frontier lifestyle, in segregated Fort Lauderdale, it was against the law for black folks to be on the streets of the white part of town after 8:00 p.m.

"Alright, let's pack up and get back to the boat." Jack motioned for Finn to help him gather their things. Finn kicked sand on the last embers of their fire while Annie and Emma hastily rolled up the blanket and towels and collected the empty Coke bottles.

As they hurried toward the boat, Jack kept a protective arm around Emma's shoulders.

Once aboard, he yanked the motor's starter cord. The engine sputtered to life, and they motored off into the darkness.

# CHAPTER FIVE

*Fort Lauderdale, Florida*
*December 25, 1941*

The puttering outboard motor was the only sound slicing through the crisp night air as their small wooden skiff glided through the dark channel. Annie trailed her fingers along the boat's weathered gunwale, gazing up at the mangrove canopy.

Jack steered the outboard one-handed out of the channel and onto the main canal, his other arm draped around Emma's shoulders. "Look at all those stars."

Emma pointed towards the southern sky. "See how clear you can see Orion's Belt."

"Wow, you mean that string of stars there?" Finn said.

Emma chuckled. "Un-huh."

Finn leaned back, holding onto the side of the boat, his face tilted skyward. "Wish I knew more about the stars."

Annie smiled. "Me and Emma, that's our specialty. She's teaching me astronomy, and I'm teaching her celestial navigation."

As they passed through Port Everglades, the warm glow of

lights aboard a docked cargo ship illuminated the water, casting rippling reflections like an oil painting come to life.

"Y'all ever wonder what it's like to be one of those sailors on a ship like that?" Finn asked.

"Maybe you'll find out soon enough," Jack replied.

"Let's not talk about that now," Emma said, her hand brushing against Jack's arm. "We still got tonight."

"Right you are, Miss Albury," Finn said. "Y'know, nights like these make me realize just how much I love this place."

Annie watched Finn's profile as he stared skyward. "Me too."

When they turned into the mouth of the New River, the channel narrowed again. Homes dotted the river banks, soft light from their windows glowing among the lush greenery.

As they neared the Finch homestead, Annie saw movement in the high weeds around an old Model T car up on bricks. A shadow crossed the yard.

She glanced at Jack. They had grown too relaxed. Emma was no longer wearing the hooded jacket.

"Hey!" a shout echoed from shore. Ernie Finch and three of his rat-faced cronies burst from the trees, sprinting for the sagging dock.

"Well, lookee there!" Ernie hollered. "If it ain't the Jeeves brats out for a moonlight cruise with their pet monkey."

"Damn," Jack quickly withdrew his arm from around Emma's shoulders. "It's that idiot, Finch." He cranked the handle of the outboard, and the engine revved higher.

Annie saw the four figures scramble to untie the battered skiff. Their outboard fired up at the first pull.

She turned to her brother. "Can't you go any faster?" Over the noise of both engines, she could hear them shouting derogatory insults.

"Oh gee, Annie. I never thought of that." Worry lines etched into his forehead.

Both boats raced up the dark river water, engines roaring. Ernie began closing in.

"We don't want any trouble, Finch," Jack called out over his shoulder. "Let us pass."

"Don't think so," Ernie sneered. "What you doing ain't right."

"We can outrun them," Finn said. "Wouldn't be surprised if that leaky ol' skiff of theirs sinks."

"Are you crazy?" Emma's eyes were wide with terror. "We can't outrun them in this boat!"

Annie reached out and squeezed Emma's hand. She wasn't going to lie to her friend and tell her everything was going to be okay, but she wanted Emma to know they would do everything in their power to prevent them from hurting her.

"Better suggestions, anyone?" Finn's hands clenched into fists at his sides.

They were coming into the docks.

Jack shouted, "Get ready to jump out and run. Finn, you take the girls. I'll hold them off best I can."

As they careened toward the dock, Jack cut the engine, and Finn grabbed hold of a piling to steady the boat.

Annie leapt onto the pier, then reached back to help Emma. As Emma grasped her hand, her foot slipped on the wet boards. She yelped and started to fall back.

Annie held tight to Emma's hand, bracing herself. Behind her, she heard the thud of boots hitting the dock.

"Y'all ain't gettin' away that easy!" Ernie hollered, his three friends joining him on the dock.

One man grabbed Finn while another wrenched Emma from Annie's grip.

"No!" Annie cried. She whirled around to see Ernie swing his fist at her brother. It connected with Jack's jaw, and he reeled backwards. Annie surged toward them, but strong hands grabbed hold of her braid and yanked downward, nearly pulling her off her feet.

"Let them be, missy," a deep voice growled in her ear. "Wouldn't want that pretty face of yours to git messed up."

Ernie threw a roundhouse punch that snapped Jack's head back. "Not so high and mighty now, rich boy!" he jeered, shoving Jack hard.

Jack bent over and barreled shoulder first into Ernie's midsection, knocking him into a couple of wooden barrels. Finch fell onto his backside.

Ernie's hand darted into the shadows, searching for something on the dock. He pulled out a long steel pipe that had been lying between the barrels. He jumped to his feet and brandished it like a sword, swinging at Jack, and connecting with his ribs. Her brother's breath exploded as he bent over in pain. Ernie swung the pipe again, and though Jack tried to duck, it glanced off his head, knocking him back. Jack staggered and fell. Annie gasped as she saw the dark red blood pour from her brother's eyebrow.

Just then a deep voice cut through the melee. "That's enough outta you boys!"

Annie sagged with relief at the sight of Cap Knight, a local fisherman, standing on the dock in his denim overalls, his meaty fists clenched at his sides.

His eyes blazed with anger as he shouted at Ernie and his cronies. "Y'all better leave these folks alone if ya know what's good for ya!"

Ernie spat curses, then jerked his chin at his pals. "C'mon, let's scram." He glared at Jack. "This ain't over, Jeeves."

They released Finn, Annie and Emma, then backed away toward their boat.

Annie rushed over and knelt at her brother's side. His brow was split and swelling, and blood covered half his face.

Cap watched as the Finch gang started their engine and

pushed away from the dock. Then the older man reached out a hand to Jack and pulled him to his feet.

"Thanks, Cap," Jack managed through gritted teeth.

"Anytime, kid." Cap nodded.

Annie stood and slid her shoulder under her brother's arm, supporting him. "Come on, Jack, we gotta get you home."

Her brother groaned.

"Can you walk?" Cap asked.

Jack nodded. "Yeah."

"In that case, get out of here. Finch boys aren't the only ones around here who won't take to you all fraternizing."

Finn held up the black rain slicker to Emma and said, "I'll walk you home. We need to make sure you're safe."

"Thank you, Finn," Emma whispered as she pulled the jacket tight around her shoulders.

"Annie," Finn said, "you take care of your brother. Get him back to the house."

She watched as Emma and Finn turned and began a brisk walk, Emma in the lead and Finn following behind her. "Right."

"I'm good." Jack's words slurred together into a single word.

"Easy now, Superman, it seems you didn't have your red cape tonight." Annie murmured as she guided her brother toward their home in Sailboat Bend. When they walked past a brightly lit house, she glanced up at his face. Dried blood crusted around his flaring nostrils and coated his chin. She guessed he might have a cracked rib or two based on the way he gingerly held his left side.

The walk home seemed to take forever with Jack leaning heavily on her shoulder. His breathing was labored, and heat radiated from his battered body. "Hold on, Jack," she urged. "We're almost there."

At last, their small house came into view. Annie fumbled for the door, hands shaking. Inside, her mother Hilda sat on the couch mending a shirt. She took one look at Jack's battered face and leapt to her feet.

"Mother of God, what happened?" Hilda grasped Jack's chin and raised his face to the light.

"Ernie Finch and his pack of hyenas," Annie said.

Their father stood in the kitchen doorway, his fists clasped at his sides. "Damn Finch family. Nothing but a bunch of hooligans."

Though Hilda's eyes had widened at the sight of her son's battered face, she quickly composed herself.

"Get him inside, Annie." Her mother's tone left no room for argument. "Let's get him to bed, and I'll take care of this."

Together, Annie and her mother helped Jack to his bedroom, supporting his weight between them. The dog followed them. Jack's breathing was ragged, and beads of sweat dotted his forehead, betraying the pain he fought to conceal. They eased him onto his bed as gently as they could. Tess jumped onto the foot of the bed and rested her head on his legs.

"Get the medical chest."

Annie nodded. She retrieved the worn wooden chest from the hallway closet, its contents meticulously organized by her nurse mother.

"Here you go, Mama." She handed over the chest.

"Leave us now, Annie. I'll take care of Jack."

She reluctantly closed the door behind her with a quiet click and stood breathing deeply in the dark hallway. The adrenaline was abandoning her now, leaving her limbs feeling weak and rubbery. She stiffened her back, then stepped into the living room.

Her Pa sat hunched forward on the faded floral couch, cap twisted in his hands, unlit pipe clenched between his teeth. At her approach, he glanced up, eyes clouded with concern. She settled into the armchair.

"What in blazes happened out there?" he asked. "I've never seen Jack take a beating like that."

"Well, Papa." Annie paused, searching for the right words. "We were on our way back from Whiskey Creek when we passed the Finch place. Emma was with us. Those boys saw us go by and... well, they started chasing us, shouting all sorts of ugly things."

She didn't mention that Jack had his arm around Emma; that detail felt too dangerous to share, even with her father.

Skeeter's expression darkened, and his hand clenched into a tight fist on his knee. "Damn those boys," he muttered under his breath. "Always looking for trouble."

"And Ernie grabbed an old pipe and got a few good ones in with that."

"Just like a Finch not to fight fair."

"Is Jack gonna be okay?" Annie asked. She knew once the words were out that she wasn't only asking about his injuries.

Before Skeeter could answer, Hilda emerged from the hallway. "He's gonna be fine, Annie."

"Thank God," Skeeter said.

"I had to put in a few stitches on that eyebrow, and he'll have some nasty bruises, but he'll be alright." She sank onto the sofa beside her husband. "His ribs are mighty bruised, but I don't think they're broken. He's got strong bones, that boy."

The quiet of the room was interrupted by the sudden noise of a car engine revving outside, followed by loud, angry shouting. Her father instantly tensed. He rose from the sofa and moved slowly toward the window.

"Stay back," he said, his voice low and full of concern.

From down the hall, the dog started barking.

Just as her father pulled back the lace curtain, a rock came crashing through the glass.

"Damn it!" her father shouted, shielding his face from the flying shards of glass. "Are you two okay?"

Her mother looked her up and down, then said, "We're fine."

"Stay here. Those no-good cowards!" Her father charged out the front door.

"Be careful, Pa!" Annie called after him. She stood there, torn between wanting to help her father and staying put like he'd instructed.

"Mama, what do we do?" Annie's heart pounded in her chest.

"Help me pick up this glass," Hilda stood wrapping her hand with the dish towel that often rested on her shoulder. The white fabric was dotted with blood. "It's nothing. Just a nick. Don't tell your father." Hilda's hands were shaking as she used the wrapped hand to brush the last shards of glass off the couch.

Annie turned to the door at the sound of her father's heavy footsteps. He entered, slammed the door behind him, and leaned against it for support.

"Are they gone?" Annie asked.

"Seems like it. For now." Her father rubbed his temples.

"Did you see who it was?"

"It was a blue truck with a bunch of fellas in the back. Too dark to get a good look at their faces." Skeeter shook his head. "But I can guess."

Hilda strode forward and took Skeeter's arm firmly.

"Come." She led him to the dining table. "We'll call the sheriff."

At that, Skeeter barked out a harsh laugh. "And what good'll that do? Sheriff's no better than that Finch bunch, you know that."

Annie sat at the table across from her parents. Her father reached for her hand and her mother's. "No, this is between us and them. We'll handle it on our own, like we always have. Keep it in the family."

Annie let go of her father's hand and shifted uncomfortably on the hard wood chair. She had promised Jack she wouldn't tell their mother about his plan to join the Navy. But after tonight, it seemed wrong to keep it from their parents.

Her voice trembled as she began. "I need to tell you both something... about Jack."

Skeeter and Hilda looked up from their whispered conversation. "What is it, Annie?" Hilda's voice was firm.

"Jack's planning to join the Navy," Annie blurted out. "He wants to be a Navy pilot."

For a moment, nobody spoke. Then her father asked, "You're certain about this?"

Annie nodded. "He told us today at the beach. He even asked Finn if he'd join him."

"Oh, Jack." Hilda placed a hand on her chest.

"Damn fool."

"He's been thinking about it for a while," Annie said. "But after what happened to us tonight, I think his mind is made up."

Hilda pressed her lips together, looking between Annie and Skeeter. "I can't say I'm totally surprised. That boy's been restless as of late."

"Well I don't like it one bit," Skeeter said. "It's dangerous being on those ships in the middle of a war."

"More dangerous than being here, with the Finches gunning for him?" Hilda asked.

"His loyalty is to this family first."

Just then they heard the creak of a floorboard and the tapping of the dog's claws on the wood planks. Jack stepped into the room shirtless, one eye swollen half-shut beneath the stitched eyebrow. His face was stony.

"Thanks for keeping my confidence, Annie," he spat out.

Annie flushed. "Jack, I'm sorry, I just thought—"

"You thought you'd go blabbing my business to everybody." Jack's voice was sharp with anger and disappointment.

"Jack..."

"Stay out of this, Ma." Jack spoke without turning to his mother. "That was my decision, and my news to share."

"Jack, I..." She felt a knot of guilt tighten in her stomach.

"You had no right, Annie."

"I thought they had a right to know."

"Damn it, Annie." Jack's voice cracked with emotion. "You always have to stick your nose where it doesn't belong."

"I didn't mean to hurt you."

"That's enough." Hilda's eyes shone with tears. "Your sister only told us because she's worried about you, son. We all are."

"I can handle myself. Don't need my little sister fighting my battles."

Hilda stood up and faced her son. "You listen to me, Jack Jeeves. We stick together in this family. We don't run off doing things on our own."

"It's not your choice, Ma." Jack's voice was quiet but firm.

Hilda wiped at her eyes and then sighed. "No. I reckon it's not."

"I've got to do this. It's the right thing." Then he wrapped his long arms around his mother's shoulders and pulled her into a hug.

Skeeter cleared his throat gruffly. "Your ma's right; it's your decision. And if you're set on going..." He met Jack's eyes. "We'll make do without you on the *Tequesta*." He turned to his daughter. "Reckon that duty will fall to you now, Annie girl."

Jack nodded, seeming to accept his father's words. "She'll do just fine. Always been better than me with the charts and the tides, anyway."

# CHAPTER SIX

*Flensburg, Germany*
*December 25, 1941*

Will's breath condensed into clouds that quickly dissipated as he shuffled down the icy road following directions given to him by his driver. The bus had deposited him on the outskirts of Flensburg, and now he was making his way towards the naval academy building at Marineschule Mürwik. He squinted into the thick fog that enveloped the landscape, rendering everything into indistinct shapes. His fingers ached, and he clenched his fists inside his pockets.

"*Verdammte Kälte*," he muttered. Damn cold.

After half an hour of trudging, his legs numb and cheeks stinging, a hulking red brick structure appeared out of the mist. The round tower topped with a peaked roof had one heavy wooden door. A spotlight formed a cone of light on the snow-covered ground.

With a sigh, he fished a cigarette from his pocket and placed it between his lips. The scratching noise of the match was lost in the wind, but the brief flare did the job. He drew deeply, savoring the burn in his lungs.

As he drew closer, rows of frosted windows glinted in the fading light, and the brick facade looked more like a prison than a naval academy.

"Well, here goes nothing," he muttered under his breath, flicking the cigarette into a nearby snowbank. Squaring his shoulders, Will strode forward into the cone of light.

The tower door swung open, and a tall German officer emerged. The officer's uniform was crisp as he raised his outstretched arm in salute.

"Your name?"

"Wilhelm Hersey."

"Follow me." The officer turned and strode around the corner into a long brick walkway leading towards a pair of massive doors. The man did not even bother to check if Will was following.

Once inside, the officer led Will through a maze of dark, narrow corridors. The musty smell of damp and age permeated the air, making it difficult to breathe. Every step of the tall German's boots on the polished stone floors echoed with an eerie hollowness.

They arrived at last before a door that opened into a dimly lit room. Inside, three men sat around a rough-hewn table, their faces etched with tension. Though they wore similar uniforms of the German army, which Will found odd given they were at the Naval Academy, the men themselves could not have been more different. As soon as the door opened, they looked up in unison.

"Sit," the officer commanded before turning away and exiting the room.

"Ah, another newcomer!" The rotund man with apple-red cheeks and a cheerful smile stood and extended his hand with a warm smile. "I'm Erich Burger."

Will dropped his duffle down on an empty bench at the table. The man's fingers felt like stale carrots in his grip. "Wilhelm Hersey."

"Baum," grunted the tall, rugged man who sat closest to him, nodding. "You can call me Max." His eyes and the single arched eyebrow seemed to tell Will not to judge him by the other two odd characters he was with.

"Adler," said the third soldier as he pushed up to a stand. The man appeared to unfold his gangly, tall body. His angular shoulders jutted in little peaks beneath the uniform that hung in folds on his gaunt frame. The eyes behind his wire-framed glasses were cast downward when he extended his hand. "My given name Jorg, but everyone just calls me Adler."

Erich pointed at Will. "Not in uniform?" The tone of his voice lifted at the end, transforming the statement into a question. "Can I assume that means you are not serving the Führer?"

"I work at the Reich's Ministry of Public Enlightenment and Propaganda. I speak English, so I was translating the Führer's messages for the English."

Erich smiled and clapped his dainty hands together. "Wonderful! I lived in Canada for several years when I was a boy, and I also speak English."

"Hmm..." Max looked around at the others. "Five years in Philadelphia," he said in unaccented American English.

They all turned to Jorg Adler. When the man lifted his head from where it seemed to have shrunk between his shoulders, Will was reminded of a turtle. "I went to public school in England, then university in Boston," he stated, returning the conversation to German.

"Strange, isn't it?" Max remarked, leaning back in his chair. "We're all here for some mysterious reason, and we all can speak English."

"Ah, another piece of our little puzzle," Erich said. "Sit,

sit," he urged, gesturing to the empty bench. "We were just discussing how none of us knows why we're here. Perhaps you have some insight?"

Will took a seat among the others. "All I know is that I received orders to report here immediately."

"Same," Adler said. "One minute, I'm stationed in Berlin, and the next, I'm pulled away for some mysterious mission. It doesn't make any sense."

"Yes," Erich agreed, his jolly demeanor dampened by the confusion that plagued them all. "We were hoping you'd have some answers."

"Sorry." Will shook his head. "But it seems to matter that we all speak English."

"Maybe they need someone who can curse at the enemy in multiple languages," Max said.

"Wait a moment," Erich said. "Are you suggesting that the Reich has brought us here *because* we can speak English?"

They exchanged glances, and then Will ventured, "Looks that way to me. We all have some connection to the English-speaking world."

"An interesting theory," Adler mused, stroking his chin. "But what could they possibly want with four bilingual soldiers at the Naval Academy?"

Their conversation was interrupted by the sound of heavy footsteps approaching the door. It swung open to reveal a stern-looking naval officer, his uniform immaculate and adorned with medals. He surveyed the room with an air of authority as the men jumped to their feet and stood at attention.

The officer spoke briskly, closing the door behind him. "Good evening, gentlemen. You may be seated. I am Admiral Wilhelm Canaris, and I will be overseeing your new assignment."

The four men returned to their seats, but now their backs

were straight, their eyes locked on the newcomer. Admiral Canaris, as most German citizens knew, was Chief of the Abwehr, the Reich's military-intelligence group.

The admiral pulled over a chair and sat in front of them. "I'll get straight to the point. You will be taking part in a top-secret mission known as Operation Pastorius."

"Pastorius?" Max again lifted one eyebrow.

Admiral Canaris sat in silence for several moments, looking up and down at the men before him, measuring them.

"You have been brought here today to be a part of the first of what I hope will be many missions to stop the Americans by hitting them at home. This mission is named after the man who started the first German settlement in America, Francis Pastorius. Today, that settlement is called Germantown in the state of Pennsylvania." He turned to Max. "You're Max Baum, right? I believe you used to live in Germantown?"

Max nodded.

"Your shared ability to speak near native English has not gone unnoticed by your superiors," the Admiral continued. He turned and spoke to each of them. "Jorg Adler, four years in Boston for university. Wilhelm Hersey, born in Indiana to an American father and German mother." Will nodded. "Erich Burger, you lived with your uncle and went to grammar school for three years in Toronto. Each one of you has been selected for this vital operation, one that requires you to speak English and to pose as merchant mariners."

"Speaking English brought us here," Will said.

"Correct. Each of you will need to play a part. You will receive new identities, close to your reality. You will be transported across the Atlantic Ocean and landed on foreign soil. In case of capture on arrival, you will need to pass as sailors. In this way you will infiltrate enemy territory, and you must pass scrutiny in encounters with locals," the Admiral explained. "Due to the urgency of this mission, your training will be swift and rigorous. Do not expect any leniency."

"Where will we be going, sir?" Adler asked.

"Details about your destination will be revealed once your training is complete," the Admiral replied. "For now, focus on mastering the skills necessary to carry out this mission."

"Understood, sir."

"Good," the Admiral nodded. "You will begin your instruction tomorrow morning at five sharp." The admiral stood, and the four men jumped to attention once again. Will watched the others and tried to salute properly.

As Admiral Canaris turned to leave, he paused in the doorway and fixed them with an intense stare.

"Prepare yourselves, gentlemen. Make no mistake, this mission, Operation Pastorius, could change the course of the war. But it will require iron discipline and absolute secrecy."

The admiral lowered his voice. "If captured, Germany will disavow any knowledge of your mission. The Reich will not come for you. And the penalty for treason and espionage is death."

He turned, and the door closed behind him.

Max broke the heavy silence first. "Well, looks like we're off on an adventure, boys."

"Some adventure," Will said. "They're sending us into the lion's den blindfolded."

Max laughed. "Blindfolded, but not unarmed." He mimed swinging a fist. "We'll give those Yankee bastards a little taste of German steel if they try anything."

Will attempted to raise a single eyebrow, amused by the bravado.

The others shifted in their seats at Max's irreverent tone. "This is not a game," Erich said. "The admiral made it clear how high the stakes are."

"Oh I'm taking it very seriously," Max replied. "But a little humor never hurt." He gave Will a roguish wink.

"America." Saying the name aloud filled him with a surprising warmth. He felt an odd mixture of terror and excitement. Having lived so long in Germany, he now even dreamed in the language. He thought he had erased all his boyhood yearnings to return to the land of his birth. But something deep now stirred inside him. "What have we gotten ourselves into?"

Max paced the room, then leaned against the wall, his arms crossed over his chest. "Well, it seems like they've hand-picked us for something big. America, huh? Didn't think I'd ever step foot there again."

"Neither did I," Will replied. "But here we are. Sounds like we are about to go on a top-secret mission we know nothing about."

Max laughed. "Hey, at least we're not stuck in the trenches like those poor bastards on the Eastern Front."

"True," Will conceded, a hint of a grin forming on his face.

"And I suppose if we have to infiltrate enemy territory, it might as well be one we're familiar with." Max slapped Will on the back with a hearty laugh. "We'll show them how it's done, won't we?"

Enemy territory. Of course, that is what they expected him to think. But he remembered Billy Turner, his best friend, who had lived in the house next to his in Valparaiso. They had collected tadpoles, built forts, shared penny candy. Billy, or Bill now, would probably be a soldier himself. It was one thing to listen to the speeches or read the newspaper about the enemy. Quite another to think of having to cross an ocean and take this war to them.

The other men spent the next few minutes discussing

their backgrounds and experiences in America while Will sat alone, deep in thought.

A sharp rap at the door silenced the others. The tall lieutenant stood in the doorway, face grim.

"It's time," he said. "Bring your kits."

They gathered their meager possessions. Will worked at shaking off the reverie as they followed the lieutenant out into the freezing night. They walked across a parade ground to another red brick and turreted building on the far side of the base.

Upon entering the dimly lit barracks, each man found his assigned bunk, and they dropped off their gear. The sparse accommodations did little to ease the tension; if anything, they only emphasized the seriousness of their situation.

"Next stop, mess hall," the young officer informed them, gesturing towards the door. They followed him obediently.

Will hurried his pace to catch up with Max. In English, he asked, "Did you ever think you'd end up on some top-secret mission like this?"

"Never in my wildest dreams," Max said in English. "I always imagined I'd be sipping cocktails on a beach somewhere, not playing pretend sailor for the Reich."

Will laughed.

"Looks like we're all quite the international bunch." Max spoke in English.

Just then, they passed by several naval cadets who eyed them with suspicion. Will assumed the Army uniforms weren't helping any.

"*Nur der Feind spricht Englisch*," one cadet said to another as they walked past.

"Only the enemy speaks English," Max translated, mimicking the disdainful tone of the cadet. He smiled and held his hands, palms up. "Look boys, we're already making friends."

"Great," Will murmured.

"Maybe we should throw a party, get to know our fellow soldiers better," Max suggested, earning a few chuckles from Jorg and Erich.

"Sure," Will replied, knowing the surrounding cadets could not understand their English. "I'll bring the champagne and caviar."

"Ah, don't forget the dancing girls!" Max added.

The stern officer led Will and his newfound companions down a dim corridor.

"Here we are," the officer announced, halting in front of a well-lit room full of tables and the noise of clattering dishes. "The mess hall." He turned and left them.

Will couldn't help but notice the hostile glares and grunts from the other soldiers.

"Something tells me we're not welcome at this party," Max whispered to Will as they joined the others in line for their meager meal: watery soup, a slice of bread, and a pat of butter.

"Looks like fine dining to me," Will said.

"Maybe we should have brought our own food," Max replied.

The four men collected their plates and found an empty table in the back of the room.

"Ah, we are in training already. Feeding us a proper American Christmas dinner. Nothing like the smell of stale bread and overcooked soup to really get you into the holiday spirit," Max said, breaking the silence that had settled over the table.

"Who needs a Christmas turkey with all the trimmings when you have this culinary feast before you?" Erich joined in as he raised his spoon to his lips with exaggerated flourish. "Truly, we are blessed."

Max tapped the hard bread with his spoon. "Hmm, just like mother used to make," he said.

The laughter soon faded as they ate in silence, each lost in their own thoughts.

Will's mind churned. Memories he had buried seemed to rise from the dead. He saw his father's face smiling with pride when Will caught his first fish. He remembered sitting on his father's knee in front of the fire and listening to the deep voice reading aloud from *The Jungle Book*. Will had wanted to be brave like Mowgli.

He glanced at Max, who was smirking as he poked at the bread soaking in the soup bowl. In just a day, he felt closer to the irreverent soldier than he had to anyone in a long time. Was it only because he too knew what a proper American Christmas dinner could be?

As they finished their meager meal, Max leaned back in his chair. "Well, boys, I hope you enjoyed your Christmas dinner. Nothing says holiday cheer like a bowl of lukewarm gruel and a side of death glares."

"We should count ourselves lucky and thank the Reich we got something to fill our bellies," Erich said, his mouth still full of food.

"Lucky indeed," Max said, lifting one lump of bread and letting it fall with a splash into his soup. "I'll be sure to leave a glowing recommendation in the guest book."

"Things will get better, I'm sure," Erich said. "Perhaps they will grant us leave for the new year. My father owns a gasthaus in Füssen. You could all come visit, and my family will feed you well."

For a moment, the four men allowed themselves to share fleeting smiles.

As they stood to leave, Max clapped a hand on Will's shoulder, his grip firm. "Stick close," he murmured, his voice low enough that only Will could hear. "I feel we're going to need to watch each other's backs."

# CHAPTER SEVEN

*Fort Lauderdale, Florida*
*January 1, 1942*

Annie stood on the foredeck, one arm wrapped around the forestay, and gazed downriver as the *Tequesta*'s engines rumbled to life. When she blew on her hands and rubbed them together, she saw a faint white cloud of her own breath. The cold front that had come through the day before had dropped the temperature twenty degrees overnight.

After days of little charter work, three young naval officers had hired the *Tequesta* for two whole days of fishing the reefs and wrecks of the Atlantic. Her father insisted she go as crew to learn all she could from her brother before he left, so for Annie, that meant two days of freedom from waiting tables.

She glanced aft at her brother, who signaled her to untie the dock lines. With the rope in her hands, she nodded to her father, who stood with the stern lines in his hand, and they looped them over the pilings and pushed the boat off in unison.

Their guests were seated back in the cockpit watching her brother as he maneuvered the engine controls. Jack stood, shoulders thrown back, eyes squinting at the water off their bow as the Navy men peppered him with questions about the boat and the sort of fish they might catch. So much for teaching her anything. Jack could never resist an audience.

She should be happy about these two days away from waitressing. This was supposed to be her day for learning how to run this boat, but she didn't know how to feel about that. Sure, she loved sailing, and she was good at it, probably better than her brother if the truth be known, but she didn't want her brother to leave.

Annie stayed at the bow, watching the river banks, and pushing back the strands of hair that had already escaped from her braid. If her brother wanted to train her, he'd have to come to her. Might as well enjoy the ride. She loved watching the bow as it cut through the water.

"Jack's got a lot to learn," her father said, patting her hand.

Annie hadn't heard him come up the deck behind her. When she turned to face him, he was smiling.

"My brother has never figured out that actions speak louder than words."

Skeeter chuckled. "Our Jack is a man of too many words, all right. But he'll come around. You just gotta be patient with him."

"Don't know why I gotta."

"You know he'll be leaving us soon enough. Less than a month now."

"Yeah. And he's supposed to be teaching me to run the boat before he goes, not grandstanding in front of the guests."

Skeeter smiled, the creases around his eyes deepening.

"Go easy on your brother. He just wants to feel important before the Navy ships him out."

She glanced back at Jack as he flung his arm through the air, and the surrounding men threw back their heads in laughter. They had cleared the jetty, and he was pointing to an area of disturbed water.

"See those birds over there?" Jack pointed towards a flock of seagulls hovering over the splashing. "That's where the fish are."

But as they drew closer to the feeding frenzy of fish, the water calmed and the birds flew off.

Annie turned back to her father. "Too busy showing off to actually find anything more than bait."

"Listen, girl," Skeeter said, his tone kind but firm, "you could captain this boat with your eyes closed. You've been reading the stars and tides since you were knee-high, and you seem to find fish with intuition more'n technique. Ain't nothing Jack can teach you that you don't already know."

"And yet you still call me girl," she said with a grin.

Her father tapped the end of her nose. "You will always be my girl. You know that."

Annie retreated to the cabin top just forward of the cockpit as the men's talk turned to U-boats. Rumors of sunken freighters and tankers in the mid-Atlantic chilled the air despite the climbing sun. Jack eyed the officers, nodding along.

"I heard on the radio that they've mined the entrances to New York Harbor and the Chesapeake Bay," one man said. "The entire Atlantic fleet is in Norfolk."

"Those are attack ships. What've we got for defense?" a much younger officer asked.

"They say the Army Air Corps is flying U-boat patrols, but the whole east coast? That's a lot of water to cover."

"Alright, gentlemen," Jack announced. "We're not going to

defeat the Krauts this afternoon. Time to get some lines in the water!" Jack throttled back on the engine, stepped to the rail and picked up one of the fishing poles.

Annie watched as her brother flicked his wrist, casting his line far out into the sea. He looked over at the officers and winked, saying, "Now it's your turn."

She helped distribute a rod and reel to each man, but as they attempted to mimic Jack's technique, their casts fell far short of his. Jack offered encouragement and guidance, his voice booming with authority as he moved between them, adjusting their grips and offering advice on timing.

Soon enough, the officers' casts were sailing out into the open water with ease. But still, no one had had so much as a nibble.

As the day wore on, the naval officers' frustration grew. The empty cooler meant to hold their catch yawned accusingly. But despite the setbacks, Jack continued to work to impress them, adjusting the bait and offering advice on technique.

"Hey sis, why don't you take the helm for a while?" Jack called out. "Let me show these officers how to catch some fish."

This wasn't the first time her brother had struck out at finding fish and asked her to bail him out.

*Let's see if we can't turn this day around*, Annie thought.

She reached into her pocket and, after checking her watch, she gauged the tides and currents. With one hand on the wheel, she lifted the binoculars, scanning the shoreline for familiar landmarks. She spotted the Hillsboro Inlet lighthouse over a mile to the north. In the last couple of hours, they had drifted at least six miles north, she calculated. A mile offshore, a pair of charter powerboats were running with their outriggers spread, their baits skimming the surface. Pelicans and terns wheeled above, diving for the baitfish.

She knew they were already at the fringes of the Gulf Stream. The sea color had changed to that deep cerulean blue. Annie coaxed more speed from the old diesel engines.

She explained to the Navy men that they were going to shift from casting to trolling, and Jack stepped in to show them how to let out their lines.

The *Tequesta* surged forward, her bow cutting through the swells. They'd be in the stream soon now.

It wasn't long before the first strike came.

A reel screamed. "Fish on!" the officer shouted.

The man reeled in a large dorado, its scales shimmering with iridescent blues and golds as it thrashed against the line.

Annie grinned. Pa was right. She didn't need Jack's training.

"Looks like we're in luck," she said, as the officers started hooking large dorado fish one after another.

Jack smiled at his sister, then called over his shoulder, "Ever caught a sail before, boys?"

The tallest officer shook his head, eyes gleaming. "We're relying on you to show us how, Captain."

Jack puffed out his chest. "Well, you've come to the right place. Ain't a fish in these waters I can't catch."

Annie bit her tongue to avoid a retort. Her brother just raised the stakes, but she'd do her best to deliver.

As the naval officers peppered Jack with questions, awe in their voices, Annie turned the wheel to head out into deeper water.

The sea itself had taught her more than any person could. And soon enough, this would be her job. Best to take advantage of the best teacher she'd ever had.

Annie kept her focus forward as the men whooped and hollered behind her. The thrill of the catch was contagious, even if she wasn't holding the rod herself.

"Nice work, Jack!" one officer called out. "You've got a helluva knack for finding fish."

Later that afternoon, Annie steered the boat back towards the dock, lost in thought. This could be her future, supporting the family business. But if all the changes she had seen in town were the price she had to pay, if sending her brother off to risk his life was the reason, then she didn't want this.

As the *Tequesta* approached the pier, Jack began cleaning the officers' fish and accepting their hearty congratulations.

"You've got a gift, son," one said, clapping him on the back. "With skills like yours, you'll go far."

Annie held her tongue, busying herself with tying up the boat. Jack's "skills" would take him away from home soon, as he shipped off to join the Navy.

Once the men disembarked, Jack turned to Annie. "These are my last days at home, Annie. I've got to go meet Emma. Wish her a happy new year. You good finishing up here?"

Annie nodded, lips pressed in a thin line. "Sure. Go see your girl."

As Jack jogged down the pier, she called after him, "Watch out for Ernie Finch. Heard he's been making more trouble lately."

"I can handle Finch," Jack called back.

Annie grabbed a bucket of soapy water and a brush to scrub down the decks. As she worked, she couldn't help but overhear the dockworkers and fishermen nearby talking about

German U-boats attacking American ships up around Boston. She paused in her scrubbing, listening.

"Did you hear that Captain O'Brien's boys are gonna join up with the Mosquito Fleet?" one fisherman asked another.

"Sure did; they're itching for a fight," the other replied, spitting tobacco into the water.

"What's the Mosquito Fleet?" a young boy asked.

"Folks who are helping the Coast Guard patrol with their own boats. Up north they call it the Picket Patrol or the Hooligan's Navy. Us Florida boys are the Mosquito Fleet."

As Annie closed the doors to the deck shuttle and the main companionway, she saw Cap amble over. When the old dockworker gave her a gap-toothed grin, she wondered if he was seeking or spreading gossip.

"Evenin' Annie. Heard those Navy men caught themselves quite a haul today."

Annie nodded. "My brother will dine out on that story for weeks."

Cap chuckled. "Bet he will. Say, word around the dock is Jack's shipping out with the Navy soon. That true?"

Annie hesitated, then said, "I'm not sure of his plans."

"Well, maybe you could pass the word on to him. Some of us were wondering if he'd be up for joining the Mosquito Fleet while he's still here."

"Some of the fellas were talking about that."

"Yeah, word come down from Washington that the Coast Guard is stretched too thin. They're wanting the locals to take up the slack. Extra eyes on the water as the war heats up and all."

Annie held his gaze. "I'll pass along the message."

Later that night, Annie sat rereading one of her favorite books, *Swallows and Amazons,* when the front door creaked open. Jack stumbled in, looking disheveled. His clothes were rumpled and dirty, and his eyes looked troubled.

Their mother jumped up. "Jack, thank heavens! I was worried sick. You said you'd be home hours ago."

"I'm fine, Ma," Jack mumbled, waving her off. He staggered off to his room without another word.

Annie watched him go. Something was wrong. She wanted to talk to him about joining the Mosquito Fleet. Maybe convince him to join that instead of the Navy. But seeing his state now, she doubted he'd be open to reason tonight.

Annie took a deep breath and followed Jack to his room. She knocked softly, then let herself in.

Jack lay sprawled on his bed, one arm flung over his eyes, an issue of *Detective Comics* resting open across his chest. Tess lifted her head when Annie entered, then rested her head back on her brother's leg and closed her eyes. At the sound of the door clicking shut, her brother lifted his arm and peered out at her.

"What do you want?"

"What happened tonight? You and Emma okay?"

"We're both fine." The way he said it made her wonder if that was true.

Annie perched on the edge of the narrow mattress. She lifted the comic book and looked at the cover drawing of Batman. "Really Jack? You wasted ten cents on this?"

"If you just want to criticize my reading material, you can leave now."

"Actually, I heard something interesting down at the docks today."

"Not interested."

"Hear me out. Some of the local captains are talking about forming something called the Mosquito Fleet. They're organizing folks like us, you know, volunteer boats to patrol for U-boats and help protect our shipping lanes."

He showed no reaction.

"It could really make a difference, Jack. And it'd be a chance for you to serve." She hesitated. "Might even be better than joining the Navy and getting sent off to protect some foreigners. Might keep you and us safer, 'cuz of you knowing these waters better than most around here."

Jack snorted. "You don't think I'd join up with those old salts and rummies?"

Annie bristled. "Those are our friends and neighbors. Good men willing to risk their lives."

"And what about you?" Jack tried to smile, but there was no humor in it. "Gonna captain the *Tequesta* out there chasing Krauts yourself?"

Annie lifted her chin. "Maybe I will. Those U-boats threaten all of us, women and children, too. Why shouldn't I help protect our home?"

"Fine. You do that. Just leave me alone."

Stung, Annie set her jaw. "Well, I damn well don't need your permission. I don't know what's got into you, Jack, but I want my old brother back."

Annie strode from the room, letting the door slam behind her.

# CHAPTER EIGHT

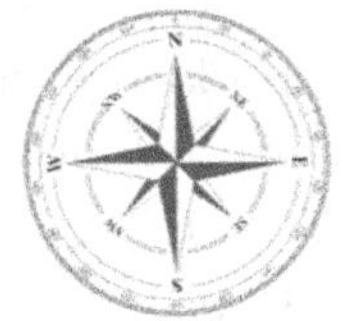

*Fort Lauderdale, Florida*
*January 2, 1942*

The lunch rush at The Deck restaurant was just winding down when Annie burst through the swinging doors into the stifling kitchen heat, her sailor hat askew. All those Navy men had recently discovered The Deck, and she'd never seen the restaurant this busy.

"Miss Cora, table three is still waiting for that meatloaf order."

"Coming right up, fresh out of the oven."

"Thanks," Annie said as she reached for the plate. She noticed the tight-lipped look instead of the usual smile as the tall cook turned back to the stove.

"Is everything okay?"

Then Annie spotted Emma leaning against the stainless steel counter, her head bowed.

"Emma?" Her friend lifted her head, and Annie saw the tears.

Miss Cora, standing tall by the grill, cast a glance over her shoulder. "This is no place for tears," she said. "And it sure isn't no place for what she's been up to."

"Look, I gotta deliver this food, or this guy's going to get the Skipper to fire me. I'll be right back." Annie crossed the kitchen and spun around backwards to push her way out the door with the plate of food in one hand and a coffee pot in the other.

After delivering the meatloaf to the grumbling naval officer, Annie hurried around the dining room making sure the few remaining customers had full coffee cups.

Back in the kitchen, Annie sidled up to Emma. "So, what happened?"

"Last night." Emma's voice was barely audible. "Jack and I—"

"Jack?"

Miss Cora swung around to face them, one fist planted on her hip. "Mm-hmm, your brother. I told her, mixin' with white boys only brings trouble."

"Momma."

"Tell me," Annie said.

"Those boys, you know the ones. They found us. At our spot, up on the North Fork."

"I know the place. We called it Jack's Hideaway. Used to hide out there when we didn't want to do chores."

"We were just talking." Emma's eyes darted back and forth between her mother and Annie. "Really. But those men..." She shuddered. "They chased us, shouting things, hateful things."

Cora sniffed. "Just talkin'."

Emma sat up straighter, her reddened eyes wide. "Momma, it's true."

Annie reached for her friend's hand. "Tell me what happened next. Where'd you go?"

"We ran and hid in Leroy's Auto," Emma said, referring to the only black-owned garage in town.

"Did they see you go in there?"

Emma shook her head. "Jack's smart. We hid behind Leroy's own old Model A. My heart was hammering so loud, I thought they'd hear it."

Annie wasn't sure how smart her brother was, seeing as he got caught to start with. "Did Leroy help you?"

Emma nodded. "Kept us safe 'til they left. Then Jack walked me home." Emma looked up at her mother's back.

"Christ Almighty," Annie shook her head.

Miss Cora swung around, both hands on her hips now. "Annie Jeeves, we don't talk like that 'round here."

"Sorry, Miss Cora. But I knew something had happened last night when Jack got home. I should have weaseled it out of him."

Cora's voice cut her off. "You best get back to work, Annie."

"Sure thing, Miss Cora," Annie said.

"And Emma," she pointed her finger at her daughter. "You and I, we'll talk more about this later."

Annie didn't move right away. Instead, she held Emma's hand a moment longer. Their eyes met and held the gaze, then with a nod at her friend, Annie headed back out into the dining room.

~

Annie and Emma stepped out of the Deck Restaurant, their workday over. Their route along Los Olas Boulevard passed busy shops, and cars lined the road, their rounded metal bodies gleaming as they jockeyed for parking spots. Even though it was late afternoon and time to head home for supper, the sidewalks were still filled with strolling housewives and men in and out of uniform.

Silence stretched between the young women as they walked, Annie in front, Emma a few steps behind. Annie wasn't used to seeing her friend with red-rimmed eyes, her face and hair mussed up. Emma usually dressed so nice in dresses her mama made, and since she'd been seeing more of Jack, she'd started wearing lipstick, too. Annie sometimes envied how pretty her friend was.

It wasn't until they reached the boundaries of Sailboat Bend and the city fell behind them, though, that Annie felt comfortable enough to fall back and walk next to her friend.

"Jack shouldn't never have taken you there," Annie finally broke their silence.

Emma lifted one shoulder in a shrug. "He thought it'd be safe after dark. We just wanted a place where we could talk, be ourselves."

Annie ran her hand across the back of her neck. "Nothing's safe round here, not for the two of you."

"I know that now."

"Emma, I hate that it's so. I wish we lived in a world where you and I could walk arm in arm and let the whole world know you're my best friend. Where we could both go to the same school. Where Jack could take you to see a picture at the Colony Theater and sit in the front row. But that's not this town."

"I know that better than you."

They walked a few more steps in silence.

"Annie, I'm scared," Emma whispered, her voice barely audible. "What if those boys come back? What if they try to hurt Jack... or my family?"

"Let 'em try," Annie said.

"Easy for you to say. You're white."

That stung. Before Annie could respond, a commotion at

the far end of the street caught her attention. Finn Taggart came running toward them, his ginger curls bouncing with each stride. His blue eyes locked on Annie, urgency written all over his face.

"Annie!" he called out, breathless when he reached them. "I've been looking everywhere for you."

"Hey, Finn." Annie felt a flutter in her stomach at the sight of him. "Is everything okay?"

Finn was bent over, hands on his knees, still trying to catch his breath. "It's Jack." He straightened up. "There are rumors swirling around the shipyard. Some local boys are planning to rough him up. They think he's—"

"Been seeing a colored girl," Annie finished for him.

"Exactly." His eyes flicked between Annie and Emma. "It's got them riled up something fierce."

Emma covered her mouth, her eyes glistening. Then she hugged herself, looking skyward. "What have we done?"

Annie reached out and took hold of her friend's shoulders. "This is not your fault."

"But we knew *the rules*. Every colored girl in this town, heck, this whole country knows better."

"Em, those are stupid rules for stupid people. Ernie's had it in for my family ever since I turned down his advances in high school. But those Finch boys are cowards." She knew once she'd said it that it wouldn't matter. Like the other night on the dock, there was strength in numbers, and Ernie showed he wouldn't fight fair.

"Annie," Finn touched her elbow. "They're not just talking. They mean to act on it."

Annie paled. If those boys caught Jack alone...

"You're right." Annie spun around and looked down the street towards home, then back at her friends. She needed to find Jack now and warn him.

"Emma," Finn said, "Look here, I'll follow you home, make sure there's no trouble for you."

Annie reached out and took hold of her two best friends' hands. "Thanks, Finn." She turned to Emma. "You get home. I'll find Jack."

Emma's eyes, still rimmed with red and swollen from crying, met Annie's as she nodded. "You be safe too, my friend. There's no telling what those Finch boys will do."

Annie watched as they walked away, Emma's slender frame dwarfed by Finn's taller presence. A part of her longed to follow, to be enveloped in the safety of Finn's company, but another part knew she had to find her brother. Now.

Turning, she took off down the street, her path homeward a blur of storefronts and passing faces. Why hadn't Jack confided in her? She had been there, right in his room, and he'd said nothing of the danger, nothing about Emma.

He didn't trust her; that's why. She was the one who broke her promise.

"Jack, where are you?" she said aloud to herself. Pa would know what to do. Then she took off at a run, racing through the streets towards home.

Annie flew up the steps and burst through the front door of the little bungalow, startling her mother, who was darning socks in the living room.

"Annie! Heavens, child, what's the matter with you?" Hilda frowned, taking in Annie's wild eyes and heaving chest.

"Ma, have you seen Jack?"

Skeeter emerged from the kitchen, his brow furrowed in concern.

"Pops, do you know where Jack is?"

"No, sweetheart. What's wrong?"

"Jack's in trouble." Annie told them where her brother had been the evening before when he'd come back late and disheveled. "Seems some of the local boys chased him and Emma last night, hooting and hollering awful things. Finn says it was the talk of his shift at Dooley's today. Says they mean to find Jack and teach him a lesson."

Skeeter closed his eyes for several seconds. "Damn it." He pulled off his cap and slapped it against his thigh. "I knew that boy was playing with fire."

Annie opened her mouth to explain further, but the crunch of tires on the driveway interrupted her. All three turned towards the window, just in time to see a familiar black sedan pull up behind their Chevrolet.

"Aw hell." Skeeter shook his head.

The car door swung open, and out stepped the imposing figure of Sheriff Walter Clark.

Tess trotted to the door and emitted a low growl.

Her parents exchanged a look, then her father tilted his head towards the hallway, signaling Annie to go to her room. She took hold of the dog's collar as her parents stepped out onto the porch, leaving the front door ajar.

Annie pulled Tess into her room and closed the door. She crossed to the window next to her desk and drew the curtains back a few inches. Sitting on her desk chair, she had a clear view of the porch.

"Evening, Sheriff." Skeeter's voice boomed. He was trying to sound casual, but making sure all the neighbors would be at their windows, too. "What brings you here?"

Sheriff Clark hitched up his belt and his gaze swept over them, his expression unreadable. "My Deputy heard some talk 'round town." He looked up at the front of their home as he shifted a wad of tobacco under his lip. "Seems your boy Jack's been mixin' with the wrong sort of company." His eyes settled on Skeeter with a squint, like he smelled something rotten.

Her father pulled out his pipe and a box of matches from

his pocket. Taking his time, he struck a match, then took several long puffs of the fragrant smoke.

After blowing out a long white stream of smoke, Skeeter finally spoke. "Jack's a good kid, Sheriff." His voice was calm and steady. "He's mighty friendly. Friends with just about everybody in this town."

"See here, Skeeter. Don't you try to play games with me. That boy of yours," Sheriff Clark hawked, turned and spat a stream of tobacco juice over the porch railing. "Folks are mighty riled up about him runnin' around with a colored girl. Ain't right, Skeeter. You know that."

Annie thought about all the times Sheriff Clark had ordered his food while staring at various parts of her body. She'd tell him a thing or two about what wasn't right. As she stepped back from the window, a hand grasped her shoulder.

She whirled, mouth opening, ready to cry out.

Jack stood behind her, and he pressed two fingers to her lips.

Relief flooded through her. She rested her forehead against his chest and took a deep breath.

Jack stepped back and tilted his head toward the window. Annie sat back down on the wooden chair, and her brother leaned over her. Together, they peered through the gap in the curtains.

Skeeter had straightened, pipe still clenched between his teeth.

"I appreciate the concern, Sheriff." His voice was loud, but calm. "But I reckon me and Hilda can handle our own. Besides, Jack's got more important things to worry about than some gal." He drew in a mouthful of smoke and blew it out in the lawman's direction. "He'll be shipping out any day now, off to fight the Jerries."

Something flickered in the Sheriff's expression, there and gone too quick to parse. He rocked back on his heels. "Don't think I won't come for the boy if I have to, Jeeves. What he's done ain't right."

Skeeter met the sheriff's gaze without flinching. "And what exactly has my son done, Sheriff? Last I checked, it wasn't against the law to walk a girl home." He puffed on his pipe again. "Of course, if some damn fools were to come after my boy, a young man headed off to fight for his country... I imagine folks round here wouldn't take too kindly to that."

Skeeter didn't give him a chance to respond.

"I'd make sure everyone knew exactly who sent those boys. How Walter Clark's thugs attacked an American hero." Skeeter straightened. "So you go on ahead if you feel the need. But this family will be ready, and everyone in this town will know just who to blame."

The sheriff's face darkened, then he looked around at the other houses on the street. He rubbed his hand across his mouth. "Well, I suppose even our local boys can scrape up some patriotism when needed." His gaze flicked to Hilda, hard and assessing. "Best he mind himself until that train whistle blows. This town don't look kindly on race-mixing, war or no war."

"I'll be sure to tell him." Skeeter's tone was neutral, but Annie could see the muscle ticking in her father's clenched jaw. "That all, Sheriff?"

Clark took his time adjusting his gun belt, letting his hand linger on the heavy wooden grip of his revolver. "For now," he said.

With a final disgusted look, Sheriff Clark turned and swaggered back round his car. He opened the door and paused. "You best get a handle on that boy." Sheriff Clark sucked his teeth in a grimace. "Otherwise, there might be consequences."

Once the taillights faded into the distance, Skeeter turned

and held the door open for his wife. Jack and Annie turned from the window and walked into the hallway.

Skeeter exhaled loudly at the sight of his son. “Glad you’re home safe, son.” Then he gestured for the family to sit down in the living room.

Pa leaned forward, his elbows on his knees. “Jack has to leave come sunrise,” he said. “It ain’t safe for him here no more.”

“But we need more time,” Ma said.

“We just run outta’ time.”

“I’m sorry, Pa.”

“No Jack,” Annie said, “I’m the one who’s sorry. I never should have broken my promise to you. You shouldn’t feel like you’ve got to keep secrets from the family.”

“What’s done is done. Jack’s been itchin’ to head off to flight school training, anyways, and Annie’s ready as she’ll ever be to take over the boat.”

Their father stood and walked to the coat closet to retrieve the family shotgun. “We’ll take shifts through the night,” he said. “Keep watch, make sure no one comes snooping ‘round.”

Ma nodded and began assigning watch shifts. Pa gave instructions, each family member nodding solemnly as their role was assigned.

“We’ll all stand watch by the front window. Get up and check the back every ten minutes. Two hours each per shift. Keep those eyes sharp,” Skeeter directed.

“Pop, I—” Annie started, but caught herself. This wasn’t the time for fear or hesitation.

“Annie,” he said, handing her the shotgun, “you’re up first.”

# CHAPTER NINE

*Wiesbaden, Germany*
*January 2, 1942*

Will sat on the wood-frame bed in his childhood room, his canvas duffle resting next to him. The bag was nondescript, military-issue, and bulged at the seams from the hasty packing. The new army uniform felt stiff and scratchy. It didn't fit him in more ways than one.

Downstairs, he could hear his mother clanking pans as she moved around in the kitchen. Lowering his head, he rubbed his hand across his eyes. He hadn't slept well on the narrow bed the last two nights. Thoughts of what lay ahead had kept sleep at bay.

The room was small, the furniture sparse; just a small wooden desk and bookshelf stuffed with novels in both English and German. Here, in this small space, he'd sought refuge from the jeers of children who couldn't comprehend his American accent or the far-off look he wore whenever he spoke of baseball or Chicago's skyscrapers.

He reached over and traced a finger along the spine of a

book left on the nightstand. It had been his father's favorite detective novel, and was now dog-eared and well-thumbed. Will remembered sitting at the small wooden desk years ago, writing his own stories in his illegible cursive script, certain that when he was grown up, he would sell those stories of gallant knights and terrifying monsters and become a famous writer.

And look at him now. Not only writing propaganda for the Reich in order to save himself from the front, but now he was agreeing to go on some mission to win the war for the real-life monsters who had taken over this country. He still wasn't able to call this place *his* country. Resting his forehead on the heels of his hands, he closed his eyes.

Visions from that last day at Marineschule Mürwik, their first psychological training, continued to haunt him. Ordered to report to the academy's basement after dinner one night, he and Max had laughed at first as they descended the narrow stone steps into darkness. The air grew colder with each step, carrying a strange metallic smell that made Will's skin crawl.

At the bottom, they found themselves in a long, narrow room with walls of sweating stone. Chairs arranged in rows faced a small stage where a screen and projector had been set up. Admiral Canaris introduced Dr. Kaufmann, a thin man in wire-rimmed spectacles who looked more like an accountant than part of a military operation.

"Sit." Kaufmann made it sound more like an invitation than an order. "Tonight we begin your ideological preparation."

Will took a seat between Max and Adler. Erich wheezed as he lowered himself into the chair behind them.

"You've been learning to play the parts of merchant sailors," Dr. Kaufmann began, his voice soft, almost hypnotic. "You have been issued new identities for this mission. Soon, you will train for survival, combat and demolition. But the greatest battle is not with explosives or knives. It is here." He tapped his temple. "Your mind will betray you in America. It will whisper that these are innocent people. That what you do is wrong. Tonight, we begin to silence those whispers."

The lights dimmed. The projector clicked on.

At first, the images were benign: American cities, factories, families at dinner. Then came the newspaper headlines: *Germans Banned from Public Pools. Speaking German Now Illegal. German-Americans Forced into Camps.*

"This is what America does to Germans," Kaufmann said over the clicking projector. "Your people. Perhaps your own relatives."

Will knew some of it was true. He'd heard about the internment camps, the suspicion that fell on anyone with a German surname.

The images shifted. Now they showed American soldiers, but the photographs had been doctored. Distorted faces transformed into leering masks, while their hands dripped with what looked like blood.

"They rape." Kaufman's voice took on a sing-song, hypnotic rhythm. "They pillage. They destroy. This is not propaganda. This is their nature. They are not civilized men like you. They are beasts who wear the mask of civilization."

Click. Click. Click. The images came faster now. Bombed German cities. Dead children. Women weeping over rubble. Will recognized some photos. They were from the ministry where he'd worked, images they'd staged for propaganda. But mixed in were actual photos, too, making it impossible to separate truth from fabrication.

"Every factory you destroy," Kaufmann continued, "will save German lives. Every rail line you cut will prevent weapons from reaching the pilots who bomb our cities. You are not saboteurs. You are the guardian angels of the Reich."

Behind him, Will heard Erich sniffle.

The images stopped on a photograph of Hitler, benevolent and paternal, surrounded by German children.

"Close your eyes," Kaufmann commanded.

They obeyed.

"When you are in America, when doubt creeps in, remember this: You are the sword of your country. Every action you take, every life you end, is a life saved here. Your mother. Your sister. Your neighbors. They sleep in peace because you do what must be done."

"Repeat after me," Kaufmann said. "I feel no guilt for righteousness."

"I feel no guilt for righteousness."

"My enemies are not human."

Will's throat tightened. Around him, voices repeated the phrase. He moved his lips but couldn't force the words out.

"Hersey!" Kaufmann's voice cracked like a whip. "I don't hear you."

"My enemies are not human," Will said.

They continued for an hour. Phrases designed to burrow into the unconscious. Images that would surface in dreams. Will had begun to dissociate, to float above his body and watch himself mouth the words. It had been the only way to endure it.

He lifted his head and looked around his childhood bedroom, the memory of Kaufmann's voice still echoing in his mind. He remembered the child he had been, angry at leaving the only home he had known in America, forced to come live in this house with a stern grandfather and a grieving mother. What would that boy think of what he was about to do?

With one last glance around the room, Will stood and hoisted the duffle's strap onto his shoulder. The worn floorboards creaked beneath his boots as he moved towards the door. Descending the narrow staircase required a practiced tilt of the head. He had grown so much since the days when he could barrel down them without a care. He slapped his free hand against one of the old beams, darkened by time and smoke, and dropped his duffle at the foot of the stairs.

The kitchen greeted him with the warm, yeasty aroma of freshly baked bread. His mother stood with her back to him, the muscles of her shoulders tense as she attended to something on the stove. The sizzle and pop of food cooking covered the sound of his footsteps.

"*Mutti*," Will whispered, not wanting to startle her.

She turned, wiping her hands on the apron tied around her waist. Her eyes, shining with tears, met his, and it struck Will how the lines on her face were now etched much deeper than he remembered.

"Two days, Wilhelm. It's not enough." Her head moved slowly from side to side.

He stepped forward, closing the distance, and wrapped his arms around her. He could feel her shaking, clinging to the fabric of his shirt as if she could hold him there, safe from harm.

"Everything will be fine, *Mutti*," he whispered into the silver strands of hair that smelled of wood smoke. He wanted to etch the moment in his memory to get him through what was to come.

When they pulled apart, she motioned to a chair. "A few more minutes, please. I don't know when I will see you again." She dragged another chair around so that they sat facing each other, knees touching. "You remind so much of your father in this uniform. Of course, his was American." A tentative smile played about her lips. "But you are about the same age now as he was when I first met him."

"You and Papa told me the story many times. The shop girl and the soldier."

The smile won, and Will saw a hint of the beautiful young woman she must have been.

"My father never approved of Jacob, but he was a good man, a wonderful father. And he was always so proud of you."

Will snorted. "I wish he'd told me that."

"He was not a talker, but he listened." She lifted a corner of her apron and dabbed at her eyes. Her chin dimpled as she struggled to say, "Perhaps too well."

"*Mutti,* that is all in the past now." Will wanted to stop her before she got started on her conspiracy theories about his father's death. Subpoenaed to testify against a group of corrupt police officers, Will's father had been shot in a dark alley two days before his court appearance. His mother never believed his killer was a thief, the story the department released. She had loved her new home country right up until the day that police officer had come to their door and delivered the news. The next day, she made plans to return to Germany with her 11-year-old son.

Will cleared his throat. "I need to go, or I will miss my train."

She stood and slid her chair back into place. When she reached for a napkin-wrapped bundle resting on the table, her smile returned.

"I made bread for you," she said, her fingers lingering on the rough fabric. "From the flour I've been saving from our rations." She handed him the parcel. "Take it. It will give you strength."

"But..."

She held his gaze for a moment, then glanced at the old family clock on the mantel, the one item she had brought from Chicago. "Some things are worth preserving, Wilhelm. Even when everything else changes."

"*Danke,*" he said, accepting the offering. Rationally, he knew the army would provide rations. Efficiency was drilled into every German citizen. And he also knew that the two of them, his mother and grandfather, would go without bread now, but to decline the gift would cause her more pain.

Will looked past his mother towards the front door. He needed to get moving.

"When will you—"

"*Mutti*, please." Will's interruption was soft but firm. "You know I cannot talk about that."

The sound of heavy footsteps signaled his grandfather's approach, and Will stepped back, bracing himself for the inevitable clash.

"Wilhelm," the gravelly voice boomed from the threshold.

The old man appeared in the kitchen doorway, his white hair combed back, his eyes dark with his ever-present anger.

"Grandfather," Will greeted him with respect, though his insides knotted at the sight of the man.

The old man stepped forward, his gait unsteady but determined, and placed a hand on Will's shoulder.

"Look at you, my boy," he said. "A loyal son of the Reich."

Will met his mother's gaze, a silent apology passing between them, before turning to face his grandfather.

"I'll do my best to make the Fatherland proud," he said, the words like bile in his throat.

"Your father may have been an American," the old man began, the corners of his mouth tugging downward in distaste, "but you had no choice in that. You are also of our blood."

His grandfather never said the words, but Will always knew in the old man's eyes, he was not of "pure blood."

"You carry the honor of the Fatherland on this journey."

Honor. Will reserved that word for his actual father. As if that madman in Berlin knew the meaning. He ground his teeth as the staunch old nationalist rambled on, heaping praises on the Reich. Will bore it in silence, but he noticed the words sounded like a rote repetition. He wondered if the old man had lost some of his fervor after three winters of war.

"Go now, fulfill your duty." His grandfather raised his arm in salute. "*Heil Hitler!*"

Will refused to return the salute. He shouldered his duffel, and with a last glance at his mother, he stepped out into the cool morning, the echo of his grandfather's words trailing behind him.

Gulping the fresh air to cleanse the bitterness from his lungs, he quickened his pace down the dirt path that led to the city streets. He needed to put distance between himself and the little cottage that no longer felt like home.

Several blocks from the train station, Will heard the rhythmic chanting before he saw them: a Hitler Youth troop practicing drill formations in a small square. Their leader, perhaps twelve, barked commands while the younger boys wheeled and turned with practiced precision.

At the sight of Will's uniform, the boys snapped to attention, arms raised in salute. "*Heil Hitler!*" their youthful voices cried out.

The boys held the pose, faces alight with pride at demonstrating their training. He knew what they expected of him, but he couldn't. After a long moment, he nodded and continued on his way.

Will arrived at the train station, the looming red brick building seeming to pulse with energy. Soldiers, families, travelers hurried about the platform, the tension and anticipation palpable in the air.

He sank down onto a worn wooden bench, the grain rough under his hand. The duffel bag landed beside him with a dull thud. The wrapped bread shifted inside, and Will extracted it from the bag. A breeze stirred, and the flap of the napkin lifted, revealing just the corner of what lay beneath. Will loosened the knot his mother had tied with such care.

As the flap of the napkin fell open, a sliver of sunlight caught the crust of the homemade bread, gilding it with warmth and highlighting the grains of flour dusted across its surface.

For a moment, the simplicity of the gift transfixed Will. He reached out, his fingers brushing the soft fabric of the napkin.

Something metallic glinted from within the folds. Frowning, he reached in and extracted a round, silver object. His father's police badge.

Will's throat tightened. He hadn't seen the badge since he'd left America, when he was just a boy. He turned it over, taking in each familiar scratch and dent.

A slip of paper fluttered free from the napkin. Will picked it up off the ground. In his mother's delicate script were the words: *Make your father proud.*

# CHAPTER TEN

*Fort Lauderdale, Florida*
*January 3, 1942*

When Annie stepped out into the cool, gray morning, rubbing her eyes after a night of little sleep, she saw Finn and Bean were already there, leaning against the old Chevy.

"G'morning, sunshine," Finn said, his crooked smile making her wish she'd put on something more flattering than her old gingham shift.

"Hardly." She shuffled past him and stood in front of Bean. "What are you doing up at this hour?"

"Jack woke me up when it was still dark," the girl said. "He told us to come say goodbye."

Annie thought of her reckless brother leaving the house in the dark to go make sure his best friend could see him off at the station. All she could think about last night as she stood her watch, and later as she tossed and turned in bed, was all the what-ifs. This war, Sheriff Clark, Jack's leaving, it all made her feel so helpless.

"Where's Jack going?" the girl asked.

The screen door swung open, and her brother strolled out with an olive-colored bag slung over his shoulder. He struck a pose with one arm held skyward.

"I'm off to fight for Truth, Justice and the American Way."

Bean's eyes grew wide. "You got a red cape in that bag?"

Jack swung open the car's rear door and tossed in his duffle.

Annie rolled her eyes. "Ignore him, girl. Despite what my brother might think, he's no superhero."

Jack turned to deliver his comeback, but the paws that landed on his thigh interrupted him. "Hey there, Tess. No, you're not coming along with us today." He squatted in the dirt next to the car and buried his face in the fur on her neck. "I'm gonna miss you, girl." The dog squirmed and licked his cheek.

Annie swallowed hard and turned away. Tess had been a gift from their father on Jack's tenth birthday, the cutest little ball of brown and white fur. She'd always been Jack's dog.

Just then, Mama emerged, followed behind by a bleary-eyed Skeeter. "Bethany, you'll ride up front with me and Pa. If we don't hurry, Jack's gonna miss his train."

Finn opened the door to the back seat. "After you," he said. Annie felt his fingers touch the small of her back as she climbed in. The backseat was going to be a tight fit, with Annie crammed between her brother and Finn. She fidgeted, trying to ignore the electricity tingling through her as their bare arms brushed together.

Her brother slid in from the other door, rubbing at one eye. "Scoot over!" Then he grinned at her discomfort. "Cozy enough for ya?"

"Cut it out." Annie gave her brother a playful swat, but she could feel her face glowing with heat.

The old Chevy sputtered to life as Skeeter turned the key.

Hilda settled in the front seat, Bean's compact form on her lap. They pulled out of the driveway and onto the street lined with boxy cinderblock homes and shotgun shacks. When he turned onto Lauderdale Trail, Annie admired the gabled roof of Commodore Brook's two-story house.

"Look at that," Finn said, pointing to the arched doors and windows of Lady Claire's Spanish-style bungalow next door. "I hear they throw some real swanky parties there. Maybe we should check it out one of these days, Annie."

"Sure, and then maybe we can hop a flight to New York City for dinner," she replied, though the thought of escaping to a world far removed from her own held a certain appeal.

"Hey, you never know," Finn said with a grin. "Stranger things have happened."

They hadn't driven more than a few blocks further when they spotted a black sedan idling in an alleyway. Through the windshield, Ernie Finch's slight frame looked dwarfed next to Sheriff Clark's hulking silhouette.

"Looks like we've got company." Pa sat up straight and gripped the steering wheel so hard his knuckles turned white.

"Damn it," Annie whispered. "Why won't they just leave us alone?"

"Keep your cool, kid," Pa said. "We're just taking our boy to the train, same as any other family."

The Chevy turned onto Broward Boulevard, and Annie felt her brother shift in his seat as they drove over the bridge crossing the North Fork of the New River, near to the not-so-secret spot where Jack and Emma had put all this in motion.

"Look at that," Hilda murmured, pointing to a great blue heron coasting down to a graceful landing on the river bank. "Even in times like these, life goes on."

Times like these. War time. Her brother was being unusually quiet. Annie wondered what thoughts were churning through Jack's mind as they drove past sights grown so familiar since coming to this town. What if this was the last time he would set eyes on this place, on his family, on her?

The very thought made her feel queasy, so she told herself to stop thinking about that.

The big car rolled to a stop outside the bustling Fort Lauderdale train station. Finn climbed out and reached back for her hand. As her feet met the pavement, Annie felt the blood reddening her face and ears again, and she released his hand before he noticed her flustered reaction. He was just being polite, and she didn't want him to know what his actions were doing to her.

"Thanks," she mumbled without meeting his eyes.

"Come on, dear," Mama said as Bean slid off her lap. The girl gazed up at Finn with a question in her eyes.

"Can I go with you?"

Finn shook his head. "You stay with Annie." He walked around the car to join Skeeter and Jack. The men headed inside to secure the ticket, leaving Annie, Bean and Ma to navigate the bustling platform.

Smartly dressed soldiers embraced weeping wives and mothers, while harried porters lugged trunks and duffel bags. New recruits inspected their kits while sizing up their fellow travelers. The loudspeaker crackled announcing the northbound train's arrival. Bean clung to Mama's hand, wide-eyed at the organized chaos around them.

"Is Jack coming back?" she asked.

Mama smoothed the girl's hair. "Of course he is."

Annie wished she could freeze time, imprint every detail of this moment in her memory. She longed to sketch the frenzied mayhem on the platform, but more than anything, she wished her brother would still be here come morning to captain the *Tequesta* as always.

"I can't believe it, Ma. Jack, our Jack, going off to fight. I thought we'd have more time. It doesn't seem real."

Hilda's eyes remained fixed on the men and women around them. "I can believe it," she said, her tone even. "After Pearl Harbor, nothing surprises me anymore."

"Just seems so hasty is all."

"Sometimes, Annie," Ma said, "the best we can do is choose between terrible options. This war..." Her voice trailed off. Then, glancing back at the uniformed men, she said, "It will demand more impossible choices before we're done, I'm afraid."

Annie opened her mouth to argue when she saw Jack, dodging his way through the throng, tickets in hand. He had his duffel slung over one shoulder. Finn and her father followed close behind.

"Got the tickets!" Jack announced, brandishing the papers like trophies. "All set."

"Good." Hilda forced a fragile smile.

As they stood together, Annie noticed the Sheriff's black car idling in the parking lot, Ernie Finch leaning against the side of it, his beady eyes watching them like a vulture waiting to swoop.

"Looks like we got ourselves an audience," Skeeter said, keeping his eyes fixed on the car.

Jack followed his gaze and grinned. "Think they came to see me off?"

Skeeter sighed, "Or chase you out, more like."

He clapped a hand on Jack's shoulder. "Doesn't matter now, son. Don't let their presence weigh on you."

"Not a chance, Pops. I want to fly more than anything." Jack's smile was genuine now, lighting up his eyes. "Nothing can ground me today."

"Thatta boy," Skeeter nodded in approval. "Just checking your bearings."

"Well, ain't this a right fine farewell committee!" a booming voice called out. Cap Knight ambled towards them, his denim overalls hanging from his broad shoulders. "Heard you were shipping out this morning."

"News travels fast in small towns." Jack met Cap with a firm handshake.

The older man thumped him on the back. "You're doing a brave thing, son. You keep your head on straight out there, ya hear?"

"Yessir," Jack said, standing taller. "I aim to do Fort Lauderdale proud."

"That's the spirit! And don't you fret none about the *Tequesta*. I'll keep a watchful eye out." He winked at Annie.

Annie bristled at the insinuation that she needed Cap's supervision, but held her tongue. This was Jack's moment.

"Appreciate it, Cap," Jack said. "Means the world."

The train whistle sounded just to the south of them, and Cap turned and vanished into the milling crowds. The loudspeaker cautioned folks to stand clear of the incoming train.

Finn stepped forward and clasped Jack's shoulder.

"Guess it's my job to keep these knuckleheads in line now, huh?" Finn's smile didn't quite reach his eyes as he gestured toward Annie and Bean.

"Knuckleheads?" Annie crossed her arms and glared at Finn through narrowed eyes.

"I'd advise you to stay away from my sister, my friend." Jack's tone danced between jest and warning.

"Wouldn't dream of it." Finn's eyes locked on hers until Jack punched him on the arm.

"I'm just warning you for your own good, brother."

Jack threw his arms around Finn. Annie heard him speak into his friend's ear. "And think about joining up."

Finn pushed back and held Jack at arms' length. "Maybe." He inclined his head toward Annie. "But someone's gotta be here to make sure your sister doesn't run wild."

"Ha! Too late for that," Annie said.

Bean tugged at Jack's sleeve next, her small fingers curling around the fabric. "You'll write to us?"

"Every chance I get, firecracker." Jack knelt down to meet her eye level, ruffling her hair. "Keep giving 'em hell, Bean."

"Always do." She mustered a brave nod.

One by one, each family member took their turn. Skeeter clasped Jack's hand, a silent communication of love and concern passing between father and son. Annie could see the tension in her father's jaw, the effort it took for him to keep his composure.

"Remember what I taught you." Skeeter's voice was rough. "And stay sharp."

"Will do, Pop." Jack swallowed hard.

Annie watched as her mother stepped forward, cupping Jack's face, a rare gentleness in her touch.

"Jack," Hilda began, her voice heavy with sorrow and pride. "War makes men of boys and widows of wives. Keep your heart true and your head low."

"I will, Ma," Jack choked out.

Annie's own throat constricted at the intimacy of their exchange. Hilda enfolded Jack in a fierce embrace that conveyed what words could not.

Then she held his shoulders at arm's length and took one last lingering look. "And come back to us."

"I promise," he murmured before stepping back, his gaze roving over each beloved face.

As the train slid into the station, Annie caught sight of a lone figure hovering on the edge of the platform. Emma Albury. Even from a distance, Annie could see the tears streaking down her friend's lovely face. She was clutching something to her chest.

Annie waved her over, shooting a furtive glance at the Sheriff. He had straightened up from the car, his eyes narrowing as he watched Emma approach.

"Emma, honey, I'm so glad you came." Annie spoke into her ear, folding her friend into a swift hug.

"I had to be here," Emma whispered back. She turned to Jack, holding out a cloth-covered basket with a tentative look on her face. "Mama sent this for your trip. It's not much, but..."

"This looks incredible, Em. Thank you." Jack's smile was affectionate but fleeting as his eyes flicked to the approaching Sheriff.

"Thank you." His fingers lingered on hers a heartbeat too long as he took the basket. Then, quick as a magician, he slipped something small and folded into Emma's palm. It vanished into her sleeve without a trace.

As the train came to a final halt, the crowd swarmed forward, seeking their correct cars. In the chaos, Emma slipped away and disappeared into the throng.

"Em!" Jack called after her. He stood on the balls of his feet, craning his neck, searching for any sign of her in the sea of faces.

Annie knew she couldn't delay any longer. She grasped her brother's arm, recapturing his attention. "Hey, try not to crash too many planes, hotshot."

Jack enveloped her in a fierce bear hug, lifting her off her feet.

Her voice was tight when she said, "Take care of yourself, okay?"

"Always do, Sis." He squeezed her so tight she couldn't breathe, then released her with a laugh.

The conductor's voice rang out, and Jack's eyes flicked toward the train.

"Go," Annie whispered, fighting back tears. "You don't want to miss your ride."

"Right. I will be back. I promise."

“Last call for the Silver Meteor to Jacksonville,” the conductor called again.

“Goodbye all!” Jack called as he stepped onto the train car, gripping the railing. “See you soon!”

The train whistle cut through the moment, shrill and ominous. Jack straightened up and disappeared up the steps and into the train.

With a groan of metal, the train shuddered into motion, steam hissing as the wheels began turning. Annie watched the train chug away, leaving only a plume of smoke rising against the Florida sky. It was all too real now.

The war had come to Fort Lauderdale.

# CHAPTER ELEVEN

*Fort Lauderdale, Florida*
*January 13, 1942*

Annie pulled on her faded overalls and fastened the buckles with a sense of relief after days spent trapped in dresses. She was feeling like herself once more as she braided her hair and prepared to leave for her charter as captain of the *Tequesta*.

"Annie," her mother called from the living room, "you don't want to be late today."

"Sure thing, Ma." Annie tucked her braid under a faded baseball cap that had once belonged to her brother.

She checked her reflection in the mirror. She wanted to look like she was a serious, knowledgeable captain. After having two charters cancel on her this week, she had wondered if she was going to fail at this job before she even got started. Then late yesterday afternoon, Mr. Crowley from down in Miami, who'd known Pa for years, came by and booked a family outing for this morning. Maybe it was a bit of a charity move, but she didn't care. They needed the work and the money, and she needed to show that Jack wasn't the only Jeeves who could run the family business.

Leaning against the doorframe, she watched her mother cut black fabric into large rectangles. Her sewing basket rested on a chair, and the scissors clinked against the table as she worked.

Annie leaned over the sink and looked out the window. She could see patches of blue sky between the branches of the live oak trees in their side yard. "Are we expecting enemy planes?"

Her mother sighed and set down her scissors. She turned in her chair and looked at Annie. "I don't know what to expect anymore."

Annie grabbed a glass and filled it with water. "I hate the way this war is changing every little thing about our lives." She gestured towards the table. "Even the dang curtains." After she took a long drink, she held up her water glass as if in a toast. "On the bright side, Mr. Crowley hasn't cancelled. At least not yet."

What she didn't tell her mother was that Finn had told her yesterday he had to work at Dooley's, so she would be working her first charter sail solo. Fortunately, she knew the Crowleys well, and they would be happy to lend a hand on the boat.

"Don't think so negative, child. You've got a job today; that's all that matters." Her mother turned back around and resumed her cutting. "By the way, we sure could use some fish. Folks say these new rationing cards are going to limit the meat we can buy."

Annie nodded and grabbed her rucksack. "Fish for mama, coming right up." She pushed her way out the screen door and started the walk to town.

When she turned down Andrews Avenue headed towards the bridge, she could already smell the fleet on the southeasterly breeze. Dozens of fishing boats lined both sides of the New River, and crowds of captains and customers thronged on the docks.

She stopped in one of the few small patches of shade beneath a coconut palm and pulled Jack's letter out of her pocket. Resting her back against the tree trunk, her lips moved as she reread her brother's words for what must have been at least the tenth time.

*Going to England sooner than expected.*

Those were the words that always made her feel nauseous.

*When they saw what I could do, they cut short my flight school training and awarded me my wings. They're sending a couple of us off to train with the RAF. And by the way, that's Ensign Jeeves to you now.*

Any hope she'd had that he might flunk out of training was now dashed. Her brother would soon fly combat missions over enemy territory.

"Damn it, Jack." Annie looked down the dock at all the men hustling to prepare for their day out on the water. "Why do you have to be so good at everything?"

A booming voice grabbed her attention, making her forget all about Jack's letter.

"Course I got them to switch." Captain Ned Hardy, owner of the *Lucky Strike*, the charter fishing boat tied up next to the *Tequesta,* leaned in toward a fellow fisherman. "Told 'em straight, you want fish on your lines or yarns to spin back home? Can't trust the *Tequesta* to deliver either one."

The surrounding men snickered and cheered, pounding

Ned on the back. Annie's jaw tightened as she recognized one man. He had come by her boat early yesterday morning to cancel his charter on her boat.

"Maybe Miss Annie could give you some net-mending lessons," another captain added. More laughter echoed down the dock.

She pulled the bill of her cap down and started walking to her boat. It was *her boat* now, and it appeared her cancelled charters had not just been random. Then Annie heard Ned's braying voice again, as he spoke to another charter captain. "See that group of New Yorkers over there."

When she stopped in front of her boat, she saw Ned point to a group of men. The four of them looked just like what he called them, a bunch of New Yorkers in their white linen pants and blue blazers. "Those fellas were gonna book the *Tequesta*, but I convinced 'em if they want to catch fish, they need a real man, not some schoolgirl running the show."

Annie's jaw clenched, her anger rising, but she held her tongue as she unlocked the companionway doors. Ned knew she could hear every word.

"Can't trust a girl to handle something as important as fishing," Ned continued, laughter bubbling from his throat.

Annie watched him jump aboard the *Lucky Strike*, then march up the deck and stop where his black deckhand was struggling while trying to stow some fishing gear.

"Hey, boy! Get a move on!" he barked as he slapped the young man across the top of his head.

"Keep calm, Annie Jeeves," she said out loud as she descended the steps into the cool interior of her boat. It wouldn't do any good to confront Ned. Not now, at least.

She plopped herself down on the leather-covered settee in the cabin and secured her rucksack in the cabinet beneath her legs. So, it wasn't coincidence that she'd lost those two charters. Ned had poached them, using the excuse that she was an incompetent female.

Take deep breaths, she told herself. There was only one way to fix this. She had to prove Ned was wrong.

"Right then." She rolled up the sleeves of her work shirt. "Let's get to it, shall we?"

The *Tequesta* had always been her father's pride and joy, and she intended to have her looking shipshape to wow Mr. Crowley and family. Annie set to work scrubbing the deck, tightening the rigging, and double-checking the engine and supplies.

*Let Ned Hardy think what he wants*, she thought.

Annie surveyed her handiwork. Now for the final touch: retrieving the launch from where she'd left it bobbing alongside the boat.

The little wooden rowboat was indispensable for ferrying supplies and towing lines. With its outboard motor chugging away, it had helped her scrub the *Tequesta*'s hull just yesterday.

Annie clambered over the railing and lowered herself down into the boat. The water lapped at the hull as she untied the painter line and gripped the oars. A few powerful strokes took her around to the davits at the stern of the boat.

Voices drifted over from the next slip, two fishermen swapping stories. Annie stopped to listen.

"Heard it straight from the radio this morning," said one in a gravelly voice. "U-boat got that British steamship, the *Cyclops*. Three hundred miles north of Cape Cod."

The other man whistled low. "The Krauts are gettin' brazen, ain't they? Heard they hit another ship just sixty miles off Long Island."

"No kiddin'?" said the first man. "Well, I'm headin' out with the Mosquito Fleet tonight. We'll show those sausage-eaters what for if they come round here."

Annie frowned. The war was creeping closer, even here.

She hoped Jack would stay safe. Her thoughts drifted back to his letter. They needed him sooner than planned. Even the thought of her brother flying combat missions over Europe terrified her.

Footsteps on the dock and the sound of wagon wheels drew Annie's attention to the dock. She stood up in the tippy little boat and saw Emma pulling a heavy wagon down the rough boards of the dock.

"Ahoy! Anybody aboard? I've got your order from The Deck."

Annie climbed up over the transom in time to see Emma straining to lift a box. "Got everything you ordered. Fresh this morning."

"Put your legs into it, not your spine." Annie leaped down to help. She grabbed the edge of the crate filled with sandwiches and containers of potato salad. The second box contained ice and bottles of pop and beer.

As they unpacked the goods, Emma's usual cheer seemed subdued. She kept glancing over her shoulder down the dock.

"You alright?" Annie asked.

Emma bit her lip. "Mr. Beck told Mama I'm not allowed at The Deck no more. Sheriff's orders."

Annie reached for her friend's shoulder. "Oh no, Em. That's not right. We've got to fight this."

"Easy for you to say," Emma said. "No good comes from fighting when you look like me."

Annie knew the truth of Emma's words, and there was nothing left to say. She reached into the pocket of her overalls. "This may or may not cheer you up." She held out the crumpled envelope. "We got a letter from Jack yesterday."

"Is he okay?"

"He's fine. You might say he's doing too good." Annie took Emma's hand and placed the envelope in it. "Why don't you take this down into the cabin and have a read? Then you can stow the food for me, okay?"

"Thanks, Annie."

Emma disappeared down the companionway ladder, and Annie transferred the provisions to the cockpit where Emma could reach them. Then, she turned her focus back to securing the wooden boat to the davits.

The sound of Captain Ned Hardy greeting his guests on board the *Lucky Strike* drifted over to her.

"Morning gentlemen! Who's ready to reel in some trophies?" Ned wasn't more than a boat length away, shouting at the top of his voice. He knew she could hear every word. "Bet you're glad you wised up and booked with me, eh?" he said, pointing towards the *Tequesta*. "A skirt running a charter boat, and one who chats with that sort." He nodded towards the cabin where Emma had disappeared, his voice dripping with disdain.

Annie's fists clenched at the insult, but she held her tongue. She had a charter to run, with or without Ned's nonsense.

"Annie!" called a voice from down the dock.

She turned to see a familiar middle-aged man approaching, his face etched with grief. His slow, deliberate steps.

"Morning, Mr. Crowley. Are you all right?"

He attempted a smile that didn't reach his eyes. "Annie. I'm afraid I have some terrible news."

Annie's stomach dropped.

"We just received word about our boy Richard. He's been out in the Philippines, under General MacArthur. He was killed trying to prevent the Japs from taking Manila."

"I'm so sorry," she said, reaching out to clasp his hand.

Annie's heart ached for him. Richard was the eldest. She pictured his smiling face, only a few years older than Jack.

Mr. Crowley nodded, blinking back tears. "I'm afraid we got to cancel our trip today."

"Of course," Annie said. She thought of the food she'd already bought for their charter, money they couldn't spare.

As Mr. Crowley turned to go, he hesitated. "Let me pay you something for your troubles."

Annie shook her head. "No, sir. You go be with your family."

With a sad smile and a nod, Mr. Crowley turned and walked back up the dock.

The loud roar of the *Lucky Strike*'s engine drew her attention back to the river.

The name of Ned's boat irritated more now than ever. She couldn't blame today's cancelled trip on Ned and his poaching. It was her bad luck.

The *Lucky Strike* began backing out into the river just as a tug pushing an enormous barge rounded the bend coming upstream heading for the already open Andrews Avenue Bridge.

"Really? Come on, Ned," she whispered, willing him to make the right choice. "Don't be a damn fool."

At that moment, she saw the crewman aboard the *Lucky Strike* fumble with the stern dock line. He dropped one end of the rope overboard into the churning water. Panic spread across his face as he realized his mistake. The rope floated on the surface for a few seconds, then disappeared beneath the stern.

The engine sputtered and then stopped as the rope wrapped the prop. Ned's boat was dead in the water and drifting into the path of the oncoming barge.

"Damn it all!" Ned shouted. He went after his deckhand with his fist raised, and the man ran for the foredeck. The *Lucky Strike* sat stranded and helpless, directly in the barge's path.

Annie didn't hesitate. She leaped into her launch, untied the painter and yanked the outboard's starter cord. The motor caught, and she twisted the throttle. The launch jumped onto a plane speeding toward the crippled boat.

"Throw me your line!" she yelled.

"Leave us be, girl! We don't need your help!" Ned spat, his wide eyes blazing with anger.

Ned's crewman ignored his boss's furious protests and hurled the rope towards Annie. She caught it with one hand. She mouthed the words "Thank you" as she secured the line to her boat and gunned the engine.

The launch strained against the weight of the *Lucky Strike*, but, inch by agonizing inch, she dragged the larger vessel towards the docks. The barge loomed like a giant steel wall pushing a foaming head of water. Annie's launch was now clear, but the barge bore down on Ned and his crew at the end of the tow rope.

She readied her hand over the cleat that connected her boat to Ned's, determined not to let his boat pull hers under. Then, the enormous bow wave curling off the corner of the barge lifted the stern of the fishing boat, and the *Lucky Strike* surfed her way clear. Annie's engine roared as it took up the slack in the towline, and the two boats pulled away as the barge's rusty side slid past them.

The tug captain shouted expletives at them as the two smaller boats rocked furiously in his wake.

Ned glared at her as she let go of the tow line, leaving the *Lucky Strike* to drift into the dock. "I didn't need your help, girl," he snarled.

Annie shrugged. Some people would never change.

After tying the lines from the davits to the launch's lifting harness, Annie climbed back up on deck and raised the little boat out of the water.

When she looked over at her neighbor, Ned's face was red

with embarrassment as his passengers collected their gear, shaking their heads.

"Sorry, folks, looks like we're out of commission today," he muttered.

The men climbed onto the dock, then glanced between their frustrated captain and Annie's *Tequesta*. They whispered among themselves before walking over and approaching her boat with tentative steps.

"Miss," one of them said, rubbing his hands together. "Um, we were wondering if your boat is available for charter today?"

Annie attempted to keep her face impassive. "As a matter of fact, I just had a charter cancel."

She paused longer than necessary, enjoying every second of the wait.

"Give me a moment to get things ready," Annie said, turning toward her boat. She knew that this was a risk, but nothing would ever change if they didn't try.

"Emma!" Annie called.

Emma poked her head out from the cabin, her dark eyes questioning. Before she could ask what was going on, Annie cut her off. "Roll up your sleeves, my friend. You just landed yourself a job today."

She turned back to her new customers. "Gentlemen, welcome aboard. Let's go catch some fish."

# CHAPTER TWELVE

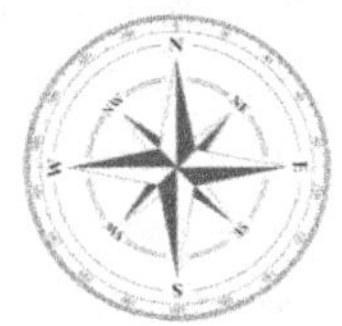

*Brandenburg, Germany*
*January 13, 1942*

"That lazy fat sack of potatoes, Erich, will make us late again." Max scowled, his angular features pinched with irritation. "The instructors don't give a damn about his beauty sleep."

A bone-chilling wind swept across the parade ground as Will and Max walked down the front steps of the red brick country house.

Max was always riding Erich. Will couldn't help but agree, but a part of him felt sympathy for the rotund soldier. And if Erich was bound to be on their team, better to work with him.

The Quenz Lake spy and sabotage school was situated on a large property composed of a requisitioned country manor house where the men slept four to a room, as well as the various training encampments scattered in the acres of surrounding forest.

Their first few days at the school, they had concentrated on firearms, cryptography, and wireless operations while they also studied American culture and slang. This week, they would start with incendiaries, explosives and hand to hand combat.

In the distance, smoke curled from the chimney of the explosives training shed, a wisp of warmth in the bleak winter landscape.

"Max, Erich's trying. Cut him some slack. We were up past midnight going over the codes. Radio encryption, cipher keys, the works. It's not so much laziness; he's just... slow on the uptake." Erich had been more interested in showing Will photos of his young wife than in studying.

"Slow?" Max scoffed. "A snail would lap him without breaking a sweat."

Will held his gloved hands up to his face and blew on them. His friend was so much funnier now that they alway spoke in English. Max's comments were brutal, but the man did always seem to make him chuckle.

Max snorted, and the plume of vapor hung in front of his face like a word bubble in comic books. "The only thing that fat-bellied fool is cut out for is the nearest Gasthaus and a beer, not espionage." He choked out a laugh. "The Abwehr's scraping the dregs if Erich's the best they can dredge up."

Will suppressed a shiver that had little to do with the cold as they moved into the shadowy forest. He had done his best to stay out of this war by hiding at the propaganda ministry. Everything happened so fast. After a short week at the Naval Academy learning to pass as a merchant mariner, now he was training in how to kill.

Max was right about Erich, though. One misstep, one fumbled transmission or missed rendezvous could spell disaster for their entire team. Will had no illusions about how long Erich, or any of them for that matter, would stand up under torture before revealing the identities of everyone.

"Maybe," Will ventured, "we could try to help him more. He won't improve if we just leave him on his own."

"If you want to help him, be my guest," Max replied. "Just don't let him drag you under."

The explosives shed loomed ahead, a squat structure of rough-hewn logs. Will and Max stomped the snow from their boots and ducked inside, the sudden warmth a shock. A blackened iron stove in the corner glowed orange through the dirty glass door. Jorg was already there, laying out blasting caps and lengths of primer cord on the wooden table. He glanced up, his eyes as pale as the ice on the lake. "Nice of you to join us."

Will started to reply, but at that moment Sergeant Klaus Schmidt, their demolitions instructor, marched through the door with a scowl, a cigarette dangling from the corner of his mouth. The man wore his blond hair long, trying to cover the reddish mottled scar tissue Will had glimpsed covering the entire back of his neck.

A crash through the underbrush and labored breathing announced Erich's arrival. He stepped through the doorway with sticks and leaves in his hair and took his place next to Jorg.

"Well, our gourmand stayed for a second breakfast." Schmidt spoke without removing the cigarette. "And only five minutes late today. I'm impressed."

"We're all here and ready to learn, sir." Will wished he could tell the ghoul his true thoughts.

Schmidt took a final drag on the cigarette before flicking it out the doorway into the snow. "Adler, the detonator kit. Double time."

Jorg retrieved a battered leather satchel and handed it to

the sergeant. Schmidt rummaged inside, his large hands oddly delicate as he extracted the day's deadly lesson.

The instructor picked up a blasting cap. "Precision is your ally. Carelessness is the bullet you won't hear coming."

Schmidt paced in front of the four of them, turning the device so that they could see it from all sides. "Gentlemen, meet the M2 electric blasting cap." The device looked like a small metal cylinder trailing two slender wires. "This little darling is what you will find in America, and when paired with a suitable explosive, can reduce a bridge, building, or vehicle to rubble with the flick of a switch."

Will stared at the detonator gleaming in Schmidt's palm. That tiny device would snuff out how many innocent lives before this war was over?

"A blasting cap is useless without a triggering mechanism," Schmidt continued. "That's where our friend the MZ-35 detonator comes in." He withdrew a rectangular block with dials and ports from the bag. "Proper preparation of the detonator is crucial. Sloppy wiring will get you blown to pieces."

Max leaned over to Will and whispered in English, "I bet our dear sergeant has firsthand experience with premature detonation. Poor fellow."

Will bit the inside of his cheek, strangling the inappropriate laugh threatening to escape.

Schmidt narrowed his eyes at the pair, sensing their inattention. "Since you two are in such high spirits, perhaps you would like to teach the class?"

Both Will and Max knew enough to keep their mouths shut.

"I thought so." Schmidt paused, his scarred neck flushing darker. "There is nothing funny about explosives. I learned this lesson the hard way in Poland." He ran his hand over the back of his neck. "My carelessness cost three men their lives."

Schmidt walked over to the table where the equipment

was spread out. "Today, gentlemen, we will learn about time delay devices. Pay attention, for your lives will depend upon it." He held up a small cap in one hand. "This is an electric blasting cap. Inside is a small charge of high explosive." He raised his other hand in a fist. "When you apply current..." He opened the fist, fingers wide. "***Boom.***"

The instructor moved down the line. Pencil detonators. Ampoules of corrosive liquid. Acid fuses that hissed and smoked. Will committed each one to memory.

"And now," the instructor said, "you will each set a charge. Imagine you are beneath a bridge, a railway trestle, a critical piece of infrastructure. You must set your charge to detonate at a precise time, then escape undetected. Begin."

Will selected his components. Blasting cap, length of fuse cord, detonator. His fingers were clumsy in the cold, but he forced himself to focus, to move with deliberate care. Beside him, Max was already done, his movements quick and sure. Jorg worked slowly, double and triple checking each connection.

And Erich... Will glanced over, his stomach sinking. Erich was fumbling with the blasting cap, and his charge was a tangle of wires and fuses.

The instructor loomed at Erich's elbow, his scarred neck flushed red. "What in God's name is this?" He snatched the charge from Erich's hands, holding it aloft. "Are you trying to kill us all?"

Erich blanched. The instructor hurled the charge down, the components scattering across the frozen ground.

"Congratulations, Herr Burger. You're dead, and so is your team," Schmidt spat. "A mistake at this stage means dismemberment at best."

Erich blanched, looking as if he might vomit.

The morning passed in a blur of explosive compounds and timing devices. By the time Schmidt told them to stow their equipment and report to the mess hall, Will's head throbbed and his fingers were numb from the cold.

As they readied to leave, Schmidt said, "At least you three won't blow yourselves into small pieces. The same can't be said for Erich."

After lunch, the trainees stood shivering on the shore of Quenzsee Lake. The jagged ice had started to break up earlier in the day, and there was now a dark expanse of water. Will shifted from foot to foot, trying to generate some warmth. Beside him, Max bounced on his toes, his lean frame coiled with restless energy.

"What's the hold up?" Max muttered. "Let's get this over with."

The camp's commanding officer, Kommandant Heinrich Vogel finally strode out of the officers' quarters, his black uniform stark against the snow. Vogel was a small, wiry man with a ferret's sharp features and cold eyes. He carried himself with the rigid bearing of a Prussian aristocrat. He surveyed them, his eyes lingering on Erich's hunched shoulders.

"Gentlemen, welcome to your first cold water endurance trial." Vogel spoke in a clipped tone. "Today, you will all swim." He paused and looked down the line of men. "Out to the buoy and back. The first man to return earns an extra ration at supper." His lip curled. "And the last... well. I advise you not to finish last. You will disrobe down to your undergarments and, on my mark, swim to that buoy and back."

Will studied the lake. The water looked dark as a bottomless well, and twice as cold. But an extra ration of food would give him strength for the combat yet to come. His stomach cramped at the thought. It had been so long since he'd felt truly full.

"Can't believe they expect us to swim in this." Max pulled his wool sweater over his head. "I'd rather face another round with the explosives."

"Me too." Will fumbled with numb fingers, tugging off his boots and socks, his trousers and shirt. The sand and pebble beach was so cold his feet ached.

Beside him, Max had already stripped down to his underwear, his lean body corded with muscle. Jorg looked pale and miserable, his skin fish-belly white. And Erich, his belly drooped over his tight underwear.

"*Ja, ja.*" Max wagged his head back and forth. "At least it'll be quick. Either we freeze or we drown."

"Or both," Will added, earning a wry smirk from Max. He couldn't shake the image of Erich's humiliation during the explosives exercise.

"Alright, men!" the Kommandant called out, and the adjutant at his side raised the stopwatch. "At the sound of the whistle, you will swim out to the buoy and back. Understood?"

"Sir, yes sir!" The men chorused as they danced around, beating their hands against their bare skin, stripped down to their skivvies.

"May the best man win," Max said through clenched teeth. Will nodded, his heart pounding not only from the cold but also from anticipating the race ahead.

"Ready?" Kommandant Vogel called, raising his whistle to his lips.

The sharp blast of the whistle sent the men running into the icy water. Will plunged forward, the shock of the water driving the breath from his lungs. Who knew that cold could produce such a stinging burn that turned his limbs numb and leaden. He struck out for the buoy, his strokes choppy. Beside him, Max cut through the water like a shark. Will gritted his teeth and swam harder, his lungs aching and his vision narrowing to a pinprick.

The red and white buoy loomed ahead, the waves slapping against its algae-slick sides. Will stretched out a hand, his fingertips grazing the slimy growth on the painted wood. He kicked harder, propelling himself around the turn. Beside him, Max executed a neat flip turn, his feet flashing above the surface. Will set his jaw and reached deep inside for a strength he wasn't sure existed. His legs churned against the icy drag of the water, and he felt himself pull ahead of Max.

They were halfway back to shore when he heard it. A strangled cry, thin and desperate. Will raised his head, blinking the stinging water from his eyes. There, off to the side. A thrashing of pale limbs, a flash of a round, terror-stricken face.

Erich. He had not even made it halfway out to the buoy...

The man flailed as he fought to stay afloat.

In the lead, Will had victory within his grasp. He hesitated, torn. The shore was so close, the promise of warmth and food almost tangible. Max churned past him.

Will cursed and veered off course, striking out for his floundering teammate. He reached Erich in a few strokes and hooked an arm around the other man's chest.

"I've got you," he panted. "Relax, don't fight me."

But Erich struggled, arms flailing, panic overwhelming reason. They went under, the frigid water closing over Will's head. He kicked hard, dragging them both back to the surface. Coughing and sputtering, his eyes rolled back in his head.

"Erich!" Will shook him. "Erich, *verdammt*! Hold still and breathe man!"

Somehow, he got them pointed towards shore. Jorg and the rest of the men passed them. The swim seemed to take hours, each stroke an agony of exhaustion. At last, Will's feet touched bottom.

Will heaved his comrade up onto the icy gravel and collapsed beside him, both chests heaving as they gulped air.

Most of the others had rushed off to the barracks. Max had already pulled on his pants, and he was pushing his arms through the sleeves of his sweater.

Icy water dripped from Will's hair, stinging his eyes as he sat up. He glared at Max. "You would have just let him drown? Really, Max?"

"I'm a survivor, Hersey," Max replied. "He's a liability."

Erich lay on the ground, wet and defeated.

Kommandant Vogel interrupted their exchange.

"Hersey! On your feet!"

Will struggled upright, his limbs shaking. Kommandant Vogel stared at him, his face dark with rage. "What was that, Hersey?"

Although he was standing there in sodden underwear, Will drew himself up and met the officer's glare. "I was saving my teammate, sir."

The Kommandant said nothing for what seemed like an eternity. "Return to your quarters and change into dry clothes," he ordered.

Will peeled off his sodden clothes in the barracks, the frigid air biting into his already freezing skin. His thoughts raced as he dressed, anger and frustration warring within him. He had made the right choice, hadn't he? Surely saving a comrade was worth more than winning some pointless race?

There was a knock at the door, and the Kommandant's adjutant handed a paper to Will. With a sinking feeling, he read the summons to report to the Kommandant that evening after dinner.

At 1400 hours, the four trainees reported for hand to hand combat training. Will stood in a circle with the others, watching as their instructor, Hauptmann Krueger, demonstrated a killing technique on a straw dummy. Krueger was a compact man with hands that moved with disturbing precision.

"The larynx," Krueger said, his thumb pressing into the dummy's throat. "Apply pressure here." He jutted his fingers forward in a quick thrust. "And your enemy drowns in his own blood." He turned to face them with a slight smile, as if he'd been explaining how to tune a radio. "Who wants to try first?"

Max stepped forward. Of course, he did. Will watched as Max replicated the move, his face showing neither pleasure nor revulsion.

"Good," Krueger said. "But you're thinking too much. When you kill, it must be automatic. Like breathing." He moved to the next dummy, this one dressed in an American army uniform.

"Look at this uniform," Krueger said.

Will remembered his mother's words; his father had worn that uniform.

"Some of you knew Americans once." His eyes found Will's. "That man is gone. The person wearing this uniform wants to destroy everything you love. Your mothers, your sisters, the Fatherland."

Krueger grabbed the dummy by the collar and reached for the knife on his belt. "When you see this uniform, don't think. They are not human. You act." In one fluid motion, he drove the knife up under the dummy's ribs. Sawdust spilled onto the floor like entrails.

"Hersey," Krueger barked. "Your turn."

Will approached the dummy. Up close, he could see they'd pinned photographs of American soldiers to its face. Young men grinning at the camera, maybe on leave, maybe writing home. His hand trembled as he took the knife.

"I said, your turn." Krueger's voice hardened.

Will gripped the knife handle, feeling its weight. He thought of Billy Turner back in Indiana, probably in uniform now. Would Billy hesitate if their positions were reversed? The metal felt cold against his palm.

"The enemy won't hesitate." Krueger stood behind him. "Strike, or be struck down."

Will thought of the faceless man who killed his father. He drove the knife forward. The blade caught on the canvas. He pushed harder, feeling it punch through into the sawdust interior. When he pulled it free, his hand was steady.

"Better," Krueger said. "Still too much thinking."

Next to him, Erich was fumbling with his knife. The blade slipped from his sweaty grip, clattering on the floor. Krueger's expression darkened.

"Pick it up," he ordered.

Erich bent down, his thick fingers struggling to grasp the handle.

"In America," Krueger said, his voice carrying to all of them, "hesitation means mission failure. Mission failure means your comrades die. Their blood will be on your hands, Burger. Can you live with that?"

Erich grabbed the knife and stabbed wildly at the dummy, missing all the vital points. Krueger shook his head in disgust.

"Again," he commanded. "All of you. Again and again until it becomes part of you. Until you dream of it. Until your muscles know the motion better than your own name."

They practiced until the photographs on the dummies were shredded beyond recognition, which was perhaps the point.

As they filed out, Max fell into step beside him. "You did

well," he whispered. "Better than I expected from a propagandist."

Will said nothing. His hand still remembered the knife's weight, the resistance of the canvas, the way the blade had finally slid home. He wondered whether that knowledge would ever leave him.

"It's just training," Max said, perhaps mistaking Will's silence for squeamishness. "Chances are, we'll never need to use it."

But Will knew better. They wouldn't teach them to kill unless they expected killing to be done.

His mother wanted him to make his father proud. His father had been a policeman, sworn to protect and serve. Would he be proud of what his son was becoming?

Will flexed his fingers, trying to shake the phantom feeling of the knife handle. Outside, snow fell again, covering the training ground in a fresh layer of white as they headed to the mess hall.

Will wasn't sure he could force himself to eat.

~

After dinner, Will hurried back to their room to freshen up before his meeting with the Kommandant. He found Erich waiting for him.

"Wilhelm," he began, then stopped, his round face flushed. "I... want to thank you."

Will nodded, unsure how to respond to gratitude for an act that might have doomed them both.

"You alone have shown me kindness here. I hope I can repay you someday."

"We'll both keep working and improving, right?"

Erich stepped forward and hugged him, then stepped

back, embarrassed. "I'm sorry. At Christmas, I learned my wife is expecting. It has made me very emotional."

"Congratulations, Erich. I have to go. I have an appointment." Will turned and left their room in a hurry.

Ten minutes later, he stood outside the Kommandant's office. He hesitated, smoothing his clothing. This moment would define his path forward. What would his father think of his son learning to see Americans as less than human?

The realization that he did not want to flunk out of this mission came as a surprise. Not because he wanted to rain death and destruction down on America. Quite the contrary. He was looking forward to returning to a country that was more home to him than Germany. Perhaps he could find answers there. Steeling himself, he knocked.

"*Herein.*"

The shadowed room was thick with the scent of cigars and gun oil. The commander sat behind a broad oak desk, a single lamp casting harsh shadows across his angular face. He regarded Will, his fingers steepled before him.

"You wished to see me, sir?" Will kept his voice neutral.

"I did." The small man leaned back, the leather of his chair creaking. "Explain your actions at the swim trial, Hersey."

Taking a deep breath, Will looked into Kommandant Vogel's eyes. "Sir, I made a split-second decision to save Erich Burger. Every member of our team is valuable. Our mission requires us to work together. Abandoning a comrade would only weaken us. Not to mention that a strange dead body washing up on a foreign shore could reveal our mission to the enemy."

The commander regarded him, his expression inscrutable. Will could feel the weight of his judgment.

"Is that all?"

"Yes, sir." Will stood up straight.

The Kommandant was silent for a long, agonizing moment. Will barely dared to breathe, cold sweat trickling down his back.

"I must confess, Hersey, I had my doubts about you. Your background, your loyalties."

Will stiffened.

"But today, you showed something. Something I did not expect. You put the mission above yourself. Above your own survival." He paused. "I am giving you a chance, Hersey. A chance to prove yourself."

"Sir?"

The Kommandant stood, his movements precise and deliberate. He rounded the desk to stand before Will.

"Your task will require the utmost secrecy. If you breathe a word of it to anyone, I will know. And I will see you hanged as a traitor." He paused, letting the threat sink in. "Am I understood?"

Will swallowed. "Yes, sir."

"Good." The commander smiled. "You, Hersey, will be partnered with a special operative. I cannot tell you his identity. You will receive your orders from Admiral Canaris once you are on your way to America. If you succeed, you will be a hero of the Reich."

Will wanted to know more, but he dared not ask. "Sir?"

Vogel leaned forward, his eyes glinting. "Do you understand, Wilhelm Hersey?"

Will saw the faces of his childhood friends back in Indiana, heard their laughter. Could he turn his back on all that he had been, all that he had loved, in service to this brutal regime? Only a fool would think he had a choice. Or a coward.

But beneath the revulsion, a voice whispered. It was his mother's. *Make your father proud.*

If only he knew how.

Will raised his head, meeting the commander's gaze. They taught the art of subterfuge at this camp, and he was an excellent student. "I will do whatever the Reich demands of me," he said. "I will not fail."

Kommandant Vogel leaned back, a flicker of something almost like respect in his eyes. "See that you don't, Herr Hersey." A pause. "For all our sakes, see that you don't."

# CHAPTER THIRTEEN

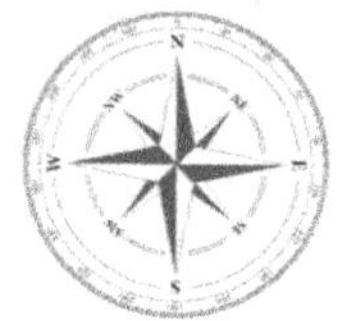

*Fort Lauderdale, Florida*
*January 15, 1942*

Annie walked north, her boots kicking up dust on the unpaved road. The afternoon sun was already starting its descent toward the Everglades, but she had to talk to Emma.

Soon she crossed the boulevard, the line dividing Fort Lauderdale's white and black neighborhoods. The ramshackle wooden buildings bore a striking resemblance to their counterparts on the white side of town, barbershops, tailors, doctors' offices, but here, every face was dark-skinned. Annie felt the weight of curious stares, but no one spoke to the white girl walking alone.

When Emma's small weathered house came into view, the tightness left her neck, her shoulders relaxed. She knew these folks, and they knew her. She rapped her fist on the door. After a moment, it creaked open, revealing Emma's surprised face.

"Annie? What are you doing here?"

"We need to talk," she said. "Can I come in?"

Emma stepped aside, ushering Annie into the living room, where the walls showed off a pair of colorful landscape paintings from the Bahamas, and the Dade County pine floors were partially covered with a rag rug.

Emma's mother and grandfather sat in matching armchairs. A faded quilt draped across the old man's lap. They looked up at Annie with a mixture of wariness and curiosity.

"Good afternoon, Miss Cora, Mr. Walker," Annie said, nodding to each of them.

"Hello, Annie." Cora rose and brushed invisible particles off the front of her dress. "Can I get you some lemonade? You must be parched from your walk."

"Thank you, ma'am." Annie sat down on the worn sofa beside Emma.

Grampa Elzo leaned forward, his dark eyes sharp and assessing. "Any news from your brother, child? We've been praying for his safe return."

Annie shook her head, a lump rising in her throat. "Not for a while. I think that means he's left for England." She shook her head. "Don't know where he is right now."

Emma reached over and squeezed her hand. Annie forced a smile. She knew Emma was as worried as she was about Jack.

Emma's grandfather had worked at the high school Annie and her brother had attended. Back then, he knew every student by name.

"You hear about Homer Jenkins?" she asked.

Word had hit town two days earlier about the death of this young man who had enlisted the day after Pearl Harbor.

Grampa Elzo frowned and gave a curt nod. "He's not the first, and won't be the last. War's like that." His soft voice carried a pain-filled tenor. "No one knows what's happening until it's too late."

Emma had once told Annie about her grandfather's experience in the First World War. The old man rarely talked about it.

Cora returned with a tray of glasses, which she set down on the coffee table. Annie accepted one, the cool condensation soothing against her palm. She took a long sip, enjoying the tart sweetness.

"These are hard times," Miss Cora said. "War changes everything."

"It does, whether we like it or not. My Pa's got that radio on whenever he's home. The news is not good," Annie said.

Grampa Elzo nodded. "What worries me most is I suspect they aren't even telling us the whole truth."

"That's why I'm here." Annie set her glass down on a doily on the side table. "You all know I've cut back on my work at The Deck. I told the Skipper that I'd fill in if he needs me, but since Jack left, I'm now the full-time captain of the *Tequesta*."

"Can't say I don't miss you." Cora smiled.

The old man fussed with the quilt on his lap. "That boat's not a job for a young lady, but ..."

Emma leaned forward, saying, "Gramps, like Mama said, times are changing!"

"Hush, child. You didn't let me finish. I know that you girls have untapped potential," he said, his voice soft but firm. "Don't let anyone tell you otherwise. Yes, the world is changing too fast as a result of the war, but too slow in other ways. It won't be easy for Annie on that waterfront."

Annie cleared her throat. "That's part of why I'm here." Pausing, she looked at each of them, connecting. "I'm sure Emma told you that a few days ago, she went out with me when I worked my first charter. Those fellas weren't real sure at first, but when they caught plenty of fish and got served sandwiches and Miss Cora's potato salad, they were plenty happy and tipped me two dollars."

Grampa Elzo's face transformed into a proud grin.

"Now, I have a proposition for Emma. For all of you, really."

Miss Cora leaned forward, her expression unreadable.

"See, Finn's not always available." Annie paused and cleared her throat. "So, I want Emma to be my full-time crew on the *Tequesta*." Her words tumbled out in a garbled rush.

Cora gasped. Grampa Elzo's eyes narrowed.

Emma turned on the couch to face her. "Annie, you know what you're asking?"

"I know, Emma. But we can do this. Like your mama said, whether or not we like it, the war is changing things."

Emma bit her lip. She looked at her mother's worried face, then shook her head. "Annie. It's too risky."

"We'd be careful," Annie insisted. Yet even she heard the naivete in her words.

"Careful?" Elzo's deep voice rumbled. "Sheriff Clark has been watchin' this family for years. He'd love any excuse to cause us grief."

Emma nodded, face pained. "What would people say about two girls crewing a boat? Let alone one who looks like me!"

"I know it's risky." Annie faced each of them. "But we can make this work if we're smart. And we are smart. Many other charter captains have black men as crew. And I can explain to folks that it wouldn't be proper for me to go out to sea alone with a man I don't know, black or white. With so many men going off to fight, people are going to have to get used to seeing women doing men's work."

Cora said, "True enough. I heard they're hiring women

down at the port to unload the cargo ships now. Not enough men to get the work done."

Annie turned to Grampa Elzo. "You're worried about Emma's future. I know that. This could help her earn enough money to go to college."

Elzo rubbed his chin, considering her words.

"The restaurant doesn't pay as well as charters," Annie pressed on. "Emma would get a fair share of the charter fee, plus a share of tips. Same as we always paid Finn. Some days those tips alone could equal a week's pay from her old job at The Deck."

Emma leaned forward. The hint of a smile curled her lips as she looked back and forth between her mother and her grandfather. Annie had a sense that something had shifted in the room.

"Fact is," Annie continued. "I can't keep on doing all this alone. Finn's working sixty hours a week at Dooley's now. And I need crew. My family depends on that money."

She waited, watching emotions play across their faces. The song of a mockingbird broke the silence from the big oak tree outside.

Elzo sighed. "You drive a hard bargain, Miss Annie. Can't say I'm not worried. But you may be right about this changing world."

He looked at his granddaughter. "Emma's future is what's important. If you two are careful, and Sheriff Clark doesn't catch wind."

"I don't know, Pa. It's dangerous work," Cora said.

"I know what the work is like," he said. "I worked on boats bringing cargo over from the Bahamas in my younger days."

Cora and Elzo stared at one another. Annie sensed a whole wordless conversation was going on between them. At last, Elzo nodded. "Alright, Annie. We trust you, and we trust

Emma. If you two think this is the best path for her, then we'll support her."

Emma's eyes widened, a brilliant smile lighting her face.

"Oh, thank you!" Emma cried, jumping up to embrace her grandfather.

Cora nodded, though her expression remained worried.

"You girls be discreet, you hear?" she said. "Don't go stirring up trouble."

"We'll be careful, Mama." Emma turned to Annie. "I can't believe this is happening."

Cora rose to her feet, smoothing her apron. "I'd best get supper on," she said, her voice tight with emotion. "Annie, will you stay and eat with us?"

"Thanks, but I should get back." Annie rose from her chair. "My family will be expecting me."

"Be safe out there," Elzo said.

Annie reached for the door. "Always," she said as she turned the knob.

~

Emma followed her outside. "Can you stay a little longer? I've got lots of questions."

"Sure"

"Follow me."

They made their way to the woodshed behind Emma's house, its rough wooden planks weathered by time and exposure.

"Up for some stargazing?" Emma asked with a grin, gesturing up towards the shed's sloped roof.

Annie returned her smile. "Race you to the top."

In moments they were clambering up the fence next to the shed, then settling onto the rough shingles. The first stars appeared above the pink clouds clustered on the western horizon. The night breeze smelled like impending rain.

More of the day's tension eased from Annie's shoulders.

Emma sat perched on the edge of the shed's roof, her legs dangling over the side. She leaned back and laced her fingers to cradle her head. "So, when do we start?"

"Tomorrow. We've got to keep the *Tequesta* ship-shape," Annie replied. "You never know when somebody's gonna come strolling down the dock and ask to go out for the day."

Annie settled back against the roof, her shoulder touching Emma's, gazing up at the vast expanse of the night sky. The stars seemed to multiply as they watched.

Emma spoke first. "You ever notice how quiet the stars get? Like they know secrets we're too noisy to hear."

"Do you remember the stories I used to tell you?" Annie asked. "About the ancient mariners, and how they used the stars to navigate uncharted waters?"

"Is that what we're doing now? Navigating uncharted waters?"

"I guess you could say that."

"In a way, the stars make sense to me in ways that people sometimes don't."

Annie laughed. "Your brain, girl. But you're right that people sometimes make no sense at all."

They lapsed into a comfortable silence, the only sound being the distant chirping of crickets.

Emma said, "You wouldn't be referring to a certain young man, would you?"

"Finn? Don't get me started. I've got nothing to say on that topic because nothing is happening."

"I got a letter from Jack," Emma said.

"Really?" Annie jerked her head up. "What'd he say?"

"Not much. Leastwise not much that I could read. They blacked out most of the parts where he was writing about the training camp. I have no idea where he was." Emma then said in a whisper. "He did say he loved me, though."

Annie chuckled. "Well, that's not exactly a news bulletin. My brother has been crazy about you since the day he met you."

Emma sighed. "I know the entire world is against us being an *us*."

"Back home up in Edgewater, at Pa's fish camp, nobody cares about stuff like that. Maybe we can all go live up there."

"Annie, marriage for us not only isn't possible, it isn't legal. But I love your brother with all my heart. Before he left that day at the train station, he gave me this." She reached into her skirt pocket. When she opened her hand, a cheap dime-store ring was in her palm. "Maybe after this war is over, the world'll change."

Again, they let the conversation pause while they listened to the sounds of the night. A mother was calling her children in for supper. In the distance, a car backfired with a loud pop.

"Emma," Annie said at last. "There's something else I need to ask you. Something important."

Emma turned on to her side and braced her head with her hand, her dark eyes serious and attentive. "What is it?"

Annie tented her fingers in front of her lips as she searched for the right words. "I sent a message to the folks running the Mosquito Fleet. I want to talk to them. Learn more about taking the *Tequesta* out on some night patrols, looking for German U-boats off the coast."

Emma sat up and turned to stare. "Annie Jeeves, what in tarnation?"

"I just want to know, Emma," Annie interrupted. "I can't just sit here and wait for the war to come to us. Every day I sit here, wondering if Jack's letter will be the last one, and I feel useless. I hate this war, and I feel like I need to do my part to make it stop. Cargo ships are being torpedoed right off our coast. I'm not saying we'd do it for sure. But it doesn't hurt to learn more about it."

She reached out and took Emma's hand, squeezing it. "I need someone I can trust out there with me. Someone who knows the stars and is a quick learner."

Emma was silent for a long moment. "Do you really think there are Nazi submarines right off our coast?"

Annie nodded. "I know there are. Maybe not down here in Florida yet, but up north. The news reports, the rumors. Cargo ships are being torpedoed just up the coast. So many men have died already, and more are dying every day. The Germans caught us unprepared. The Coast Guard, the Navy, we have little to defend ourselves with, and nobody knows what the Germans are planning."

This time Annie sat up. "I can't protect Jack, not where he is. But maybe I can protect someone else's brother. Maybe I can make a difference, even if it's just a small one."

Emma stared at her for a moment, then closed her eyes and sighed. "You're so brave, Annie," she said. "Braver than I could ever be."

Annie sat up and shook her head. "I'm not brave, Emma. I'm just stubborn. And I'm scared, too. Scared of what might happen out there, scared of losing the people and the life I love."

She took a deep breath, her grip on Emma's hand tightening. "But I'm more scared of doing nothing. Aren't you?"

Emma was quiet for a long moment, her gaze fixed on the dark night sky. Then she nodded.

"Sometimes, I'm afraid I'll never see Jack again, and I feel like I can't breathe," Emma said at last. "But when I'm with you, it feels like anything is possible. I feel that we're just like those ancient mariners, navigating through this uncertain world, searching for something better. Somewhere beyond this small town."

"It's a mighty big world out there beyond this small town," Annie said.

"Okay." Emma sat up and faced Annie. "I'll do it if you decide to. Got no idea what I'll tell Mama and Granddad, but I'm a grown woman, and I will figure that out." Emma put out her hand, and they shook on it. "I will sail with you, Annie Jeeves, off to hunt for German submarines." Emma laughed. "Or wherever you need me to go."

# CHAPTER FOURTEEN

*Fort Lauderdale, Florida*
*January 21, 1942*

"So, how did you get out of going to church this morning?" Annie sat cross-legged on the deck working to mend a torn sail while Emma applied varnish to the handrail with smooth brush strokes.

"Mama wasn't happy about it, but she didn't argue. I said it was your fault."

Annie sighed. "Thanks."

"Actually, you saved me from another morning trying not to fall asleep at Mount Hermon." Emma dipped her brush in the varnish. "Think I'm going to get struck by lightning for saying that?"

Annie squinted skyward. "Not a cloud in the sky. I think you're safe."

Finn's muffled voice followed a loud clatter from below deck. "Annie! Need your help!"

"Coming!" Annie slid out from under the sail.

The interior of the *Tequesta* was dim and close. Finn

hunched over the engine, muttering as he adjusted a stubborn valve. His red hair stuck up in tufts and sweat soaked his undershirt.

"I need a three-eighths wrench," he said.

Annie rummaged through the toolbox.

"Here it is."

He extended a bare, muscular arm in her direction. When he took the tool from her, his fingers brushed against hers. She pulled back her hand.

"Thanks."

She hoped the dim light had hidden the color in her cheeks.

Then she heard a strange voice outside. She couldn't make out the words, but the tone was assertive, not friendly. Her curiosity piqued, she climbed the steps and saw a well-dressed, older man with an air of authority conversing with Emma.

"Excuse me." Annie stepped into the cockpit. "Can I help you?"

"Good afternoon." His hands rested in the pockets of his tweed jacket. "I'm looking for Captain Jeeves."

"You're looking at her."

The man's eyes widened. "You're the captain?"

"Yep."

He ran his fingers through his hair.

"Well then. I'm Fuller Mansfield. Coast Guard Officer in Charge of the Mosquito Fleet. I received a message from a Captain Jeeves."

"Yes sir. That was me."

The man opened his mouth and then closed it again. He looked so perplexed, Annie was on the verge of laughing. "And who is the owner?"

"That would be my father, Skeeter Jeeves."

"I see. And is Mr. Jeeves aboard?"

She took a deep breath and pushed down her frustration. "My father works at Dooley's. Look, no sense standing out here in the sun, Mr. Mansfield. Why don't you come aboard for a cold drink?"

The man hesitated for a moment, his eyes sweeping over the *Tequesta* as if assessing its worthiness. Then he nodded. "Very well."

"Welcome aboard." Annie stepped aside and gestured toward the companionway ladder.

When she followed him below, Finn had emerged from the engine compartment. Emma slipped around them in the crowded cabin and opened the ice box.

"Ah, company, I see." Finn wiped his fingers with a rag.

"Mr. Mansfield, this is my friend Finn. He helps maintain the *Tequesta*."

Finn extended a grease-stained hand. Mansfield shook it before settling onto the settee.

"And you already met Emma."

He nodded. "Happy to make your acquaintance."

He didn't look happy.

As Emma poured the iced tea, Annie sat across from their visitor.

"Thank you," Mansfield said. He took a sip, grimaced, and set the glass down.

Annie regarded him before she spoke.

"Mr. Mansfield, I appreciate you coming by. I'm the one who sent word that the *Tequesta* would like information about joining the Mosquito Fleet. Not my father."

The man looked relieved. "Oh, you just want information. I'm happy to share that with you."

"Why don't you fill us in on what the Mosquito Fleet is all about?"

"Well, Florida's got 1,197 miles of shoreline, and we simply don't have enough Coast Guard vessels to patrol it all. Until we can get more patrol boats built, civilians are stepping in to help. The job of the Mosquito Fleet, otherwise known as Coast Guard Auxiliary Flotilla No. 2, is to patrol the waters off South Florida. The men in this fleet perform the vital functions of rescuing survivors and reporting sightings of U-boats or any other suspicious activity, but they never, ever engage with an enemy vessel."

Annie slid off the settee and went to the chart table. She pulled out a faded chart of the South Florida coast and the Bahamas.

Mansfield spread it out on the table and leaned in close to read the dozens of pencil annotations. "Your father's quite the navigator."

Finn stepped away from the galley. "It's not her pa who recorded all those notes. That's Annie's work."

The man looked at Annie, then back at the chart. He pressed his lips together. "Well, you see this area here." Mansfield pointed to the narrow stretch of water on the chart between the southern Florida coast and the Bahamas. "It's a pinch point. The best defense for our cargo ships is that the ocean is vast. But here, ships have to bunch together, which will make them easy targets. We haven't had any action off our waters yet, but it's only a matter of time. Especially with cities like Miami resisting mandatory black-outs because they say it's bad for tourism. Bright lights on shore make the outlines of our cargo ships easy targets."

Annie swallowed hard, imagining the destruction those U-boats could cause.

"We're not defenseless," Mansfield said. "Most of our patrols launch after nightfall. You see, U-boats run on battery power when they're submerged, but they have to surface at night to run their diesel engines to recharge the batteries. We're outfitting some of our boats with radio sets so they can report any sightings."

"So, what do we have to do to join?"

"I don't think you understand, Miss Jeeves; this isn't some pleasure cruise we're talking about. The Mosquito Fleet's work is dangerous business and not suitable for..."

Annie cut him off. "Emma and I are both twenty years old, Mr. Mansfield. We're women, not girls."

"Emma?" Mansfield said.

Annie swallowed nervously and pointed to her friend standing in the shadows. "Emma is my crew."

Mansfield glanced at Emma and shook his head. Annie saw the corner of his mouth rise in a half smile. "You're not serious."

Annie tried to keep her voice level. "With all due respect, sir, I'm very serious. This war is bringing lots of changes to our little corner of the world. There aren't enough men to both fight overseas and protect the coast at home. You might have to adjust your idea of what those protectors look like."

"Miss Jeeves..."

"No, sir. I'm not finished. That woman," Annie pointed at Emma, "she is smarter than any man I've ever known. She may not have much experience on the water, but there is no one I would rather have by my side when I am trying to solve a problem."

"Sir, if I may," Finn said. "I've known Annie since we were kids. She's got more seamanship in her pinky than most sailors I've met. Why, just last October we hit a bad squall offshore. Zero visibility. I was struggling to keep us pointed into the waves. But Annie took the helm and steered us straight back to Port Everglades." Finn held up both hands. "I can't explain it. She's got a sixth sense concerning navigation, and she's fearless. There's no one I'd trust more to captain a boat, man or woman."

Annie glanced at Finn, surprised and touched by his passionate defense.

The Coast Guard officer looked unconvinced. "Even if that's true, the *Tequesta* is hardly fit for open ocean patrols. The Gulfstream will toss this boat around like a cork out there. She's what, thirty feet?"

"Thirty-eight," Annie corrected. "And she is tougher than she looks. My father used to sail her to the Bahamas. Madeira framed and pine planked, built for sponging, and she's weathered her share of storms. Including the big hurricane back in '26."

Mansfield ran his hand over the chart. "I don't know."

"Then let me make this clear," Annie said. "We aren't asking for any special treatment. We're asking to be treated as equals, as fellow Americans who want to contribute to the fight against the Nazis."

He leaned back with a sigh. "You're a persistent young woman, Miss Jeeves." He looked around. "All of you. I'll give you that. But I'm afraid my answer is still no. The risks are simply too high."

Annie opened her mouth to argue further, but Mansfield held up a hand to silence her. "The Nazi U-boats prowling our shores make any hurricane look like a spring squall," Mansfield said. "I've seen what they can do, the ruthlessness of their attacks. They think nothing of strafing the lifeboats of the ships they torpedo. That's what you'd be facing out there. Can you honestly tell me you're prepared for that?"

"Are any of the fishermen up and down this dock prepared for that?" she replied. "How does *anyone* prepare for something like a war?"

Mansfield put his elbow on the table and rested his face in his hand. He stayed that way for more than a minute. He looked tired when he raised his head. "I must admit you have a point. I volunteered when I was just 19 years old back in 1917. I served on convoy escorts in the Atlantic. I saw what their U-boats can do. I heard the cries of men in the water and watched as others burned to death. These experiences never leave you. They haunt your dreams. Miss Jeeves, I was raised to protect women from seeing such sights."

"Yes, sir. I understand that. When I first sent you that message, it was just to learn more about the Mosquito Fleet. But you stirred up a hornet's nest when you told me that neither we nor the *Tequesta* were good enough for your fleet."

"That was not my intention."

Emma stepped forward and placed her hand on the chart. The contrast between the color of her hand and the paper was stark. "Sir, I appreciate your concern for us, but every day I walk the streets of this town, my life is at risk. The men who live on your side of town, including the Sheriff, were not raised to protect me. The time I've spent out at sea with Annie is the safest I've ever felt." Mansfield lowered his eyes.

"Emma and I, we're not naïve little girls. We know there are risks, but we're willing to face them. My brother is a Navy pilot risking his neck right now in the skies over Europe. Every day he goes up, he puts his life on the line. All I want —" Annie met Emma's eyes. "All *we* want is the chance to do our part, so Jack and other brothers, fathers, and sons can come home again."

For a long, tense moment, Mansfield said nothing. Then, he reached up to rub his forehead. "You're either the bravest young women I've ever met or the most foolhardy," he said. "All right, Miss Jeeves. Against my better judgment, *I* will accept the *Tequesta* into the Mosquito Fleet, Flotilla Number Two—on a probationary basis."

Annie's face broke into a grin as she reached across to shake his hand. "You won't regret it, sir."

"I might if my wife hears about this."

Annie laughed. "So what's next?"

"There's some paperwork. Come to my office in town. We'll get you on the list to get a radio. That might not happen for a while. There are shortages." He looked back and forth between the two women. "I hope you're ready for the reaction you're going to provoke."

"Trust me. I'm the only woman charter captain on the dock, and Emma is my crew, so I reckon this won't be much worse than what we've already seen."

"Don't be too sure."

"So, without a radio, what do we do if we see a submarine?"

"You get out of there as fast as you can," Mansfield said. "You head straight back to port and report the location, what direction it was traveling, and any markings on the bow that you might see with binoculars. Your job is to be our eyes and ears out there," he said. "If you spot a U-boat, you get us that information fast as you can, so we can divert ships and send out planes with depth charges. Under no circumstances do you ever approach an enemy vessel. Understood?"

Annie nodded. "Understood, sir."

"Yes, sir," Emma said.

"Good." He stood and turned towards the companionway ladder. "I'll be in touch when I can secure a radio for you."

He paused at the top of the ladder and looked down.

"Up and down the East Coast of the United States, civilians are volunteering to go out in small boats to patrol the coast. These are men who are either too old to fight, disabled or who have a criminal record. In some places they treat us like a joke, call us the Hooligan's Navy. But a pair of young women?" He shook his head. "I didn't see this coming."

Annie and Emma exchanged smiles.

"I just hope you understand what you've signed up for," he said. With that, he stepped off the boat and disappeared.

# CHAPTER FIFTEEN

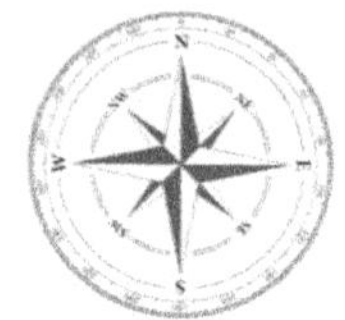

*La Rochelle, France*
*January 22, 1942*

The rain pelted Will's face as they walked through the cobblestone streets of La Rochelle. Max, Erich, and Jorg huddled close, their collars turned up against the biting wind that whipped off the Atlantic. Each man carried a bag with their American clothing, shaving kits and various personal objects related to their new identities. Their target loomed in the distance, rising from the mist: the silhouette of the enormous concrete U-boat bunker at La Pallice.

"How much farther?" Erich struggled to keep pace.

"Not far now." Will observed the empty streets. Even in the downpour, the absence of civilians was unnerving. La Rochelle had become a ghost town.

As they rounded a corner, Erich halted, his gaze fixed on a nondescript building across the street. "Wait. I need to stop here."

Will exchanged a puzzled glance with Max. "What for?"

"I have to see someone."

Jorg adjusted his dripping glasses. "Who could you possibly know in France?"

"Family." Erich's cheeks flushed. "Won't take long, I promise. Here." He handed Will his duffel bag.

"Fine." Will sighed. "But make it quick."

Erich crossed the street and knocked on a nondescript door. The others exchanged baffled looks. Will thought back to the pension where they'd stayed the night before shipping out. He recalled the concierge slipping an envelope to Erich right before they checked out. He hadn't given it much thought.

Max lit a cigarette. "What's the story with our Bavarian simpleton?"

Will shifted his weight, unease prickling his spine as he studied Erich waiting on the stoop like an overeager schoolboy.

Jorg's eyes widened as the door swung open. "Friends in high places, apparently."

The tall man who stepped out onto the stoop was older than Erich, in his fifties maybe. He wore a crisp black uniform, and the silver death's head on his cap gleamed in the weak light.

"Who in God's name is that?" Max whispered. He reached out, offering the cigarette to Will.

Will took a deep drag and passed it back to Max.

"An SS-Obergruppenführer," Jorg said.

Will watched with disbelief as Erich engaged in hushed conversation with the Nazi officer. Their rotund friend stood at attention, and his usual jovial demeanor had vanished.

Max tossed his cigarette butt into the gutter. "What the hell is going on?"

Before Will could respond, movement caught his eye. An old Frenchman, hunched against the rain, pedaled his rusty bicycle down the street. His beret was soaked, and his thin patched coat offered even less protection from the cold.

A screech of tires tore through the noise of the rain. Will whipped around to see a French policeman on a motorbike racing up the street from the other direction. As he passed, the old man's bicycle began to wobble across the slick cobblestones. The Frenchman saw the danger and tried to steer around it, but his foot slipped off the pedal and he lost control. He careened straight into a deep puddle that exploded in a geyser of muddy water, splattering across the polished black boots of Erich's SS acquaintance.

The officer let out a bellow of rage. He pushed Erich aside and advanced on the old man lying in the street next to his bicycle. Spittle flew from the officer's thin lips as he spewed a torrent of guttural German epithets. The Frenchman cringed, shaking hands raised in supplication.

*This can't be happening*, Will thought.

The SS-Obergruppenführer's hand moved to his holster, drawing his Luger with practiced ease.

Every fiber of Will's being longed to step forward, to stop the inevitable. But he couldn't make his feet obey, paralyzed by the same shameful instinct for self-preservation that had brought him to this godforsaken place to begin with.

So he stood there. Watching. Complicit.

The gunshot cracked through the air, and the old Frenchman collapsed. A pool of blood spread, mingling with the rainwater on the cobblestones.

"*Mein Gott*," Max whispered.

Will stared at the sightless eyes, pressure building at the back of his throat. He glanced at Jorg, his face a grim mask of resignation.

Erich stood rigid, his colorless, cherubic face focused only on the gun. The SS officer turned to him, his eyes burning with an icy fury. They spoke in hushed tones, and then Erich nodded, a stiff, mechanical gesture. The officer stalked away, disappearing into the house as swiftly as he had emerged.

Erich crossed the street without a glance at the body. He walked with the mechanical precision of a man trying not to think.

"Let's go." His voice was unrecognizable.

"Erich," Will began, "what—"

But Erich cut him off with a sharp shake of his head. Will searched those wide blue eyes for some sign of the good-natured young man he'd known. The man who dreamed of returning to his family's gasthaus, who carried photos of his pregnant wife like precious talismans.

"We must go," Erich said. "Now."

The team plodded on through the rain-slicked streets. Will's mind kept replaying the old man's fall.

"Papers," shouted a stern-faced guard, a rifle slung across his chest.

Will fumbled in his pocket, his fingers numb from the cold and shock. He produced his documents.

The guard's eyes flicked between Will's face and the photograph. "Purpose of travel?"

"Military assignment."

The man waved them through one at a time.

The roar of the waves breaking against the stone seawall grew louder. Rain was still falling, but it had slowed enough that he could see where they were going. They passed a series of narrow streets and continued along the edge of the harbor until they reached a wide boulevard lined with tall trees on both sides. From there, Will could see the massive concrete walls of the U-boat bunker.

The four men showed their papers at three different checkpoints before they arrived at the main entrance to the submarine pens. Each time, the guards checked their names against a list in a black leather-bound book and then waved them through saying nothing. It was as if the SS officer's murder of the old man hadn't happened. But every time they stopped, Will felt the tension among them grow tighter.

When they got to the last guard post, one soldier took out a flashlight and shone it into each of their faces. "You're late," he said.

Max stepped forward. "We met with difficulties in the city."

The soldier shrugged. "That does not concern me." He handed Max the papers, then turned and opened the iron gate.

A uniformed officer stood waiting. "Follow me."

They fell in line behind him, their footsteps echoing on the slick concrete floor. The officer led them through a warren of dimly lit passages, the air heavy with the stench of diesel and human sweat. The thrum of generators and the distant clang of metal on metal echoed from the darkness ahead.

When they arrived at the end of the tunnel, the structure opened up to display two sub pens, the black water occupied by one U-boat. Though the lofty conning tower and sinister deck guns appeared enormous, all of it was dwarfed by the massive bunker surrounding the vessel.

Alongside the boat ran a narrow concrete quay lit by bright white spotlights. Sailors and civilians hurried onto the gangplanks, carrying bags of supplies over their shoulders. In the empty slot alongside, a fuel barge lay tied to the boat with a black hose snaking along the sub's deck.

"Welcome to your new home, gentlemen," a different naval officer greeted them at the base of the gangway and introduced himself as Oberleutnant zur See Fischer.

The submarine rose on a swell and pulled against the groaning ropes that held it to the dock.

"Follow me. I'll show you to your quarters," Fischer said.

After climbing down ladders and threading their way between men, equipment, pipes and gauges, the officer led them to a compartment where torpedoes lay in cradles on the floor, while above them narrow pipe berths hung from chains. The officer stopped.

"The four of you are assigned to these two bunks. You will sleep in shifts, like all the men aboard. The other men here will tell you when you eat." Fischer looked at his watch. "We will leave in two hours. Leaving the vessel is forbidden." And with that, he turned and left them.

The journey across the Atlantic aboard the U-boat was worse than Will had expected. After they left La Rochelle and made their way out into the open sea, Erich became so seasick that he could hardly stand. Fischer explained to them that the submarine could make 18 knots under diesel power at the surface even with all the sea motion, but a mere 7 knots when below the surface where the motion eased. They would only dive if there was a reason, some danger present, so Erich would have to suffer.

The other men who shared their compartment made them miserable with their complaints about the stench of Erich's vomit. Will tried to empty the bucket into the latrine as often as he could.

On the third day of the voyage, Will sat wedged between the torpedo and the cold side of the hull trying to read a paperback book he'd borrowed. As his bookmark, he used the postcard of Valparaiso, Indiana they issued him as part of his new American identity. He knew the beach in the photo. His father had taken him there once.

From the hammock above, Erich moaned he was going to die.

Max let out a strangled laugh. "If only, Erich. If only."

Will closed his eyes, trying to steady his breathing. The oppressive closeness of the submarine's interior pressed in on him from all sides. He could almost taste the recycled air, heavy with the stench of vomit and sweat.

"How do you stand it?" Max whispered.

Will glanced up, surprised to see beads of sweat on Max's forehead despite the chill. "The submarine?"

Max nodded. "Feels like being buried alive."

Before Will could respond, Fischer appeared at the hatchway. "The Kapitänleutnant requests your presence in his office. All of you."

Erich groaned again. "Even me?"

The sailor's expression didn't change. "All of you."

As they wove through the narrow corridors, Will recalled the disjointed path that had led them here: from the day they'd recruited him, to meeting the others at the Naval Academy, to the weeks of training at Brandenburg. *This is it*, he thought. *At last we're going to learn the details of what will happen next*.

The Kapitänleutnant's office was no larger than a closet. The man himself stood behind a small desk, his weathered face impassive as he regarded the four men.

"Gentlemen," he began, "it's time you learned the details of your mission." He broke the seal of a thick envelope, and extracted a sheaf of papers.

Will held his breath, aware of Max's tension and Erich's labored breathing.

The Kapitänleutnant skimmed the document before he spoke. "They've divided you into two teams. One gets dropped off on the coast of New York; the other, at a location in Florida."

The small office seemed to shrink as the Kapitänleutnant read a second page in silence.

"So, your mission is twofold: sabotage of American infrastructure and gathering intelligence to relay to our U-boats offshore."

Will felt a chill colder than the metal walls of the submarine. Sabotage, he thought. Not just spying, but actively destroying.

"The equipment you'll need is already aboard," the Kapitänleutnant continued. "You will have weeks to familiarize yourselves with it during the voyage."

Jorg shifted, his voice low. "What kind of sabotage, sir?"

"Bridges. Power plants. Factories. Shipyards." The man's words fell like hammer blows. "Anything to cripple their war effort."

Will's stomach churned. Places full of Americans. So much for not killing. He glanced at Max, saw the same revulsion reflected in his friend's eyes.

"Your American clothing and papers are in a crate on board," the Kapitänleutnant said, then he handed each of them a single sheet of paper. "These are the details of your cover stories. During the rest of the voyage, you will memorize every word."

"Homework," Max said under his breath.

The Kapitänleutnant's smile was thin and humorless. "We will send you ashore with all the supplies in the crates they sent for you. Explosives, weapons. I recommend you bury them immediately somewhere close to the beach."

"And if we're caught during the landing?" Max asked.

He shrugged. "Your supplies make it obvious you are spies. Among your equipment, you will each have a cyanide capsule. Your presence in America will be disavowed by the Reich. None of you would hold up under torture by the Americans. Think of it as your duty to the Fatherland."

Will's mind tried to make sense of what he was hearing.

*They expected us to kill ourselves if captured.* The weight of it all pressed down on him.

"Questions?"

The men looked at one another, but no one spoke.

"Very well." The Kapitänleutnant cleared his throat. "One more thing. Hersey, you are partnered with Burger for this mission. You are going to Florida. Baum and Adler, you're the second team, and we will drop you at an island off New York."

Will froze. He turned, searching the Kapitänleutnant's face for any sign of a mistake. There was none.

"Sir?" Will's voice cracked. "I thought Max and I—we trained together."

"This is not up for discussion, Hersey."

Will glanced at Max. His stoic expression had cracked, revealing a flicker of dismay. Partnering with Erich felt like a death sentence before the mission had started.

Erich, oblivious to Will's distress, beamed. "We shall be a fine pair, ja?" His high-pitched voice grated on Will's frayed nerves.

As the others filed out, the Kapitänleutnant said, "Hersey, a word."

Will's stomach clenched as he watched Max close the door.

"Sit," the Kapitänleutnant commanded, gesturing to a chair.

Will sank into it, his legs weak.

"I received a direct order from Berlin that Erich Burger is to be paired with the strongest operative. Hersey," the Kapitänleutnant said. "These orders say that is you."

Will leaned forward, dread coiling in his gut. "Sir?"

"Burger's uncle, a high-ranking SS officer, requested that you are to ensure his nephew's safety during this mission."

The implications hit Will like a punch to the gut. He was

to be Erich's babysitter, responsible for a man who could barely tie his own shoelaces.

"I... understand, sir."

The Kapitänleutnant's gaze hardened. "I don't think you do, Hersey. Burger's uncle is not a man to be crossed."

Will's mind replayed the scene on the street. The encounter in La Rochelle, the SS officer's brutal act, Erich's pale face. It clicked into place with sickening clarity.

"Do you have a family, Hersey?"

"Yes, sir. My mother and grandfather."

"The SS-Obergruppenführer is a hard, uncompromising man. For the sake of your family, I hope Burger will return home in one piece."

Will swallowed the bile that threatened to betray his composure. When he spoke, his voice trembled. "I'll... do my best to keep him safe, sir."

The Kapitänleutnant leaned back, his chair creaking. "That is all, Hersey. Dismissed."

# CHAPTER SIXTEEN

*Fort Lauderdale, Florida*
*February 5, 1942*

The first hint of dawn cast pale grey shadows across the water as Annie and Finn guided the *Tequesta* into her dock on the New River. It was a relief to be back in port after the night they'd had. The patrol had started out calm, but turned nasty. The wind clocked around to the north when the cold front blew through, and wind against current caused the waves to grow tall and steep.

Annie stood on the stern trying to get some feeling back into her fingers. She'd been nursing a cup of coffee that had gone cold hours ago. The wind-chill factor must have dropped the temperature near freezing.

Finn came up behind her. "Rough out there last night."

She watched as he turned the spaghetti-like pile of rope into neat coils hanging from his rough palms. She liked the way he pursed his lips off to one side when he concentrated on a job.

"Thanks for agreeing to crew. I knew something was up

yesterday afternoon when the wind went westerly. Emma's been doing great on the boat, but she's not ready for a night like we just had."

"If I had to be out on a night like that, I'm glad it was with you. I knew you'd find your way home. Even once the rain got so bad we couldn't see the lights in the entrance channel."

She didn't know what to say.

Finn smiled. "Did you ever think we'd end up here?"

"What do you mean?"

"Patrolling the damn Gulf Stream looking for Nazi submarines?"

Annie shrugged. "Not much surprises me these days. And I could swear I heard something last night. It sounded like what they say a sub sounds like when it surfaces."

"You mean that whale that surfaced off our bow?" Finn laughed.

"Shut up," she said, reaching for one of the jib sheets. "How do you know it wasn't a U-boat blowing air out the air tubes at the surface?"

He looked over at Annie and shook his head. "I can't believe you thought that was a U-boat surfacing."

She laughed. "Well, I've never heard one before."

"No kidding. That's because they're all way out in the Atlantic where they belong. For now, anyway."

"Hey, we are supposed to be patrolling for them, right? They've sunk ships up north, and they'll come down here, one day. How can you be so sure what that noise was?"

She'd heard a loud exhale followed by a whooshing sound. It had been dark and so windy last night, she couldn't be sure of anything.

"I told you, Annie, it was just a whale breathing."

"All right. You win."

Finn's grin widened as he hung the coiled lines on the side

of the cabin. "I can't promise not to laugh if you mistake another sea creature for an enemy vessel."

They spent the next half hour cleaning up. When they finished, they locked everything up tight and stepped onto the dock together.

The lights of the city were still on in the early morning darkness, but the streets were empty. The wind had died down, but it was still chilly as hell.

"Maybe we'll get lucky next time," Finn said. "That cold front sure stirred things up."

Annie suppressed a smile. She wondered what he thought when he said the words 'get lucky.' They wouldn't be lucky if they ever encountered a real enemy sub, but she was pretty sure his thoughts didn't go where hers went. She watched him with occasional sidelong glances as they walked through the quiet streets. "What do you think it's like on a submarine when the weather gets all riled up like that?"

"Long as they can stay below the surface, they're fine. Problem is, they have to surface to recharge their batteries. They need fresh air. That's when they're vulnerable."

"Hmm," she said. But she thought, *Kinda like me*.

By the time they got back to the Jeeves' house in Sailboat Bend, the red-streaked clouds were giving way to morning sunlight. They entered quietly, taking care not to disturb anyone inside.

"I'll go wake up Bean," Annie whispered, tiptoeing towards her bedroom. Finn nodded and followed close behind.

The young girl was curled up under the blankets in Annie's bed. Her fiery red hair spilled over the pillow, framing her peaceful expression. Annie shook her shoulder, rousing her from sleep.

"Bean, time to get up."

Her blue eyes fluttered open, then she scowled and began rubbing the sleep from her eyes.

“Do I have to?”

“If you want to help fix breakfast, you do.”

"Okay," she mumbled, sitting up in bed. "Did you catch any U-boats?"

Finn sat down next to her and brushed the hair off her face. "Nothing but whales, kiddo." Bean giggled and crawled out of bed. Still wearing her pajamas, she joined them as they headed to the kitchen.

In the small, cozy space, the three of them moved with practiced ease, preparing breakfast together. Annie stirred oats into boiling water while Finn made toast.

Bean climbed onto the stool next to the counter and pulled down three bowls. She set them on the countertop. Annie poured hot water from the kettle into the teapot and took down two cups for herself and Finn. Bean preferred warm milk instead of tea, even though she insisted it made her feel like a baby.

“Hurry up, you guys,” she said. “I’m starving.”

While Bean spread the butter and marmalade on slices of bread, Finn filled their bowls with oatmeal. Then they carried everything over to the table and sat down.

Finn sipped his tea with his elbows on the table. “I just might sleep through my whole day off.”

Annie yawned as she sprinkled brown sugar on her oatmeal. “Me too.”

“Me three,” Bean said. “I got scared when that wind started blowing and making scary noises. Your ma came in and sat with me so I could go back to sleep.”

Finn reached over and roughed up his sister's hair. "Maybe you and me'll both take a nap, Squirt."

She pointed a finger toward her chest. "I even still got my PJs on."

Annie was washing the breakfast dishes when a sharp rap at the front door made her flinch, almost dropping a plate. She glanced at Finn, who shared her perplexed expression. Visitors this early were rare, especially on a Sunday morning.

"I'll get it." Annie dried her hands on a dish towel, then made for the front door.

Taking a breath, she turned the knob and pulled the door open. On the porch stood a tall man in a naval officer's uniform. He removed his hat, tucking it under his arm.

"Good morning, miss. I'm Lieutenant Andrews from the Naval Air Station," he said. His voice was grave. "Are your parents at home?"

"Of course, come in," she said, stepping aside and gesturing for him to enter.

As she led him toward a chair in the living room, she glanced over her shoulder at Finn and Bean, who were still sitting at the kitchen table staring at her. Before he took a seat, her father and mother emerged from the hallway wearing robes over their pajamas.

"Is there something we can help you with, Lieutenant?" Skeeter asked, trying to maintain a calm demeanor.

"Good morning." The officer stood and reached out to shake hands with each of them in turn.

"I'm sorry to bother you folks so early in the morning." His voice was soft, almost apologetic.

Skeeter motioned for him to have a seat while Hilda sank onto the couch.

When everyone was seated, the silence in the room seemed as thick as fog. The officer looked from one person to another, his gaze lingering on Annie's parents before shifting back to her again. “I’m very sorry,” he began. He cleared his throat, then started again. “There’s no easy way to say this.” He paused for a moment, then took a deep breath and continued. “Your son’s plane crashed while returning from a reconnaissance mission yesterday afternoon. There were four souls on board.”

“Oh my God,” Hilda said, covering her mouth with one hand. For a moment, she just stared at the officer, her eyes wide open. Then she closed them and turned away from him.

“Engine failure. As they were going down, Ensign Jeeves, who was technically still in training, radioed back important intelligence that will save lives.” The man wiped his hand across his mouth. “There were no survivors,” he added.

“Jack?” Hilda’s voice was barely a whisper. “No, that can’t be true.” Her head swung from side to side as if she could make the words go away by denying them. “He wasn’t even supposed to be there.”

Skeeter reached out and put his arm around her. “Hildy,” he whispered, his voice hoarse.

“Again, I’m very sorry for your loss.” The Navy man stood.

Annie felt like she was tumbling headlong into an abyss. She wanted to scream, to cry out, but she couldn’t make a sound. The man’s mouth was still moving, but she didn’t hear anything except the wind rushing past her ears.

The man was walking out the door.

Her parents had collapsed on the couch in each other's arms. They were crying. She had never seen her mother cry.

Finn was kneeling in front of her, grasping her forearms, shaking her. He was crying too. He was trying to say something, but the wind was all she heard.

She glanced at him through tear-filled eyes. Then she buried her face in his shoulder and sobbed.

No, no, no.

She heard her father’s voice. He sounded very far away.

"I'll take your mother to our room and stay with her for a while," he said. His voice was different too, almost as if it belonged to someone else.

She felt as if her heart was being torn apart inside her chest. She wanted to scream, to cry, to run until her legs gave out and she couldn't move anymore. But most of all, she just wanted to be alone.

"I can't." She stood up, then ran down the hall. The door to Jack's room was closed, as usual, but there was no more usual. Never would be. Nothing would ever be the same again. Not here at home, not anywhere.

When she reached her own room, she slammed the door behind her and threw herself onto the bed. Burying her face in the pillow, she screamed as loud as she could. Over and over until her throat was raw, and she didn't have any breath left. When the screaming stopped, the silence rushed in to fill the empty spaces, and all she could hear was the sound of her own heartbeat pounding in her ears.

~

She was still lying there, limp from sobbing, listening to the steady thump-thump of her heart when she heard a soft knock on her door.

"Annie," Finn said. "Can I come in?"

She considered pretending she hadn't heard him. She didn't want to talk to anyone right now. Didn't want to see the pity or listen to anyone tell her how sorry they were that Jack was gone. But if she didn't answer, he'd just keep knocking until she did.

"Go away." Her voice sounded muffled against the pillow.

"Please, Annie." There was an edge of desperation in his voice, and for a moment it made her angry. Why couldn't everyone just leave her alone? Wasn't it bad enough that she had to go through this at all? Now they wanted her to talk about it too?

"I can't."

The door creaked open, and she rolled half over. Finn was standing in the doorway. He looked as lost as she felt. Pale face. Dark circles under his eyes. Neither of them spoke. Then he crossed the room and sat on the bed beside her.

"You don't have to say anything." He reached out to take her hand. When he touched her, she started crying again.

He lay next to her and held her close while she sobbed. His shirt was rough against her cheek. She could hear his heart pounding in his chest. She closed her eyes and let herself sink into the warmth of his body. He didn't comfort her with words. Instead, he simply held her, rocking her back and forth like a child.

When the tears stopped at last, she pushed herself up and wiped her face with the sleeve of her sweater.

"I'm sorry," she whispered.

Finn sat up and shook his head. "Don't apologize, Annie. He was my best friend in the world, you know," he said. "I can't remember not knowing him."

Her own loss was so enormous, she had ignored Finn's. "I know. You guys were like brothers."

"I wish I had gone with him." His voice faltered as he swallowed back his own tears. "Maybe things would have been different."

"All the maybe's. They're going to haunt us now."

"I can't help thinking that there must have been something we could have done..."

"Emma." She blurted out the name.

"What?"

"I need to tell Emma." Annie tried to stand, but she wobbled and sat back down again.

"No, Annie. You're in no shape to go anywhere."

She turned to look at him. "Finn, he's dead! And Emma is in love with him."

"I know." He sighed and ran his fingers through his hair.

"She's *my* best friend, Finn."

"And now he's not coming home."

It was true. Jack wasn't coming home. Never again. The tears threatened to start again, but she blinked them away.

She tried to stand again, and this time there was no wobble. Her eyes were dry by the time she reached her bedroom door.

Finn was stretched out on her bed, his arm flung over his face.

"Don't go," he mumbled into the crook of his elbow.

"I have to."

He raised himself onto one elbow and tried to focus on her. His hair hung down in front of his eyes. "You're not thinking straight, Annie."

There was no point in trying to explain this to Finn. He would never understand how she felt about Emma. About any of it. She turned away from him and closed the door behind her.

Emma.

When Annie crossed through the living room, she was aware of little Bean, sitting alone on the couch. Then she was outside, walking, then running.

What was she going to tell Emma? How do you tell someone the man she'd dreamed of spending the rest of her life with is dead?

A car honked when she crossed Broward Boulevard, and she wasn't even sure how she'd got there.

Then she was standing on the front steps of the Albury

house. She took a deep breath. *Get a hold of yourself.* Her chest felt as though it was being squeezed. She couldn't breathe. But there wasn't time for that now. She had to do this.

Annie knocked on the door. Her knuckles were white against the dark wood.

The door opened, and Emma stood in front of her, smiling. "Annie! I was just on my way to church. I didn't expect..." She looked closer at Annie's face and the smile disappeared. "What is it? What's wrong?"

"Emma." Her voice broke. She cleared her throat and tried again. "It's Jack."

"What about him?"

"His airplane..." Her throat closed and the words came out no more than a whisper. "He's gone." she said.

Emma's eyes widened and then narrowed again. "No!"

"I'm sorry."

"What? How?" Emma started shaking her head. "No. Not Jack."

Annie nodded. "Yes. Our Jack."

And then, with a cry that sounded more animal than human, she raised her fists and began flailing them at Annie's head and shoulders. Though her words sounded like screams, she was repeating, "No, no, no," over and over again.

Then the fight was gone, and Emma collapsed into Annie's arms. Her friend was trying to speak, but the words came out only as moans. Annie held onto her, feeling her own tears begin to fall again. She clutched at Emma's coat, holding her close, rocking her. They swayed together on the doorstep, their bodies leaning into each other for support.

Annie heard footsteps on the dirt behind her.

"Annie?"

She turned and saw Finn standing in the yard with red-rimmed eyes.

"Finn. What are we going to do? How—"

And then he was moving toward them, his arms reaching out to take both women in his embrace. He held on to them for several minutes. Annie'd thought she was done with crying, but the tears flowed again. When Finn pulled back just far enough to look into Annie's eyes, she saw the depth of his pain.

Emma stayed where she was, leaning against Annie's shoulder. Her eyes were closed. Her hair was loose and hung down over one side of her face. Droplets of water from her morning shower shimmered in the sunlight. Annie stroked her hair.

Finn cleared his throat. "Emma?"

She opened her eyes and stared straight ahead at nothing. Her skin looked chalky, her face expressionless, except for the tear tracks that glistened on her cheeks.

"What can I do?" he asked.

"There is nothing left. Jack is gone."

# CHAPTER SEVENTEEN

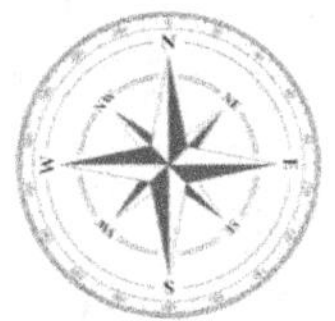

*Fort Lauderdale, Florida*
*February 19, 1942*

Annie and her parents sat on hard wooden chairs at Evergreen Cemetery, their eyes fixed on the newly-dug grave. Jack's flag-draped coffin rested on a stand next to the gaping hole in the ground. A mockingbird sang in the oak branches overhead, and the red hibiscus blooms scattered along the hedge nodded in the light breeze.

*But it felt wrong*

"Beautiful day." Her father's voice cracked as he spoke, eyes cast downward, his calloused fingers fidgeting with his cap.

"Too beautiful," Ma snapped.

Her mother's words echoed her own thoughts. Hilda sat ramrod straight, but her black dress hung loose and wrinkled. She stared at the coffin, her thin lips pressed together, her chin dimpled by the strain.

Annie blinked, fighting the sting of her own tears. She

would not cry, not here in this cemetery with its indifferent beauty.

A small crowd of townspeople, most dressed in black, fanned out around the family. Finn and Bean stood just behind their seats, both of them leaning for support on her parents' chairs.

Annie recognized Jack's old flight instructor from Merle Fogg Field, but she couldn't remember the man's name. He bent over Bean's shoulder and murmured words of condolence to Annie's parents, then his face turned to her. His lips moved, but the rushing in her ears swallowed the sounds.

She glimpsed her old boss, Fred Beck, from The Deck Restaurant and averted her eyes. Two Navy men flanked the gravesite at attention, white hats gleaming. One of those men had been the officer who'd brought the news two weeks ago.

Had it only been two weeks? The days had blurred into one endless twilight as she had stayed in her room with the curtains closed. She'd counted the cracks in the ceiling and listened to her mother's muffled sobs through the walls. Pa kept trying to coax them both to the table, where eating his flavorless food was more of a chore than a pleasure. Finn had come by daily, Bean too, but she'd turned them all away.

And the *Tequesta*'s lines had grown green with algae as she sat idle at the dock. Too many memories there.

Annie blinked, realizing the minister was speaking about Jack.

"Lord, we gather here today to celebrate the life of Jack Jeeves, a brave young man who made the ultimate sacrifice for his country." The preacher droned on, his words lost to the infernal buzzing in Annie's ears.

She crossed her ankles and worked to keep her breathing slow and steady. Her disobedient mind drifted back to Jack's booming laugh, his goofy grin. She saw him playing in the surf with Finn, running up the beach in that golden dusky light.

Her fingers twisted the coarse fabric of her new dress. The getup felt like a straitjacket, constricting her ability to breathe. It should be Jack sitting here in an ill-fitting suit, smothered by sympathy. If one of them had to die, it should have been her. Everyone loved Jack.

The minister's words skittered across Annie's consciousness, unable to penetrate the haze that had settled over her thoughts. She caught snatches here and there - "brave," "sacrifice," "hero."

She shifted on the hard wooden chair, her dress scratching against her skin. Jack would've howled with laughter seeing her trussed up like this, hair all pinned up, feet stuffed in new patent leather shoes, her body shrouded in a costume better suited for a spinster librarian than his tomboy sister. She could almost hear his voice, teasing her about the lace collar itching at her neck.

"Aww, don't you clean up nice, Miss Antsy Pantsy?" he'd say under his breath. "Bet you can't wait to shuck those shoes and dive into the river, clothes and all."

A laugh bubbled up in her throat, escaping in a strangled hiccup that earned her a sharp glance from her mother. Annie bit the inside of her cheek until she tasted blood. Even muffled by a mahogany box, Jack somehow managed to get her in trouble.

The service dragged on, an endless blur of prayers and memories. Annie wanted to scream, to rage against the unfairness of it all. Twenty-three was too young to be a memory. Too young to be relegated to past-tense.

The minister's voice faded, replaced by a solemn silence. The two Navy men stepped forward, their movements precise and practiced. Annie watched, her throat tight, as they folded the flag draped over Jack's casket.

Crisp corners. Sharp creases.

Her father's hand trembled as he accepted the triangular bundle.

They all stood and approached the grave. One by one, the mourners filed past, each placing a single flower on the polished mahogany. White lilies and crimson roses. Annie clutched her lilies, waiting. She couldn't do it, wouldn't say goodbye.

Skeeter cleared his throat. "He woulda liked this spot."

Annie's gaze drifted to the cemetery entrance, her heart clenching at the sight of Emma standing in the shadow of a sprawling oak, flanked by her mother and grandfather. Even from a distance, the pain in her friend's eyes was palpable.

*Emma.* Annie ached to go to her. Damn these stupid rules. Why on God's earth did it make sense to prevent loved ones from sharing pain at a grave? "Emma." She said her name aloud and raised her palm.

"Annie." Her father's voice lifted with caution. He'd caught sight of the trio at the cemetery entrance. He placed his hand on her forearm and lowered it. "We have to stay here and accept the condolences of the others."

A flash of red caught Annie's eye, and she turned to see Bean barreling towards her, braids flying. The girl threw herself into Annie's arms, almost knocking her off balance.

"Annie!" Bean cried, her small body shaking with sobs. "I'm gonna miss Jack so much."

Annie hugged her, burying her face in Bean's vanilla-scented hair.

Finn appeared at Annie's side, his hand coming to rest on the small of her back.

Annie leaned into him, but even as Finn's arms encircled her, the numbness remained.

She closed her eyes, and a sob caught in her throat. She couldn't do this, couldn't bear the weight of her grief, the endless parade of sympathetic faces and hollow platitudes.

Annie extracted herself from Finn's embrace, her movements stiff and jerky. She couldn't breathe, couldn't think. The press of bodies, the murmur of voices, it was all too much.

"Sorry. I need to go," she choked out. "I can't... I can't do this."

"Annie, I know."

She shook her head. No, nobody knew.

Her father turned to her, his brow furrowed with concern. "Sweetheart, let's go home."

"No!" The word burst from her lips, sharp and jagged. "I can't get in the car. I need to walk. I need, I need to be alone."

Her father protested, but something in her wild-eyed expression must have stopped him. He nodded, his eyes glistening with unshed tears. "Alright. We'll see you at home."

Annie turned, her gaze seeking Emma. The other girl stood apart from the crowd, her face a mask of quiet sorrow. Annie walked towards her, each step an effort.

She stopped in front of Emma. No words could counter the pain in her friend's eyes. Annie pulled her into a fierce hug.

"I'm so sorry," Annie whispered, unsure if she was apologizing for not going to see her friend these past weeks, or for not inviting her to sit with the family at the funeral, or for everything that had kept her and Jack apart. When they pulled back, Annie saw in Emma's dark eyes that here was someone who knew what she was feeling. Someone who would understand. She squeezed her eyes tight, feeling that black ball of grief rising, threatening to explode.

With a curt nod, Annie turned and ran. She ran from the cemetery, from the suffocating sympathy, from the wooden box that held what was left of her brother. Her feet pounded against the earth, the slap of her ill-fitting shoes on pavement echoing in her ears.

She ran until the cemetery was far behind her, until her lungs burned, and the hot tears stopped flowing.

At last, the manicured lawns gave way to the bridge across the New River. She slipped off the shoes that had chewed through her heels. Barefoot, she ran through the ramshackle buildings along the town wharf and down onto the farthest end of the docks. Only then did she allow herself to collapse. Alone at last.

Annie sat on the weathered planks, her legs dangling over the edge, her toes skimming the water. She rubbed her eyes and wiped her nose with the back of her hand. The shiny black shoes rested on the dock behind her, with her bloodied anklet socks stuffed into the toes. The creak of ropes and slap of water against hulls were the only sounds breaking the stillness.

Across the New River, she watched a flock of egrets take flight, their wings beating a steady rhythm against the cloudless sky. Beneath the surface of the dark water, small fish were darting around the pilings.

Lost in thought, Annie didn't hear the approaching footsteps until a voice said, "Rough day, eh?"

She glanced up to see Fuller Mansfield standing over her, tweed jacket draped over one arm. Without waiting for a reply, he dragged over a small wooden barrel and lowered himself down beside her with a grunt.

"Mind if I join you?" he asked, gaze fixed on the river. "I came down to the dock to talk to some captains, and I saw you sitting over here."

She looked up at the face of the man in charge of the Mosquito Fleet. His brown hair was combed straight back, and his gaunt cheeks gave him an air of quiet authority.

Annie shrugged. She wasn't in the mood for conversation.

Mansfield seemed content to sit without speaking, something Annie appreciated. She continued staring out at the water, wishing she could sail away from this place where every sight and sound brought up some memory of her brother.

After some time, Mansfield cleared his throat. "I know there's not much I can say," he began. "Losing someone. Well, it leaves a hole that nothing can ever fill."

He paused as his voice seemed to catch, and Annie heard him clear his throat. He waited several minutes before he tried to speak again.

"My older brother died in Europe in '17. In the trenches. I was just a young sailor then, not much older than you. The war ended before I saw too much action." The man kept his eyes focused on something across the river. "That was a long time ago, but I still think of him every day."

They sat in silence then for a long while, the only sound the whisper of the breeze through the mangroves. Annie studied Mansfield's profile, the sharp lines of his face softened by the afternoon light.

"I wanted to express my condolences," Mansfield said at last, his gaze still fixed on the horizon. "Your brother's loss is a tragedy. He was a brave man."

Annie swallowed past the constriction in her throat. "He loved flying. Didn't want to talk about anything else. Ever since we were kids, and he saw a plane land on the road one day in front of Pa's car, all he ever wanted was to be a pilot."

"And he achieved that dream," Mansfield said. "That's no small thing, Miss Jeeves."

Annie blinked back tears again, surprised by the compassion in Mansfield's voice. She had expected platitudes, not understanding.

"I also wanted to thank you for joining the Mosquito Fleet. We need all the help we can get, especially now."

Annie frowned. "Why? What's happened?"

Mansfield sighed, his shoulders slumping. "That's what I came down here to talk to the captains about. They're here, Annie. Yesterday, the Germans torpedoed a cargo ship, the *Pan Massachusetts*, off Cape Canaveral. Eighteen men dead, twenty rescued. It's the first one sunk by a U-boat off our Florida coast."

Annie felt as if something had sucked the air from her lungs. "No, not now, not here."

She thought of her old home up north, Skeeter's Fish Camp, where she and Jack had spent their childhood. It wasn't just Jack. They were all vulnerable. The war, which had always seemed so distant, was very close now.

"Those poor men. Their families." She knew the words weren't enough, but she didn't know what else to say.

Mansfield nodded, his jaw tight. "We knew it was coming, but we're never really prepared."

Annie turned back to stare out at the river once again. She had always known that the war was raging just beyond the horizon, but Canaveral? That was so close to Skeeter's Fish Camp. So close to home.

Mansfield seemed to sense her disquiet. He placed a gentle hand on her shoulder; his touch was light but reassuring. "I know it may seem trivial on this day after your loss."

"All those men. No, that could never be trivial."

He nodded. "This is a terrible reminder that our mission matters. Transporting supplies for our boys. Patrolling for U-boats. It's critical work."

He held Annie's gaze. "I want to express my gratitude for your being part of it. I know I wasn't exactly welcoming when you first volunteered, but that's changed. These days, everyone needs to step up. We need your skills. And your spirit."

Annie managed a small, appreciative smile.

"Thank you for telling me."

Mansfield rubbed his knees. "We'll talk soon."

He stood, brushing off his tweed trousers. "I'll leave you to your thoughts, Miss Jeeves. Remember, we need you sharp."

Annie nodded, barely registering his departure. Her eyes remained fixed on the river's swift current and a graceful dragonfly that flew inches above the sun-dappled surface.

A flicker of movement caught her eye down in the darker depths. Something gray and bulky glided beneath the surface, heading upstream. Annie leaned forward, squinting against the glare of the sun on the water.

Then the creature breached, and a loud "whoof" of exhaled air broke the stillness. Annie's eyes widened as she recognized the whiskered nostrils and then the smooth, rounded back.

"Hello manatee," she said aloud.

The gentle giant's back rolled along the surface, its movements slow and deliberate. Annie watched, transfixed, as it navigated the river with surprising grace for its size.

*Jack would've loved this.*

She tracked the animal's progress upstream as each pump of her mermaid-like tail formed an upwelling and a patch of growing concentric circles on the surface of the water.

After the manatee vanished, Annie sat in contemplative silence. The river flowed onward, toward the ocean, where the hunters now roamed. She breathed in the warm, briny air.

She pushed to her feet, picked up her shoes and walked down the dock. It was time to face the *Tequesta*.

# CHAPTER EIGHTEEN

*Fort Lauderdale, Florida*
*February 22, 1942*

Annie lay in bed, both hands behind her head, staring at the ceiling. She guessed from the faint light in the room that it was not yet 7:00. Tess had sprawled out on the white chenille bedspread with her own head pillowed on Annie's leg. She reached down and stroked the dog's head, scratching behind her ears.

Surveying the room that had been her refuge these past few weeks, she crinkled her nose at the mess. Nautical charts and books had overtaken her tidy bedroom, their musty boat smell filling the air. She had intended to use them to study for her work with the Mosquito Fleet, but that was before...

Above her desk, pinned to the wall, hung Annie's most prized possession: a treasure map based on the family's fish camp up in Edgewater, Florida, drawn when she was nine years old.

In the top right corner, she had drawn a fancy compass rose with the fleur de lis pointing north. Below that, in her best penmanship, she had written "The Treasure Map" in black ink with the tails of the T and M curling around under the words. She had outlined the Mosquito Lagoon and the village of Edgewater, with arrows pointing to Skeeter's Fish Camp and the creek where she and Jack had discovered the old abandoned skiff.

Annie did not know where she got the idea to create that map, but she remembered the day she had sketched it out. She presented it to Jack with instructions to find the treasure she had hidden under the X.

Closing her eyes, she pictured Jack's mischievous grin and infectious laughter. She would give anything to have him there to tease her one more time.

"I miss him so much," she said. She reached down to stroke Tess's fur. "Every day."

Tess whined once, low in her throat.

"Yeah, I know you do, too." Annie closed her eyes, and Tess nuzzled closer, her wet nose pressing against Annie's palm.

The muffled sounds of her parents moving about the kitchen drifted through the closed door. Her mother hadn't cooked a proper meal since the news of Jack's death, and her father had stopped shaving, his stubble now a patchy beard. They moved past each other like ghosts, communicating in grunts and gestures. She knew her mother would still be in her bathrobe, her hair in curlers. Pa would be in his undershirt. It had been like this for weeks now. No one within their small circle of family and friends seemed to know how to navigate this world without Jack.

Annie heard the kitchen door bang open and the pounding of heavy footsteps.

"Mrs. Jeeves?" Finn's voice sounded breathless and frantic.

Annie sat bolt upright in her bed.

Then she heard her mother's voice, soft and hesitant. "Finn. What's the matter?"

"I'm sorry to barge in like this, but where's Annie?"

"She's in her room."

The silence that followed told her that her mother had not even asked him why he needed to see her. She imagined him standing in their kitchen, his red hair curling from the humidity. Annie had not seen Finn since the funeral, but she had heard that he had gone back to work at the shipyard.

Finn's voice again. "Annie! Where are you? I need to talk to you."

She stumbled out of bed, her loose hair falling around her shoulders. The pajamas she wore—pants too long, sleeves hanging past her wrists—once belonged to Jack. She grabbed her robe off the hook and slipped it on.

"I'm coming!" she yelled as she tied the sash around her waist.

When she walked into the kitchen, a part of her hoped her parents would be there talking to Finn. She wanted to find them discussing something–anything–to show they had not become zombies. She saw the closed door to their bedroom, the untouched breakfast dishes still on the table. They had retreated again.

Finn looked up at her, his face flushed, his mouth open, still catching his breath. His hair was dark with sweat.

"What's wrong?" she said. "You look like you've seen a ghost."

"It's good to see you, Annie. I've missed you."

"Is that what you came here to tell me?"

"No, it's another ship. A tanker this time. *The Republic*. Torpedoed by a U-boat just before daylight. She's the biggest tanker been hit yet."

Annie shook her head. "Another? So soon? Where?"

He paused. "Jupiter."

"*Jupiter?* My God. That's not far."

Finn nodded. "I heard about it on my way to Dooley's. Everybody's talking about it. Figured you'd want to know. Said she'd sailed out of Houston on her way to New York with a full load of crude. They took a hit before dawn, but she didn't go down. Not right away, anyway. They tried to get into the Port of Palm Beach, but didn't make it. They drove her up onto the beach near Jupiter so she wouldn't sink."

"Casualties?"

"It's not clear yet. I heard a yacht picked some crew up. A Coast Guard cutter picked others up, but some are still missing."

Annie stared at the ceiling. "Jupiter?" she said. "That's about fifty nautical miles north." She looked at Finn and saw her own wild eyes reflected in his. "I've gotta go. I need to get dressed and get down to the boat." She drew a deep breath. "There may still be men out there in the water."

Finn swallowed, then said, "You know I want to go, but with all the time I already lost, I've got to think of Bean. I have to get back to work. If you mean to take the boat out, you'd best ask Emma to crew for you."

Annie nodded. "No worries. But this is something that I have to do."

"Annie, are you sure you're ready?"

She blinked away the wetness in her eyes. "I'll be fine."

He crossed the room and wrapped his arms around her. He whispered in her ear, "You stay safe, Annie girl." Then he turned, and the screen door slammed behind him.

She reached for the back of a wooden chair to steady her dizziness. *Breathe*, she told herself. Then she returned to her room and peeled off her pajamas. After digging around in a pile of clothes on the floor, she pulled out her old overalls. When she had dressed, she sat down on the bed, leaned over, and stroked Tess's head. The dog's eyelids drooped and the corners of her mouth turned up in a blissful canine smile. Annie scratched the dog's ears.

"Yeah, I miss him too, girl," she said. She pressed her cheek against the top of Tess's head. The dog's fur tickled her nose and the tops of her lips.

Annie sighed, sat up, and patted the dog's side. "But Jack wouldn't want either of us moping around. He'd tell us to get off our arses and get to work. We've got to fight back, girl. Are you ready?"

Tess barked, and Annie went to her desk, pulling her rucksack out from under a pile of charts. She grabbed a pair of shorts, a few pairs of underwear, a clean T-shirt and stuffed them into the bag. She set her sextant case on the bed. Not likely to need it, but better safe than sorry. She slipped her navigation dividers and parallel rulers into her bag. Then she pulled her chart tube out from under her bed, opened it up, and added the charts of the Florida coastline. She'd make do with these. She didn't need to bring her complete collection.

In the kitchen, Annie paused. The door to her parents' bedroom was closed. She looked around the quiet kitchen. She couldn't take another day of this. After helping at the shipwreck site, she would continue up north and visit Woody at the fish camp, their old home.

Annie gathered up food: two apples, a half loaf of bread, and a couple of cans of Campbell's soup. After stuffing them into her rucksack, she walked over to the small writing desk in the kitchen's corner and pulled out the chair. Using one of her father's pencils, she wrote on a notepad:

*Dear Ma and Pa,*

*I'm going to take the Tequesta out to join the search for survivors off Jupiter, then continue on to the Fish Camp. I'll send word when I arrive.*

*Love, Annie*

She folded the note in half and placed it on the kitchen counter near the sink. Then she grabbed her rucksack, whistled for Tess, and left.

The morning air was already thick with humidity when Annie stepped onto the dock and quickened her pace towards her boat. She saw several empty slips where other members of the Mosquito Fleet docked their boats.

Tess ran ahead and jumped aboard the boat, sniffing at the closed hatch. Annie wondered if the old dog hoped she might find Jack there after all. On the walk to the docks, she had considered going to ask Emma to accompany her. They hadn't seen each other since the funeral, and they hadn't spoken there. How could she explain to Emma that she wanted to be alone right now? Not even her best friend, who was suffering in her own right, would be welcome on this trip. It was just going to be Annie and her ghosts.

Once inside, she hurried to check the supplies on board, her mind racing through what she'd need for the journey. Water tanks—full. Enough diesel to get her there and back, with a bit to spare. As she worked, she heard footsteps on the dock. When she popped her head out the hatch, she saw Mansfield approaching, his suit and tie looking out of place in the Florida heat.

"Hello, Annie," he said, his voice cool and controlled. "Heading out?"

She straightened up and wiped her palms on her overalls.

He took off his jacket and slung it over one shoulder.

She paused for a moment and then said, "Yeah, I heard about the *Republic.* Thought I'd take Emma and do a little look-see up there off Jupiter." She shouted as if her friend was below deck. "Emma? You got those cans stowed down there?"

Mansfield's brows rose in surprise, but he didn't question her further. Instead, he offered a curt nod and with the words, "Well, you be careful out there. Those U-boats, they aren't to be trifled with," he walked on down the docks to take the lines of an approaching boat.

When the Tequesta cleared the harbor entrance, Annie slowed the engine and turned the boat's bow into the southeasterly wind. She tied off the wheel and went forward to grab the main halyard. Her movements were precise and deliberate, the way her father had taught her. It had been weeks since she'd raised sail aboard the *Tequesta*, and she realized now how much she had missed the sea.

She pulled the halyard to lift half the sail, then wrapped the line once around the winch and continued pulling it until the sail was all the way up. She cleated it off and gave the line a final yank to set it tight. Then she released the boom vang and topping lift and headed back to the helm.

The silence surrounded her, interrupted only by the slight sound of water sliding past the hull. She set the mainsheet and moved to the foredeck to haul up the big genoa headsail. When she raised the canvas, the southeast breeze filled the headsail, and the boat heeled over as she picked up speed. Annie moved back to the cockpit, took a seat on the windward side, and pulled the headsail sheet to get the proper trim. Then she adjusted her course to north-northeast.

Annie figured once she got into the Gulf Stream current, she'd be doing eight or nine knots over the bottom. The tanker was only fifty miles up the coast. She should be off Jupiter by late afternoon.

By the time she arrived at the wreck site, the sun was low in the west, and she had to strain to see the ship that had run aground on the beach. Her father had once told her that tankers carried a crew of about forty men. Had they all made it? She scanned the horizon, but there was nothing. Not a single boat in sight.

She zigged and zagged offshore, searching the surface for any sign of life, but she saw nothing as the light faded from the sky. She was too late.

Tess climbed up into the cockpit and placed her head on Annie's lap. She was trying to tell her something. Perhaps that it was dinner time. "Just a few minutes more, girl."

The bow of the *Tequesta* rose and fell in the swells, and Annie could feel the current carrying them north. At four knots through the water with the Gulf Stream running three knots from the southeast, she calculated she'd reach the search area in half an hour.

Just above the horizon, she watched the first star of the night appear in the sky. Beneath it, the outline of a tanker slowly making its way south against the Gulfstream made her think about the men on board. She wondered if they were aware of what had happened in these same waters in the last twenty-four hours.

Annie shivered and rubbed her arms. Tess whined, pressing against Annie's legs.

"It's getting cold out here, girl." The air had turned chilly, and it was time to fix herself and Tess some dinner. They had a long night ahead. But the air felt wrong, too still.

Annie was still looking up at the stars when the concussion from the explosion hit, almost knocking her off the cockpit seat. She grabbed the coaming and held on, the shockwave vibrating through her body. Tess darted into the cabin.

Out at sea, where she had just seen that ship, she now saw flames shooting into the air.

Boom! A second explosion, louder than the first, sent up an even bigger fireball. Thick smoke billowed into the sky, obscuring the starlight as two more explosions followed one after the other.

"My God." Annie shook her head. How could anyone survive that inferno?

When she tried to stand and reach for the binoculars, her legs felt weak, her muscles trembled. The bright flames ruined her night vision. Around the *Tequesta*, the water appeared black. She was several miles offshore, and the wind was light, but she could still see the fire's reflection on the water. It appeared as though the sea itself was aflame. The smell of burning oil reached her, the stench making her feel nauseous at sea for the first time in her life.

Annie adjusted her course to head east to intercept any survivors being pushed north by the Gulf Stream. She sheeted in the sails, but the *Tequesta* was no race boat, and she couldn't point well upwind. The fire was out there, even closer now, and still burning like a torch on the horizon.

Closing her eyes, she pictured the chart of the Florida coast in her mind. They were north of Jupiter Inlet. The tanker was about ten miles offshore and a good three miles south of her position. She was making about four knots through the water, but the Gulf Stream was running at three knots from the southeast, pushing her sideways. If she could hold her course, she'd soon arrive, not to where the ship had been hit, but to the area where any survivors would be as the current carried them north.

When Annie opened her eyes, all trace of the ship was gone, though there were still flames burning the oil on the water. She shook her head again. How on earth could an enormous ship like that just disappear? The fire was burning so hot, it was unlikely anyone could survive.

Was she crazy driving her wooden sailboat ever closer to the fire? As the distance shrank, Annie felt the heat on her cheeks from the flames on the water.

Tess reappeared at the top of the companionway ladder.

"Sorry, girl. I know you're hungry. But I've got to stay out here for now. There might be survivors."

The dog climbed out into the cockpit and came over to sniff at her and lick her face. Then the dog stopped and turned her head, her ears cocked at an alert angle. Then she turned and jumped onto the side deck and disappeared on the dark foredeck.

"Tess, come! Here girl, you know you're not allowed out on deck."

Tess erupted in a volley of loud barks. Annie jumped and peered forward into the faint light offered by the fire. The dog stood at the bow, ears perked, and her body tense and alert.

Annie stared out at the dark water. What was it? What had Tess heard or seen?

She sighed. Of course, the dog was already a little jumpy tonight. Maybe it was dolphins, freaked out by the explosion as they all were. But now, as the fire was burning itself out, it had grown quiet. All she heard was the whoosh of the water against the hull, the boat creaking, and the flutter from the wind in the sails.

The dog started barking again.

"Tess! Hush, girl!"

Annie moved forward, keeping one hand on the cabin top, the other on the lifelines. The boat was rolling in the light wind and the two to three-foot swells. She stopped behind the dog and scanned the horizon. No lights, no ships. Squinting, she tried to see what the dog was looking at. Tess was standing at the bow, her nose pointed forward. She was staring at something about ten degrees off the starboard bow.

"Tess, you silly dog." Annie reached out and grabbed the dog's collar. "Come on back. It's not safe for you on deck. Good girl."

With her hand on the dog's head, she stopped. Out of the darkness, on the top of a swell, she saw something bobbing in the water.

Annie squatted, peering out into the night. In the quiet, she felt her pulse pounding in her temples. She thought about the German U-boat out there somewhere, perhaps even beneath her at this moment. What was it? What had the dog seen?

She turned and hurried into the cabin. Where was the damn flashlight? Her fingers fumbled through the jumble of tools and rags. She felt the cool steel and grabbed it.

Tess was still staring into the darkness, a low growl in her throat.

*Whatever this is, please don't let it be a U-boat.*

Annie aimed the light into the black night, but it reflected off the mist in the air. Tilting it lower, she swept the beam across the water. Then she stopped and swung it back over the last area.

*What was that?* Something was floating there in the waves, much closer now. She looked up and blinked. She turned off the light. Was she seeing things?

When she switched the light back on and looked again, the doubt was gone. This was no hallucination. The shadow hardened, and she saw the faint outline of a man clinging to a piece of wood. He lifted his hand and gave a weak wave.

# CHAPTER NINETEEN

*The Atlantic Ocean off Jupiter, Florida*
*February 22, 1942*

Will Hersey's arms churned through the water with powerful strokes. He lifted his head to breathe and looked back over his shoulder. The overturned rubber boat bobbed fifty meters away. Beyond it, the flames that engulfed the tanker lit the night sky. Erich had stopped screaming intelligible words. Now he just screamed.

One minute he and Erich had been in the rubber boat, hurriedly launched off the deck as the U-boat submerged beneath them. They were paddling as fast as they could, trying to get out of the way of the tanker bearing down on them. Then all hell broke loose.

The world exploded. He couldn't see. Couldn't breathe. When Will crawled his way to the surface, their boat was upside down, drifting away, and he heard Erich crying for help. He swam to his teammate, but the man in the water was no longer Erich.

Mad with panic, his teammate kept pushing Will under the water, trying to climb up his body like a pole to keep his own head in the air. While Will had controlled Erich back in Brandenberg, this Erich was not the same man. This man had allowed his panic to devour his sanity.

When Will tried to push away, the madman's grip on his clothes was like an iron clamp. Again and again, Erich pulled or pushed Will's head under water as they both floundered.

Will opened his eyes. The water was opaque black. He saw nothing except the silver bubbles of his own breath rising.

Air was all he wanted. Summoning his remaining strength, Will punched Erich in his chest. He heard the whoosh of the man's exhale. The grip loosened, and Will kicked his way to the surface. He pulled in deep breaths. Choked, coughed.

And then he had swum as fast as he could away from the man it was his sworn duty to protect.

Another explosion tore through the night, illuminating the sky with a bright ball of fire. The sea around the ship was alight with burning oil. Will realized the wind was driving the inferno closer to him. The rubber boat was nowhere in sight. He forced himself to swim faster, widening the gap between himself and his teammate.

*Damn you, Erich.* His legs were cramping from the cold water. He had to keep swimming. Keep his blood flowing.

He rolled over onto his back, lifted his head and looked back at the ship. The entire front half of the ship was ablaze, and the windborne flames were spreading like an orange, undulating carpet. His cheeks felt the heat from the burning oil.

Even from the top of the swells, he could no longer see the man who had nearly killed him. But the flames were after him now. Will turned and continued his crawl stroke.

His lungs burned from the heat and smoke. He'd experienced nothing like this. The water was freezing, but the air felt and tasted like it was on fire.

He had to keep moving, had to get away from the flames that were chasing him. But his once powerful strokes were becoming weaker, his muscles not responding. He was so damn tired. He felt as if he could sleep right here in the water.

When he turned his head for his next breath, a wave slapped his face and filled his mouth with seawater. Coughing and gagging, he tried to tread water. Air, he needed air to clear the burning salt water in his throat. But the cold had become a debilitating ache in his arms and shoulders, and he could barely keep his head above water.

His mind was growing fuzzy. He could see the flames dancing across the water, but the ship was gone. He had to keep swimming, had to stay ahead of the fire. Legs numb, and the cold had crept up into his groin. Eyelids heavy. The warmth from the flames tingled the skin on his face even while the icy water was lapping at his chin.

Then he saw it out of the corner of his eye. It was just a shadow floating in the water. He almost swam past it. Turning, he lifted his leaden arm and reached for it. His fingers grasped the edge, and he pulled the wooden hatch cover to his chest. He clung to it with both arms, and his head fell forward. The wooden splinters scratched his cheek, but he did not care. He could not let go.

The cold seeped into his bones, his skull, his brain. His thoughts were thick and sluggish, and yet, he wanted to make some sense of the events that had gotten him here.

As though it were a dream, he saw himself and Erich blinking at the setting sun as they had climbed up onto the sub's deck. The Kapitänleutnant had brought their sub to the surface and sent them out on the deck to inflate the rubber boat. The sea was smooth, the wind light.

Kapitänleutnant said he would take them closer to the coast. He and Erich were chatting and sharing a smoke, excited at the prospect of getting to land. The whole team came on deck, and Will and Max joked about how they would meet up for drinks in New York.

Then they sighted the tanker on the horizon. All the others rushed down the hatch, the dive signal sounded, and the black deck slid beneath the water.

Will and Erich had been left paddling their rubber boat alone in the path of a tanker.

The cold was so intense, his whole body was shaking. He was afraid he might lose his grip on the wooden hatch. His mind kept drifting away. It must have been another U-boat that fired the torpedo that exploded the tanker. What was its number? Where did it come from? He had not seen it on the surface, but he had seen the white streak of the torpedo. And then fire everywhere.

"Wilhelm."

He lifted his head and looked around. Just the sea, the stars and the orange glow in the sky behind him. Did he imagine it?

"Wilhelm, what are you doing?"

He closed his eyes, and he could see her. He opened his eyes, and there she was, her hair piled up on top of her head, her long neck rising out of the water.

"*Mutti*?"

He squeezed his eyes shut, but she was still there, smiling at him, the way she used to when he was a boy. He could see the tiny lines around her eyes. He wanted to reach out and touch her hand. He wanted to feel her skin.

"I'm cold, *Mutti*. So cold."

She reached out and touched his face. Her fingers so warm on his skin. He tried to reach up and touch her, but his hands were numb.

He let his head fall back into the hollow between his arm and the hatch cover. His brain was not working right. He felt so very tired.

Through the haze of pain and cold, Will's eyes caught a flash. A speck of white fluttering amidst a sea of endless black. An apparition. A ship sailing toward him in the distance.

"Can't trust your senses," he muttered to himself, his words slurred and barely audible. "It's not real."

But then, as if in defiance, a sound pierced the silence: a dog barking.

He squinted, straining his eyes against the ripples of water that distorted his vision, and there, a man atop the deck, busily lowering the sails. His face was obscured by shadow, but the flashlight he held aloft revealed his figure, clad in loose overalls that billowed with the wind.

"*Mutti*?" he whispered. *Did you send him?* Or was this yet another phantom?

*Please.* He rested his head on his arm as it draped over the hatch cover. *Please let this be real.*

With every fiber of his being, he prayed that the sailboat and its enigmatic occupant would prove to be more than a figment of his imagination.

His legs had stopped moving, and he fought to keep his eyes open. His vision blurred, and the horizon seemed to move up and down. He blinked, trying to focus, but he could see only a few hundred feet. Nothing. He was alone.

He had seen his mother, but she was not there, and neither was that boat. And he definitely had not heard a dog. It made no sense. The oblivion of sleep would be so sweet.

When he was next awakened by the barking dog, it was so loud, he thought the animal must be right next to his head. He had no strength left to turn his head in the direction of the sound. The dog barked again. Surely, it was a dream. Dogs do not bark in the middle of the ocean.

Then he heard the faint sound of an engine, and he saw a white smear.

He lifted his hand and waved it, palm out, at the boat. He wanted to tell them to go away, but he did not have the energy. He just wanted to sleep. It was not real. He was not thinking straight. He was too tired.

The dog kept barking, but then something landed on his shoulder. He turned and saw the figure in overalls standing on the deck, holding a coil of rope. Long hair? *A woman?* She was waving her arms and shouting.

*He must be dreaming.*

She hauled the rope out of the water and coiled it. There was a loop in the end. She pointed at him. Then she pointed at the rope and at her own head. He did not know what she wanted.

The woman began shouting again, and he opened his eyes. She had picked up the coil of rope again and was swinging it back and forth. She was going to throw the loop to him. He had to get ready to catch it. He tried to lift his arm, but it would not move.

Then she threw the rope. The loop was flying through the air, and he watched it as though it were in slow motion. The loop landed on the hatch cover, splashing water into his eyes. The woman was shouting again, pointing at the rope as it slithered off his arm, toward the black water.

He grabbed it.

Will slid one arm through the loop, then the other.

The woman on the boat began to pull, and he slid forward on the hatch cover. The dog was barking and jumping up and down, and then the woman dropped to her knees on the deck. The water foamed around him as she hauled him closer.

He let go of the hatch cover and reached up. She grabbed his wrist.

"See here, it's a rope ladder. I can't haul you up on my own. You've got to get your foot on the ladder and help."

She had a firm grip, and when his foot found a rung, he pushed with an effort he didn't think he still possessed. She pulled him up, grabbed the belt on his pants and slid him onto the deck. She collapsed on the deck next to him. The dog was barking and sniffing him all over. The animal's fur was rough against his cheek.

He lay on his back with his eyes closed. He could feel the boat rolling beneath him, but he felt nothing else.

"Can you hear me?"

He nodded.

She placed a hand on his shoulder. "You're going to be all right now," she said. "You're safe. You're going to be all right."

The dog was still sniffing and brushing up against him. She pushed the dog away. "Down, Tess. Leave him alone. Go to the cockpit. Go on."

Will watched the dog disappear from his view. Then he dropped his head back onto the deck. He closed his eyes.

The woman was talking to him again. Then he felt her strong hands under his arms. She lifted him into a sitting position, then pulled his arm over her shoulder. She wasn't very big, but she pulled him to his feet. He tried to help her, but his legs did not want to work.

She half dragged him across the deck, and he had to duck his head under a pile of sailcloth. She slid him down a ladder. His feet touched the cabin sole, and he collapsed into a sitting position beside the base of the ladder. He sat there with his head resting on his knees.

She was talking to the dog again. He opened his eyes. The dog was lying on the floor in front of him, sad eyes looking up at him. The young woman had her hands on her hips, and she was shaking her head.

"Good God," she said. "You were on that tanker."

Will opened his mouth. He wanted to say something, but he did not know what. He closed his mouth. The boat rolled, and he had to close his eyes again.

"It's okay," she said, her voice steady. "You don't have to talk. Just breathe. You're lucky we were on patrol."

Will opened his eyes again. He did not understand what she was talking about.

"Listen," she said. "Take off those wet things. I've got to check on things topsides. Gotta outrun that burning oil slick." She dodged around him and climbed back up the ladder.

Will stared at his sodden clothes. It was good to be out of the water and the wind, but he was still so cold. He was sitting in a narrow passageway. Behind him, he felt heat from the engine as it revved up inside that compartment. A small galley on one side, a table and bench on the other.

He had to get out of these wet clothes, but his body was shaking out of his control. His fingers fumbled as he searched for the buttons on his jacket.

The dog's toenails clicked on the ladder, and then he felt the animal's warm breath on his neck. The rough tongue licked the salt water on his face.

The woman stood in the companionway looking down. "You're not even out of those wet things yet?"

He lifted his limp hands. "Ah—"

"Move over, Tess," she said. "Let me help him." She stepped down the ladder and dropped to her knees beside him. She unfastened the buttons, pulled the jacket off his shoulders and then began to unbutton his shirt. He saw her fingers on his bare skin, but he felt nothing.

"You're freezing," she said. "We've got to get you warm."

She pulled his shirt off, and he watched her as she rubbed up and down his arms. He could not feel her touch, but he could see her fingers on his skin.

Then she was kneeling in front of him, untying his shoes.

"Come on, sailor," she said. "You've got to help me here. You can't go to sleep on me yet." She began to unbutton his trousers.

She had her head down, her fingers working fast. White skin showed through the part in her hair, and her long braid curled around her neck.

Then she slid across the floor to his feet and yanked hard on his pant legs. He nearly fell over as she pulled the heavy, wet trousers free.

Sitting on the floor in a puddle wearing only his underwear should have embarrassed him, but he felt only gratitude.

"I'll get the stove going." She pushed her way to a stand. "We'll have some hot tea in a few minutes, but first—" She took his arm and pulled him to his feet, before lowering him to a seat on the bench. After reaching into a cabinet behind the bunk, she took out a stack of blankets and tossed them on his lap. "Wrap yourself in these."

Will watched her as she lit the stove, her every movement purposeful. The scratch of the match, the poof of the initial spark.

He was still struggling to unfold one of the blankets when she turned around. The *tsk, tsk* sound she made as she wrapped the thick blankets around him, tucking them in under his chin, made him think of his mother. He could feel the warmth of the wool on his cheek, but the rest of his body was still so cold. She spread another blanket over his legs, then rubbed up and down his back and arms. "We've got to get some heat into you," she said. "Friction will help. I want you to rub your legs, like this." She demonstrated, and he tried to make his body move, but there was a disconnect between his brain and his hands.

The kettle whistled, and she turned to the stove. After pouring the water and adding sugar, she handed him the steaming mug. It took so much effort to wrap his fingers around the handle.

"Now for some soup."

She had not asked him anything. Yet. The fog in his brain was clearing. She assumed he'd been on that tanker. He didn't even know the name of the ship. Think. Work out a story to tell her.

He lowered his head to meet the cup halfway and took a sip of the hot tea. So sweet. He took another sip.

There was no way he could tell her the truth. He was not who she thought he was. He did not even know who he was.

He was German. He was American. He was a sailor, a spy.

He was a man who had saved himself and left Erich to drown.

Saying nothing was the best course. He didn't need to fake confusion, exhaustion, or sorrow. He would say very little. For now.

Wrapped in the blanket, Will felt the stinging burn as his limbs came back to life. He had been so cold. The heat from the tea was spreading down into his belly. He was afraid to let go of the cup for fear he wouldn't be able to pick it up again.

The cabin was small, but it was cozy. Better than a submarine. The stove was throwing off heat, and the air filled with the smell of the food she was preparing. He was so tired, but he didn't want to close his eyes. He watched her move about the galley, bracing herself each time the boat rolled, her arms reaching into the lockers, her fingers opening cans.

He knew he should be thinking about what to say to her, but he couldn't control his thoughts. His vision was blurring.

He blinked his eyes, trying to stay awake. His head felt heavy, and he could feel his eyelids drooping.

The dog rested her head on his knee. Her breath came in rhythmic puffs. *Be cautious*, he told himself, but he was so tired. This young woman and her dog seemed harmless enough. Kind.

He had to think. He had to stay awake.

His vision was fading. The sounds in the cabin grew more distant. He was sinking into the darkness. His eyes closed, his head fell forward, and the mug slipped from his hand.

# CHAPTER TWENTY

*Ponce Inlet, Florida*
*February 23, 1942*

The swells rolled in from the Atlantic behind her as Annie gripped the spokes of the big wooden wheel, her feet spread wide. She lined up the boat's bow on the narrow entrance to Ponce Inlet. The tide was flowing out, turning those swells into standing waves in the narrow channel. Worse, the sandbanks that formed in the inlet were always shifting, and the channel markers were out of date and useless.

The trick, she thought as she inched the boat forward, measuring the size of each swell, was to get through the inlet riding the set's biggest wave over the outer sand bars and into the river without running aground. And without the boat skewing sideways and broaching. It was all about timing.

Pa had been right when he taught them that the most dangerous part of any trip was going in and out of port.

The *Tequesta* bucked and yawed when a breaking wave collided with the stern. Annie glanced over her shoulder and saw the biggest swell yet bearing down on her. She gunned the engine and soon the stern lifted. She smiled for the first time in a long while at the thrill of acceleration as the big old boat surfed over the bars in a neat straight line.

Her overalls were stiff with dried salt, her black rain jacket flapping in the breeze as the boat glided off the wave. With the excitement over, exhaustion pulled at her eyelids. She hadn't slept all night. Blinking it away, she focused on turning south and navigating the inland passage to Skeeter's Fish Camp.

Her passenger emerged, his blond hair tousled, eyes squinting in the sudden brightness. Tess followed him into the cockpit. She had spent the night keeping watch over him.

He stretched, yawning, then hugged himself against the bite of the cool wind. He wore his own trousers again, still damp from the night before, and an old fisherman's pullover she'd set out for him that had once belonged to her father.

"Sleep well?"

He nodded, like a man waking from a long slumber. "Where are we?"

It was the first time she had heard him speak. "Ponce Inlet."

He looked around at the wide expanse of water and the low, scrubby shoreline. A pair of pelicans cruised past.

"It's beautiful." He spoke in a monotone.

Tess barked at the familiar shoreline. Annie smiled. "Yes. It sure is."

There was heavier traffic than usual. A few small fishing boats puttered along, their wakes fanning out behind them, and a northbound shrimper. The houses and docks that clustered on shore made up the familiar little town of New Smyrna. She could navigate this stretch in her sleep. The engine puttered and spat as she slowed to make sure her wake didn't disturb the houses along the shore.

He sat on one of the cockpit seats and watched her steer,

saying nothing. She wondered what he was thinking, if he was grateful, or angry, or simply numb. Men were such mysteries, even the ones she thought she knew well.

They had made it through the town, and there were no more boats ahead. Just home, and Woody, the fish camp's caretaker.

She killed the engine, and the lagoon fell into a soft, lapping quiet.

"Gotta save fuel these days," she said.

They ghosted along at four knots under just the mainsail. Annie stripped off her rain jacket and let the wind dry her sweat-dampened skin. The man continued to stare at the shoreline, his eyes tracking something distant and unseen.

"How long?" he asked.

"What?"

"Until we get to wherever you're taking me."

"An hour. Maybe less."

He nodded again, with the same slow bob of the head. He looked as if he wanted to say something, then thought better of it and retreated back down the ladder into the cabin.

"There's bread and an apple in the galley if you're hungry. Coffee in the thermos."

Annie sat down on the aft seat and drew her knees to her chest. She couldn't imagine what he had experienced out there. She closed her eyes and let her mind drift.

The night had been a blur of cold, fire and fear. The explosions. Knowing the enemy was right there. Then finding a survivor. Getting him aboard had taken a Herculean effort, one she still wasn't sure how she'd managed. His lips had been blue. She'd stripped off his wet clothes, rubbed his cold, white skin, wrapped him in every blanket she could find.

She remembered the man's body, well-muscled, yet defenseless, and how she'd hesitated a bit too long when undressing him.

A few minutes later, the companionway doors creaked open, and he emerged again. He ran a hand through his hair, which had dried in a wild, salty tangle. She wondered what it would feel like to run her own fingers through that hair. A hot flush of shame followed the thought. Jack was gone, and here she was, thinking of a strange man's hair. She pushed it away, blaming the exhaustion.

"Thank you," he said. "For everything."

"Couldn't just leave you out there."

He moved to sit closer to her, and she tensed.

"I've never been to Florida," he said. "It looks strange."

"Strange how?"

He thought for a moment. "Empty. Like it's waiting for something."

She could see what he meant. The shoreline was sparse and flat, dotted with a few fishing shacks, slash pines, dwarf oak trees and saw palmetto.

Will rubbed his palms together. "What's your name?"

"Annie," she said. "Annie Jeeves."

He waited, as if expecting her to ask something. When she didn't, he said, "You can call me Will."

She gave a short, dry laugh. "Is that your name?"

"It's what my friends call me."

Annie considered this. "Are we friends, then?"

"I hope so."

She stood and stretched. "We should get ready to dock. My family's fish camp isn't far now."

Will nodded and rose, waiting for instructions. She liked that he didn't assume anything, that he let her take the lead. Most men she knew were insufferable know-it-alls. A slight smile curled her lip when she thought, *even Jack*.

Annie adjusted the course. An osprey took flight from its nest atop an abandoned piling. The air was heavy with the smell of salt and mangroves.

"Why do you do this?" Will asked.

"Do what?"

"Sail this boat all alone."

She didn't answer right away. He didn't want her life story. Family fish camp, a dead brother.

"It's what we do," she said. "In Florida, we call ourselves the Mosquito Fleet. We go out to look for U-boats, to pick up survivors from ships that get torpedoed. Most able men are gone off to fight, so we're an odd lot. Older men, those unfit to serve. Some folks call us the Hooligan's Navy."

Annie knew his real question was why is a young woman doing this.

As they neared Skeeter's Fish Camp, Annie brought the sails down and started the engine. The familiar shoreline was a hodgepodge of neat buildings, makeshift docks and a dirt launch ramp. A few skiffs and runabouts bobbed in the water, their paint peeling and sun-bleached. This place—unchanged since her childhood—was home.

Will looked to her for direction. She pointed to a dock near the end of the row, its planks warped and mottled with algae. "Grab a line and when we get close enough, jump down and tie us to a piling."

The *Tequesta* puttered into the dock's embrace. Will moved with surprising grace. He looped the line around a piling and pulled it tight, then looked to Annie for approval. She gave a curt nod and cut the engine.

The engine sputtered and died, leaving only the sound of water slapping against wood and the distant cries of seabirds.

"Annie-girl!"

She turned to see Woody striding down the sandy path, his limp more pronounced than she remembered. The tall, black man had been a fixture in her life for as long as she could remember, more family than hired help.

Annie jumped from the boat onto the dock. "Woody!" She ran to meet him.

They embraced, and his body felt smaller, more frail. When she looked up into his dark, lined face, his eyes were wet, but he smiled.

"It's been too long," he said. Then he reached down to scratch Tess's ear.

Annie nodded.

"How's the family?" he asked.

"Getting by," she said. "You know how Ma is. And Skeeter's being Skeeter."

Woody chuckled. "Yeah, still tinkering with that old Chevrolet, I reckon." He paused, his expression turning somber.

"Any news from Jack?"

Annie busied herself with a dock line and shook her head. She wasn't ready to talk about that yet. News traveled slowly to Woody up here. She worked up a smile and changed the subject.

"Emma and Miss Cora send their love."

Elzo, Emma's grandpa, and Woody went way back. They were like kin, after serving together in the last war.

A shadow passed over Woody's face. He stared at the ground, digging his toe into the sand. "I should visit." He spoke more to himself than to her.

"Ah, Woody. They know you're busy keeping this place open for us."

He waved her off. "Come now." He wrapped his arm around her shoulders. "Tell me what you've been up to."

Annie took a deep breath. "I'm part of the Mosquito Fleet now. Patrolling the coast for U-boats."

Woody's eyebrows shot up. "Is that so?"

"Just temporary. Until things settle back down."

Woody's gaze shifted to the dock where Will was unloading a small duffel bag. "Who's the blond fella?"

Annie bit her lip. "That's Will. My first rescue. Pulled him out of the water last night."

"From one of them two tankers?"

She nodded. "I went out to search for survivors from the *Republic* off Jupiter. But I was too late. Then I was right there when the other ship got hit."

She blinked and saw the flames again, smelled the smoke that had stung her eyes and lungs. The sound of explosions echoing across a placid sea.

"That would have been the *W.D. Anderson*. I heard about it on the radio."

Will approached. She put a hand on Woody's arm and turned to Will.

"Will," she said, "this is Woody. He's been our caretaker here at the fish camp since, well, as long as I can remember."

Will extended a hand.

"Pleased to meet you," Will said.

Woody grunted. "Come inside. I'll fix us some hot tea."

The three walked up the path to the main house, a ramshackle two-story structure that looked as if a strong sneeze might topple it. Annie had always loved its crooked lines and peeling paint.

Inside, Woody led them to the kitchen, where an old wood-burning stove took up most of one wall. The rest of the room was a clutter of mismatched cabinets and enamelware. Annie sat at the rough-hewn table, but Will lingered near the doorway, as if ready to bolt.

Woody put a kettle on and turned to Annie. "How'd the boat handle?"

"Like a dream. We got knocked around pretty good out in the Gulf Stream but she held steady."

Will spoke up. "You built this place?"

Woody shook his head. "Her grandaddy built the house. I just look after it." He eyed Will with a mixture of curiosity and suspicion. "The house has history."

Woody turned back to the stove. "So," he said over his shoulder, "you were looking for survivors from the *Republic*?"

Annie sighed. "Tess and I didn't find any. Will was a lucky catch."

She saw Will's jaw tighten.

The kettle whistled, and Woody poured three mugs of tea. Will took his but didn't drink at first, instead letting the steam curl around his face.

"Man on the radio said they felt the explosion all over Jupiter. It even broke a few windows," Woody said. "Damn shame. All those men."

Annie glanced at Will. His eyes looked forward, unfocused.

"I sure felt it from a few miles off," she said. "The explosion lit up the entire sky. There was nothing I could do. She was all in flames." She turned to Will. "I don't know how you survived."

He didn't move.

Woody stroked his chin. "That's two in a week. Krauts are getting bolder."

"It takes some kind of monster to kill all those men in cold blood."

Silence settled over the room. Annie thought of the night before, of the flames on the water. Of Will, cold and lifeless in her arms.

Woody broke the silence. "You'll be staying, then?"

Annie nodded. "Just until he's on his feet."

"I reckon he can stay in Jack's room. I'll make up the bed," he said, then added, "You should get some rest, girl. I reckon you been up all night."

"Will needs the rest more than me."

Woody's eyes flicked to Will, then back to Annie. "As you say."

Annie stood. "I need to get some things from the boat," she said. "Will, can you give me a hand?"

They walked back to the dock in silence. The sun was baking the sand and wooden planks with a Florida ferocity. When they reached the *Tequesta*, Will stopped and turned to her.

"Why are you doing this?"

She met his gaze, those blue eyes searching her face. She didn't have an answer that would satisfy him.

"Because we're not monsters," she said, and immediately regretted the flippant tone.

Will held her stare for a moment longer, then looked away. "Your friend doesn't trust me."

"Woody's not the trusting sort. He fought over in France during the last war with a unit called the Harlem Hellfighters. They suffered a lot of casualties. This war reminds him of that, I think. It's hard on those who fought what they thought was the *War to end all wars*."

Will said nothing to that.

"Come," she said. "Let's get this done."

They boarded the *Tequesta* and started gathering the garbage and the wet clothes. Annie draped the blankets Will had used over the table to air out, while Will emptied the used cans into a crate. Annie worked quickly. Will moved slower, his actions more deliberate.

She thought of Jack, of how he would have jumped into the task with a reckless energy, making a game of it. Her brother had never been one to take life seriously, and that was part of his charm.

"Annie."

"He asked you about Jack. I saw the look on your face. What happened?"

How was she going to talk about this? Even with a stranger. "Jack is, or was, my older brother. A pilot. He went to fight this damn war, and now he's gone." She stopped there. She didn't want to cry again.

"I'm sorry. Woody doesn't know?"

She pressed her lips together and shook her head.

"I would have died if you hadn't come along."

She was grateful for the change of subject. "I don't know how you survived that explosion. But I'm glad I was there to help you."

"Thank you." He looked down, almost as though he were ashamed of having survived.

Back at the house, Woody caught up with them as Annie placed the food on the kitchen counter.

"Annie," Woody said.

She turned to face him.

"It's good what you're doing. Being part of the war effort."

She gave a weak smile. "I'm just filling in. It's not forever."

"Still," Woody said, "you're defending us against the Germans. That takes courage."

She knew he meant well, but his words made her uncomfortable. She needed to tell him about Jack, and she couldn't even find the courage to do that.

# CHAPTER TWENTY-ONE

*Skeeter's Fish Camp, Florida*
*February 23, 1942*

Annie led Will up the creaking stairs to the second floor. The banister was slick with decades of hand oil, and she ran her fingers along it, remembering how she and Jack used to slide down its length, laughing and shrieking like banshees.

At the top of the stairs, she paused. Will stopped behind her, waiting.

She walked to the first door and opened it. The room was just as she'd left it, a frozen diorama of her childhood. The iron bed with the patchwork quilt hand sewn by a grandmother she'd never known, and the pine dresser. She had taken most of her books and drawing supplies to the Lauderdale house when they'd moved. Sunlight filtered through the lace curtains. She dropped her wet clothes on the floor.

Annie closed the door and turned to Will. "Come on," she said, leading him farther down the hall.

They stopped in front of another door, this one adorned with a small brass plaque that read "Captain Jack." Annie traced the letters with her fingertip. She'd bought the plaque for him with her allowance, and he'd crowed about it for weeks, showing it off to everyone who came through the house.

She opened the door and stepped inside. The room was a shrine to her brother's boyhood dreams: model airplanes hung from the ceiling, a telescope perched by the window, and stacks of superhero comic books lay on a set of shelves resting on bricks. The narrow bed was neatly made. His matching quilt, sewn by the same grandmother, draped over the foot.

Will stayed in the doorway. Annie walked to the center of the room and turned in a slow circle, taking it all in. "This was my brother's room," she said. "He's the reason I can tie a bowline and read a chart. The reason I'm not afraid to captain that boat out there."

Memories cascaded over her. Jack teaching her to swim in the lagoon, showing her how to rig a sail, recounting tall tales of pirate adventures. He'd been her hero, and then her equal. And now he was a gaping absence in her life.

"You're lucky," Will said.

Annie looked at him, confused. The ache in her heart didn't feel lucky.

"To have all this."

She didn't know what to say. Were they lucky? Her family had its share of troubles, and lately it seemed like they were sinking under the load. But they were still here, still together. Except for Jack.

"Take what you need." Annie pointed to the dresser, though his very presence in that room felt like a violation. "The clothes should fit."

Will didn't move. "Are you going to be okay?"

No, she would not be okay, not now, not for a long time. "I'll be fine."

Will stepped into the room, and she moved past him to the doorway. She watched as he ran a hand over the dresser top, his touch gentle, almost reverent.

"Thank you," he said again.

She nodded, closing the door before he could say anything more.

Annie made her way downstairs and into the kitchen. Woody was busy filleting a fish, working with the precision of a surgeon.

"I had this in the icebox," Woody said, holding up the translucent slabs. "Thought it might make a decent supper."

Annie's stomach growled. She couldn't remember the last time she'd eaten a decent supper. "It'll be more than decent," she said, taking a seat at the kitchen table.

After a few minutes, Will appeared and hovered near the doorway, his stance unsure. Woody noticed and gestured with his knife. "Sit. It won't kill you."

Will sat in Jack's usual spot without knowing it. Woody set glasses and a pitcher of water on the table and watched her. She forced a smile.

Then, Woody leaned against the counter, crossing his arms. "So, Will. How'd you end up on the *Anderson*?"

Will took a sip of water, swirled his glass, and then set it down.

"I signed on in Charleston. Needed the work. The Anderson was running the Maracaibo-New York route. Good pay for dangerous waters."

"Deckhand?" Woody asked.

Will nodded.

Annie studied his face. He seemed composed, but there was a distance in his eyes, as if he were recalling someone else's life.

"Must have been rough," Woody said. "Being away from home."

Will shrugged. "You get used to it."

Annie asked, "Where is home, Will?"

He looked at her, then at Woody. "Indiana," he said. "A small town near the lake. Close to Chicago."

That was the first concrete piece of information he'd volunteered.

Woody pushed off the counter and retrieved a cast-iron frying pan from a cupboard, then turned to the stove. "You ever work on the lake?" he asked Will.

"Some," Will said. "Summers. As a kid. Not on a ship. The *Anderson* was my first real job."

The conversation lapsed into a comfortable silence, the kind that occurs when men are occupied with their hands. Woody cooked the fish in butter, letting the natural flavors speak for themselves. He served it with a side of boiled potatoes, their skins cracking from the heat.

They took their plates to the dining room. The familiar hutch filled with chipped porcelain took up one wall, and one of Woody's paintings of the lagoon hung on another.

Woody sat and bowed his head. Annie followed suit, peeking to see what Will would do. He waited a respectful moment, then started eating.

The fish was tender and flaked apart with the touch of a fork. Annie savored each bite.

Will ate with purpose, pausing only once to say, "This is good. Thank you."

Woody nodded. "It's red fish. Caught it right out there." He pointed his fork toward the lagoon. "Yesterday."

Annie wiped her mouth with a napkin. "So, Will. Do you have a family waiting for you in Indiana?"

"No," he said. "It's just me."

Annie wasn't sure if he meant he had no family or that they weren't waiting for him. She suspected it was the latter.

"I've never been that far north," she said. "What's it like?"

Will chewed his last bite, then swallowed. "Cold," he said. "And crowded. Compared to here."

Annie imagined him in a bustling town, perhaps wearing a flat cap and woolen coat, mingling with factory workers and shopkeepers. It didn't fit. He had a quiet manner about him.

Annie wanted to press him, but he was like a clam, shutting tighter the more you pried. She was afraid to get Woody started talking because the conversation would inevitably lead to memories of Jack. They finished the meal in awkward silence.

"I'm sorry." Will dabbed at his mouth with a napkin. "But I need to lie down." He rose and turned to Woody. "Thanks for the fine dinner."

Will walked into the kitchen and placed his plate on the counter. Then he disappeared upstairs.

Woody cleared his throat. "Strange fellow."

Annie turned back to her plate, poking at the remnants of fish. "He's been through a lot."

"Maybe," Woody said, not sounding convinced.

"Why don't you like him?" she asked.

Woody sighed and rubbed his temples. "It's not that I don't like him. I just..."

"Just what?"

"That boy's hands are too soft for a deckhand. And he holds his fork like my old lieutenant. European style."

"Maybe folks do things different up north."

"I just don't trust what I don't understand."

Annie thought about that. About the things she didn't understand: the war, her family, herself.

"Woody," she said, "he's not a mystery. He's just a man who's been through something. The other men on that ship surely died. She sank so fast. One minute she was there, and then she was gone. Nothing left but a huge burning oil slick."

"In war, everybody wants to be a survivor, but it gets complicated when folks start asking, ***why you?***"

~

When they'd finished washing the dishes, Annie stepped out onto the porch into the bracing cold of the night air. The sky was a dome of pinprick stars, the kind you only saw during the dry season in Florida when the nights were cold and clear. She heard the door creak open and close behind her, and Woody stood beside her.

"You must be freezing, Missy," Woody said. "I'll be right back."

He returned with an old quilt and wrapped it around her shoulders. "There you go," he said. "That should keep you warm."

She grabbed the corners with her fists and folded her arms across her chest. "Thanks."

They stood side by side, leaning against the porch rail. The fish camp was quiet, save for the occasional creak of a boat down at the dock or the distant call of a night heron.

"You want me to sleep here in the house tonight?"

"No, you go on home to your cabin. I'll be fine."

"You sure 'bout that?"

"Woody," she said after a long silence. "I know you mean well, but..."

He cut her off. "He's an enigma, Annie. And not a harmless one."

She sighed, sinking deeper into the quilt. "You don't even know him."

"Neither do you," Woody said. "But I know his type."

Annie turned to face Woody. "What type is that?"

Woody gazed out at the dark silhouette of the mangroves

on the shore. "A man with nothing to lose is a dangerous man."

"He's not dangerous."

"He's hollow, Annie. Empty. Like a shell the hermit crab has abandoned."

"He's been through a trauma," she said. "It'll take time for him to come back to himself."

"Exactly," Woody said. "He doesn't behave like a man who just lost his buddies. He's too... controlled."

"People grieve in different ways."

Woody turned to her, his eyes hard but not unkind. "I know about grief, Annie. I know about loss. Don't forget that."

"Woody," she said, "the things you saw, the things you did in the war... Did it change how you see the world?"

He frowned, pondering her question. "It made me see more clearly, I suppose. The world was always like this. I just had my eyes opened."

She nodded. "You never talk about it. About what you went through."

"Would it have helped you to know?"

"I don't know. Maybe."

He straightened and drew in a deep breath. "We were young, like Jack. Thought we were invincible. That the war would be a grand adventure." He paused and rubbed the palm of his hand across his mouth. "That first week." Woody shook his head. "We got shelled so hard we couldn't even bury our dead. Just piled them in the trenches like cordwood. After that, the adventure didn't seem so grand."

Annie bit her lip, not sure she wanted to hear the rest.

"Elzo and I made a pact," Woody continued. "Whoever came back would look after the other's family. We thought it was a noble thing." He shook his head. "In the end, it was just another burden."

"Is that why you've stayed with us? Out of obligation?"

Woody looked hurt. "Annie, you are my family, and this is my home. Don't ever think otherwise."

She nodded. "I just mean... I understand why you're loyal to us. But can you see that maybe Will had some loyalties? That he's trying to honor them?"

Woody didn't respond. Instead, he turned his gaze back to the mangroves.

"I hate war," she said. And in bringing Will here, she'd brought the war home.

Woody remained still, but she could tell he was listening.

"I hate what it's done to us. To Jack, to you, to Elzo. And now to Will."

A shooting star arced across the sky and burned out above the tree line.

"Woody." Her voice sounded hoarse. She swallowed and tried again. "I need to tell you something. It's about Jack."

The old man turned and wrapped his arms around her. "I know, Annie-girl. I saw it in your eyes the minute you stepped off the boat."

# CHAPTER TWENTY-TWO

*Skeeter's Fish Camp, Florida*
*February 24, 1942*

Annie perched sideways on the porch railing, sipping her second cup of coffee. The morning air smelled of low tide. Tess had run off to Woody's cabin to see if the old man was up.

A pelican dove on the bait fish congregating around the dock pilings, and the sound of the splash bounced off the old house. The quiet was one of the many things she missed about the camp. And the lagoon reflected a perfect image of the clouds and blue sky overhead. It was almost like being inside one of those dream-like paintings Woody and several of his friends used to paint down by the shoreline on Sunday afternoons.

The only thing missing was the sound of her brother's feet pounding down the stairs and then that goofy, tousled-haired yawning face of his, feigning sleepiness just before he tried to pull some prank on her.

Behind her, the floorboards creaked.

"Good morning, Will."

"Morning." His face looked scrubbed, and his wet hair combed. He smelled of coconut soap. He certainly wasn't a bad-looking fellow. "You found the coffeepot." He held a steaming mug with both hands.

He nodded. "I can see how this place could grow on you."

She stood. "Come on. I'll show you around."

He followed her down the porch steps.

"The little orchard's around back. We've got oranges, key limes, and even a few grapefruit trees we planted one year."

When they reached the back of the house, the scent of citrus filled the air. The trees were heavy with green fruit.

"My pa, Skeeter Jeeves, he inherited this place from his folks," she explained as they walked through the trees. "I never knew my grandparents. They passed from the Spanish flu before I was born. But they moved to Florida when Pa was just a baby, and they homesteaded this place."

Will walked alongside her, his hands shoved deep in the pockets of his trousers. He said nothing, just nodded, his eyes darting around as if mapping the terrain. From time to time, she felt his gaze on her face, and she did her best not to let her skin flush.

"When the fruit is ripe, Woody sends some down south to us on the train. Course there's plenty for him, too. See that garden over there?"

She pointed towards the tidy plot where green rows of vegetables, tomatoes, cucumbers, beans and squash sprawled in the sandy soil. "Used to spend hours out here with Mama, pulling weeds and picking beans 'til our fingers ached. Now it's Woody's. He sends some down to us, feeds himself, and still has enough left to sell at the market in New Smyrna."

They stopped near a rusted water pump where the citrus trees gave way to a tangled mass of scrub and palmetto.

"From here, our land continues all the way out to the

main highway. This area used to be a lot wilder. Pa would take tourists out to hunt wild pigs. He'd come home saying, 'you should've seen their faces when they'd spot one of them razorbacks!'" She smiled, remembering. "Course, most times they'd miss clean, but they'd still go home with tall tales. Used to be lots of wild animals in these parts: bobcats, deer, brown bears. Too many folks living around here now. Bunch of fat raccoons are about all that's left." She pointed into the bush. "When Jack and I were kids, we built forts in those woods. Played pirate and conquistador." She paused, then added, "He always made me be the Indian."

A ghost of a smile curled on Will's lips. "I can't picture you losing that fight."

"Oh, I gave him a good beating more than once." She giggled, and it felt good.

"It must be nice having a family. A place to call home."

"It is." Annie turned away from the woods and surveyed the property. "We were lucky." *Until we weren't.*

She closed her eyes for a moment against the sudden wave of hot grief that washed through her. Get control. Move. She walked ahead at a brisk pace, and she could hear Will trotting to catch up.

They left the garden and followed another winding path, this one strewn with crushed oyster shells they'd collected from an old Indian mound. The path took them past several rectangular, unpainted wooden buildings.

"What are these?" Will asked when he caught up with her.

Annie cleared her throat and hoped her voice would sound steady. "Back when we lived here full time, tourists rented out these cabins from October to April. Folks from up north came down for our Florida sunshine, to go fishing and hunting with my pa. That open field over there was for those that camped, either in tents or we had a few tin can tourists."

Will's eyebrows lifted. "What?"

"You know, those funny-looking camping trailers? That's what we'd call those folks."

Will nodded.

"The cabin at the end down there with the flowers planted out front? That's Woody's." Annie thought she could see the old man's silhouette in the back window.

As they walked back towards the lagoon, the silence between them returned. Annie needed the time to get her fluctuating emotions under control, and she wasn't sure what to make of Will. He was a puzzle with too many missing pieces. She had to admit she found him intriguing, though. And his eyes. They were the color of tropical water over a sandy bottom.

The bait shack stood on stilts at the water's edge, its weathered planks bleached gray by the sun, and the sign that read, "Skeeter's Bait and Tackle" was missing several letters. An odd collection of old license plates, road signs, and boat nameplates surrounded the door.

Annie climbed the steps and waved at Will to join her. "This was where the real work happened," Annie said. "We'd net shrimp, catch crabs, dig for clams. During mullet season, the entire camp smelled like a bait shop." She opened the door to the shack, and the scent of salt and fish guts wafted out. "Take a whiff. Dried fish. It's an acquired taste."

Will stood in the doorway, not entering. "You've got a whole operation here."

Annie shrugged. "It's a living. Or it was. After the crash of '29, the tourists stopped coming. Pa tried to find a job around here, in Edgewater or New Smyrna, but there was no work. We could eat off the land and sea, but paying the taxes on the land became a problem. Mama got work as a nurse at the new hospital they built down in Fort Lauderdale. That's where we live now. Pa works at the shipyard there."

She closed the door.

She started walking back toward the main house, and Will followed. Annie's mind filled with questions. Why wasn't he hurrying back to his job, his comrades? She knew better than to ask outright; people like Will only revealed what they wanted to, and no more.

They reached the house's sprawling wide front porch. Annie stopped at the bottom of the steps and turned to Will.

"You're welcome to stay as long as you need to," she said.

Will looked up at the house, then back at Annie. "Thank you," he said. "I appreciate it."

"It's a good life here," she said.

Will nodded, his eyes distant. "Yeah, lucky you."

They climbed the steps to the porch and sat on the bench outside the front door.

"So," Annie said, breaking the silence. "Tell me about your family."

Will stared out across the still water. "Not much to tell," he said.

She waited for him to say more, but he didn't. "Do you have any brothers or sisters?"

He shook his head.

"And your parents?"

"They're fine."

Annie bit her lip. She knew he was holding back, but she didn't understand why. It wasn't like she was asking for state secrets. "You must miss them," she said.

Will shrugged. "I suppose."

Looking out across the camp, she sighed. "You know, when Jack first shipped out, it was awful not knowing."

"It's different for us," he said. "My family, we're not that close."

She turned back to him. "You don't have to lie, you know. We're just talking."

Will's gaze snapped to hers, a mix of wariness and weariness in his eyes.

"Life on that tanker... it was hell."

His voice was so soft, Annie had to lean in to hear the words.

"I hated every minute. The noise, the fear, the endless horizon. I just want some peace."

Now she was getting somewhere.

"There was this guy on the boat. It was sorta' up to me to look out for him." His voice cracked. "I watched him die out there in the water. Right in front of me. And I couldn't do a damn thing about it."

"Do you think there were any other survivors?"

"I don't know. I doubt it."

Annie studied his face, searching for the lie Woody was so sure existed. But all she saw was genuine pain.

"How long have you been at sea?"

"Long enough to know it's not what I want."

"What do you want?"

Will took a deep breath, his chest rising and falling. Then he turned and looked straight into her eyes. She couldn't look away. No man had ever looked at her that way before.

"What I want..." He looked across the lagoon. "It's to start over. A fresh start. If that's even possible."

They sat in silence for a long time. Annie had a thousand things she wanted to say, but none of them seemed right.

Will broke the silence. "Do you have any cigarettes?"

She shook her head.

"I should go." He stood up, lifted his arms and stretched.

"To get cigarettes?"

He glanced back at her, a gentle smile revealing a dimple. "No, no. I have to leave. You understand that, don't you?"

Annie's heart sank. "Not really. Where will you go?"

"North, maybe. I don't know. Somewhere."

"You *can* stay, you know. At least until you figure things out."

Will looked down at her, his eyes unreadable. He reached out, placing his fingertips on her shoulder. "You have no idea how tempting that is." Then he yanked his hand back. "Thank you for the offer, but I don't want to be a burden."

"You wouldn't be. You need time to figure things out."

He reached for the door, then stopped. "I appreciate everything," he said. "But I can't stay."

"You should go to the authorities," she said. "They can help you. The people in town here are good folks."

"I don't want people treating me like a hero or a survivor."

Annie didn't know what else to say. She believed him, but she also knew how alone he must feel. How alone he was.

"Let's go," she said, stepping past him and heading for the kitchen. "Let me at least give you some clothes and food. We haven't even eaten breakfast."

Will hesitated, then followed her into the house. The screen door slammed shut behind them. Annie led him to Jack's old bedroom and opened the closet. She pulled out a few shirts and a pair of trousers, then handed them to Will.

"These things should fit," she said.

Will took the clothes. "Thank you."

Annie left the room and went to the kitchen. She could hear Will changing, the rustle of fabric and the soft thud of his shoes as he moved around. She packed a flour sack with bread, cheese, and an apple, then took some money from the jar on the counter.

When Will came into the kitchen, he was wearing Jack's blue-checked shirt. It hung loose on his frame, but it suited him. Annie handed him the sack, and he stuffed his old clothes inside.

"There's a bus station in New Smyrna," she said. "It's not a long walk. You can catch a ride north from there."

Will took the flour sack and looked at her, his eyes softer now, less guarded. "You've been very kind, Annie" he said. "But there is something. I don't have the right to ask. I owe you my life."

"What is it?"

"I don't want to go back to sea, but I signed a contract. This is my chance to make a new life for myself." He reached out and wrapped his fingers around her forearm. "Promise you won't tell anyone about me. About me surviving. Give me a chance to start over."

She looked down at his hand on her arm and felt the heat through the fabric of her shirt. If only it were possible to give Jack a second chance.

She nodded. "Of course."

They walked to the front porch, and Will opened the screen door. He turned to her in the doorway.

"Goodbye, Annie."

"Good luck, Will."

She watched him walk down the sandy path, his figure growing smaller and smaller until he was just a speck in the distance. Annie wondered if she would ever see him again, and if she even wanted to.

Annie found Woody in the kitchen, chopping onions, with Tess lying on the rag rug at his feet. The sharp smell made her eyes water. She wiped them with the back of her hand and leaned against the doorframe.

"You're late for breakfast. I'm already working on lunch."

"I'm not hungry."

"Where's the new guy?" Woody asked, not looking up from his work.

She hesitated. "Will. He left."

Woody paused, then he continued chopping, slower this time. "Left? Just like that?"

"He said he needed to go north. To start over. He says he doesn't want us to tell anybody about my finding him."

"Start over," Woody repeated. "Sounds like he has it all figured out."

Annie walked to the counter and picked up an onion. "He was in a bad way. He saw another man drown before I saved him. I think he just needs some time."

Woody nodded, then put the vegetables into a big pot on the stove. "It's probably for the best," he said. "We have enough going on without taking in strays."

She bristled at his words. "Pa would have given him a chance."

"Maybe," Woody said. "But Skeeter's not here, is he?"

Annie didn't have an answer for that.

Woody walked to the sink and washed his hands. "Don't get me wrong, Annie. I feel for the guy. But I can't say I'm sorry to have seen the last of him."

"I know." But she didn't have to agree with him.

Woody hung the dishtowel on the stove. "Let me know when that gumbo's ready."

Annie watched him walk away, her mind turning over his words. She wondered if he was right, and if Will was gone for good.

~

That night, Annie tossed and turned, the sheets a hot, tangled mess around her legs. Her mind wouldn't quiet, with thoughts of Will and Jack and her father swirling in her head. She got up, wrapped herself in her robe, and paced the hallway, its wooden floor cool on her bare feet. The house was eerily silent, the quiet that amplified every creak and groan of the old structure.

She wandered into the living room and looked at the photographs on the wall. There was Jack and her as kids, holding up a massive tarpon with proud, gap-toothed grins. Another showed her parents on their wedding day, young and hopeful. The last was a recent one, taken just before Jack shipped out. All four of them stood together, a united front. A family.

A soft thud came from the front porch, and Annie's heart got a jump-start. Maybe Tess had changed her mind about sleeping with Woody. She hurried to the door and peered through the screen. A figure stood in the shadows, tall and lean.

"Will?" she called out.

The figure stepped into the dim light. Finn.

"Annie. Can I come in?"

She opened the door and Finn staggered in, his movements stiff. She noticed a bruise on his cheek and dirt on his clothes.

"What happened to you?"

He shrugged. "Caught a ride with a trucker. Don't think he was too happy when I bailed out."

"You jumped?"

"He wanted me to work off the ride. Figured I'd rather walk."

Annie led him to the kitchen and lit the stove under the tea kettle. Finn sat at the table, his shoulders slumped. She could see the exhaustion in his eyes, the weariness that went beyond physical tiredness.

"Why are you here, Finn?" she asked.

He took a deep breath. "Everyone at home is talking about the *W.D. Anderson*. About how it got sunk by a U-boat right off the coast. I knew you were headed north, right in the path of all that. I couldn't sleep for worrying."

Annie's chest tightened. "Worrying?"

Finn looked up at her. "About you, Annie... I don't know. I thought you might have got caught in it or something."

"I left a note for Ma saying I was gonna head up here."

"Yeah, I know. But we hadn't heard from you. You wrote that you'd send word."

"Finn, I'm fine."

He ran a hand through his hair, making it stand on end. "I know that now. But Annie, you didn't even call to let us know."

"You know there's no phone out here. I was going to go into town today, but I was too tired. I don't need a babysitter."

He flinched, and she regretted the words. His sudden appearance had thrown her off balance. Why did she feel guilty?

"Finn," she said, softer now. "I'm sorry. Thank you for coming."

He leaned back in his chair, closing his eyes for a moment. "I couldn't stop thinking about you, wondering if something had happened to you. I was useless at work. The *Tequesta*'s a big boat for you to sail all alone."

Annie's mind flashed to that day with Emma, when she had told her that Finn's feelings were obvious to everyone but her. She had dismissed it, thinking Emma was just teasing her. Now she wasn't so sure.

The tea finished brewing, and Annie poured two cups. She slid one across the table to Finn, then sat down with her own. The steam rose in soft, lazy curls.

"Annie, do you remember when my ma died? How your family took us in?"

"Of course," she said. "You and Bean are family to us."

He nodded. "We grew up together. I just... I need you to know something."

Annie didn't like where this was going. It felt like a goodbye. She wasn't sure she could handle losing him, too.

"Finn, whatever it is, you can tell me."

He looked at her then, really looked at her, and she saw the conflict in his eyes. The hurt and the hope warring for control.

"I just want you to be happy," he said. "That's all."

Annie's thoughts raced. She remembered the times Finn had been there for her: when Jack broke his leg and she was scared out of her mind, when their old dog Max died when she was 9 years old, when Jack left for the war. She'd always had a crush on him, as far back as she could remember. But after losing Jack, it felt wrong somehow to want to be happy.

"Thank you," she said. "That means a lot."

Finn took a sip of his tea, then set the cup down. "The Mosquito Fleet went out after the *Anderson*, you know. To look for survivors."

Annie's stomach knotted.

"They found only one. A single man clinging to a piece of wreckage."

Annie gripped her cup, the ceramic warm against her palms. She pictured Will, alone in the water, the flames of the burning ship lighting up the night.

"Do you know his name?"

"Frank Terry," Finn said. "They say he dove off the tanker's deck when he saw the torpedo headed for them."

She stayed silent. She wanted to tell Finn about seeing the explosions, feeling the heat of flames and saving a man. But she had made a promise to Will.

"Annie," he said, breaking the silence. "Is there something you want to tell me?"

She looked at him, at the boy who had grown into a man before her eyes. At her brother's best friend, at her friend. She had never kept secrets from him.

"It's late. We should get some sleep. You can take Jack's room. The bed's all made up."

She led him upstairs, the floorboards creaking. The house felt different with Finn here, smaller, more charged. At Jack's door, they paused.

"Goodnight, Annie," Finn said, his voice low.

"Goodnight."

As his door closed, Annie stood still in the hallway. Her mind filled with images of Will walking away, of Finn's worried face on her doorstep. She wandered back downstairs to the kitchen, filled a glass with water and took a long drink.

The ticking clock was the only sound in the quiet house. She leaned against the counter in the dark. *What am I doing?* she thought. Will's secret felt like a physical weight on her chest.

She set the glass down with a soft clink. Outside, the wind rustled through the palmettos, a familiar sound that usually soothed her. Tonight, it only emphasized her restlessness.

# CHAPTER TWENTY-THREE

*Edgewater, Florida*
*February 24, 1942*

The rumble of an automobile engine approached from behind on the desolate highway, and Will considered sticking his thumb out. He remembered seeing men doing that when he was a child riding in the back seat of his parents' car. His father had explained that it was a way of asking for a ride. But in Brandenburg, the instructors had taught them to avoid interaction with local people if possible. The white car rolled past. He turned his face away from the cloud of dust kicked up by the tires.

The midday sun bore down on his neck, and sweat trickled between his shoulder blades, soaking into the borrowed shirt Annie had given him.

*Annie.*

He tried to force her from his thoughts, but her image remained floating in his vision no matter which way he looked. Those intelligent eyes seemed to catalog his every movement, searching for information he couldn't give.

He took another step, wincing as his blistered heel rubbed against the worn leather of his borrowed shoes. Three miles since he'd left Skeeter's Fish Camp, and already his throat felt like sandpaper. The cloth sack of food and clothing hung from his right hand, swinging with each stride.

His mind wandered back to her despite his best efforts. He pictured the curve of her waist as she'd leaned against the porch railing that morning, her kind eyes when she'd offered him clothes, food, and shelter.

*Damn it.* His mission was in tatters, and here he was daydreaming about a woman who would despise him if she knew the truth.

Their rubber boat had capsized in the wave generated by the tanker's explosion. He could still hear Erich's panicked cries, still feel the icy Atlantic water filling his lungs as he fought to stay afloat. Their radio equipment, codebooks, explosives, forged identification papers—all gone to the bottom of the sea.

But his actual mission, the mission his life and the lives of his family members depended on, was also gone. Erich... poor, bumbling Erich had never stood a chance. The man could barely swim, and he suffered unrelenting seasickness, yet the Reich had sent him on a mission that required crossing the Atlantic Ocean in a submarine and paddling ashore in a tiny inflatable craft.

When their boat flipped upside down, Will had reached for his partner, had grabbed his flailing arm as the waves battered them. But when Erich's panicked thrashing pulled them both under, again and again, Will had made a choice. He'd broken Erich's grip with a sharp blow and kicked away, watching his partner's pale face disappear into the black water.

"I had to," Will whispered to himself, squinting at the

shimmer of heat rising from the asphalt ahead. There was no option where we both survived.

Erich had trusted him. More importantly, Erich's uncle had trusted Will to keep his nephew alive. Now Erich was dead, and Will was as good as. Even if he somehow made it back to Germany, a bullet awaited him there. If not from Erich's uncle, then from his *Abwehr* superiors for failing his mission.

Will ran a hand through his salt-stiffened hair. Max and Jorg were supposed to be landing in New York about now. Different boat, different mission, same overall objective. Were they successful where he had failed? He had no way of knowing, no means of contacting them.

All that was left of his mission brief was the arranged contact date. Tomorrow night, he was supposed to send a Morse code message from Jupiter, Florida to the waiting U-boat that would signal whether he and Erich had successfully established themselves on American soil. The agreed signal for 'mission proceeding' encrypted in a sequence of flashes toward the dark sea.

But what would he signal? That the mission was a disaster? That the rubber boat had capsized, the equipment lost, Erich drowned? That he, Will, was wandering aimlessly along a Florida highway with no documents, no money, and nowhere to go?

The distant rumble of another engine pulled Will from his thoughts. He glanced over his shoulder to see a large black car approaching from behind. He forced himself to keep walking at the same steady pace. Don't run. Don't look suspicious.

The car slowed as it neared him, matching his pace for several excruciating seconds, and he saw the badge insignia along with the word POLICE in bold white letters.

Will kept his eyes forward, his stride deliberate. Then the

cruiser accelerated past him, and Will exhaled hard through rounded lips.

But seconds later, the brake lights flashed red, and the cruiser pulled onto the shoulder. Will's mouth went dry as the driver's door opened, and a stocky officer with a wide-brimmed hat stepped out. The man hitched up his pants and turned to face Will, his expression as hard and flat as the Florida horizon.

"Hey there," the officer called out, one hand resting on his holster. "Where you headed, son?"

Will felt sweat break out across his skin, but not from heat this time. His training kicked in. Stand up straight, look respectful but not frightened, maintain eye contact but don't stare, speak clearly but not too confidently.

"J-Jacksonville, sir," Will stammered, then cursed himself for the slip. *Calm. Stay calm.* "Looking for work at the shipyards."

The officer squinted at him, the deep creases around his eyes suggesting he'd spent a lifetime squinting at people he didn't quite believe. "Where you from?"

"Indiana, sir," Will replied. "But I was down at Skeeter's Fish Camp, looking for work there. They didn't need anybody, so I'm heading back north."

The officer's gaze swept over him, taking in the borrowed clothes, the cotton sack, the dusty boots. "You got identification, son?"

Will's heart hammered. "No, sir. Lost my wallet swimming in the lagoon. That's why I'm heading to the city." He gestured northward, hoping the officer wouldn't ask for details he couldn't provide.

The sun beat down on them both as the officer considered him, seconds stretching into what felt like hours. A bead of sweat trickled down Will's temple, and he resisted the urge to wipe it away.

At last, the officer's hand dropped from his holster. "You look like you could use a ride to the bus station."

It wasn't a question.

The interior of the police cruiser felt like an oven, the vinyl seat scorching the backs of Will's legs through the thin trousers. Will sat stiff-backed, the borrowed flour sack clutched on his lap, as the officer slid behind the wheel with a grunt. The cruiser pulled back onto the highway, and Will watched through the side window as the scrubby palmettos and pine trees blurred past, trying to ignore the sick feeling in his stomach.

"Where'd you say you were from again?" The officer's eyes remained fixed on the road ahead.

"Indiana, sir," Will replied, keeping his voice steady.

The officer pulled a cigarette from the pack on the car's dashboard and stuck it in his mouth. "Long way from home."

"Yes, sir."

A heavy silence filled the car. The officer contorted himself to one side and pulled a lighter from his pocket. He lit the cigarette and took a deep drag.

Will counted his heartbeats, focusing on his breathing: not too fast, not too shallow. The training had been thorough. How to control physical reactions, how to maintain a cover story under pressure. But sitting inches from an American law enforcement officer while pretending not to be a German spy was testing the limits of that training.

"You hear about that tanker?" The officer's question cut through the silence. "The *W.D. Anderson*? Got torpedoed just off the coast a few days back."

Will swallowed. "I heard something about it."

"Germans," the officer spat out the window. "Sinking our ships right off our own damn shore." He glanced sideways at Will. "You know what else they're saying?"

Will shook his head, not trusting his voice.

"They say these Kraut sailors speak perfect English. Can you believe that?" The officer's voice rose. "They come ashore from those U-boats, blend right in with regular folks. Going to the movies, buying beer, walking around like they belong here."

Will kept his face neutral, even as he felt sweat beading along his hairline. "Is that so?"

"Damn right it is," the officer continued, warming to his subject. "Fellow over in Palm Beach swears he served beer to two fellas last month who turned out to be German sailors from a submarine. Said they knew all about American baseball, could talk about the Yankees and everything."

The cruiser hit a pothole, jolting Will against the door. The officer didn't seem to notice.

"My buddy down in Key West? He's Navy. Says they've caught Germans with Florida driver's licenses. Maps of bridges, power stations. Goddamn spies right here in Florida!" The officer's face had reddened, a vein pulsing in his temple. "Boy, I'd sure like to get my hands on one of them Krauts."

Will's mouth felt like cotton. "What would you do if you caught one?"

The question slipped out before he could stop it. Stupid, stupid mistake.

The officer took his eyes off the road to look at Will, then laughed. It wasn't a pleasant sound. "Well now, that'd depend on whether he was feeling talkative." He tapped his nightstick against the dashboard. "These foreign types, they don't always understand English so good. Sometimes they need a little encouragement."

Will forced a small, uncomfortable laugh. "I suppose they would."

"Course, the FBI boys would try to take him off my

hands." The officer shrugged. "But not before I got to have a little chat with him first."

Will turned to look out the window again, pretending to be interested in the passing landscape. He was aware of the pistol on the officer's hip, the handcuffs dangling from his belt. One wrong word, one suspicious gesture, and this ride could end very differently than he hoped.

The small coastal town came into view, a collection of weathered buildings clustered around the intersection of two highways. The police cruiser slowed as they approached the bus station, which was little more than a wooden bench beneath a sagging awning.

"Bus to Jacksonville should be along in about twenty minutes," the officer said as he pulled to a stop. He tossed his cigarette butt out the window, then pointed to the north end of the small platform. "That's where you'll want to wait."

"Thank you, sir," Will said, reaching for the door handle. "I appreciate the ride."

The officer nodded once. "Stay out of trouble, son."

Will forced himself to walk at a measured pace toward the bench, even as he heard the cruiser's engine revving behind him. Only when he heard it pull away did he allow his shoulders to slump in relief.

"Last call for northbound service to Jacksonville!" a driver called from beside a dusty Greyhound. "All aboard who's coming aboard!"

Will stood motionless, watching as a few stragglers hurried toward the bus. His hand tightened around the sack Annie had given him. North was the logical choice. Max and Jorg would be in New York by now, perhaps already establishing their network of contacts, laying the groundwork for the intelligence operation they'd spent months planning. If Will hurried, he might find them somehow. Maybe Max would know what to do about Erich. Maybe he could salvage this Florida disaster by doing great things with the team up north.

But as the driver climbed aboard the bus and the doors began to close, Will made no move toward it. Instead, he thought of Annie. Not just her face or her form, but the intensity in her eyes as she'd shown him around her family's fish camp. He recalled her quiet competence as she navigated the boat.

The northbound bus pulled away in a cloud of exhaust, leaving Will alone on the platform. He knew what he should do. He knew what a loyal soldier would do. Max and Jorg wouldn't hesitate. They would continue the mission, regardless of the cost.

Yet he couldn't forget the way Annie had looked at him in Jack's room. In the few hours he'd known this American girl, she'd shown him more kindness than he'd experienced in years of service to the Reich.

Perhaps he could just disappear here in America. Find a small town, change his name, get a job. Maybe this *was* his chance at a fresh start.

Then, he heard the Kapitänleutnant's warning, the words echoing with the clarity of a final order. *The SS-Obergruppenführer is a hard, uncompromising man. For the sake of your family, I hope Burger will return home in one piece.*

His family. Was the threat real? He remembered the Frenchman lying in the street in a pool of blood.

"*Mutti,*" he said aloud. A woman walking by on the street turned and stared at him. He couldn't take that risk. He reached into his trousers pocket. When their rubber boat overturned, he had lost everything except for what had been in his pockets. He touched the cool metal of his father's police badge. He had to try.

Without fully understanding his own decision, Will turned away from the now-empty northbound platform. He marched to the bench marked for southbound service, sat down, and placed his flour sack beside him. The next bus wasn't due for hours, but he didn't mind the wait.

There was no way the *Abwehr* could know Erich was dead. The contact point with the U-504 was south of Jupiter. He would find a light to signal the sub even if he had to steal it. They had trained him in subterfuge. He could lie better than most after writing propaganda for years. It would be easy to convince them that everything was going—how did the Americans say it? Hunky dory.

If they knew about his lies, his superiors would call it treason. His comrades would call it cowardice. But as Will settled onto the hard wooden bench, he couldn't bring himself to care about their judgment. For the first time since he'd been assigned this mission, perhaps for the first time since he'd moved to Germany, he was making a choice for himself.

And that choice was leading him back to Annie.

# CHAPTER TWENTY-FOUR

*Mosquito Lagoon, Florida*
*February 25, 1942*

Annie cracked eggs with a flick of her wrist, the yellow centers plopping into the cast-iron skillet like yellow suns in a Milky Way. She wore her mother's old apron, the one with the embroidered largemouth bass on it.

She heard heavy footsteps crossing the porch. The look on Woody's face would make it worth getting up before dawn.

He pushed open the screen door. "Smells good in here."

"Morning, Woody."

"You're up early." He rubbed his palms together.

"Remember this sight, old man. Won't happen again soon." She smiled as she handed him a cup of coffee.

"Well, I'll be damned. Miss Annie making breakfast in the big house kitchen. Never thought I'd see the day. And it's not even light out yet."

Annie smiled. "Finn showed up last night. Said he thumbed his way from Lauderdale."

Woody cleared his throat. "That so? Jack used to—"

"I know," she cut in. "I know."

The eggs crackled and popped as Annie poked them with a wooden spoon. She remembered the way her brother had once held that spoon like a sword, thrusting it at her, repeating, *All for one, and one for all* with a terrible Spanish accent. She was never any good in the kitchen, but Jack, while he was silly, could cook.

The kitchen door swung open, and Finn strolled in, his ginger hair an uncombed mess, his eyes bleary. Tess was at his heels, wagging her tail so hard, she looked like a hula dancer.

"Morning," Finn said, stretching. He wore the same clothes as yesterday, wrinkled and tired-looking. A dark bruise bloomed on his left cheekbone.

Woody turned around, and his grin made him look ten years younger. He clapped a hand on Finn's shoulder. "Well, I'll be. Finn Taggart. I haven't seen you in a dog's age." He stretched out a hand.

Finn took it, then pulled the old man into a bear hug. "Good to see you, Woody."

Woody stepped back and squinted at Finn's face. "What's that shiner you're sporting there?" He gestured at the purple bruise on Finn's cheekbone.

Finn dabbed the bruise with his fingertip. "Occupational hazard of hitch-hiking. Got to be quicker on my feet, I reckon."

"Or keep your nose out of places it don't belong," Woody said.

Finn winked. "Now where's the fun in that?" He sniffed the air. "Smells mighty good, Annie girl. You spoil us."

She jabbed at the eggs with the spoon. Damn. Her eyes burned, and she blinked fast.

It was Jack who had started calling her *Annie girl.*

She turned back to the eggs, dividing them into portions. "You're lucky, Finn. Could've been worse."

"Yeah," Finn said. "I suppose."

Silence settled in the room. Annie remembered the last time the three of them were here—the laughter, the plans. They were teenagers. That was before the family moved south. Now, the country was at war, and Jack was dead. Get a hold of yourself, Annie.

She plated the food. Fried eggs, bacon, slabs of Woody's homemade bread. Finn would be hungry after traveling all night.

"Just glad you made it in one piece," Woody said.

Finn shrugged, smiling. "It was worth it. Hadn't heard any news from this one," he nodded towards Annie, "and I was wondering if she'd taken on the Krauts single-handed."

Her eyes lingered on his tanned forearms as he reached for the coffeepot.

Stop it. She carried the plates to the table, avoiding his gaze. He had no right to still make her want impossible things.

Finn dug into his breakfast with relish. "This is swell, Annie. You've outdone yourself."

"It's just eggs and bacon." She poured herself coffee, breathing in the steam.

Woody sopped up egg yolk with his bread. "Don't sell yourself short, Miss Annie. These vittles are fit for a king."

A door inside of her had closed that morning when the Navy man delivered the news about Jack.

Finn reached across the table and snagged a slice of bacon off Woody's plate. "Remember when we tried to build that raft out of driftwood? We must've been, what, ten years old?"

Woody chuckled. "Oh, I remember. You three hooligans, hammering away with rusty nails and rotted boards. Surprised you didn't get tetanus."

"Or what about the time Jack convinced us we ought to go out and catch us a wild pig?"

Woody almost choked on his coffee. "Do I ever remember that. I think I told you kids that there was a wild boar that lived in the woods out there."

"Yeah, you told Jack that, but he was the only one of us who believed you. That boy was determined. So, we scrounged up some rope, and Jack had a flashlight. He took us out there into the woods to look for this pig. We walked for hours."

Annie said, "I don't think we saw a single animal, not even a bird."

"Yeah, but then you got tired, and you wanted to go back, so you and me, we did. But Jack, he was determined to find him a pig, so he stayed behind."

"I was asleep when he came back," Annie said. "But I remember he woke you up."

Finn laughed. "Yeah, he told me to come see what he'd caught. He had that flashlight under his chin, lighting up his face, and he was grinning from ear to ear. He said he'd tied the boar to the back bumper on the truck."

Annie laughed. "And you *believed* him?"

"I was just a kid. I didn't know any better. I followed him out there to the truck, and he shone his flashlight on the back bumper, and sure enough, there was a rope tied there. He told me to grab hold of the rope and pull the pig out of the woods. I grabbed that rope, and I pulled on it, but nothing happened. Jack said to pull harder, so I did. I pulled with all my might, and suddenly I'm holding a rope with an old boot tied to the end."

Annie tried not to, but she broke out into full-throated laughter. Her braid fell over her shoulder, and she pushed it back with her palm.

Finn looked very pleased with himself. "When I looked at

Jack, he was laughing even harder than you are now. He was jumping up and down, holding his sides, and running around in circles."

Woody said, "That boy sure did love a good joke."

Annie's laughter died down, and she put her hand over her mouth. Her eyes clouded over, and she blinked back the tears.

What was she doing? She wrapped her hand around the handle of her coffee cup and squeezed.

She had been laughing. How could she laugh when her brother was dead? The tightness in her chest felt like she was having a heart attack. Or maybe it was just a symptom of a broken heart. She wanted to run out of the house and keep running. Most of all, she wanted to be alone.

The table fell silent. Finn looked at her, but he said nothing. He just sat there watching her.

"Annie? You okay?"

Her chair scraped against the floorboards as she stood. "I have to get back to Fort Lauderdale. There are clients waiting to take the boat out. I've been gone too long already."

Woody frowned. "Now, hold on just a minute. You only just got here."

"And now I have to leave." She began clearing the plates. "I have responsibilities, Woody. Charters, the Mosquito Fleet. People are counting on me."

Finn looked up. "You're really going, then?"

Woody set down his coffee. "You could stay a few more days. It's not like Skeeter's gonna fire you."

"I'm needed back home. Plus, the season's starting. Tourists will be swarming in, and with all the soldiers in town, there's plenty that want to go out fishing. We need the money now more than ever."

Silence settled over the table, heavy and uncomfortable.

They all knew why. The family had one less earner with Jack gone.

"I'm leaving in an hour," she said. "That'll give me time to pack provisions to take back to Mama."

Woody started to protest the premature departure, but Annie cut him off. "I wish I could stay. It's been good to be here. But I have responsibilities."

Woody stood. "I'll go to the garden. Start picking what's ready."

Finn stayed seated as Woody left the room. Annie could feel his eyes on her, studying her.

"Annie." His voice was gentle, like a parent talking to a child. "We're just worried. That's all."

"I know." She turned back to the sink. "I need to clean up and get started packing."

As Annie scrubbed the dishes with single-minded focus, Finn remained silent. Then, he stood, walked to the sink, and picked up a dish towel. "I'm coming with you."

She paused, sponge dripping onto the plate. "What?"

"To Fort Lauderdale. I'm coming with you on the *Tequesta*." His tone left no room for argument.

Annie turned away from him. "Finn, that's not necessary. I can handle the boat on my own."

"Course you can." He took a step closer, his expression softening. "But you don't have to. Besides, you'd be doing me a favor. Saving me from hitchhiking again."

"Look, I appreciate the offer, but I need this time alone. To think. To..." She swallowed past the lump in her throat.

Finn's hand settled on her shoulder. "I get it, Annie. I do. But shutting yourself away won't help. Trust me, I've tried."

She knew he spoke from experience.

"Annie, I need a ride home, and getting to spend more time with you would be a bonus."

The tightness in her shoulders eased. She was tired of

arguing with him. "Okay. You can come. But don't run your mouth the whole time."

"I promise, you'll barely know I'm there."

They finished the dishes in comfortable silence, the splashing water and clink of plates filling the room.

Annie folded the dishtowel. "We'll need to check the sails, top off the fuel tanks. Woody will help us get the food on board. This will save him a trip to the railroad station."

"I'll head down to the smokehouse and pack some fish."

She nodded. "Sounds good. We'll leave in an hour. I want to take advantage of these northeasterly winds."

~

Annie walked back toward the boathouse. She had hoped the sail south would give her time to think, to sort through her feelings. Now she'd have to do it with Finn watching her.

She stepped down onto the foredeck of the *Tequesta* and ran her fingers along the seams of the sails on the bowsprit, checking for wear. She tied down the rigging, pulled the ropes tight, and checked the engine oil. Then she went about organizing the gear and the food. She packed Woody's smoked fish and the oranges and grapefruits in the forepeak, so the load on the boat would be balanced. They'd still have room to cook and sleep in the sea berth.

"Annie," Finn called from the dock. "I'm ready."

She climbed out on deck and took his duffel. Tess didn't wait to be invited aboard.

Woody cocked his head to one side and stuck out his lower lip in a pout. "Hate to see you go."

"I know. Look, thanks for not saying anything to Finn about, *you know*."

"Ain't none of my business."

"I made a promise, and well, I guess I ought to keep it.

Hopefully, this war will be over soon, and the world can get back to normal. Can't wait 'til we're all back living here the way it's supposed to be."

"A wise man once said *Don't waste your life waiting for the perfect life when there's a perfectly good one right in front of you.*" He looked down the dock at Finn, who stood on the foredeck, waiting to take the bow line.

"You mind your own business, old man. Come here and give me a hug good-bye." They embraced.

"No goodbyes, Annie girl. Just I'll see you soon." She stepped aboard and started the engine while Woody untied the dock lines and tossed them to Finn.

As the boat slipped away from the dock, Finn waved to Woody, then moved to the mast, waiting for her signal.

"Just the main, I think, until we get out of the inlet."

Annie adjusted the rudder, feeling the wind catch the sail. When she pulled in the sheet, the boat heeled over, cutting through the water with a graceful, powerful motion.

Annie focused on the water ahead. The channel was wide, but it felt small today. At least they had a favorable tide. They sailed until they approached the town of New Smyrna, where they could see the outlines of houses and docks, the occasional boat puttering along.

"Do you remember when we used to race?" Finn said, breaking the silence. "Down the river, out to the inlet?"

Annie didn't answer. She remembered. They'd spent whole summers racing each other, first on dinghies, then on larger boats. Jack had always been there, cheering them on, giving her tips. Those were the best times, the three of them together.

Finn sat down on the cockpit coaming, and one leg bounced in a staccato rhythm. He appeared to be looking at the shoreline to the east of them, but his eyes remained focused on something beyond the horizon.

"I should have been there. For him. For you."

She turned away, pretending to check for boat traffic behind them. The wind whipped her hair into her face. She knew what Finn was thinking about. Jack in that airplane, going down alone. It was always there, hanging between them. The truth was neither of them could have saved him, but grief didn't pay any attention to the truth.

"You're here now, aren't you?"

He turned to her and tried to smile, then returned his gaze to the water.

The northeast wind kicked up after noon, and Annie found the sweet spot around a mile offshore where they could not only avoid the northbound Gulf Stream but also ride the countercurrent to speed their trip home. True to his word, Finn kept to himself, either steering the boat or stretched out on the bunk below. They made great time and found themselves just off Port St. Lucie after nightfall.

Finn took the first night watch, and he woke Annie at midnight. "Wake up, sleepyhead. Your turn to battle the elements."

She pulled the wool blanket over her head and moaned.

He sat on the edge of the bunk, pulled the blanket down and brushed the hair off her face. His touch was gentle. She reached for his hand and held it cupped against her cheek for a few seconds. Then, she opened her eyes and found him staring at her.

"I can't keep pretending," Finn said.

"Don't." Annie's voice cracked. "Not yet. Please."

He leaned down and kissed her forehead. When he sat up, he leaned his head back and took a long breath. After a beat, when he turned down to face her, a half-smile curled his lips. "You awake now?"

She nodded, heart pounding.

He ran the back of his hand across her cheek. "Dress warm. It's chilly out there tonight."

He stood and returned to his post at the helm. When he was gone, she closed her eyes and ran her fingertips across the skin of her forehead.

*Stop it*, she told herself. *You're going to ruin everything.*

Annie dressed in an extra sweater and pulled Jack's old black oilskin jacket on. She lifted the collar on one side and smelled the lining. God, she missed him.

On her way up the ladder, she cleared her throat, intent on making her voice sound normal. "You go get some sleep now," she told him. "Hurry while the bunk's still warm."

"You should be able to see the entrance to Lake Worth in a few hours," Finn said. "The Jupiter light was quite dim when we passed. Probably couldn't see it more than a couple of miles from shore. I guess that's to keep the Germans from using our lights." Then, Finn ducked into the cabin.

Annie settled into her seat at the stern, one foot resting on the wooden wheel. She squinted over her shoulder at the black night off her starboard quarter. The Jupiter Light was right back there, but she couldn't see it.

It was here. Only a few days ago. The vivid memory of the explosion, the heat of the burning oil, came flooding into her mind. The sick feeling as the ship vanished. And then Tess barking, the man in the water. Will.

When she started wondering where he was at that moment, she stopped herself. *No. Think of something, anything else.*

The sounds of the boat were hypnotic: the creak of the rigging, the continuous swoosh at the stern as the stern wave crested behind them. Annie set her mind to wander, hoping it would find a safe topic. She thought about the last letter her brother had sent. She'd read it a hundred times. He'd been thrilled to be flying and getting to see the world. That was all he'd ever dreamed of. Maybe he wouldn't get to do a million other things, but at least he got that.

Annie enjoyed night watches, especially when the boat was sailing at full speed, charging through the water on a broad reach. The moon had set earlier, and the night was so black, it was nearly impossible to see the horizon. She made up stories, sang songs, and went below for a cup of tea from the thermos Finn had left her. They were just north of the Hillsboro lighthouse when she heard a low rumble she hadn't heard before.

The noise grew louder. Annie sat up, her ears straining to pinpoint the source. It was the unmistakable growl of a diesel engine. Her eyes scanned the horizon, and she spotted a dark shape moving against the backdrop of stars. It was heading toward shore and about to cross their bow a half mile ahead.

She slipped down to the cabin and shook Finn. "Wake up," she whispered. "Something's out there."

Finn rubbed his eyes and sat up. "What is it?"

"Come see."

Tess had been sleeping in the bunk with him, and when she stirred, Annie commanded her to stay. On her way to the deck, she grabbed her sketchbook from the chart table.

They tiptoed to the deck, crouching low. The diesel engine was louder now, and Annie could make out the silhouette of a conning tower blacking out the stars. The dark shadow crossed their bow moving at about six knots. Her pulse throbbed in her neck.

"Is that...?" Finn started, but Annie put her hand on his mouth to shush him.

She put her lips to his ear. "It's not a whale."

They watched as the submarine glided through the water,

its wake a phosphorescent trail. It was close enough now that Annie could see figures on the deck, their outlines sharp against the night sky. At the speed they were traveling, the *Tequesta* would soon pass the sub to starboard as it approached the coast.

"Smell that?" Finn whispered.

She nodded. The wind carried the faint scent of cigarette smoke.

A flash of light caught her eye. Annie turned to the shore and saw it again, a brief burst of flashes. The sequences were nothing like what her brother had taught her. She counted: three long flashes, pause, two short flashes, pause, five long flashes. Maybe it was Morse code, but she couldn't decipher it.

The submarine's engine cut, and the vessel drifted to a stop. The night fell quiet, and the water rushing past their hull sounded way too loud. Annie held her breath, her body rigid with tension.

"Why aren't they diving?" Finn whispered. "Surely they can see our sails."

Annie didn't answer. She could not take her eyes off the submarine on their beam. Her thoughts were a jumble of fear and curiosity. This was real, wasn't it? This was happening.

Another burst of flashes from shore.

She looked at the compass, took a bearing, and jotted the numbers down in her sketchbook. Then she scooted across the bench and waited for a dim flash from the lighthouse off their stern. There. Another bearing.

The submarine remained motionless, its crew eerily still. Annie's mind jumped to the burning tanker, all those men who died. Was this the same U-boat?

"We should call the Coast Guard," Finn said, his voice tight.

"With what?" Annie snapped. "A message in a bottle?"

Finn fell silent, and Annie regretted her harshness. She was scared, more scared than she'd ever been, and the fear was making her sharp.

Fuller Mansfield had promised them a radio, but it had not yet materialized.

They waited, neither moving nor speaking. The standoff stretched into minutes, each one an eternity. Annie's mind played out scenarios: the submarine opening fire, a landing party coming ashore, their sailboat being rammed and sunk. She gripped the rail so hard her knuckles whitened.

Without warning, the diesel engine sputtered to life. The submarine began to turn, its conning tower slicing through the water. It moved slowly at first, then picked up speed, heading back out to sea. Annie watched until it disappeared into the moonless night.

"Annie," Finn said, breaking the spell. "Did you see the light?"

She turned to him, her eyes wide. "Someone was signaling to them."

"It could have been anything. A fisherman, a tourist."

"It was Morse code, Finn. Someone on shore is communicating with them."

Finn rubbed his thighs, his face troubled. "It was probably nothing."

Annie looked out at the dark horizon, her mind considering other possibilities. "Maybe," she said. But she did not believe that for a second.

# CHAPTER TWENTY-FIVE

*Fort Lauderdale*
*February 26, 1942*

It was almost noon by the time Annie guided the *Tequesta* alongside the Fort Lauderdale docks on the New River, the boat's single-cylinder engine thumping a steady rhythm.

Finn leaped to the dock, and she tossed him the stern line.

Ned Hardy stood on the foredeck of his charter boat, *Lucky Strike*. "Dangerous work for a girl." He spat a brown wad of tobacco into the river, just missing the *Tequesta*'s stern.

"That's why I bring Finn along," she said. "For the girly stuff."

Hardy leaned against an outrigger; old fish blood stains peppered the front of his once-white captain's shirt. The odor of stale rum wafted across the water. "You been gone a while."

"Just out fishing."

"Yanking nets with your daddy is one thing, but patrolling for U-boats is serious business."

Annie closed her eyes for a couple of seconds and took a

deep breath. The sun's warmth felt good after a long night of bucking the Gulf Stream. She didn't bother looking over at Hardy. "It's all fishing, Ned."

Hardy grunted. "Men's work."

Finn stepped forward. "Careful, Ned. Annie's got a mean right hook."

Hardy snorted. "Yeah? I'd like to see her try."

Annie's fingers twitched at her sides, but she forced a smile. "Maybe later. Right now, I've got more important things to do."

Hardy's laugh followed her as she walked forward to hand Finn the spring lines, but she ignored him.

"You okay?" Finn asked.

"Fine," Annie said, though her chest felt tight. She glanced toward the *Lucky Strike*, where Hardy was still watching them with that smug grin. "Plenty of other fishermen on this dock are decent fellas, but my dock space has to be next to him."

Finn nodded. "He and Jack used to get along fine, Annie. I reckon he misses Jack, too, and you remind him of that every time he sees you."

She'd never thought of Ned like that. "You're a smart fella, Finn Taggart."

He grinned. "Glad to see you're coming round to noticing that."

"Let's get to work. We've got all these crates of food and a boat to wash down."

"What do you say I fetch your dad and the Fumblebee? This lot's too much to carry," he said, nodding to the crates of food stacked in the hold.

"That sounds like a plan."

Annie watched him weave through the bustle of the dock, fishermen unloading their hauls, charter captains prepping for the day's tourists. Then, he disappeared when he turned onto the main avenue. She'd started this sailing trip wanting to be alone, and now that she was, she already missed him.

Annie shook her head, thinking she was acting like a fool. The boat needed her right now, and there was plenty of work to be done before she could head home and sleep.

At that moment, she spotted Fuller Mansfield aboard another patrol boat. She hesitated, then cupped her fingers around her mouth and shouted, "Mansfield!" Her voice cut through the din of working men and boat engines.

Mansfield looked up, his weathered face squinting against the midday sun. Annie waved, and he gave a curt nod. She beckoned him with a hand. He held up a finger, then went back to his conversation with the other skipper. Annie waited, shifting from one foot to the other.

Eventually, Mansfield made his way down the dock.

"I need to talk to you. In private."

He studied her for a moment. "All right. But make it quick."

Annie waved him aboard the *Tequesta* and down into the cabin. Charts, bedding and oilskins cluttered the small space. She cleared room for them on the settee.

"Alright," Mansfield said. "What's so urgent?"

"We saw a U-boat," she said. "On our way back from Ponce Inlet last night. Close enough to catch the reek of tobacco smoke."

Mansfield's expression didn't change, but his shoulders tensed. "Go on."

"There was a light," she continued, her eyes fixed on his face. "Coming from the shore. Flashing. Short ones, long, then short. Like a signal."

He leaned forward, his gaze sharpening. "Slow down. Are you sure what you saw was a U-boat and not just a fishing boat?"

Annie shook her head. "There was no moon, so it was

dark. But we could see the conning tower and the men on deck. And the engine. That was the first thing. I realized there was a boat nearby when I heard the engine."

"If you were that close, they would have been able to see you, too."

Annie nodded. "We were under full sail, so they must have seen us. But even if they did, they must not have seen us as a threat. I guess they figured we were just a fishing boat."

"If it was that dark, how can you be sure what you saw was a U-boat?"

She sighed. "Finn was with me. He saw it too. It was between us and the shore." She grabbed her sketchbook off the chart table and opened it to the page her pencil marked. "I sketched this outline of the conning tower and the deck. There were men down on the forward deck and others in the conning tower."

Mansfield took the book and examined drawing. "Tell me about the signaling. What exactly did you see?"

"Short and long flashes," she said. "I don't know Morse code well enough to read it, but the pattern was distinct. It went on for several minutes."

He handed her back the sketchbook and crossed his arms. "A U-boat communicating with someone on shore?"

"I know." Annie nodded. "It sounds wild. But I could pinpoint that location on shore to within a quarter of a mile, maybe closer."

Mansfield's eyes were wide open, but unfocused. He sucked in his lips and sighed.

"I know these waters," she said. "This coast. The numbers next to the drawing—those are some rough bearings I took off the compass."

He uncrossed his arms and turned to her. "It's not that I doubt your abilities, Miss Jeeves. It's just a lot to take in. " He moved toward the hatch, pausing with a hand on the ladder.

He turned back and said, "We should equip the *Tequesta* with a radio."

"We've been waiting for a long time."

"You know we don't have enough to outfit every boat," Mansfield said. "But you've just jumped up the list.

"Thank you."

Mansfield stroked his chin, the stubble making a soft rasping sound. "It's important for you to convey every bit of information to us. It's hard to know what little piece of knowledge can make a difference." He reached for the ladder, then turned back. "Lives could depend on it. Tell me more about the lights. What makes you so sure it wasn't just someone looking for their dog with a flashlight?"

Annie closed her eyes for a minute to see those lights again in her mind's eye. "It was deliberate. A series of short and long flashes. Then darkness." She opened her eyes again. "Sorry, I can't remember the exact sequence. I couldn't tell you if the Germans were signaling back to the shore because, like I said, we passed them on the seaward side. But the flashing light on land—someone on land was signaling the sub."

Mansfield removed a notepad from his jacket and scribbled something. "We'll need to train you on signaling and Morse, too, so you can recognize real signaling."

"Yes, sir." There was something in the tone of his voice when he said real signaling that made Annie wonder if he believed her.

"I'll talk to my superiors," he said.

"Thanks."

"And Annie, if you think of anything else, let me know. You never know what little detail may be important."

"I will." She was glad his back was to her as he climbed into the cockpit. The lie of omission had tasted bitter.

After he left, Annie opened the sketchbook to the page

marked by the pencil. She might not read Morse code yet, but she could recognize 'real signaling' when she saw it. Then she turned back one page to a drawing of Finn sitting on the foredeck. One more page back, and there was the sketch she'd drawn from memory that night she couldn't sleep. Will's eyes stared back at her from the page. What was she thinking? A survivor from the *W.D. Anderson*. That was more than a 'little detail.'

She began unloading the crates Woody had sent for her parents. She included the dorado they had caught off Boca Inlet on their trolling line. Finn had gutted it and placed it in a crate with the remaining ice from the boat.

She thought about the U-boat as she worked, about the men inside it. Were they as tired as she was? As hungry? Would they sink more ships because of her promise to Will? But she told Mansfield about the U-boat they'd seen last night, and he didn't seem to believe the lights on shore mattered, nor take any interest in her bearings.

She climbed back out on deck and went to fetch the hose. "Did you hear about the *WD Anderson*?" one dockworker said, loud enough to carry over the din. Annie's ears perked up.

"Yeah," another replied. "Poor bastards. Went up like a powder keg."

Annie tried to tune it out, but something big as U-boats torpedoing ships right offshore would dominate dockside gossip for the next month or more.

"They pulled one guy out of the drink. Still alive, can you believe it?"

"Yeah, tough as nails, that one. Says he was on deck and saw the torpedo heading straight for them. Dove straight overboard. He's the only man who survived. Reckon he's headed home a hero now."

Annie exhaled. She opened the tap and began washing the salt off the boat.

At least they weren't talking about Will. For now, he was still her secret, and she would keep the promise. But he'd never told her how he and his friend survived that initial explosion.

Annie had just finished hosing off the boat when a familiar honk cut through the morning air. She looked up to see Finn waving from the passenger seat of the Fumblebee.

Her father killed the engine and got out, stretching his lean frame and lifting a hand to wave at her.

"Annie," Skeeter called. "You ready?"

"Just about," she said. "Finn, can you help me carry these crates?"

When they had finished loading the car, her father closed the door to the back seat.

"Your ma's gonna appreciate all that fresh food," he said. "How were the conditions on the way back?"

"Calm enough. We saw a U-boat up off Jupiter."

Skeeter's face tightened. "Did you now?"

She met his gaze, waiting for the lecture. Instead, he just nodded.

"Be careful, Annie. This isn't like before."

She knew he was referring to the times when she was just a girl, when she had accompanied him on some runs offshore to pick up Bahamian liquor during Prohibition. They had dodged the chasers offshore and the revenuers on land.

"We're always careful," she said.

"You don't need to share that bit of information with your mother."

"Agreed." Selecting the information she shared was becoming a habit.

Finn returned, carrying the last wooden crate filled with vegetables.

Annie took the crate from him.

"Do you need a ride?" she asked. There wasn't much room in the back of the car.

Finn shook his head. "I'll manage. See you tomorrow?"

"Sure," she said. "Thanks again."

Finn lingered for a moment, then walked off toward the main road. Skeeter watched him go, then looked at Annie.

"You know, he was worried about you," Skeeter said.

Annie sighed. "I know, Pa. We're all trying to figure things out. It's complicated."

The familiar sight of the Jeeves' family home came into view as they pulled up the gravel driveway. Annie felt a surprising surge of emotion at the sight of her mother, Hilda, standing on the porch. She stood, one hand shading her eyes as she watched their approach.

"There's Ma." Her father's voice carried a forced cheerfulness.

As they climbed out of the car, Ma descended the porch steps. Her green eyes, usually so sharp, held a muted look that Annie had grown accustomed to since Jack's death. But at least she was out of bed, out of her room.

"Welcome home." Ma's voice wavered. "You look tired, dear. How was your trip?"

Annie swallowed hard. "Just the usual, Ma. Nothing to worry about."

"Well, come in then. I've got coffee on." She climbed back up the steps and opened the screen door.

Annie hung back, watching her mother's movements. There was a heaviness to them, a sadness that seemed to permeate the surrounding air.

"She misses him something fierce." Pa stood next to her, holding a crate of vegetables.

Annie nodded, her throat tight. "We all do."

Inside, the kitchen was familiar, but Jack's absence was a

palpable thing, an actual empty chair at the table that no one dared fill.

As her father regaled Hilda with tales from the docks, Annie sipped her coffee. She wondered if part of that feeling of wrongness came from her. She'd seen this war up close now in the flames of a burning tanker, the exhaustion of a half-drowned survivor, the dark shadow of the enemy's most lethal weapon. And here at home, in the new lines on her parents' faces.

The weight of her promise to keep Will's secret pressed down on her. But as she looked at her mother's tired eyes, her father's forced smile, she knew she couldn't add to their burdens.

"Annie?" Hilda's voice cut through her thoughts. "Are you all right?"

Annie plastered on a smile. "Just thinking about the tides for tomorrow's charter," she said. "Nothing to worry about, Ma."

# CHAPTER TWENTY-SIX

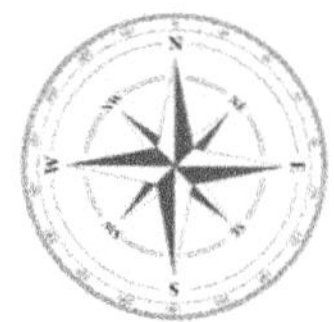

*Fort Lauderdale*
*March 3, 1942*

Annie knelt on the *Tequesta*'s deck, scrubbing fish blood stains from the pine planks with a stiff brush. On their last charter, they had a fellow from South Carolina who insisted on killing fish his way. The decks and the fish had suffered.

She rubbed her eyes, exhaustion blurring her vision.

"How's it going down there, Emma?" Annie stretched her neck to look down the companionway.

"Mr. Brunton's trying to pass off these second-rate vegetables again." Emma poked her head out of the hatch. "Says the war's making everything expensive."

Annie pushed loose hair off her face. "War's just his excuse to squeeze more profit. What makes folks think they should make money off misery?"

"Anyway, almost done down here. These provisions should last us through the week." Her dark eyes studied Annie's face. "You look like you haven't slept."

She hadn't. Not for several nights. Too many dreams of fire and flames.

Annie started to answer Emma, but a movement down the dock caught her eye. A familiar figure approached through the maze of moored boats. Surely, her eyes must be playing tricks.

Will.

No mistaking that blond hair. It was him. He looked different, cleaner, more polished in pressed new clothes and a crisp white shirt. His hair was combed, and he carried himself with the careful posture of a man trying to blend in.

Emma followed her gaze and tensed. "Who's that?"

"Someone I know," Annie said, setting down her brush. She wiped her hands on a rag as Will stepped onto the dock.

"Hello, Annie." His voice was steady, but she caught the nervous tension in his stance. "It's good to see you."

"This is a surprise. I didn't expect to see you again." Annie glanced at Emma, who had retreated partway down the companionway, listening but giving them privacy. "You said you were headed north. To start over."

Will's eyes swept the opposite river bank before settling back on her. "There was something I needed to do first."

"In Lauderdale?"

"Sorta. How've you been?"

"It's been busy." Annie studied his face, searching for the vulnerable, half-drowned man she'd pulled from the ocean. "The war's brought lots of new folks to town. Seems they all want to go fishing."

He nodded, his fingers drumming against his leg.

"Listen, Annie, I need to talk to you." He glanced at the companionway. "Somewhere private. Could you meet me later at Hardy Park?"

"Why not talk now?"

"Please, Annie." The way he said her name made something flutter in her chest. "It's important."

She knew she should say no. She remembered Woody's words. *You can't save everyone.* Something about this felt wrong. Yet.

"What time?"

"Six o'clock. By the banyan tree."

Against her better judgment, she nodded. "I'll be there."

Will stepped closer to the boat's edge, close enough that she could smell the soap on his skin. His fingers brushed her forearm, lingering a moment too long.

"Thank you." Then he turned and walked away, disappearing into the crowd of dockworkers.

Emma's head popped back up from the companionway. "Who was that handsome stranger?"

"Just someone passing through." Annie avoided her friend's gaze.

"That man's got trouble written all over him, Annie."

Annie picked up her brush and scrubbed harder at the already-clean deck.

"It's a long story."

"Is Finn part of that story?"

Annie set down her brush and looked at her friend. "I need to clear my head. Are you about done down there?"

"Almost. Just need to store the last of the cans from Brunton's."

"Would you mind locking up the boat? I need to stretch my legs. Meet me at the Stranahan house?"

Emma cocked her head and stared at Annie. "I'll be on my way in fifteen minutes."

The afternoon was overcast and the air thick with humidity as Annie walked along the waterfront toward the Stranahan house, her and Emma's unofficial sanctuary.

Mrs. Stranahan had been the first schoolteacher in town

forty years back when she was a new bride. With her husband, they ran the first Indian trading post and ferry to cross the river. Now a widow, she was always friendly with all the young folk in town, and she didn't care if they were white, black or Seminole Indians. Everyone was welcome at her door.

As she walked, Annie felt her anger simmering, at Will, at herself for keeping secrets from Emma. The weight of everything unsaid sat heavy in her chest.

Mrs. Stranahan met her at the door. "Why, Miss Annie Jeeves. I haven't seen you in ages."

"Good to see you too, ma'am." The older woman swung the door wide, but Annie glanced down the porch towards the river.

"Dear, you look like you've got some thinking to do. The porch and dock are yours."

"Thank you, ma'am."

Annie bypassed the comfy chairs under the covered porch, and sat at the dock's edge, letting her feet dangle over the dark water. Emma appeared a few minutes later. Mrs. Stranahan followed her with a tray of sweet tea and cookies.

"Such troubled times." Mrs. Stranahan spoke softly, touching Annie's shoulder. "I'm so sorry about Jack, dear. I pray this war ends soon."

After she left, Annie took a deep breath. "Em, I need to tell you something."

"Go on."

Annie exhaled. "I'm sorry. I was—"

Emma cut her off. "Are you?"

"What?"

"Sorry. I know you've been keeping something all bottled up. Not telling is making you sick."

"I wanted to tell you when I first got back. But I

promised I wouldn't. It turns out that's a promise I can't keep."

"I'm listening."

"After the funeral when I sailed up to Edgewater, I rescued a man. A survivor from that tanker. The *W.D. Anderson*."

"What? And you're just now telling me this?"

"Yeah, I know. I saw that ship get hit and burn. It was awful. I was sailing away from that burning oil slick when I found him. I pulled him out of the water. He was half-dead. Off Jupiter."

Emma pursed her lips, then repeated, "Off Jupiter."

"I know I should'a told you. His name is Will. And that's the man who came by the boat today."

"Why's it taking you so long to tell me this?"

"I promised him I wouldn't tell anybody."

"Not to say his name? Or to say anything at all?"

"Both. He says he doesn't want to go back to sea. Says he signed a contract, and he's afraid they'll make him go back. He almost died out there. Most of the men he worked with on that ship are dead. He wants to start his life over, least that's what he said. He doesn't want anybody making a fuss over him. And that's something I can understand, can't you?"

"Okay, I can understand that. But why did he come here to find you?"

"That, I don't know. When he left the fish camp that day, he said he was going north. To start a new life. Where people wouldn't feel sorry for him. It's like he's got survivor guilt. Was a heck of a surprise to see him show up here. He said he wants to talk."

"Talk?"

"He wants me to meet him later across the river at Hardy Park."

"And you're going? A man who wants you to keep secrets,

showing up during wartime?" Emma shook her head. "Annie, you're too trusting. Always have been."

"You sound like Woody. But I understand wanting to start fresh," Annie protested. "Don't you ever wish you could just disappear? Become someone new?"

"I'd trust Woody's instincts if I were you. He and Granddad are wise old men. Starting over's one thing. But what's he disappearing from? And what does he want from you?" Emma's voice was gentle but firm.

"I'm just trying to help him."

"Be careful, Annie. You might think you're helping him. But what if he's saving himself at your expense?"

# CHAPTER TWENTY-SEVEN

*Hardy Park, Fort Lauderdale*
*March 3, 1942*

Will gripped the rusty chains of the swing, his shoulders tense despite his effort to appear relaxed. He'd found this park when he'd first arrived in Fort Lauderdale, and he was surveying the town, getting his bearings, and looking for a place where he could set up camp. He remembered places like this, parks where he had played as a child. Before *Mutti* had taken him back to Germany.

The mission they had trained for was simple: gather information about the harbor defenses, sabotage any military installations, factories or shipyards. Admiral Canaris's instructions echoed in his mind: ***Be charming, be American, find a local who knows the waters.*** And he had found Annie Jeeves.

Riding the bus south, he had considered how to continue the fiction that Erich was still alive. If he could pull off some sabotage, find some information to relay during his next contact with U-504, they would believe both men had made it to shore. He did not want to help the Reich, but his mother's life was at stake, as was his own.

He was learning how to survive in this country. The people were friendly, gullible. He'd learned that many homes in Florida were vacation homes for rich people from up north. This winter, the war had kept many away. The fellow at Brownie's Bar told stories about the homes where he did yard work. So, Will had hitch-hiked up the coastal highway and found a small beach bungalow filled with nice clothes and food. He'd even found a big old lantern for signaling. Stealing came easy when your life, and those of your loved ones, depended on it.

So, he had made contact and told them he had befriended a local who would make an excellent asset. What the *Abwehr* hadn't accounted for was how Annie's smile would affect him, how each conversation would feel less like an assignment and more like coming home to a place he barely remembered.

What was he doing? This meeting needed to be business only, but Will found his attraction to Annie Jeeves irresistible. He shouldn't be here. He should find someone else. Could he betray the woman who had saved his life?

He looked up and watched as Annie approached, her dress fluttering in the breeze. Her guarded hesitation pricked at him. Was she afraid of him? How could he reconcile his desire to protect her while feeding her lies?

*Remember why you're here*, he reminded himself. *Remember Berlin. Remember what happens to agents who fail.*

He looked up, careful not to appear too eager. "Annie." Her name felt right on his tongue, perhaps the only honest thing he'd spoken since arriving.

"Will."

"You came."

"I said I would."

Will shrugged. Her honesty was disarming.

"You look like a grown man trying to fit back into his childhood," she said.

He laughed, caught off guard by the truth she had spoken. For a moment, his mission receded, and he was himself.

"Why did you want to see me again?"

Will patted the swing beside him. "Maybe I enjoy your company."

She settled into the canvas swing, close enough that he could detect the faint scent of lavender. "You traveled a long way in the wrong direction just to enjoy some company."

He didn't know what to say about that.

"Where are you staying in town?"

"A room," he said, then reached into his jacket pocket and pulled out a tarnished silver cigarette case. Instead of a cigarette, he removed a piece of cardboard, folded in half. "Ever heard of Valparaiso, Indiana?"

Her fingers brushed his as she took the water-stained postcard he'd slid from the tin. Will swallowed hard. The postcard was part of his well-rehearsed cover, close enough to the truth to be simple to remember. The silver case, tucked in his back pocket, had been just enough to keep it from turning to pulp in the Atlantic.

"See there? That's the lifeguard tower where I worked summers. I walked along the beach selling candy and soda pop. I was just a kid." As he spoke about swimming at Blackhawk Beach, genuine homesickness crept into his voice. He had missed America, the land of his birth, even as he had trained to undermine it.

"Sounds like a nice place," she said. "Why'd you leave?"

Will looked away. "I thought I wanted to go to sea. Didn't know I'd end up almost drowning in it."

"I'm glad I found you," Annie said.

"Me too."

He steered the conversation toward her then. This was

safer ground. Asking questions, being the attentive listener. Her face animated as she spoke about mapmaking and charting waterways. She was beautiful in her passion, and for moments he almost forgot his purpose.

Until she mentioned Whiskey Creek.

"It's this little inlet off the canal, south of the port," she said. "Can't get there by road, only by boat. On the ocean side, there's a white sand beach, and on the canal side, there's this shallow entrance through the mangroves that's hard to find. Nobody goes there much, so my friends and I, we kind of made it our secret spot."

His eyes flicked past her toward the harbor, his mind cataloging potential targets.

"During Prohibition, my pa used to meet Bahamian boats out in the Gulf Stream, load up with liquor and smuggle it in to offload on the beach at Whiskey Creek. The revenuers couldn't find the entrance, and if they chased the rum runners in there, the creek was too shallow for the government chaser boats. Back in those days, they used to call this town 'Fort Liquordale'."

Will leaned forward, his interest now both genuine and professional. The location was exactly what they had asked him to find: an unpatrolled beach with access to the port.

"Do many people know about this Whiskey Creek?" he asked, then regretted his eagerness.

Something shifted in her expression. A flicker of suspicion? Had he pushed too hard?

"You're very interested in our coastline."

Will forced a casual shrug and a smile. "Just curious. Maybe you could take me there sometime?" He softened his voice, allowing real longing to seep into it, longing not for military intelligence, but for more moments with her.

The thought disturbed him. He was compromising himself, allowing feelings to interfere with duty.

She turned her face away, and he couldn't tell what she was thinking until she spoke. "Will, what's the real reason you came here?" She faced him again. "You said you had to talk to me about something."

"Would it frighten you if I told you I just had to see you again?"

She didn't answer him right away. She handed him back the postcard and stared at him, her eyes flicking back and forth, examining his.

"I need to get home." Annie stood to leave.

Will jumped up and spun around in front of her, blocking her path. "I can't stop thinking about you, Annie. When I was in that water, certain I was dying, you were like an angel pulling me back to life." He took her hand in both of his. "Come away with me."

She opened her mouth, but he continued before she could turn him down. "We could get away from this war and start over. Somewhere no one knows us." He felt as though the words coming from his mouth were beyond his control.

Annie just stared at him, and for a moment, he allowed himself to get his hopes up.

Then, she pulled her hand free. "My folks expect me for dinner. I really must go."

They stood facing each other. Will wanted to kiss her. He wanted to tell her the truth. He did neither.

"Will I see you again?" she asked.

He felt hot joy in his chest. He hadn't lost her. "You can count on it." He wanted to say more. He wanted to confess. Instead, he said, "Goodbye, Annie."

He turned and walked through a tall hedge. When he was certain she could no longer see him, he stopped and stepped off the path. She was going home, and he needed to know where her home was. He followed at a distance, keeping to the dark side of the hedge.

Suddenly, a young man appeared, blocking her path. His clothing was dirty. Will tensed. The man's voice was high-pitched, like a dog whining for attention. "Miss Jeeves, out here all alone in the dark."

"Ernie Finch." So, an acquaintance. Not a stranger. "I am not in the mood for your foolishness."

The man's face twisted into a snarl. Will remembered Erich's uncle with mud on his boots in France. Weak men expected respect.

"Didn't think you were the type to go sneakin' around with strange men." He shook his head in mock disappointment. "Guess I was wrong."

"Go home, Ernie." She said it like she meant it, but Will heard the slight quiver in her voice.

Ernie stepped closer. He was shorter than Annie. "Should've known. Little trash girl, meetin' her trash boy."

"Go home," she said again.

His hand shot out. Grabbed her wrist.

Just as Will reached for the bush, Ernie said, "Sheriff Clark always said you Jeeves were a little high and mighty, thinkin' you're better than folks like me."

He stopped and stepped back into his hiding place. What was this man's connection to the Sheriff? Will held back. He couldn't afford trouble with the American law.

The little man snorted and coughed, then spit a wad of something disgusting at her shoes. "But you ain't got Jack watchin' over you anymore, Annie."

"Let go," Annie demanded.

"Maybe you oughta be more careful who you run with."

She opened her mouth to speak, then decided not to.

"Who was he?" Ernie demanded, jerking his chin toward where Will had disappeared. "Never seen him 'round here before."

"None of your business."

"Everything in this town is Sheriff Clark's business," he hissed. "Which makes it my business too."

Annie said nothing.

A sheriff meant records, questions he couldn't answer. Will remembered the police officer back in Edgewater.

"You ain't that pretty," Ernie continued, his voice dropping lower, uglier. "What's he want with you, huh? Must be somethin' else he's after." Finch's hand lifted, reaching for the buttons on the front of her dress.

Annie swatted his hand away, but something primal and protective surged within Will.

He stepped out from behind the hedge. "Let go of her."

"Who the hell are you?" Finch cocked his head to one side and let go of Annie.

Will positioned himself between them, shoulders squared, back straight. His Brandenburg training took over.

"That doesn't matter."

"You her bodyguard now?" Finch's voice cracked. "You think you're gonna play hero?"

Will remained silent.

"I think you're gonna walk away," Will said at last.

Finch shifted, calculating his odds.

"Tell you what." Finch crossed his arms high on his chest and glared at Annie. "I think I'll have to report that you been keepin' some mighty interesting company." He sniffed, then turned around and began walking.

Only when Finch had vanished did Will turn to Annie, examining her face, then her wrist where Finch had grabbed her.

"Are you alright?" he asked.

"I'm fine. I can take care of myself."

Will looked toward downtown, aware of the danger the Sheriff represented. Not just to his mission, but to her. His attraction to Annie was a liability he couldn't afford, yet he couldn't deny it. The mission demanded he use her. His heart demanded he protect her, even from himself.

"I hope you can." Will turned and began walking away. He heard her call after him.

"Will?"

But he couldn't answer. He couldn't tell her he was the threat she should fear most.

# CHAPTER TWENTY-EIGHT

*Fort Lauderdale*
*March 20, 1942*

A faded aeronautical chart stuck in a pile of books caught Annie's attention. She was sitting cross-legged on the wooden floor of her brother's room. When she slid out the faded paper, she saw Jack's handwriting.

"Look, Mama. His notes from when he first started taking flying lessons."

Her mother glanced over from where she sat on the bed, sorting clothes into two piles. "We'll never finish cleaning this room out if you insist on talking about every last thing."

Having a day off after weeks of almost daily charters was great, but she hadn't planned on spending the day helping clear out her brother's room. Yet, here she was.

Annie looked around at the boxes and bookshelves and heaps of her brother's belongings. Airplane models. His old Rand McNally globe on his desk. She reached up and spun it with her fingertip, like when she and Jack used to dream about where they would go someday.

She sighed. Would she ever stop missing him like this? Tears welled up again. Why did everything have to make her remember all the times he had teased her, fought her, taught her?

She pulled open the last desk drawer and saw her own artwork inside. The stack included everything from treasure maps in a childish scrawl to detailed pencil charts of the depths and banks of the New River. With the back of her hand, she wiped her damp cheeks. “He kept everything I ever drew for him,” she whispered, more to herself than to her mother.

Her mother dropped a fresh box in front of her.

“I heard the Army’s starting a paper drive. Put all those old papers in here.” She set a brown paper bag next to Annie.

“Mama. It would be like throwing away our childhood.”

Hilda leaned in to see what Annie had found. She took one map and looked it over.

“He’s not coming back,” her mother said. She dropped it onto Annie’s lap.

“I know that.” She knew it was just her ma’s way of coping, but she didn’t have to like it. Annie held up a folded chart. “But Ma... These are precious memories. Kinda’ like a piece of the past.”

Her mother cut her off with a sweep of her hand. “Men dying by the thousands. Boys younger than you shipping off every day. You want to wallow in dreamland while your father’s working himself sick and the world burns?”

“You make me sound foolish for wanting to remember the good times with Jack.”

Her mother pursed her lips and looked around the room as though Jack might give her the words to put some sense into her daughter. “Annie. Annie.” She shook her head. “Did you hear about that German countess? Arrested right in Palm Beach last week long with the whole family. They were on holiday, or so they said. Spies, more like. There's no telling who people are these days."

"German spies. Hmm." She had never told her parents about the lights she had seen up around Hillsboro Light or the U-boat she had passed so close. She didn't want to add to their troubles. "Just because we've got this war now doesn't mean it's going to last forever. Things'll get back to normal someday."

"Annie, our local Japanese farmers and their families are being relocated to internment camps. Burnt bodies are washing up on our beaches right here in Florida. The world's gone crazy. It's best you stop dreaming that things are going back to normal someday."

Annie folded the map tighter, creasing Jack's handwriting.

A knock sounded from the front of the house. Her mother gave her one last glance and left the room.

Annie stayed on the floor. A front had come through the night before. Cold seeped up through the floorboards, but she didn't mind. Together with Jack, she had spent hours sitting on this floor, drawing or dreaming. She started a pile of the maps she would keep and threw the rest into the paper bag.

Then she heard footsteps in the hall.

"Annie?"

She looked up to see Emma framed in the doorway. No lipstick today. Her hair braided. A new dress with green and red flowers, and an enormous pocketbook on her shoulder. Eyes red-rimmed but dry.

"Hey," Annie said, wiping her face. "Come in."

Emma stepped over a box and asked, "You been crying?"

Annie shook her head. "It's just the dust."

Emma's gaze drifted across the room, settling on the stack of papers and photos on top of the desk.

"Your mama said you were packing up Jack's things."

"Donating most things. War effort."

Emma knelt beside her, slow. "Can I keep something? To remember him by?"

"Course you can." Annie reached across the floor to a stack of black and white photos. With one finger, she pushed several photos aside until she found the right one. A close-up of Jack at the helm of the *Tequesta*, squinting into the sun. She picked up the photo and handed it over. "How about this?"

Emma took it, touching the photo with one finger. "He loved that boat."

"Em, he *loved* you."

She slipped the photo into her purse. "Thank you, Annie."

"You want to help sort through his books on that shelf? Two piles. One for those you think I'd like and the other for the library. And feel free to take any for you."

After several minutes of working, Emma spoke up. "You know who I saw yesterday?"

Annie shook her head.

"Jedidiah. Used to work at Leroy's Garage. Remember him?"

"Sure."

"He told me he tried to enlist at the Naval Air Station. They turned him away. Said no coloreds."

Annie stared at her. "But that's ridiculous! Jedidiah can take apart an engine and put it back together blindfolded. He'd make a fantastic mechanic."

"That's what he told them. They said he could work as a civilian steward. Serving food to white officers." Emma's voice remained steady, but her fingers curled into fists in her lap. "He has two years of college, Annie. Mechanical engineering. Not good enough for fixing their precious planes, but plenty good enough to serve their coffee."

Annie exhaled hard. "Mama was just saying the whole world's gone crazy, and she's right. Hitler's putting people in camps because of their religion, and we won't let folks fight him because of their skin color. Makes about as much sense as a screen door on a submarine."

Emma laughed. "You sound just like your brother when you talk like that."

"Yeah, well, he wasn't wrong about everything."

From down the hall, they heard the radio start playing in the middle of the Andrews Sisters' new song, *Don't Sit Under the Apple Tree with Anyone Else but Me*.

"So," Emma said. "You met with that mystery man again. What's his name? Will?"

Annie flinched. "It was nothing."

"Uh-huh. You lie worse than Bean."

"He wanted to talk. I didn't. End of story."

Emma put up her arms in surrender. "Okay. Be like that. Just so you know, you're not fooling me. I saw the look on your face when you saw him."

"Clearly, he's not interested in me because I haven't seen a sign of him in over two weeks."

They continued to work in silence for over an hour. The light in the room grew dim.

Emma was the first to speak. "Say, on the way over here I saw there's a new show at the Sunset. It's called *The Maltese Falcon*. We ought to celebrate having a day off. Wanna go see it?"

# CHAPTER TWENTY-NINE

*Fort Lauderdale*
*March 20, 1942*

Dinner was loud. Easy. Almost normal. Finn and Bean had arrived, and the table was full again. Annie let herself laugh for the first time in days.

"I hear you young folks are headed to the picture show tonight," Annie's mother said, passing the last biscuit to Bean.

"Yes, ma'am," Emma replied. "*The Maltese Falcon* is playing at the Sunset."

"That detective picture?" Skeeter looked up with sudden interest. "Heard it's good. Bogart's in it."

"Jack wanted to see it," Annie said, and the table fell silent. She cleared her throat. "I think he'd like us going."

Her mother's eyes glistened. "I think you're right."

When the three of them left the house, the sky was deep violet, with stars pricking through. The warmth of the dinner lingered as they walked in the cool night air. She knew Emma felt it too when her friend dared to link arms with her. Finn skipped ahead, jumping and swatting at the leaves on the trees, and the girls laughed. It had been too long since they had all laughed together.

The closer they got to the theater, the busier the sidewalks grew. They weren't the only ones headed out to see Bogart.

"You think there's any seats left?" Emma released Annie's arm as they approached the theater.

"If they still got candy, that's all I care about." Finn grinned and licked his lips.

Annie fell back a pace, watching Finn's easy stride, the confident set of his shoulders.

He looked back to check on her, but his eyes slipped past her. His smile vanished.

"What's the matter, Finn?" Annie turned around, but the street was empty.

"I don't know." Finn stopped. "I thought I saw something."

"Like what?"

"Like someone back there. Tailing us."

"Who'd do that?" She had no sooner said it than she thought about Ernie Finch.

"Come on." Finn waved for Annie to catch up, then forced a grin. "Maybe someone who doesn't like candy?"

She took one more look down the dark street, then slipped her arm through his. "Let's get there before they run out."

The Sunset Theater stood like a beacon halfway down the block on Andrews Avenue, its neon marquee glowing against the darkening sky. A small line had formed outside the main entrance, teenagers in their Sunday best, couples arm in arm, boys in uniform, while a separate, shorter line of black patrons waited at a side door.

"You'll get the candy and meet us inside?" Annie handed Finn some coins. He nodded and headed for the marquee.

The scent of roasting peanuts mingled with car exhaust in the evening air as Annie stood with Emma beside the narrow side entrance marked *Colored Only.* She glanced once toward the theater's front, where Finn had disappeared into the white folks' entrance with his handful of change and a list of candy requests tucked in his palm.

"I told you I don't need any candy." Emma adjusted the bobby pins behind her ear.

"Doesn't mean you won't eat it."

Inside, the stairwell smelled like waxed floors and something older, wood and damp paper and the faint mildew of long summers. Their shoes clacked on the worn steps as they climbed to the balcony. There people were already murmuring greetings while settling onto creaky seats at the front, wooden benches at the back. As children, she and Jack had often sat in the balcony, but at twenty-years-old, Annie wasn't a child anymore. She didn't care. Being crammed together up on the hard wooden seats with Emma was always more fun.

They found three empty seats near the front of the balcony. From there, the screen looked small but clear, framed by ornate molding and flanked by dusty red velvet curtains. The sound of the crowd below, white folks chatting and laughing, rose in uneven waves, muffled and far away. Annie's nerves were dancing in her belly. She didn't see Finn yet.

Then the lights dimmed.

The low buzz of conversation sank into silence, broken only by the sudden *click-click* of the projector flickering to life behind them. The screen flared white, then faded into the grainy black-and-white footage of an American flag whipping in the wind.

Annie felt Finn's presence before she saw him. His

shoulder brushed against hers as he slipped into the seat on her other side, warm and smelling of popcorn grease. He leaned in close and whispered, "Got everything but the Chuckles. Sold out."

His breath tickled her ear.

She turned, heart kicking up a notch in the dark, and saw the glint of his grin. He passed her a small paper sack, still warm, with Milk Duds and two Baby Ruth bars inside.

He reached around in front of her and placed a Tootsie Roll in Emma's hand.

On screen, the narrator's voice rose above martial drums:

"*Singapore falls to the Japanese in a stunning defeat for the British Empire...*"

Footage flickered of palm trees silhouetted against smoke, British troops with grim faces marching into captivity, the Union Jack lowered in slow motion.

The theater was hushed, all eyes on the screen, where American soldiers boarded transport ships, waving at the camera. Then women in overalls smiled from factory lines, sparks flying from welding torches.

"*Here at home, America answers the call*," the narrator declared.

"*On the farms, in the factories, in every neighborhood across this great land, freedom marches on.*"

Emma snorted, and Annie felt the movement in the seats surrounding hers.

The drums swelled. The flag flew. And the newsreel ended with an appeal for war bonds.

*The Maltese Falcon* pulled them into the dark streets of San Francisco. Humphrey Bogart's Sam Spade with his sharp suits and sharper tongue. The mysterious woman with her web of lies. Annie leaned forward, forgetting the war, forgetting Jack, forgetting everything but the story unfolding before her.

Then came the scene where a character named Gutman

revealed his gun. The sudden crack of the gunshot made Annie gasp and jump in her seat. Without hesitation, Finn's hand found hers in the darkness.

Annie froze, aware of every point where his skin touched hers. She'd known Finn her entire life, had clutched his hand countless times as children racing through the woods around Skeeter's Fish Camp. But this was different. His thumb moved, brushing over her knuckles, and a shiver raced up her arm that had nothing to do with fear.

She didn't pull away. Instead, she relaxed into his touch, their joined hands resting on the armrest between them. On her other side, Emma seemed lost in the film, unaware of the small but seismic shift taking place.

On screen, Sam Spade continued his investigation, trading barbs with the femme fatale. But for the next hour, Annie existed in two worlds: the crime-filled streets of the film and the small, electric space between her hand and Finn's.

As the film reached its conclusion, with Spade turning in the woman he loved to the police, Annie wondered what Jack would have thought—both of the film and of her. Would he approve of this tentative something growing between his sister and his best friend?

~

The night air wrapped around them as they left the theater, still caught up in the film's spell.

"That ending," Emma said, shaking her head. "I can't believe he turned her in."

"She killed his partner," Finn pointed out. "What was he supposed to do?"

"I know, but still." Emma sighed. "The way he looked at her, you could tell he loved her."

Annie nudged her friend's shoulder. "Since when are you such a romantic? I thought you'd be on the side of justice."

"Maybe I'm both." Emma pulled her sweater tight around her shoulders. "Justice and romance don't have to be enemies."

They turned off onto a quieter street that would take them north toward Emma's neighborhood. The streetlights were fewer here, the shadows between them deeper.

Emma stiffened beside Annie. "Let's cross," she whispered, but it was too late.

Following Emma's gaze, Annie spotted them: three figures lounging against a brick wall in an alley. Even in the dim light, she recognized Ernie Finch's wiry frame. Her stomach clenched.

"Well, look at what we got here, boys," he called, his high-pitched, nasal voice carrying in the quiet street. "Miss High-and-Mighty Annie Jeeves out for an evening stroll."

"Leave us alone, Ernie." Annie slipped her arm through Emma's.

"Or what? You gonna call your dead brother back to save you?"

Annie turned her head aside and bit her tongue.

Finn stepped forward. "Back off, Finch. Show some respect."

The other boys spread out like a net, blocking the sidewalk ahead.

"We're just heading home," Finn said.

Ernie spat on the ground. "Ain't talking to you, Taggart." His gaze slid to Emma. "Don't you all know there's laws about who you can take to the picture show?"

Annie felt Emma flinch. She pulled her friend's linked arm in tight and said, "We're not looking for trouble."

Ernie's laugh was ugly. "Course you're not, sweetheart. But you found it anyway, bringing your colored friend through decent parts of town after dark." He leaned forward, the smell of cheap liquor heavy on his breath. "Jack wouldn't like seeing his sister hanging around with..."

"Don't you dare speak his name."

"Big talk from a girl who gives it up to this ginger orphan." He jerked his chin toward Finn.

"That's enough," Finn said. "Now step aside before I make you."

"You and what army, Taggart?"

It happened fast after that. Ernie lunged at Finn, who ducked the first swing but caught the second square in the jaw. He staggered back, recovered, and drove his shoulder into the boy's midsection, sending them both crashing into a stack of empty crates outside a storefront.

"Run!" Finn shouted at Annie and Emma, just before another of Ernie's gang caught him from behind.

Emma pulled at Annie's arm, but Annie pulled free. "I'm not leaving him!"

"Two against five, Annie! We need help!"

Before Annie could respond, Ernie was on her, his bony fingers digging into her arm. He shoved Annie against the brick wall.

"You little—" he began, but Emma swung her purse hard into the side of his head. Ernie yelped and let go.

Then she saw Finn go down under the weight of the two other attackers. They were kicking him now, vicious blows to his ribs and back as he tried to curl into a protective ball.

"Stop it!" Annie screamed, launching herself toward them. "You're going to kill him!"

A recovered Ernie caught her around the waist, spinning her away. "Not so tough now, are you?" he hissed in her ear. "Let's see how you like..."

He never finished the sentence. A shadow detached itself from the alley, moving with startling speed.

One moment Ernie was holding Annie; the next, he was sprawled on the ground, blood streaming from his nose where a fist had connected with it.

That face under the brim of a flat cap. It was Will.

He stood tall and broad-shouldered over Ernie's fallen form. Then, he turned to the two boys still kicking Finn, grabbed one by the collar, and sent him tumbling into a trash can.

"What the hell?" the remaining attacker backed away, eyes wide.

Will helped Finn to his feet with one hand while keeping his eyes on Ernie.

The bully struggled to his feet. Blood still streamed from his nose. He touched his face. "It's broken."

"Be thankful that's all that's broken," Will replied.

One of his crew tugged at Ernie's sleeve. "Come on, man. Let's get out of here."

Ernie's eyes darted between Finn and Will, calculating.

"This ain't over." He pointed a bloody finger at Annie. "Your friends can't protect you forever, Jeeves."

"But we can tonight," Will said.

Ernie spat blood onto the sidewalk, then jerked his head at his gang. "Let's go." They retreated down the dark street.

Annie looked at Finn. His left eye was swelling, and blood trickled from a cut above his eyebrow.

"Are you all right?"

"Been better."

Emma stood beside her, clutching her purse, her breath coming in quick gasps.

Finn nodded to Will. "Thanks."

Will tipped his hat. Without another word, he faded into the darkness.

Annie stared into the alley where Will had vanished. She hadn't seen him in weeks, and then he appears when she needs him? The timing was too perfect, too convenient, like maybe he'd been the one watching them earlier? The thought should frighten her. Instead, she felt oddly protected.

Finn groaned, wiping blood from his mouth. "Who the hell was that?"

Annie exhaled. "I don't know. Lucky timing, I guess."

Emma's eyes met hers. Annie looked away.

They dropped Emma off at her porch. Her mother opened the door, eyes scanning their faces, the blood on Finn's jacket. "Thanks for getting her home safe." Miss Cora closed the door before they could say good night. They exchanged a look as they heard the lock click.

Annie and Finn walked the familiar path to the Jeeves' house in silence. The cold night air smelled of smoke from the fireplaces in the few homes that had them.

As they passed the stretch of the road where Finn had suggested they were being followed, Annie felt certain he'd been right. Whether it was Ernie or Will was the question.

They walked in silence until Finn stopped and braced himself stiff-armed against a fencepost.

"Finn?"

"Just... give me a second." He took a ragged breath. "It's just now hitting me. Keep thinking about those bastards. How many of them there were. How I couldn't protect you and Emma."

"You did protect us."

"No, I tried, but I couldn't have done it alone."

Annie didn't know what to say.

Finn spoke up again. "You know the part in the movie where Bogart kissed her, even knowing what she was?"

"Before he turned her in, you mean?"

"Yeah." He stopped walking. "I keep thinking about that. How sometimes you know something's going to hurt but you do it, anyway."

"Finn."

"I'm planning to enlist, Annie. In the Navy. Soon as Bean's settled somewhere safe."

She opened her mouth to protest, but he rushed on.

"I know what you're going to say. But watching those newsreels, remembering that U-boat we saw so close to shore. I just can't stay home any longer."

"Yes, you can." Her voice shook, torn between rage and pleading. "You can't leave. Jack is dead, Finn. And now you want to run off to join the Navy? Haven't you learned anything?"

"Annie, this isn't about Jack."

"Isn't it?" She was crying now. "First my brother, and now you want to go, too?"

"Annie, this is all about you. Protecting you. And Bean." He stepped closer. "Tonight, every bruise was worth it to keep you safe. But Ernie Finch is not the real enemy."

"Protecting us? It sounds more like you're abandoning us." She turned her back to him so that he couldn't see her tears.

"That's not fair, Annie. You know that's not true."

"Just go." She did not turn around.

"If that's what you want." He waited for her response, but she stayed silent. "All right then. Good night, Annie."

She heard his footsteps moving away toward the cottage he shared with his sister. When she could no longer hear him, she wrapped her arms around her midsection and let out a loud sob. Then she straightened and spun around, but he was gone.

# CHAPTER THIRTY

*Fort Lauderdale*
*April 2, 1942*

Annie's eyes burned from staring at the black water, searching for periscopes, debris, or survivors. Anything that didn't belong to the familiar Gulf Stream currents. Eight hours into their patrol, there was nothing but darkness and the steady slap of small waves against the hull.

Shifting her weight on the wooden seat eased the stiffness in her back. She'd volunteered for the midnight-to-dawn watch, but she hadn't managed any sleep on her off watch.

The cabin hatch slid open.

"Anything?" Emma asked.

Annie shook her head. "Just water and more water. What are you doing up? You should be sleeping."

"Can't. I think I'll make us something hot to drink." Her head disappeared back into the cabin. The soft glow of a kerosene lamp lit the underside of the mainsail. Annie stood up and slid the hatch closed. They were sailing without running lights, and all the port lights were blacked out on the inside.

The hatch opened half an hour later, and Emma emerged carrying a battered thermos and two metal mugs. Her dark eyes focused on keeping the thermos upright. She had come a long way in her ability to move around on the rolling boat, but her sea legs weren't quite second nature yet.

She settled down in the cockpit and began unscrewing the cap. "Here." Steam and the rich scent of coffee rose between them as she poured. "Thought you might need something strong enough to keep you awake. I mixed some of the last of the coffee with the chicory."

Annie smiled as she took the cup, letting the warmth seep into her palms. "Thanks."

In the moonlight, Emma's dark skin glowed like polished mahogany, and for a moment, Annie was struck by how beautiful her friend was. No wonder Jack had fallen for her.

"I heard a tanker got hit off Bermuda last week," Annie said. "Navy's keeping it quiet, but Fuller told me before we left."

Emma's face tightened. "It's been quiet for a while. Maybe the first U-boats had to return to Germany to resupply."

"They'll be back. That's what we're out here for," Annie said, trying to sound more confident than she felt. The *Tequesta* was just a wooden sailboat with an auxiliary engine, hardly a match for a German submarine. Up until now, they'd counted on the Germans not seeing them as a threat, but she'd heard about a patrol boat up north that had been rammed and sunk.

"Gramps told me they found another burnt body washed up near Lauderdale Beach yesterday. Young man. They think he was from that merchant ship that went down off Cuba."

"I'm afraid we'll find more bodies washing up before this

is over," Annie said. She remembered how, back at Christmas, they'd thought this war would be over by now.

They sat in silence for a while until Emma finally spoke up. "I haven't seen Finn around lately."

"No, not since he told me he wants to enlist."

Emma set down her mug. "So you haven't spoken to Finn in two weeks?"

"We've spoken. About boat supplies and weather patterns. I don't have anything more to say to him."

"Annie." Emma's voice held gentle reproach. "He'll be leaving soon."

"I know."

"Do you? You may come to regret throwing away time you can't get back." Emma paused. "Unless this is about that stranger. Will."

Annie gripped the wheel. "What about him?"

"You haven't mentioned him since that night."

"There's nothing to mention. He walked away. I haven't seen him since."

"But you've thought about him."

Annie didn't deny it. Will haunted her thoughts. His mysterious appearances, the way he'd fought to protect her, then vanished. Twice.

"I don't understand him," Annie finally said. "Or what he wants."

"Maybe that's the appeal." Emma studied her. "Finn wants to enlist, and that terrifies you. But Will? He's already gone. No risk of losing what you never had."

"That's not—"

"Annie, people change. They leave. And sometimes they don't come back." The pitch of Emma's voice rose. She cleared her throat. "You know what Jack told me once? He said you were the bravest person he knew, but you were also the most afraid of change."

"Em, the world was better before. When everything made sense. And besides, Jack didn't know everything."

"Annie, from my view, this world has never made sense. Maybe Jack didn't know everything, but he knew you." Emma paused. "And he knew Finn loved you long before you figured it out."

Annie's head snapped around. "What?"

"Oh, come on. The boy's been mooning over you since we were in high school. Jack used to tease him about it something awful."

"Finn? He never said anything."

"Because you were his best friend's little sister."

Annie pressed her palms against her eyes. "This is all wrong. The timing, everything."

"There's never a right time in war." Emma's voice was gentle. "Trust me, I know. Jack and I kept saying we'd wait until things were different, until people would accept us, until the world made sense." Her voice caught. "We ran out of time."

Annie felt tears threatening. "I don't know how to let Finn go."

"It's not up to you. If you love him—and I'm pretty sure you do—don't let him leave without telling him."

Emma stood, collecting the mugs. "My turn to check the charts."

Annie reached out and touched her friend's wrist. "Thanks, Em. You stay down there and get some sleep, too. Captain's orders."

~

The *Tequesta* slid deeper into the open water, leaving the sheltered coastline behind. Annie adjusted the trim of the mainsail, feeling the boat respond like a living thing. The boat made sense to her, and it comforted her. She knew how the old girl would react when she trimmed a sail or put the wheel hard over. It was like they were dance partners, and while Annie took the lead, she had complete confidence her partner could follow. Men, however, were completely unpredictable.

Of course, she loved Finn. But was she *in love* with him? Did she even know what that meant?

Annie flexed her stiff fingers on the wheel. The night air had grown cooler as they moved farther from shore, salt spray occasionally misting her face when the bow cut through a larger swell.

She basked in the sound of water against hull and wind through canvas. Annie had grown to love this nocturnal symphony, so different from the daytime chaos of crowded docks and shouting men.

Then, an unfamiliar sound interrupted her thoughts.

Annie straightened, her senses alert. A distant mechanical grumble.

"Emma."

Her friend was already coming up the companionway. "I heard it through the hull." She held the binoculars. "Where's it coming from?"

Annie inclined her head toward the southeast. "Out there."

The sound was irregular, a deep, muffled churning noise. It wasn't the steady rhythm of a fishing boat or the powerful thrust of a Navy patrol. This was something else, something trying to move quietly but not quite succeeding.

Emma scanned the darkness through the binoculars.

"Can't see anything yet. Too dark."

Annie squinted, willing her eyes to penetrate the gloom.

Then she saw it. A darker shadow against the night horizon, more visible when not looking directly at it.

"There," she whispered, pointing. "Just off the port bow, about forty degrees."

Emma swung the binoculars, her body going still as she focused.

"I see it." Her voice was faint. "Can't make out what it is, though. Too far and too dark."

Annie spotted the black smudge, visible only when the other vessel and the *Tequesta* crested waves at the same time. The mechanical sound grew louder, then began to fade again, as if the source were changing direction.

"Could be a fishing boat?"

"Not likely at this hour," Annie said. "But possible."

The sound faded until it was indistinguishable from the ambient noise of the ocean.

"What do you think?" Emma lowered the binoculars, the whites of her eyes bright.

Annie considered their options. Fuller had been explicit: observe and report, nothing more. They weren't equipped to chase unknown vessels in the darkness.

"Could've been anything," she said. "Fishing boat running without lights, Bahamian trader, maybe a pleasure craft stupid enough to be out at night."

The unspoken alternative hung in the air between them. A German U-boat surfacing to recharge batteries under cover of darkness, preparing for another day of hunting Allied shipping.

Emma retrieved the logbook from below, her pencil scratching against paper as she noted the time, course, and their observations. Their patrol had suddenly acquired purpose.

"Take the helm. I'll go calculate our position." Annie took the logbook and descended to the chart table. She plotted their location based on dead reckoning, the last lighthouse bearing she'd taken, estimating their drift.

Emma's face appeared in the companionway. "We should radio it in."

"Not yet. There are no other ships in sight, and if it is a U-boat, we'd just be announcing ourselves."

"You're the captain."

Emma returned to her bunk, and Annie returned to the helm. The adrenaline rush, not the coffee, made it easy to stay awake now.

"Think it was a U-boat, Jack? That wasn't just any boat. You felt it too, right?" Sometimes on night watches, she talked to her brother.

So far, he hadn't answered.

In another couple of hours of sailing, they'd reach the harbor entrance. Fuller Mansfield would be waiting for their report. She'd have to find a way to convey her certainty without sounding foolish.

A splash off the starboard bow caught her attention. Then another, closer to the boat. A sleek gray body arched through the water, followed by another, then a third. Dolphins. The bioluminescence glowed pale blue in their wake. They raced alongside the *Tequesta*, diving beneath the hull only to reappear on the other side, performing an elegant water ballet that never failed to lift Annie's spirits.

"Dolphins, starboard side!"

Emma emerged from the cabin, her tired face lighting up at the sight. She leaned over the gunwale to watch the playful mammals.

"Never gets old, does it?" Emma said, smiling.

Annie shook her head. "Jack used to say they were good luck."

"Then we could use about a dozen more," Emma said.

The dolphins stayed with them for several minutes, riding the pressure wave created by the boat's bow. Then, as suddenly as they'd appeared, they veered away, heading toward deeper water.

Annie tracked their departure, her gaze following their path toward the shore. That's when she noticed it from the corner of her eye. A quick, bright flash from the shoreline. She squinted, focusing on the spot. There it was again. A deliberate, rhythmic flashing.

Annie scanned the entire horizon all around them, but there was no sign of a vessel. Of course, she would not be able to spot a periscope.

"Emma," she said. "Take the wheel."

Annie ducked into the cabin, retrieving her hand-bearing compass from its bracket. When she returned to the deck, the flashing had grown faster, more urgent.

"What is it?"

"Don't know yet. Something flashed on shore."

Annie raised the compass to her eye, steadying herself against the boat's motion. She aligned the sight with the source of the flashing, waiting for the magnetic card to settle. Bearing: two hundred and twenty-three degrees. She logged the number in her mind, then swung to take another bearing on the Hillsboro Inlet Lighthouse. Three hundred and twenty degrees.

"Could be just someone moving their blackout curtains."

Annie shook her head. "Too bright. Too deliberate." She lowered the compass.

She climbed below and grabbed the parallel rulers and dividers at the chart table. She plotted their position based on the lighthouse bearing, then used the dividers to measure the distance to the point where her second bearing line intersected the coast. Six nautical miles south of the lighthouse, give or take. The area was sparsely populated. Wealthy winter residents who'd fled north after Pearl Harbor, had left their beachfront properties vacant.

Perfect for someone who didn't want to be noticed.

Annie climbed back into the cockpit. She watched another series of flashes.

"Morse code?" Emma asked.

"Looks like it. I just started learning it. This is coming too fast for me."

Emma was watching the shore through binoculars. "It's stopped," she reported. "The flashing. It's stopped."

Annie took the binoculars and scanned the shoreline where she'd seen the signal. Now that the sky was growing lighter, she was fairly certain the signal had been coming from the only two-story house on that stretch of beach. Had the sender spotted them? Or had they simply finished transmitting whatever message needed sending?

"Mark it in the log, exact time the signal stopped. And our best estimate of the location."

Emma nodded, returning to the logbook. When she'd finished, she said, "You really think it's connected to that boat we heard earlier?"

"I'd bet Jack's best fishing rod on it," Annie replied.

~

As they rounded the last bend in the river, the waterfront came into view, already alive with morning activity. A pair of elderly men sat on the municipal dock with cane poles, more interested in conversation than catching anything. The normality of the scene struck Annie as almost jarring after a night of patrolling for U-boats.

The *Tequesta*'s bow nudged against the dock pilings. Emma secured the bow line, looping it around the cleat in a figure-eight pattern.

"Can you finish securing the boat?" Annie asked.

"You go on. It's important."

Annie jumped onto the dock, with the chart and logbook tucked under her arm. She headed toward the small office the Coast Guard Auxiliary had set up for the Mosquito Fleet. She doubted anyone would be there this early, but she had to find out.

To her surprise, she spotted Mansfield himself standing outside the door, deep in conversation with a man in Army uniform. Whatever they were discussing, it wasn't good news.

Mansfield caught sight of her approaching and broke off his conversation. "Jeeves," he called, using her last name as he always did, despite her repeated requests to call her Annie. "Good timing. How was patrol?"

"We need to talk, sir," Annie said, glancing at the uniformed officer. "It's important."

Mansfield studied her face, then nodded. "Harris, this is Annie Jeeves, one of our patrol boat captains. Annie, Lieutenant Commander Robert Harris, ONI, Office of Naval Intelligence."

The intelligence officer was tall and lean, with close-cropped dark hair beneath his officer's cap.

"Ma'am," he said with a curt nod.

"Lieutenant Commander." Annie wasn't sure whether she was supposed to shake his hand or salute, so she just smiled. She turned back to Mansfield. "We saw something last night."

"Let's take this inside," Mansfield said, unlocking the office door.

The room was small and utilitarian, with maps pinned to the walls, and a radio setup in the corner. Annie spread her chart on the desk, pointing to the marked location.

"Spotted an unidentified vessel last night around 0200 hours. Here, roughly six miles offshore. Couldn't make out the details, too dark, too far, but the engine noise was unusual. Similar to the last time I sighted a U-boat, but farther away. We couldn't confirm." She flipped open her logbook. "However, at approximately 0445 this morning, we observed a signal being transmitted from shore. Light flashes, regular intervals, probably code, definitely intentional."

"Where exactly?"

Annie turned the page to the small chart she had sketched as they were motoring upriver. She pointed to the spot she'd marked with pencil. "It was coming from here," she said, tapping the intersection of the lines. "A stretch of beach north of Pompano. The signals stopped as it started to get light, probably when they spotted our boat."

Mansfield and the Lieutenant Commander exchanged glances.

"You're certain about this location?" Mansfield asked, studying the chart.

"Yes, sir. I took bearings. Twice, to be sure."

"And you saw no vessels in the vicinity that might have been receiving these signals?" Lieutenant Commander Harris asked.

Annie shook her head. "None visible on the surface. But we had seen and heard the other vessel earlier in the vicinity. At sea, it's unlikely we'd spot a periscope."

The ONI officer pulled Mansfield aside, speaking in low tones. She heard fragments. "Imagination... reliable sources... just a girl."

Then Mansfield shook his head. "I'll vouch for her," he said loudly enough for her to hear.

After a moment, they both stepped back to her.

"Miss Jeeves," Lieutenant Commander Harris said. "Could you identify this location if you saw it from land?"

Annie nodded. "Yes, sir. I'd recognize the house."

"Good. Let's go."

"Now?"

"Now," Mansfield confirmed, already reaching for his hat. "Lieutenant Commander Harris has a vehicle outside."

Questions buzzed in Annie's mind as she followed the men outside toward a military jeep parked around the side of the building. A young man sat behind the wheel, snapping to attention as the officer approached.

"North along the coast." Harris turned to Annie. "You'll need to direct us when we get close to the location."

Annie climbed into the back seat beside Mansfield, aware of her rumpled clothes. She grabbed hold of her braid and tried to keep the loose hairs out of her eyes. The jeep lurched forward, weaving through Fort Lauderdale's morning traffic.

They turned north on the coastal highway that ran along the barrier island. To their right, the Atlantic stretched out beyond the white dunes. To their left, beach houses and small hotels dotted the landscape, many of them shuttered.

As they approached Pompano, Annie studied the terrain, matching it to the mental map she'd formed earlier. "Slow down," she said. "It should be somewhere along here."

The driver reduced speed. Annie scanned the beachfront, looking for anything that matched what she'd seen through her binoculars.

"There," she said suddenly, pointing to a large, white-painted house set back from the road among a stand of Australian pines. "That's where the signal was coming from."

Lieutenant Commander Harris nodded to the driver, who pulled onto a narrow driveway. The two-story house with a wrap-around veranda faced the ocean.

"Stay in the vehicle," Harris instructed the driver. To Annie and Mansfield, he said, "Follow me, but stay behind until I've secured the premises."

The lieutenant commander drew his pistol and approached the house. Annie and Mansfield followed at a distance.

Shutters covered the windows, and no smoke rose from the chimney despite the cool morning. Harris tried the front door, found it locked, and moved around to the side of the house. Annie and Mansfield trailed behind.

At the rear, Harris discovered a door with a broken lock. He motioned for them to stay back, then slipped inside, weapon ready.

Long minutes passed. Annie shifted uneasily. Finally, he reappeared at the door.

"It's clear," he said. "You both need to see this."

Most of the interior of the house was dim, windows shuttered. The furniture was draped in white sheets. But as they followed Harris through to a bright sunroom facing the ocean, Annie saw signs of recent occupation.

A telescope on a tripod stood by the window, positioned for a clear view of the Atlantic. Beside it lay a powerful flashlight with a jury-rigged shutter attachment that could create the dot-dash patterns of Morse code. On a nearby table, empty food cans and dirty plates suggested someone had been living there for days, perhaps weeks.

"My God," Mansfield said, picking up a pad of paper covered with notations. "Times, dates, ship movements."

Annie stared at the evidence. Someone had been using this abandoned beach house to track Allied shipping and signal the information to German submarines offshore.

"There's more," Harris said grimly, leading them to a back bedroom.

A bed stood unmade in one corner. A pile of clothes lay on the floor, civilian clothes. Whoever had been here had dressed to blend in.

"The radio's gone. Managed to take that, but it was a hasty departure," Harris said, touching the coffee mug on the desk.

"He must have spotted us when the light started to come up."

The ONI officer nodded. "Which means he's in the wind now."

Harris turned to Annie and Mansfield. "Let's step outside. I need to speak with both of you."

They followed him onto the veranda.

"What you've seen here today is classified," Harris said. "You can't discuss this with anyone, not your crew, not your family, not each other after today. As far as anyone knows, you reported a suspicious light, nothing more. We investigated and found an empty house. End of story."

"But sir," Annie began, "my crew already knows about the signal."

"Tell them exactly what I just said. An empty house. No evidence. A false alarm."

Annie glanced at Mansfield, who nodded slightly. "He's right. If word gets out that we've found a spy nest, he or they will simply change their methods and locations. We need them to think they're still operating undetected."

The logic made sense, but the idea of lying to Emma again didn't sit well with Annie.

"There's something else you should understand," Mansfield added. "If someone saw your boat and felt threatened enough to abandon this post, they knew a vessel spotted them. The *Tequesta* is a unique boat. They may be able to recognize it."

Annie reached for the porch railing to balance herself. It hadn't occurred to her that she and Emma might be targeted for their reporting.

"So, what do we do?"

"Keep to your routine," Harris said. "But be vigilant. Report anything unusual immediately. Not just at sea, but in town, on the docks, anywhere. And remember, not a word about what you've seen here today."

Annie nodded, though her mind was already racing ahead to all the precautions she'd need to take.

The jeep ride back to Fort Lauderdale passed in silence. By the time she reached the dock where the *Tequesta* was moored, the morning was well advanced.

Emma was gone. Annie would have to face her later, would have to look her best friend in the eye and tell her what she'd been ordered to say. An empty house. No evidence. A false alarm.

# CHAPTER THIRTY-ONE

*Fort Lauderdale*
*April 14, 1942*

Annie leaned over the nautical chart spread across her bed, her pencil tracing the intricate contours of the Florida coastline. She'd been up since dawn, cross-referencing the old chart against her observations from recent patrols.

"Annie!" her mother called. "Come down here, please."

"I'm working, Ma." Annie didn't shift her eyes from the chart.

"Annie Louise Jeeves, get down here this instant."

Annie sighed and set down her pencil. Using all three of her names meant Mama was serious. She rose from the bed, and stretched to work out the stiffness from sitting hunched over for hours.

She traipsed down the hall, stopping short when she saw Finn standing in their front room. Her mother stood beside him.

"Finn." Annie looked from one to the other. "What are you doing here?"

"I invited him," her mother said. "I've been helping him work out arrangements for Bethany."

Annie's stomach tightened. "Arrangements?"

"Someone needs to look after her when I ship out," Finn said.

"You might have mentioned this to me."

"Hard to mention anything when you won't talk to me," Finn said.

Her mother picked up a basket from a side table. "I need to tend to the garden out back. You two sort this out."

The screen door banged shut, leaving them in awkward silence. Annie crossed her arms, aware she was wearing her oldest work dress with pencil smudges on the sleeves.

"You could have talked to me," she said.

"I tried. You kept finding excuses to avoid me." Finn shifted his weight. "Look, Annie, I know you're angry."

"No, not angry."

"I'm not doing this to hurt you."

"I already lost Jack."

He took a step closer. "I know."

She closed her eyes as a rush of heat made her dizzy.

"But Annie, we're losing time right now. You've barely spoken to me in weeks. If something happens to me over there, is this really how you want to leave things?"

"Don't say that." She turned her head aside. "I can't even think about that."

She wanted to tell him that she couldn't bear to lose him, to tell him how much she loved him.

But before she could begin, someone knocked at the front door. She turned back to face him. The lines etched on Finn's face made him look older, but in his eyes, she saw hope.

She held up one finger, then moved to open the door. Through the screen, she could see a man in a rumpled suit, wire-rimmed glasses sliding down his nose.

She opened the screen door. "Can I help you?"

The man removed his hat, revealing sandy-blond hair that fell forward into his eyes. "Miss Jeeves? My name's Frank Chandler. Fuller Mansfield suggested I speak with you."

Annie blinked in confusion. "Oh. I—"

She glanced back at Finn, who was already heading for the back door. "I should go," he said.

"No, wait!" Annie reached out, caught his arm. To Chandler, she called out, "Could you please give us a moment?"

"Of course." Chandler stepped out onto the porch and turned to face the street.

Annie turned to Finn, her hand still on his arm. "Finn, I need to meet with this man. It's important. But we're not done talking."

Something shifted in his expression. "Let me know when you have time. I'll let myself out through the back." He slipped into the kitchen and soon after, she heard the back door close with a bang.

She wasn't good at this. Jack might be gone, but he still cast a long shadow over her life. Things were so much easier when they were kids. Annie stood inside, staring at the ceiling, trying to compose herself. She needed to talk to this man outside. Whatever Chandler wanted, she felt her morning was about to become even more complicated.

"Mr. Chandler, how can I help you?" She opened the screen door.

He turned to face her. "Is there somewhere we might talk privately?" He reached into his breast pocket and withdrew a small leather wallet, which he flipped open to reveal an official-looking identification card with his photograph. "I'm with the United States Government," he said. Annie noticed he held it just far enough away that she couldn't read the fine print.

He returned the wallet to his pocket. "I work at a new agency. We coordinate intelligence reporting."

Annie crossed her arms. "And what does that have to do with me?"

The man tapped his fingers against his thigh in an odd rhythmic pattern. "Fuller mentioned your talent for observation. Your eye for detail."

"Mr. Chandler, I'm already doing night patrols. If Mr. Mansfield had something to ask of me, why wouldn't he ask me himself?"

"Because this isn't Coast Guard business," the man said. "It's something more sensitive." He glanced around the porch, then lowered his voice. "I'd rather not discuss the details here. Would you be willing to walk with me?"

Annie hesitated. There was something about Mr. Chandler that unsettled her, but also intrigued her.

"Just a moment," she said, and stepped back inside, letting the screen door swing shut.

In the kitchen, her mother was sitting on a stool, snapping beans into a bowl on her lap. "Who is that?" she asked without looking up.

"A Mr. Chandler," Annie said, reaching for her shoes by the door. "He says he knows Mr. Mansfield. Wants to talk to me about some government agency."

Her mother looked up, eyebrows raised. "Government work?"

"I'm not sure yet," Annie admitted, slipping on her canvas shoes. "But I'm going to find out. We're just going to walk down to the river. I won't be long."

"Annie, you be careful. These are strange times, and people aren't always what they seem."

Annie nodded. "I'll be careful, Mama. And I'll be back for lunch."

She returned to the porch where Chandler waited, hat back on his head.

"Alright, Mr. Chandler," she said, pulling the door closed behind her. "Let's walk."

They turned onto Waverly Road, where larger homes faced the north fork of the river. Many had docks extending into the water where fishing boats and pleasure craft bobbed in the current.

"You grew up in Edgewater, at a place called Skeeter's Fish Camp," Chandler said after they'd walked half a block in silence. It wasn't a question.

Annie glanced at him. "Yes. My family moved here in '37."

"Because of the Depression?"

"Because people hadn't been able to afford to go fishing or camping for a while." She felt irritated by his presumption, accurate though it was. "My father was a fishing guide. No tourists, no business."

Chandler nodded, his eyes fixed ahead. "And you attended Fort Lauderdale High School, graduating in June 1940." He pulled a handkerchief from his pocket and cleaned his glasses with methodical strokes.

Annie's steps faltered. She hadn't expected him to know so much about her. "Mr. Chandler, I'd appreciate knowing what this is about before we continue this inventory of my life."

He replaced his glasses and folded the handkerchief with precise movements. "I'm trying to establish that I'm not approaching you out of the blue, Miss Jeeves. Fuller Mansfield recommended you, but I need to confirm that his assessment is accurate."

"Anybody can watch what's going on around them."

"Fuller mentioned your keen ability to observe, record, and analyze. Your talent for map making." He glanced at her.

"Your artistic abilities. He said you can sketch anything with remarkable accuracy after seeing it only once."

Annie flushed, uncomfortable with the praise, yet unable to deny it. Since childhood, she'd been able to recreate faces, and places with near-perfect recall.

"That's a bit of an exaggeration," she said. "But I do have a memory for details."

"Combined with your interest in navigation and mapmaking," Chandler continued, "it makes for a unique set of abilities."

They walked past a row of royal palms lining the street. A man watering his victory garden, nodded to them as they passed.

"Tell me about your work with the Mosquito Fleet." He smiled as though he found the name amusing.

Annie considered her response. "We patrol the coastline, watch for suspicious activities, and report anything unusual."

"What do you look for when you're on patrol?" he asked.

"Changes," Annie said. "Anything that's different from the last time. A boat that doesn't belong. Lights where there shouldn't be lights. That sort of thing."

"And your sketching. How does that fit into your patrol work?"

"I don't sketch for the Mosquito Fleet," Annie said. "But I've always kept sketchbooks, and I update our charts or sketch my own. I record things that interest me, or that might be useful later."

"May I?" He gestured to a small stone wall that bordered a property ahead. Without waiting for her answer, he sat and withdrew a small notebook from his inside pocket.

Annie remained standing, watching as he flipped through several pages. He turned the notebook toward her. "Does this look familiar?" he asked.

It was a sketch. Annie recognized it as Port Everglades.

"It's the port," she said. "Though it's not quite right. The channel markers are in the wrong positions, and this section here," she pointed without touching the page, "shows water depths that are inaccurate. Anyone using this to navigate would run aground."

Chandler's eyes narrowed. "How recently have you been to the port?"

"A couple of days ago. We were out on patrol."

"And you're certain these depths are wrong?"

Annie nodded. "Absolutely. The channel was dredged last year to accommodate larger naval vessels. It's deeper than before here, but shallower up here where they dumped the fill." She studied the sketch. "This drawing combines old information with new. See here? This building was only completed two months ago, but the channel depths are from at least two years back."

Chandler closed the notebook and returned it to his pocket. "Excellent observation, Miss Jeeves. That's the sort of information we're looking for."

"We?" Annie said.

He stood, adjusting his hat. "Let's continue our walk. There's a quiet spot ahead where we can speak more freely."

They were nearing the stretch where the homes gave way to vacant lots where the houses disappeared and the land grew wilder.

"There," he said, nodding toward a bench in a vacant lot. "We can talk there without being overheard."

Annie sat at one end of the bench, angling her body slightly toward Mr. Chandler. The water before them glittered with sunlight, broken only by the wake of a passing boat or the splash of a jumping fish.

Chandler gazed out at the water for a long moment. "Do you consider yourself a patriotic person, Miss Jeeves?"

Annie frowned at the unexpected question. "I suppose I

do. But I imagine most Americans would say the same these days."

"Perhaps. But there's a difference between supporting the war effort and being willing to take personal risks for your country."

Annie felt a chill. "You think I should be taking more risks?"

"You possess the skills that make a good intelligence operative," he replied. "Fuller Mansfield speaks highly of your observational abilities, your memory for detail, your quick thinking. Before we continue," he said, reaching into his inside pocket, "I need to ask you to sign this." He produced a single sheet of paper. At the head of the document there was an official government seal and the words *Oath of Secrecy*.

*I, Anne Jeeves, do solemnly swear that I will not, directly or indirectly, disclose, reveal, or communicate, or make available in any way, shape, or form to any unauthorized person any classified information or any information obtained in connection with my association with the office of the COI. I fully understand that failure to comply with this obligation will result in severe penalties including prosecution under the Espionage Act of 1917.*

At the bottom was a line for her signature and the date.

She looked up at Mr. Chandler. "You want me to sign this paper before you've even told me what this is about?"

"I do." His voice was matter-of-fact. "What I'm about to share with you is classified information. If you're unwilling to keep it confidential, I can't proceed." He tapped a finger against the document. "This isn't a commitment. It ensures that our conversation today remains between us."

Annie considered her options. She could refuse to sign and walk away now. Or she could sign and discover what government work Fuller Mansfield thought her suited for. She wasn't committing herself to whatever it was this man was offering. Her curiosity won out.

"Do you have a pen?" she asked.

Chandler produced a fountain pen from his breast pocket. Annie signed her name with a fluid motion.

"Thank you." He blew on the paper to dry the ink, then returned the signed document to his pocket. "Now we can speak freely." He settled back on the bench. "Have you heard of the COI, Miss Jeeves?"

Annie shook her head.

"It's a new agency, formed by President Rosevelt since the start of this war. COI stands for Coordinator of Information. It's dedicated to collecting and analyzing information or intelligence related to national security. I work for the counterintelligence branch here on the home front." He paused, allowing her to absorb this information. "We believe there is at least one German agent operating in South Florida, possibly more."

Annie nodded. "I guess I can tell you then that I am aware of that."

"Yes. Your actions in the field brought me here today. It's not widely known yet, but two ships were hit recently off Cape Canaveral. The Gulf America and the Leslie. This is a region rich in targets both at sea and on land with Port Everglades and the military installations nearby. The Naval Air Station, the Coast Guard facilities, the shipping channels."

Annie thought of Port Everglades, and how the port was building and expanding every day.

"Several months ago, a partially-inflated rubber boat washed ashore off Ponte Vedra. And more recently, we have intercepted odd radio transmissions. They're in code, of course, but our cryptographers have broken some of it."

"Sent from around here?" she asked.

He nodded. "The house you led us to was probably the location. But he or they will have moved now."

Annie thought about all the vacant homes in the area. Plenty to choose from.

"That's where people like you become invaluable, Miss Jeeves. We need eyes and ears in the community. People who know the area, who can recognize what belongs and what doesn't, who notice minor changes and inconsistencies."

"What would you want me to do?" she asked.

"Observe. Report. Nothing that would put you in direct danger," he said. "You would continue your normal routines. Your fishing charters, your Mosquito Fleet duties, but with a heightened awareness. We'd be particularly interested in newcomers to the area, especially those showing interest in the port or military facilities. People asking unusual questions, taking photographs, making sketches."

"Like me," Annie said, with a hint of irony. She had sketchbooks filled with drawings of the harbor, boats, and coastline.

"Like you," he acknowledged with a small smile. "Which is why you're well-positioned to recognize others doing the same with less innocent motives. You know the difference between an artist's interest and something more calculated."

Annie considered what he was proposing. It didn't sound like he was asking her to do anything she wasn't already doing.

"There would be compensation, of course. Not substantial, but something to acknowledge your time and risk."

Annie shook her head. "I wouldn't do it for money."

Chandler studied her for a long moment. "That's why Fuller recommended you, Miss Jeeves. He said you have not only the skills but the character for this work."

"And if I notice something suspicious? What then?"

"You would have a way to contact me discreetly. I would

assess the information and determine next steps." He paused. "I should be clear, Miss Jeeves. This work requires absolute discretion. You couldn't discuss it with anyone. Not your family, not your friends, not your coworkers. As far as the world would know, you're simply Annie Jeeves, skipper of the *Tequesta*."

She thought of her mother, who worried when she was an hour late returning home; of her father, who still saw her as his little girl despite her twenty years; of Emma, her best friend, who shared everything with Annie. And what about Finn? Could she keep a secret part of her life hidden from them all?

"I don't expect an answer today," he said. "It's a significant commitment, and not one to be made in haste. Take some time to consider it." He reached into his pocket and produced a small white card with nothing on it but a telephone number. "When you've made your decision, or if you observe something that can't wait, you can reach me at this number. Ask for Mr. Drake. That's the name I use for these contacts."

Annie took the card, its simple white surface belying the complexity of what it represented. "And if I decide not to get involved?"

"Then you destroy that card, forget this conversation ever happened, and continue with your life." Chandler picked up his hat and placed it back on his head. "But I hope you'll say yes, Miss Jeeves. Not to be overly dramatic, but your country needs people like you."

He rose from the bench and offered his hand. Annie stood and shook it.

"However you decide," he said, "I trust you'll honor the confidentiality agreement you signed. What we've discussed here goes no further."

Annie nodded. "I understand."

Mr. Chandler tipped his hat, turned, and walked away, leaving Annie alone with a small white card in her hand.

She slipped the card into the pocket of her skirt and sat back down on the bench. What just happened? There was the river that she knew and loved, but the world around it had changed. It was one thing to see a telescope and cans of food in a house and be told to forget she had ever seen it. Quite another to be asked to look for spies in her community.

As she walked toward home, the neighborhood looked different. Yes, there were the same weathered cottages with their tin roofs and screened porches. The same neighbors going about their morning routines. But Annie saw it all through fresh eyes, each detail now laden with potential significance. Who lived in that yellow house on the corner? The man washing his car across the street—had he moved in before or after Pearl Harbor? The radio antenna rising from behind the Petersons' house. Had it always been that tall?

Annie's hand drifted to her pocket, feeling the slight stiffness of the card through the fabric. She could destroy it when she got home. Tear it into tiny pieces and flush it away, pretend the morning's conversation had never happened.

But she knew she wouldn't.

When she turned onto Coontie Court, she saw Will leaning against an oak tree. He was only a couple of blocks from her house. She couldn't remember telling him where she lived.

His eyes looked shadowed and tired. She thought he looked different. Older. Thinner.

"Annie?" Will flicked a cigarette to the ground.

"Will. What are you doing here?"

"I've been looking for you. I wanted to see you."

"Me?"

"You weren't at your boat." Will ran a hand through his

hair, and Annie noticed it was longer than the last time she'd seen him.

"Guess I've been busy," Annie said. She wondered how he knew where to find her, but wasn't sure she wanted to know the real answer.

"I've been trying to stay away. You've done enough for me. But I don't know folks around here."

She opened her mouth to say something, but she didn't know where to begin.

"Look," Will said. "About the other night."

"That was almost a month ago. You just disappeared, Will. You seem to do that a lot."

"Your friends were with you."

"An answer for everything, huh?"

"It's not like that. I'm trying to find work," Will said.

"Oh. Well, that shouldn't be hard from what I hear. Able-bodied men are needed everywhere."

Will pointed down the road toward her house. "Want to walk?"

Annie hesitated. "All right. Just for a bit."

Will fell into step beside her.

"You didn't think I'd stick around, did you?" Will asked.

"It's been a while, so I thought maybe you'd gone back north. Like you said you wanted to."

"Not yet," Will said. "Not until I have to." And then he added, "I can't stop thinking about you, Annie."

The truth of it was that she thought about him, too. Wondering where he was, remembering drying him off that night and wrapping him in blankets. He was an intriguing man.

"I have to get home, Will. I promised Mama I'd be back for lunch." She knew she could invite him, but she decided against it.

"Annie, does your father know anyone who's hiring?" Will's voice had an urgency she hadn't heard before.

"I don't know," Annie said. "Maybe at Dooley's shipyard."

Will's face lit up. "Yeah?"

"They almost always need help."

"I'd really appreciate it if you could find out."

"I'll ask," Annie said.

They walked together a few more paces, and Will studied her with those sharp eyes. "You seem different," he said. "What's up?"

"Nothing," Annie said too quickly.

"You sure?"

She didn't answer.

They reached the corner of the next street, and Annie stopped.

"I should go," she said, not meeting his eyes.

"You won't forget to ask about Dooley's," Will said.

"Promise I won't."

The screen door creaked as she pushed it open and prepared to lie to her mother about where she'd just been and who she had talked to. She'd been right when she told herself earlier that this day was about to get a whole lot more complicated.

# CHAPTER THIRTY-TWO

*Fort Lauderdale*
*April 18, 1942*

The boards creaked under Annie's bare feet as she walked down the dock with the picnic basket hooked on her arm. Behind her, Emma juggled Jack's oilskin jacket and a crate of Coca-Cola bottles—supplies for their outing to Whiskey Creek.

Finn was bent over in the launch, checking the outboard motor. When Emma had shared her plans for this Saturday picnic, she'd failed to mention Finn. He glanced up when he heard their footsteps, and his smile revved her pulse up a notch.

He groaned when she handed him the picnic basket. "Your mom outdid herself. Feels like enough to feed us for a week."

"Woody sent a food shipment on the train," Annie said. "The chickens are laying, and we've got egg salad sandwiches."

Emma set her crate down on the dock. "I doubt the food will last that long with Finn around."

Mama had been up since dawn, packing food as if they were embarking on a transatlantic voyage rather than a day trip to Whiskey Creek. Annie suspected Emma had let her in on the secret third mouth to feed.

As she surveyed their preparations, she felt a strange hollow sensation in her chest. The last time they'd gone to Whiskey Creek, Jack had been with them.

"We should head out before the tide changes," Annie said. "I'd rather ride it downriver than fight it."

"Hold up!" a male voice called from the shore.

Annie recognized the voice. Will jogged down the dock toward them, wearing khaki pants and a buttoned shirt a size too big for his frame. His blond hair was combed back, but the breeze had already loosened several strands.

Annie saw Emma stiffen. "What's he doing here?" she whispered.

"I don't know." She hadn't seen Will since their encounter near her house several days ago. She'd asked her father about job opportunities at Dooley's, as promised, but Will had never followed up.

He reached them, out of breath. "Morning," he said, nodding to each of them.

Finn straightened up in the boat. "Well, I'll be damned! You're the fella from outside the Sunset last month, aren't you? The one who jumped in when Ernie Finch was causing trouble?"

Will shrugged, looking self-conscious. "Just didn't like the odds. Three against one didn't seem fair."

Finn extended his hand. "Thanks, buddy. You throw a mean right hook."

Will took the offered hand, a half-smile on his face. He

introduced himself, then said, "Been a while since I've been in a scrap like that."

Annie exchanged a look with Emma, whose brows had drawn together.

"You heading out?" Will asked, nodding toward the gear in the boat.

"Picnic at Whiskey Creek." Finn spoke before Annie could say anything. "Perfect day for it."

"Sounds nice."

Annie remembered telling Will about the spot.

A silence followed. Emma shifted her weight from one foot to the other, her hands on her hips. Will smiled at her like an over-eager puppy.

Finn, oblivious to the tension, broke the silence. "Hey, why don't you join us? Plenty of room in the boat, and more than enough food."

"I wouldn't want to intrude."

"Not intruding if you're invited," Finn insisted. "Right, Annie?"

Annie felt Emma's eyes boring into her. She knew what her friend was thinking: they knew next to nothing about this man. But she also recalled the way Will had looked the night she'd found him in the water. Lost and desperate.

"There's room," Annie said. "If you want to come."

Will's face brightened. "I'd like that. Thanks."

Emma turned away.

"Well, hop in," Finn said, moving aside to make room. "We're burning daylight."

Will stepped into the launch and settled himself on the center bench. Finn resumed his inspection of the outboard motor while Annie untied the painter. Emma remained standing on the dock, hesitating.

Emma leaned close. "You sure about this?"

Annie glanced at Will, who was engaged in conversation with Finn. "He helped Finn. And he's..." Her voice trailed off.

Emma sighed. "Don't say I didn't warn you." She stepped into the boat, choosing the bow seat furthest from Will.

Finn pulled the starter cord on the outboard, and the engine sputtered to life with a cloud of blue smoke. Annie stepped in, pushed them away from the dock, and settled on the center seat next to Will.

The breeze picked up as they moved into the center of the river. Emma pulled out the hooded jacket, which she slipped on despite the warm April day. She tugged the hood forward, obscuring her face from view.

Annie watched her friend's ritual. She reached for Emma's hand and squeezed it, but her dark eyes remained lowered in the shadow of the hood.

Will glanced between the two young women, his brow furrowing, but he said nothing. Instead, he turned his attention to the passing scenery, the grand houses set back from the water, their docks jutting into the river.

As they rounded a bend, Annie tensed. The Finch property came into view. The ramshackle collection of buildings included an old fishing boat up on blocks and a sagging dock where Ernie's younger brothers often lounged.

Finn cut the engine to low idle, reducing its noise. Annie and Finn scanned the shoreline, alert for movement. The Finch dock appeared empty, but that didn't mean there weren't eyes following them from behind curtains.

Sensing the tension, Will asked, "That's where those boys live?"

Annie nodded. "The Finches. Bad news all around."

"Keep your eyes open," Finn advised. "Ernie's daddy is the worst of the lot."

They passed the property without incident, and Finn opened the throttle again. Emma remained hunched beneath her hood, but Annie felt her friend's tension easing as they put distance between themselves and the Finch place.

The river widened, the houses grew more sparse, and soon they were approaching the juncture where the canal merged into Port Everglades.

They had to dodge around a Bahamian trader heading for a spot on the dock between a Coast Guard patrol boat and a cargo ship flying Navy colors. Will turned in his seat, eyes wide and tracking the moving crane offloading steel drums onto the dock. "Do they refuel the patrol boats here, or just resupply?" he asked.

Annie blinked. "I don't know," she said. "Both, I think?"

"Mmm." Will's gaze lingered on the docks. Then he smiled, catching her watching him. "Just curious. I've never seen a working port during wartime."

Once clear of the entrance channel, Finn steered them toward the opening to Whiskey Creek, partially hidden by a tangle of mangroves. He slowed the outboard as they navigated through the narrow channel, the murky water dappled with shadows.

"It's like another world," Will said.

Annie couldn't disagree. Whiskey Creek had always felt separate from the rest of Fort Lauderdale, a secret place preserved by its inaccessibility.

As they rounded the last bend, the creek opened into a cove. Beyond that, they could see the strip of sand that separated the mangroves from the vast Atlantic. Finn cut the engine as they drifted toward shore, the sudden silence broken only by the calls of gulls.

"We're here," he announced, jumping into the knee-deep water.

Will helped pull the boat onto the pale sand and tied the boat to a mangrove root.

Annie turned to give Emma a hand to climb out of the

boat, while Finn grabbed the picnic basket and some of the gear.

Annie stood for a moment. How many times had they come here with Jack?

"You okay?" Finn asked.

Annie blinked. "Fine," she said. "Just remembering."

Finn nodded, "Hard not to."

Emma joined them, having shed her jacket. She linked her arm through Annie's. "He'd want us to enjoy it."

Annie forced a smile. "I know he would. I don't know how you stay so strong."

They meandered through the Australian pines and the sea grass. It was not the explosive run of their last visit. Soon, the white sand beach stretched before them, empty and inviting. To the north, the outline of the jetties at the entrance to Port Everglades was just visible. Will followed a few paces behind, observing the port and the surroundings.

Annie spread the faded quilt across the sand. Emma unpacked the picnic basket, arranging egg salad sandwiches, a jar of dill pickles, Mama's lemon cookies, and the bottles of Coca-Cola. Finn took off to gather driftwood for a small fire. Meanwhile, Will stood apart, watching them.

"You gonna help or just stand there looking pretty?" Annie called to him, immediately regretting the flirtatious edge to her words.

Will's smile widened, though his eyes remained watchful. "What needs doing?"

"Help Finn with the wood," Emma suggested. "Fire won't build itself."

Will nodded and moved off to follow Finn. Annie watched them for a moment, Finn's easy, open stride contrasting with Will's more measured movements. She caught Emma's raised eyebrow and shrugged.

"What?" she asked.

"Nothing," Emma said, but her expression said otherwise. "Just wondering why he's really here."

"Because Finn invited him." Annie arranged the napkins.

"Mmm-hmm," Emma hummed. "Seems you got your hands full, girlfriend."

Before Annie could respond, the men returned with armloads of wood. Finn dropped his pile with a theatrical groan and flopped onto the quilt.

"I'm starving," he announced. "Feed me before I waste away."

Emma rolled her eyes but handed him a sandwich. "For the drama queen."

Will set his wood down more carefully and accepted the Coke Annie offered. Their fingers brushed, and Annie felt a small jolt.

Finn began discussing his work at Dooley's. "Keepin' me busy," he admitted. "But it's good work. Busy as all get-out since the war started."

"What kind of ships are you building?" Will asked.

"Sub chasers mostly. They say we might start on some minesweepers, too. Navy's ordering them fast as we can build 'em."

Annie watched Will. There was something *too* deliberate about his questions, a focus in his blue eyes that reminded her of Frank Chandler.

"Must be interesting work." Will leaned forward. "Are they hiring?"

Finn shrugged. "Depends on the day you ask. We're still ramping up production." He took another bite. "They're hiring new workers every week. Depends on what they need."

"I'd love to see it. The shipyard, I mean."

"Not as easy as it used to be to stroll in," Finn said. "They've got guards at the gates now. ID badges. Got to go through security checks."

"Even workers?"

"Especially workers." Finn laughed. "The military's worried about sabotage. A guy got fired last week just for having a German-sounding name."

Will looked surprised. "Seems extreme."

"War makes people jumpy," Emma said.

Will turned to Annie. "What do you think?"

"Better safe than sorry, you know." *Or at least he should.* "Especially with U-boats sinking ships right off the beach."

"Must be nice working at the port." Will waved his hand toward the harbor.

"Dooley's is inland. Upriver from town." Finn went on, oblivious of Annie's discomfort. "They expanded the facility back in January. Doubled the production capacity."

Will took a long drink of Coca-Cola. "Sounds like steady work."

Annie changed the subject. "Finn won't be there much longer anyway," she said.

"Oh yeah? You planning to enlist?"

Finn nodded. "Already signed the papers. Need to finish a project at the yard before I go, though."

"Navy?"

"Figure I might as well use what I know. Boats and engines—that's about all I'm good for."

"You're good for plenty," Emma said.

Annie stared out at the ocean.

Finn said, "I always intended to follow Jack."

"Jack didn't have a choice," she snapped.

"Not much of one on when he went," Finn said, "but you know he was always gonna go. He wanted to fly. It's the right thing for me too, Annie."

"The right thing," she repeated. "Like it was the right thing for Jack to go die in his first month over there? That kind of right thing?"

"Annie!" Emma's eyes were wide with tears.

Finn's face paled. "That's not called for, Annie."

"None of it's called for!" Annie's voice cracked. "And don't tell me you want to follow Jack. Jack is dead."

The words hung in the air. Emma covered her mouth with her hand. Finn looked as if Annie had slapped him.

Will sat motionless, his eyes moving from face to face.

"I'm sorry," Annie whispered, already backing away from the quilt. "I shouldn't have— I need to walk."

She turned and strode toward the shoreline, blinking hard against the sting in her eyes. Behind her, she heard murmured voices but couldn't make out the words over the pounding of her pulse.

The wet sand at the water's edge was firm beneath her feet as she walked, arms wrapped around herself.

So much had happened, but it had barely been two months since the officer had come to their door with the news about Jack. Two months of her mother crying in the kitchen when she thought no one could hear, of her father spending longer hours working on the car, of town folks asking how the family was holding up.

And now Finn would be leaving soon, too.

*I want to tell him how much I love him, but I can't stop being hurt about his leaving.*

Annie kicked a piece of driftwood, sending it spinning into the gentle surf. She walked until the voices behind her faded. The rhythm of the waves and her bare feet sinking in the sand grew hypnotic and welcomed calm in her mind.

She slowed when she realized how far she'd come. She glanced at the stand of Australian pines that lined the beach. Her spine prickled with the eerie sensation that she was being watched.

# CHAPTER THIRTY-THREE

*Fort Lauderdale*
*April 18, 1942*

Annie turned, scanning the tree line, the empty stretch of beach behind her.

Movement caught her eye back in amongst the trees. A man moving in the deeper shadows. He walked, hands in his pockets. When he stepped into the sunshine, she recognized the blond hair.

"Thought you might want company," he called out.

Will caught up with her and stood looking out at the ocean.

"I lost someone too," he said. "My father. I was only eleven years old."

The declaration caught Annie off guard. "I'm sorry."

Will shrugged. "It was a long time ago." His head hung down, and he stood absolutely still.

She sensed he was struggling to make a decision. At last, he reached into his pocket and withdrew something. When he opened his fingers, she saw what looked like a tarnished policeman's badge.

"This belonged to my father."

She could see him swallowing, struggling to find the words.

"Someone shot him and left him to die in the street. They said it was a thief, but my mother always believed it was another police officer. My father was preparing to testify against other police. He was a good man."

She reached out to touch his arm and he flinched. "I'm so sorry," she said. Will slid the badge back into his pocket.

Annie started walking again. "I shouldn't have said those things to Finn."

"You're afraid of losing him, too."

Annie nodded, unable to speak past the tightness in her throat.

"Come here." Will opened his arms.

Annie hesitated only a moment before stepping into his embrace. His shirt smelled of sweat, and his arms were solid around her shoulders. She closed her eyes, allowing herself to be held, to feel something other than grief and fear.

"It's okay to be scared."

Annie pulled back to look at his face. "Have you ever been scared?"

He turned his head aside. "I was scared that night I met you."

His gaze dropped to her lips then. Annie leaned forward. Their lips met, hesitant at first, then with surprising hunger. Annie's fingers slid over his shoulder, feeling the solid warmth of him beneath the thin fabric.

The kiss deepened with a rush of heat. For a moment, she forgot everything, Jack, Finn, the war, Frank Chandler, and the white card hidden in her sketchbook.

She pulled back, breathless, her hands still resting on Will's shoulders.

His eyes were darker now, intent. "I'm sorry.

"Slow," Annie whispered. "We should take this slow."

Will's smile transformed his face, lightening the shadows in his eyes. He took her hand, his fingers intertwining with hers.

"Slow it is," he said.

They walked along the shoreline, the waves rushing over their bare feet. Annie felt light. The guilt would return, she knew that, but for now, she allowed herself this brief respite.

And if a little voice whispered questions about Will's interest in the shipyard, about the too-specific nature of his questions, she pushed it aside. Not now. Not today.

They crested a small dune, and the coastline stretched south. It was time to turn around.

Annie opened her mouth to speak, when something ahead caught her eye. An unusual shape in the water. She squinted against the glare, shielding her eyes. She tried to make sense of what she was seeing. Something dark and cylindrical bobbed in the gentle swells about fifty feet offshore.

"What is that?" she asked, pointing.

Will followed her gaze, his body tensing. For a split second, she thought she saw recognition flash across his face.

"Not sure," he said.

"An abandoned boat, maybe." But even as she said it, Annie knew it was something else. The long cylindrical shape was too uniform. "Or an unexploded torpedo."

Will released her hand and moved toward the water's edge. "I don't think so."

"Will, wait!" she called. "That thing could be dangerous."

Annie followed, her sense of unease growing. As they drew closer, the shape grew clear. Cylindrical, perhaps ten feet long, with a small translucent dome rising from its center. Metal, not wood. The sun glinted off a section that wasn't coated in sand and seaweed.

"My God," Annie said. "Is that what I think it is?"

Will didn't answer. He was already wading into the shallows, water splashing around his knees.

"It's a baby submarine," she whispered.

"A one-man midget sub." Will remained calm. "German design. Must have broken off from a U-boat."

Annie stared. "How do you know that?"

"Read about them. Navy newspapers. Been spotted up and down the coast."

Will gripped the curved metal surface and pulled himself up to peer inside the translucent dome. His entire demeanor changed, his movements becoming precise, economical, almost mechanical.

"There's someone inside." He sounded detached. "Dead."

Annie covered her mouth with her hand. Then she stepped forward. "Are you sure?"

"Very." Will hauled himself higher and straddled the cylinder, like a rider on a horse. He grabbed the base of the dome and lifted.

A nauseating smell engulfed them. Annie staggered backwards and pinched her nose.

Will peered into the dark hole. "He's wearing a German uniform. Been dead a while." He leaned forward and reached down into the small craft, balancing on its curved surface.

Frank Chandler's words echoed in her ears: "We believe there is at least one German agent operating in South Florida, possibly more." She studied Will with fresh eyes.

"We should go back," she insisted. "Tell the authorities."

"In a minute. I want to see if there's anything to identify him."

"Will, that's not our job!"

But he had already ducked his head back inside the

hatch. Annie waded closer, torn between curiosity and mounting alarm. Will was behaving strangely: too comfortable with the grim discovery, too familiar with the vessel itself.

From her position, standing on her tip toes, Annie could just make out Will's hands as he searched the body. His movements were efficient, checking pockets, examining insignia. She saw him remove several folded papers from the dead man's jacket, studying them before checking if she was watching.

"Find anything?" She kept her voice steady.

Will tucked something into his pocket with a quick, furtive movement. "Just standard identification, papers, tags. Nothing unusual."

"What did you just put in your pocket?"

Will's expression flickered. "Nothing important."

"Show me."

"Annie, it's nothing." Will's tone was placating. "Just a souvenir."

"A souvenir? There's a dead man in there!"

"I was joking," he blurted. "I didn't take anything. Look." He turned out his pockets, showing their empty contents. But Annie had seen him tuck something away.

"Will, what's going on? How do you know so much about this thing? Why are you so calm about finding a dead body?"

His face hardened. "I told you. I read the Navy papers. And I've seen dead men before, on the tanker, when it went down." He slid back into the water beside her. "We should go tell the others."

Annie stepped back, keeping distance between them. "I think you should go," she said. "Tell Finn and Emma what we found. Have them take the boat to the port and alert the authorities."

"And you?"

"I'll stay here," Annie replied. "Someone needs to make sure nobody else messes with this."

"I don't think you should stay alone."

"I'll be fine," Annie insisted. "Go now. It's important that authorities get here as soon as possible."

Will turned and began wading back to shore. Annie watched him go, trying to reconcile the man who had kissed her with the cold efficiency he'd displayed examining the dead German. Frank Chandler's warnings seemed less paranoid with each passing minute.

As Will disappeared around the curve of the beach, Annie turned back to the submarine. She didn't approach the hatch or attempt to look inside. Instead, she waded around the craft, committing every detail to memory, the construction, the damage patterns, the markings on the hull.

She finished her inspection and moved back to shore, finding a spot on the sand where she could keep the submarine in view. The sun was low behind the trees now, throwing long shadows across the sand. Annie's wet dress clung to her skin, but she hardly noticed.

Annie lost track of time as she waited. She had expected Finn and Emma to return with help, but as the minutes stretched into what must have been well over an hour, anxiety gnawed at her stomach.

Where were they?

A distant mechanical rumble interrupted her thoughts. Annie straightened, expecting to see someone walking down the beach. Instead, two small boats approached on the ocean side, out from Port Everglades. Sleek, military-gray craft with mounted guns. Men in uniform crowded the small vessels.

Annie jumped up, waving her arms overhead.

The first boat cut its engine about twenty yards out. Six men jumped over the side, splashing through the shallows.

They wore sidearms. Behind them, more uniformed men were preparing to deploy a small raft toward the submarine.

Two of the men approached Annie while the others established a perimeter around the beach.

"Lieutenant Doran, U.S. Navy," the first man said. He was older, perhaps in his forties, with deep lines etched around his eyes. "You reported this?"

"My friends did," Annie corrected. "I stayed to make sure no one else came near it."

"You're alone then."

"Yes. My friends went for help." She swallowed.

The lieutenant turned back to her. "Your name, miss?"

"Annie Jeeves."

The younger officer wrote it down in a small notebook.

"Well, Miss Jeeves, I need you to leave this area. This is now a restricted military zone." The lieutenant's tone softened. "I understand your friends are expecting you back at the boat you arrived on, so I'll have one of my men escort you to your picnic site."

"But—"

"This isn't a request, Miss Jeeves," Lieutenant Doran cut her off. "This incident is now classified under wartime security regulations. You are not to discuss what you've seen with anyone—not your friends, not your family, not even the friend who looked inside the submarine. Do you understand?"

Annie thought of Frank Chandler and his confidentiality agreement. "I understand."

"Good." He gestured to one of the perimeter guards. "Petty Officer Collins will escort you back."

They walked for about ten minutes before Annie spotted what remained of their picnic site ahead. Emma and Finn sat side by side on the quilt beneath the watchful eyes of a uniformed officer.

"Annie!" Finn jumped up. "Are you alright? They wouldn't let us come back for you."

"I'm fine." Annie smiled at him.

Petty Officer Collins indicated Finn with a curt nod. "This is the man who was with you?"

"No." She swung her head around. "Where's Will?"

"He's not with you?" Emma asked.

Annie's stomach dropped. "No. He went to find you. To tell you about the submarine."

"He did," Finn said. "Then he said he was going back to wait with you."

"Sir," the remaining officer addressed Finn, "you need to pack up now. This entire area is being closed off."

"Let's go home." Finn lifted the picnic basket. "Now."

The officer escorted them to their small launch, watching as Finn stowed their gear and helped the women aboard.

Finn fired up the outboard, and they pulled away from shore. Annie glanced back at their picnic spot, now crawling with military personnel.

As they rounded the bend and the activity faded from view, Emma exhaled. "What on earth did we stumble into?"

"I don't like it," Finn said. "Any of it. Especially not with Will disappearing the way he did."

Annie stared at the water. Could Will be the German agent Frank Chandler had warned about? She couldn't reconcile that possibility with the man who had held her on the beach, who had understood her grief over Jack, whose kiss had made her feel alive for the first time in months.

Whatever secrets Will carried, however deep his lies ran, Annie vowed she would learn the truth.

And next time, she wouldn't be distracted by a kiss.

# CHAPTER THIRTY-FOUR

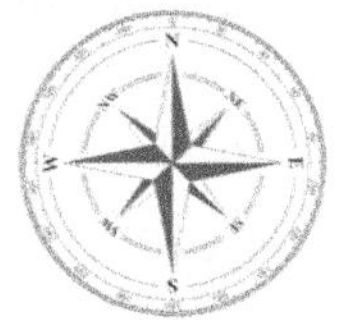

*Fort Lauderdale*
*April 18, 1942*

Will watched Finn and Emma disappear down the path towards their beached launch. The U.S. Navy installation in Port Everglades was a short boat ride away. He had maybe thirty minutes to disappear before the American military arrived.

The folded papers he'd taken from the dead sailor felt heavy against his chest. He'd slipped them inside his shirt with the practiced ease of someone who had grown accustomed to taking what wasn't his.

Will glanced down at the remains of their picnic. He grabbed the black oilskin jacket Emma had worn on the trip down the river, then turned away from the water's edge, and trotted toward the dense vegetation that bordered the eastern edge of Whiskey Creek. The sun hung low now, and soon the light would fade, giving him better cover.

Annie. He'd thought he could forget her, go about his business of sending coded messages to the U-boats, maintaining the facade that he and Erich were working together while limiting the information he shared. Annie was still back there, waiting by the submarine, expecting him to return. Her face flashed in his mind, those sharp, observant eyes that missed so little. Feeling her lips pressed against his.

But everything changed when she saw him remove those papers. Now, he'd ruined everything. He couldn't go back to her.

Will pushed deeper into the scrub, wincing as palmetto fronds sliced at his exposed skin. The vegetation grew dense as he moved away from the beach, the ground beneath his feet changing from sand to the spongy surface of decomposing leaves. Mosquitoes whined near his ears, their hunger relentless.

He didn't have a plan. He knew only that he could not be there when the authorities arrived. Annie would tell them about his tampering with the body. His cover story would never hold up under scrutiny, not without the forged identity papers that had gone down with their rubber boat. As his instructors had drilled into him during training, the punishment for espionage in America was death.

Annie had explained that the only access to Whiskey Creek was by boat. Now, his only escape would have to be by water.

A branch snapped beneath his foot, and Will froze. A night heron called somewhere ahead. No human voices, no crackling radio transmissions suggesting pursuit. Not yet.

Will wiped sweat from his forehead and continued moving, angling north. Annie had described this place as a barrier island. He would come to the end.

Kapitänleutnant Hardegen of U-123 would be expecting to contact him before dawn. Will had heard the sailors talk about this highly decorated officer as he had crossed the

Atlantic. Had the beached vessel back there come off of U-123?

The discovery of the midget submarine would change things. Plans had to be adjusted. The sealed orders he'd removed from the dead pilot's pocket might be the key to understanding what had gone wrong and might earn him the good graces of his new German contact.

But visions of Annie kept intruding on his tactical calculations. The way she'd looked at him on the beach. The trust in her eyes hardening into suspicion as she'd watched him search the submarine.

She's an obstacle as his trainers at Brandenburg would say. And it was his mission to get rid of obstacles.

As he pushed through the bush, he thought again about Max. He wished he were here in Florida. When he'd had Max by his side, Will had been the perfect pupil, absorbing everything from clandestine communications to killing techniques. Now, it seemed he couldn't get anything right. If he wanted to save his mother, he needed to forget about the girl.

Max would know what to do about Annie.

A fish splashed in the creek to his left, the sound making him start. Will's training reasserted itself. He dropped lower, moving with the silence they had beat into him during endless drills in the German countryside. Twenty paces, pause, listen. Twenty more paces, pause, listen. The rhythm of survival.

The distant whoosh of the ocean off to his right kept him on course. Soon, he neared the northern tip of the island. Will paused again, listening. Something moved in the undergrowth nearby. Possibly a raccoon or possum, but he remained motionless until he was certain it posed no threat.

He continued forward, pushing through a dense patch of prickly brush. Annie wouldn't be waiting anymore. By now, she'd be talking to the authorities. Describing him. Telling them everything she knew.

The thought shouldn't have bothered him. But it did. Somehow, in the weeks he'd spent establishing his cover in Fort Lauderdale, Annie Jeeves had slipped past his defenses.

"Weakness," his grandfather would have snarled. "Sentiment is weakness."

Will reached the northernmost point of the barrier island just as the western sky turned a deep shade of red. Across the dark channel, the lights of Port Everglades shimmered, so close yet separated by a half-mile stretch of roiling water. He crouched in the shadow of a knobby mangrove, his muscles coiled, watching and waiting. He'd noted when they passed the docks that afternoon that the military installation was on the southern end, the commercial docks on the north side.

Will studied the water before him. The incoming tide created swirling eddies visible even in the dim light, ripples catching the distant dock lights. Good luck at last. The flood tide would help carry him across the channel towards the docks rather than sweeping him out toward the ocean.

He glanced in both directions, searching for the telltale silhouettes of patrol boats. Nothing visible, though he knew they were out there somewhere. Coast Guard vessels and civilian boats alike now watched for German submarines. They'd be especially alert as the news spread of the midget submarine.

The midget submarine. Will's hand went to his chest, confirming the documents were still there. Whatever mission the pilot had been on, it had failed. The small craft was damaged—whether from American depth charges or mechanical failure, Will couldn't tell. But the papers might provide critical intelligence about German naval operations in the area.

Decision made, Will untied and removed his shoes, tying the laces to his belt. He spread out the oilskin jacket, placed the stolen documents inside and rolled it all up into a bundle. Then he lifted his shirt and tucked the bundle under his shirt and into his pants. After a last scan of the channel, he eased himself down the bank and into the water.

The saltwater embraced him, cooler than the humid air but not by much. Will slipped forward, keeping his movements silent, his head low in the water. The tide tugged at him, stronger than he'd expected. He angled his body against the current, stroking toward the distant lights.

With each pull of his arms, memories of training surfaced. The Brandenburg camp, where Abwehr agents were forged from promising recruits. Swimming across the icy Quenz Lake in January, and deciding to go back for Erich. The man's eyes still haunted him.

Salt stung his eyes and nostrils. Will switched to a breaststroke, keeping his head higher to better track his position. The distant hum of machinery grew louder.

A spotlight swept the water about two hundred yards to his right. A patrol boat making its rounds. Will took a deep breath and ducked underwater, using the small waves to mask his presence. The light passed without pausing, continuing its path across the water.

His feet found no bottom even as he neared the commercial docks. Will's muscles screamed for rest, but he pushed on, focusing on the closest loading dock, a dark wooden structure extending from the shoreline.

With a last surge of effort, he reached the barnacle-encrusted pilings beneath the dock. Will clung to one, allowing himself thirty seconds to recover before hauling himself up onto the lowest crossbeam. He lay there for a moment, cheek pressed against the rough wood, panting. The successful crossing meant little. He was now in the heart of enemy territory, soaking wet and conspicuous.

Water ran in rivulets down his clothes as he pulled himself onto the dock proper. Will retrieved his canvas shoes from his belt and slipped them on, not bothering to wring out his socks.

He straightened his shoulders and adopted the hunched posture he'd observed in the dockworkers. His shoes made a squishing noise as he walked, but he couldn't help that. Head down, purposeful stride, nothing to attract attention. Just another laborer who'd had the misfortune of falling into the water. He hoped it was a common enough occurrence that it wouldn't raise eyebrows.

Will passed a small group of men unloading crates from a truck, nodding when one glanced his way. The man returned the nod without interest, turning back to his work. Will fought the urge to walk faster. Hurrying would draw attention. Instead, he maintained a steady pace, moving with the confidence of someone who belonged, dripping clothes, squeaky shoes and all.

The port sprawled before him, a maze of warehouses, vehicles, and stacked cargo. Somewhere beyond lay Fort Lauderdale, and with it, decisions he wasn't yet ready to make. His hand went to the waterproof jacket wadded up and stuffed into his waistband.

Will moved among the stacks of cargo crates with practiced confidence, just another shadow in a port filled with men working the night shift. Dockworkers minded their business, focused on the rhythm of loading and unloading, their faces illuminated by cigarettes or the occasional sweep of distant floodlights. Will kept his head down, his posture relaxed.

A foreman shouted orders nearby, directing a crew loading

crates onto a flatbed truck. "Careful with those! They're marked fragile for a reason." The men worked with the efficient movements of those who had performed the same task countless times, passing wooden crates hand to hand up a human chain.

Will paused, observing the operation while pretending to shake water from his shoes. The truck was nearly full, its cargo bed stacked with wooden crates stenciled with "INDIAN RIVER ORANGES" in bold black letters.

Leaning against the cab, the driver smoked a cigarette while checking his watch. Will recognized an opportunity. This truck would leave soon, likely headed into Fort Lauderdale or up the coast to Palm Beach. Either direction would serve his purposes, putting distance between himself and the submarine discovery.

Will circled around, keeping cargo crates between himself and the loading crew. He approached the truck from the blind side, noting the canvas covering draped over the stacked crates. The rear gate was secured, but the canvas sagged, leaving a gap along one side.

He made himself inconspicuous behind a stack of empty pallets, waiting for the right moment. The foreman approached the driver, clipboard in hand. "You're good to go as soon as you sign this."

Will watched the driver push off from the truck, drop his cigarette, and grind it under his heel before taking the clipboard. The moment both men were focused on the paperwork, Will moved, swift and silent, to the rear of the truck. He slipped his fingers under the canvas at the gap, tested to ensure it would widen enough, then pulled himself up in one fluid motion and rolled beneath the covering.

The pungent sweetness of oranges enveloped him, so strong it made his eyes water. Will lay still among the crates, breathing through his mouth, listening to the muffled voices outside. Footsteps approached—the driver returning—followed by the creak of the cab door opening and closing. The engine rumbled to life, vibrations traveling through the wooden bed to Will's spine.

He wedged himself more securely between two crates as the truck lurched forward. The motion rocked him, wooden corners digging into his back and sides. Will adjusted his position, creating a small space where he could lie without being visible should someone check the cargo.

The truck slowed as it approached the exit checkpoint, then stopped. Will held his breath, listening to the murmur of voices as the driver presented his paperwork. A long moment passed. Then, with a jerk, the truck sped up again, turning onto a main road leading away from the port.

Only when the sounds of the port faded behind them did Will allow himself to relax. His hand went to the bundle pressed to his abdomen, confirming the documents were still secure. He should examine them, but his thoughts kept returning to Annie. The look in her eyes as he'd kissed her on the beach. The intoxicating taste of that kiss. Then, the growing suspicion when she'd caught him taking papers from the dead German. She was smart, too smart. Her Mosquito Fleet patrolling had already cost him one safe house. Soon, she would put all the pieces together.

Annie. He'd seen the human cost of this war through her eyes. The grief for her brother, the determination to protect her world. It was a world that now would never accept him. But the moment he let Erich die, a return to Germany had become a death sentence for his family as well.

The truck rumbled onward through the darkness toward Fort Lauderdale. Will closed his eyes. His stomach roiled at the overwhelming sweet citrus scent. His wet clothes grew cold as the wind blew through slats in the sides of the truck.

Tonight, though he wanted to warm his hands in his pockets, he was ashamed to touch his father's badge.

He didn't want to hurt Annie. He wasn't that man, was he? He wanted to protect her.

But he also intended to survive.

# CHAPTER THIRTY-FIVE

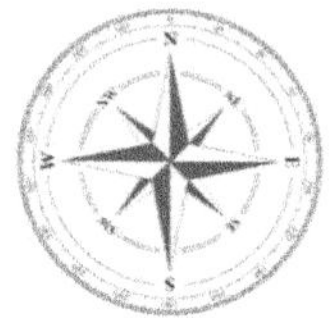

*Fort Lauderdale*
*April 21, 1942*

Tess trotted ahead of Annie, nosing at every fence post as they walked the six blocks home from the vacant riverside lot. The dog had provided perfect cover for Annie's early morning escape to a clandestine meeting with Frank Chandler. No one questioned a girl walking her dog.

When Annie had returned from the Whiskey Creek adventure on Saturday night, she had gone straight home, to her room and opened her sketchbook. She removed the white card with the telephone number, but her family did not have a phone in the house, nor did any of their neighbors. The only telephone she had ever used was at the Deck, and it was closed on Sundays.

She had placed the call from the Deck restaurant on Monday morning and asked to speak to Mr. Drake. The woman on the line told her that Mr. Drake would meet her at nine on Tuesday morning at their usual spot.

Chandler had already heard about the midget sub incident, though he was surprised to learn Annie was the one who found it.

Then she described Will's suspicious behavior and his unexpected disappearance. Chandler had barely blinked, just scribbled notes in that small leather book of his, asking pointed questions about Will's too convenient arrival on the dock.

When she mentioned the submarine, Chandler's pencil stopped moving. "Describe exactly what he removed from the submarine."

Annie closed her eyes, remembering. "Papers. Several folded sheets of paper. He slipped them inside his shirt. When I asked him about them, he lied and said he hadn't taken anything."

"Did you see any markings? German text?"

"No, but the way he handled them. It was clear they were valuable to him."

"You did the right thing coming to me," Chandler had said. "You may have helped us identify a German sympathizer or an actual enemy agent."

As she walked back home, the words *enemy agent* repeated in her mind. Annie wasn't convinced. That kiss.

Tess barked at a squirrel, lunging at her leash. Annie yanked it back.

"Settle down, girl."

A military truck rumbled past, loaded with young men in uniform. They whistled and waved. Annie ignored them, her thoughts stuck on Will's face. Those blue eyes had looked at her with such tenderness on the beach. She didn't want to believe it had all been an act.

Was that the reason she *still* hadn't told Chandler about how she met Will? How could a German spy be crewing on an Allied tanker? Nothing about Will made sense to her. There had to be an explanation.

She turned down Coontie Court toward home. Mrs. Ferguson was watering her impatiens, the radio on her porch blaring news about rationing. Two doors down, the Millers had hung another blue star in their window, their second son gone to war.

Annie turned into her own driveway. The white clapboard house looked tired, with the paint peeling at the corners. No gold star in their window. Her parents were certainly proud of Jack, but preferred to grieve in private. She released Tess from her leash, and the dog bounded ahead, disappearing around the side of the house.

The screen door creaked as Annie pushed it open. The familiar smell of today's lunch—bean soup with ham hock filled the kitchen. Her mother stood at the counter, her back to the door. A loaf of fresh bread cooled on the windowsill.

"That you, Annie?" Her mother didn't turn around.

"It's me." Annie hung her hat on the hook by the door. "Smells good in here."

Her mother's movements were quick and jerky as she stirred the soup on the stove.

"Is everything okay, Ma?" Annie asked.

"Oh, your father forgot his lunch bucket this morning." Hilda nodded toward the counter where she'd laid out wax paper. "He was in such a rush."

Annie watched as her mother wrapped thick slices of bread, nestling them alongside a jar of the bean soup, still warm from the stove.

"You sure you're okay?"

"Of course." Her mother's smile was too bright as she turned. "Just tired, is all. Double shift at the hospital on Sunday."

"I can take that to Pa," Annie offered.

"Would you? I'd be grateful." Her mother tucked everything into the metal lunch pail and handed it to Annie. "And be careful around the yard. Those guards get twitchy if you don't have a good reason for being there."

"It's not my first time at Dooley's. I'll ride the bike over."

"Best get it to him before noon," her mother said. "He gets cranky when he's hungry, and they're pushed to the limit with those new patrol boat orders."

Annie pedaled across the Andrews Avenue bridge, the lunch pail balanced in the bike's front basket. It would have been faster to take the little launch up the river, but with gasoline being rationed, today she'd take the longer trip through town and overland to 20th Street.

She swerved to avoid a convoy of olive-drab trucks rumbling east toward Port Everglades, then turned onto the rutted dirt road that led to Dooley's Dry Dock and Shipyard. Ahead, the skeletal frames of half-built vessels rose against the sky.

A guardhouse marked the entrance. An older man in an ill-fitting uniform raised his hand as she approached.

He barked, "Halt!" Then, his face broke into a grin. "Good morning, Annie"

"Morning Mr. Oliver." Annie gestured to the lunch pail. "Bringing my pa his lunch."

The guard squinted at her. "Skeeter forgot it again, eh? He's working in Building Three." He scribbled something on a clipboard and then handed her the paper. "Here's your visitor badge. Keep it visible. Stay on the main paths, and don't go near the restricted areas. They're marked with red lines on the ground." He handed her the badge. "And don't take no pictures."

Annie pinned the badge on her blouse. "No camera, sir. Only Pa's lunch."

He stepped outside and lifted the red and white striped barrier. "You can leave your bicycle over there."

She propped it up against the stack of lumber Mr. Oliver had indicated and grabbed the lunch pail.

The shipyard sprawled before her, a maze of workshops, and partially constructed vessels. As she got closer to the dry dock, the noise hit her like a physical force: hammers pounding and saws screeching. Men shouted to be heard over the din. The air tasted of sawdust and metal, with an underlying tang of sweat.

Annie navigated around puddles left from the early morning rain. Mud splattered her shoes.

Building Three stood at the far end of the compound. Two men in coveralls passed by, headed that way, deep in conversation.

She started after them, then hesitated. It was a long walk back to that corner. A sign pointed toward the dry docks: RESTRICTED AREA - AUTHORIZED PERSONNEL ONLY. Her father sometimes worked there when they needed help with engines. Maybe she should check there first? She knew half the men who worked here, and Mr. Oliver had to read the rules to everybody whether or not they applied to them. What was it Jack used to say? It's easier to beg forgiveness than to ask permission?

The path to the dry docks cut between tall stacks of lumber, creating a corridor of rough-hewn wood. Annie walked, lunch pail swinging at her side. The noise of the main yard faded, replaced by the more distinct sounds of metal on metal and the hollow echo of men's voices bouncing off water.

She rounded a corner and stopped short. A massive boat sat in a wooden cradle. Workmen swarmed over it like ants, welding, painting, installing equipment. Annie recognized the design from Fuller Mansfield's descriptions: a subchaser, built to hunt German U-boats.

She was about to continue toward Building Three when a

movement caught her eye. A man in khaki pants and a light cotton shirt moved along the edge of the restricted zone with apparent purpose. He paused near a stack of steel pipes, glanced around, then slipped between them toward the dry dock.

Annie stepped behind a stack of crates. There was no mistaking his profile, the set of his shoulders, the careful way he moved.

What was Will doing here? He looked different. His hair was slicked back, and he wore wire-rimmed glasses she'd never seen before. But no doubt it was him. How had he gotten past security?

Will straightened and looked around again. Annie ducked lower. When she peered back over the crate, he was moving away, heading deeper into the restricted area.

Annie followed, keeping to the shadows. She tracked him past the enormous boat to a smaller structure where uniformed men were unloading large crates from a truck.

Will stood watching the workers, his back to Annie. Something bulged under his jacket, a rucksack or bag, she couldn't tell which. One worker called out to him, and Will responded with a casual wave. He belonged here. Or at least, he wanted everyone to think he did.

Annie moved closer, slipping from shadow to shadow like she'd learned to do when hunting with her father. Twenty feet away. Fifteen. She could hear his voice now as he spoke to one of the workmen, but couldn't make out the words.

Will gestured toward the crates and asked something. The worker shook his head, turning away. Will's shoulders tensed. He glanced around again, and for a split second, Annie thought he looked directly at her hiding place.

She pressed herself against a wooden pallet, not daring to breathe. When she looked again, Will was moving away, heading toward a cluster of smaller buildings at the far end of the dry dock.

Annie hesitated only a moment before continuing to follow.

The maze of half-constructed vessels swallowed Will's figure. Annie cursed. She'd lost track of him between stacks of lumber and steel nearly twice her height. She paused at the intersection of narrow pathways, straining to hear footsteps over the constant din of hammering and shouting. Nothing. She turned left toward the machine shop, where he'd seemed to head, her tennis shoes silent on the packed dirt.

This section of the yard was quieter, the buildings farther apart. Perfect for someone who didn't want to be seen. Annie slipped between two storage sheds, squinting in the sudden dimness. A pile of rusty chains lay coiled on the ground. The air smelled of grease and mildew.

She had almost reached the end of the narrow passage when powerful arms grabbed her from behind. One wrapped around her waist like an iron band while another clamped over her mouth, stifling her cry.

"Stop following me," a familiar voice whispered.

Annie's body reacted from years of wrestling with her older brother. She bit down hard on the hand covering her mouth, tasting salt and dirt. Behind her, Will cursed. His grip loosened just enough for her to drive her elbow into his ribs with all her strength. Air whooshed from his lungs.

She spun free, ready to run for help. Will lunged forward, shoving her against the shed wall. His forearm pressed across her collarbone, pinning her.

"Are you crazy?" Annie spat. "Will! Let go of me!"

His face was inches from hers, his expression nothing like the gentle man who had kissed her. His eyes were wild. He looked all around to see if anyone was watching, and a muscle twitched in his jaw.

"Why are you following me?"

Annie pushed against his arm. "What's wrong with you?"

"Answer my question, Annie."

Had she imagined the man on the beach? Had she been so taken by those blue eyes she made up a story in her mind? "Why are you skulking around Dooley's? And what happened to you at Whiskey Creek? How did you get back to town?"

His breathing wheezed next to her ear. It wasn't from exertion.

"Talk to me, Will."

The pressure against her collarbone eased, but he didn't back away. "I have a job interview here."

"In the restricted area? I want to believe you, but what's stuffed under your jacket?" Annie's fear gave way to anger. "Stop lying to me."

Will glanced over his shoulder, then back at her. "You have no idea what you're getting involved in."

"Then explain it to me." Annie twisted her torso, creating space between them. "Show me what's in the bag."

"No."

"Then I'll shout for security." Annie took a deep breath, ready to shout.

Will's hand shot up, covering her mouth again. His touch was softer this time. Annie jerked her head away, and he released her.

"You kiss me one day and threaten me the next?" Her voice shook. "What's wrong with you?"

Something flickered in Will's eyes—regret? Fear? It vanished too quickly to identify. "I'm fine."

"Really? You're not acting fine. I've been trying to help you, trying to keep your secrets like you asked. But you keep acting like —" She didn't want to say the word "spy."

"You know who I am. But it's complicated."

"A survivor from the *W.D. Anderson*." Annie watched his

face. "Is *that* even true? Why didn't you report to the authorities?"

"I did report." Will's eyes shifted left. "They asked me some questions and let me go."

"What was the name of the Anderson's captain?"

Will hesitated a beat too long. "Matthews."

"And the naval officer who debriefed you?"

"Lieutenant..." Will's face hardened. "I don't have to explain myself to you."

"You do if you don't want me screaming for security." Annie folded her arms across her chest. "If you're really here for a job interview, who are you meeting?"

Will shifted his weight, the rucksack under his jacket making a soft rustling sound. "Mr. Johnson. The foreman."

"There are six foremen at Dooley's. Which building does this Johnson work in?"

Will's jaw clenched. "Building Four."

"There is no Building Four."

Pain flashed across his face. "Are you trying to trap me, Annie?" His voice had changed. More sorrow than anger.

"I think you're the guilty one." Annie's heart pounded so hard she felt light-headed. "What did you take from that dead man?"

His hand shot out and gripped her wrist. "Stay away from me, Annie. I don't want to hurt you."

A siren wailed somewhere in the yard, its pitch rising and falling. Both of them froze.

Men's voices shouted in the distance. "Accident in Building Two!"

Footsteps pounded past their hiding place. Will's grip on her wrist loosened. Annie yanked free and shoved past him, back into the main pathway.

"Guards!" she shouted. "Over here!"

She turned around just in time to see Will swing around

the stack of lumber, and he was gone. A security guard rounded the corner from the main pathway, his hand on his holster.

"What's going on?" The guard's eyes narrowed.

"Sorry, sir. I heard the alarm. It scared me. I'm bringing lunch to my father. Skeeter Jeeves, and I guess I got turned around."

The guard's face softened at the familiar name. His eyes flicked to the badge pinned to her dress.

"This is a restricted area. I ought to call this in," the guard muttered, hand still on his holster.

"Please, sir," Annie interrupted. "My father's expecting his lunch. Mr. Oliver told me he's in Building Three today, but that's such a long walk, and I knew he sometimes worked here, so..."

The guard considered this. "This is wartime, Miss. Best to follow the rules from now on." He then jerked his thumb over his shoulder. "Go give your pa his lunch, then get outta here."

Annie found her father bent over a table covered with disassembled engine parts, his massive forearms streaked with grease. His pipe dangled from the corner of his mouth, smoke curling up past the brim of his cap. Three other men worked alongside him. None of them looked up as Annie approached.

"Pa?"

Skeeter Jeeves straightened, wincing as he pressed a hand to his lower back. His face broke into a grin when he spotted her.

"Annie!" He reached for a rag that looked dirtier than his fingers. "What brings you to this den of grease monkeys?"

She held up the lunch pail. "Ma sent this. You forgot it this morning, so I rode the bicycle over."

"Thank you, sweetheart." He nodded to his co-workers. "My daughter, gentlemen."

The men tipped their caps, murmuring greetings. One of them, a lanky fellow with a shock of white hair, winked at her.

"Lucky man, Skeeter. My kid would let me starve before pedaling all the way out here."

Annie forced a smile. "Would have been here sooner, but I got caught in that alarm. Where should I put this?"

"Over there on the bench is fine." Skeeter pointed to a wooden workbench scattered with tools and blueprints. "Everything all right at home?"

"Fine." Annie set down the pail and glanced around the workshop. "Busy here, huh?"

"Round the clock." Skeeter tapped his pipe on the sole of his boot, emptying the ash. "Now that we're about finished with that sub chaser, the Navy wants these patrol boats yesterday. Not enough men to do the work."

Annie picked up a small gear, turning it over in her fingers. "I ran into someone who said he was looking for work. A job interview."

"That so?" Her father reached for a wrench. "Send him my way. We're hiring just about anyone with a pulse these days."

Annie's heart skipped. "Really? I thought there'd be all sorts of, I don't know, background checks. Security clearances."

Her father laughed. "For the mucky-mucks designing the ships, sure. But for regular workers? They check your name against a list of known troublemakers, make sure you're not fresh off the boat from Germany, and put a tool in your hand."

"So, if someone came in looking for work..."

"They'd hire him on the spot." Skeeter gave her a curious look. "Why? You asking for that same friend?"

Annie shook her head. "Just wondering." She forced lightness into her voice. "How's the engine coming along?"

Her father launched into a detailed explanation of the patrol boat's propulsion system. Annie nodded, but her mind was elsewhere.

Will had lied. There was no job interview. If there had been, they'd have hired him. Which meant he was at the shipyard for another reason, a reason that involved sneaking into restricted areas and making notes on sub chasers. And how had he got in?

"...so we had to rebuild the transmission." Her father finished his explanation, studying her face. "You sure you're alright, Annie? You look like you've seen a ghost."

"Just tired." She managed a smile. "I should get going. I promised Ma I'd be back home for lunch."

Skeeter nodded, then surprised her by pulling her into a quick, grease-stained hug. "You're a good girl, bringing my lunch all the way out here. Jack would be proud of how you're helping your old man."

The mention of her brother sent a familiar pang through Annie's chest. What would Jack think of her fascination with Will? Of her failure to report him, even now when she had every reason to?

"See you at home."

"Tell your mother I'll be home on time." Skeeter turned back to the engine.

Annie retrieved her bicycle. As she pedaled back toward town, her decision crystallized. She would report everything she knew about Will to Frank Chandler. Saving him at sea, Will's presence at the shipyard, his suspicious behavior, the rucksack.

What if Will wasn't just suspicious? What if he was

dangerous? And she had kissed him. She'd been a fool, and she had to make it right.

Annie pedaled hard, her legs burning with the effort as she raced home. The man she thought she knew was gone, if he had ever existed.

When her home came into view, something was different. The back bedroom window was open, white curtains billowing. Jack's window. Her mother never opened that window.

# CHAPTER THIRTY-SIX

*Fort Lauderdale*
*April 21, 1942*

Annie hopped off her bicycle and hurried inside. The house felt too quiet. No radio. No clatter of dishes or pots.

"Ma?"

No answer. She walked down the hallway, past her own room. The door to Jack's room stood ajar. Her mother stood in the center of the room, a stack of clean sheets in her arms. The bed was stripped, mattress bare.

"Ma?"

Hilda startled, turning with red-rimmed eyes. She wiped at her cheek with the back of her hand. "Annie. Didn't hear you come in."

"What are you doing?" Annie stepped into the room.

"Changing the sheets." Her mother snapped a sheet open. "Give me a hand. This room has been closed up too long. Getting musty."

Annie moved to help. Together they smoothed the sheet

over the mattress, tucking hospital corners just as her mother had taught her.

"Ma, what's really going on?"

Hilda's hands stilled on the pillowcase she'd been stuffing. "Promised I wouldn't say anything yet."

"Promised who? About what?"

Her mother sighed and sat down on the fresh sheets. She patted the space beside her.

Annie sat.

"Finn came by after you left to walk the dog this morning." Her mother fidgeted with the hem of her apron. "Finn got his orders. He's leaving for the Navy on Friday."

Annie's hand flew to her mouth. "Mama, no." She tilted her head back, and her hand slid to her throat. She felt the pulse in her neck pounding beneath her fingers. "He can't."

"He can, Annie. And he is."

"But what about Bean?"

"That's why I'm making up this bed." Hilda smoothed a wrinkle from the sheet. "Bean will stay with us while Finn's gone. She'll sleep in here."

Annie stared at Jack's model planes, turning in the breeze from the open window. The Wildcat had always been his favorite.

"Finn said it was time." Hilda stood, moving to straighten the collection of baseball cards on Jack's dresser. "Said he couldn't keep watching other men go off to fight while he stayed home. You knew this was coming, Annie. We all did."

Annie pictured Finn in a Navy uniform, sailing off to face the U-boats.

"Hon, I tried talking him out of it when he first came in askin' if we could look after Bethany. But his mind was made up."

Finn had been talking about it for a long time, but a part of Annie had refused to believe it would ever happen.

"Finn said he'd try to find you." Her mother took a deep breath. "He wanted to tell you himself."

Annie stood and walked to the window.

"Bean's excited about staying with us," her mother said. "Thinks it'll be like having a big sister."

Annie nodded, unable to speak. First Jack. Now Finn. The war kept taking pieces of her world, one by one.

Annie turned from the window. "I should go find Finn."

Annie paused at the door, looking back at the room. Her mother sat on the bed, her head bowed, twisting a handkerchief. The space already felt different. Still Jack's but preparing for someone new.

~

Where would Finn go? She had already checked Finn's house, Dooley's, even The Deck. Annie hurried down Las Olas Boulevard, dodging her way through the shoppers on the sidewalk.

Her pace slowed as she passed the Champ-Carr Hotel where sailors on leave lounged on the steps, their white uniforms bright against the Mediterranean-style stucco. Finn wasn't there.

Then the realization struck. Of course. The boat. Ma said he was looking for her. Finn would be at the *Tequesta*.

She turned on her heel and ran.

Finn sat in the stern, bent over a length of rope, his fingers working a complicated knot. He hadn't noticed her yet. For a moment, Annie stood watching him, the afternoon sun catching the copper in his hair, wondering if this was how she'd remember him while he was gone. Head bowed in concentration, shoulders strong beneath his thin cotton shirt, but still here, still safe.

"That rope's getting the better of you."

He looked up, and for a moment his face was unguarded—relief, fear, and something else. Then the familiar smile appeared, the one that made her insides flip despite everything.

"Hey, Annie."

She climbed aboard, careful to sit close, but not too close.

"Ma told me," Annie said, her voice tight.

His hands stilled on the rope. "I was coming to find you so I could tell you myself."

She sniffed. "A bit late for that."

Finn's jaw tightened.

Annie sat beside him, their shoulders touching. The familiar smell of teak oil and rope surrounded them.

"When do you go?"

"I ship out on Friday." Finn's voice was steady. "Training in Jacksonville first. Then they're sending me out to the Pacific."

When she said nothing, he continued. "Those U-boats are right off our coast, Annie. You and me, we've seen them with our own eyes. If we don't stop this war now, there may not be a world left for any of us. I can help. I know boats and engines. The Navy needs men like me."

She stood. "You've got this all figured out, don't you? How long have you and Ma been planning this?"

"It wasn't like that."

"Then what was it like?" Her voice rose despite herself. "Because from where I'm standing, it looks like everyone in my life thinks I'm too fragile to handle the truth. First Jack had a run-in with the Finch boys and didn't tell me, now you and Ma are treating me like I'm some child who can't be trusted with decisions about my home."

Finn stood too, reaching for her. "We didn't want to burden you—"

"Burden me?" Annie laughed. "I've been running the boat business, holding my folks together after Jack—" Her voice cracked. "But apparently I can't be trusted to know that Bean needs a place to stay?"

"Your mother offered, said Jack's room was just sitting empty," Finn said. "I didn't ask."

"That's worse! That means you both decided I didn't need to know. You both looked at me and thought, 'Better not tell Annie. She might want to have a say about who lives in her dead brother's room.'"

She saw him flinch at that, and she knew she'd gone too far. Finn just sat back down, but she could see the veins in his forearms from how hard he gripped that little piece of rope.

When he spoke, she had to lean down to hear his words. "Annie, your Ma has always been like a second mother to us. She understands Bean. About us not having anyone else in the world. I didn't have to ask. She offered." Finn tilted his head sideways to look up at her. "Bean's got no one but me, and now—"

Annie plopped herself down on the seat next to him. "Now she'll have us." She crossed her arms and sat up straight. "If you'd asked me, that's what I would have said. She'll have us."

"I know." His voice was rough. "I know you would have said yes. That's not why—"

"Then why?" She turned to face him. "Why couldn't you trust me with this?"

"Because talking to you about taking care of Bean means admitting I might not come back to do it myself."

Annie felt her anger dissolve into something else, something that hurt worse. "So you made plans with my mother because it was easier than looking me in the eye and saying you might die?"

"Yes." The admission came out raw. "I'm a coward when it comes to you, Annie. Always have been."

"You're not a coward," she said. "You're just an idiot who thinks protecting me means keeping me in the dark."

"Your whole family does it," Finn said. "Even Jack—"

"Jack kept secrets, and that hurt." The words came out flat and hard. "He thought he was protecting everyone by not telling us about him and Emma, about his plans, about that night hiding out in Leroy's Garage. And look how that turned out. So forgive me if I'm tired of the men in my life deciding what I can and cannot handle."

Finn was quiet for a long moment. "You're right. I should have told you."

"Yes, you should have."

"I should have told you everything. About enlisting, about Bean, about..." He stopped, swallowed. "About how I've felt about you since we were kids."

"Finn..."

"No, let me finish." He turned to face her. "I need to say this while I still can. While I'm still brave enough or stupid enough to try."

He reached for her hand, then stopped, his fingers hovering just above hers. Asking permission.

She grabbed his hand, intertwining their fingers.

"I've loved you since that summer you taught yourself to read the stars," he said. "You dragged me out on the dock at the fish camp every night for weeks, made me lie on that scratchy blanket while you figured out how to use that old sextant. You were so determined to navigate by the stars, like the old sailors did."

"And you fell asleep most of the time," Annie murmured.

"No." His thumb traced circles on her palm. "I never slept. I just... I couldn't look at the stars when I could look at you. The way your face lit up when you found Polaris. How you'd grab my hand and use my finger to trace Cassiopeia." His voice grew rough. "I knew then I was in trouble."

"That was years ago."

"Eight years, three months." He gave her a crooked smile. "I've gotten very good at pretending you don't affect me."

"Why pretend?"

"Because you were Jack's little sister, and I lived in Jack's shadow. Because the two of you were going places— making maps, navigating the boat, first mate, then captain. Because I was just the kid who fixed boat engines and got into fights with the Finch brothers."

"You were never *just* anything." The words came out fierce. "Not to me."

Something shifted in his expression. "*Annie...*" He took a deep breath then continued. "Then after we lost Jack, both of us felt like it was wrong to want to be happy. Like we didn't deserve it."

She lifted her free hand to his face, feeling the slight roughness of stubble, the warmth of his skin. "All those times you walked me home. All those mornings you just happened to be at the dock when I needed help with the boat. That wasn't a coincidence, was it?"

"No."

"Why now?" she asked. "Why tell me all this now when you're leaving?"

"Because I'm scared."

Finn's admission came so fast she almost missed it.

She looked up, surprised. Finn never admitted fear.

"Not of dying," he continued. "But of not coming back. Of Bean growing up without me. Of missing..." He gestured, pointing back and forth between them. "Whatever this might be. Because if you don't feel the same—"

"Finn." She leaned closer, close enough to feel his breath on her face. "Stop talking." She pressed her fingers to his lips. "For someone so smart, you're incredibly dense. I'm not going to wait three more days for you to figure out that I—"

He kissed her fingers, then moved her hand aside. "Say it."

"What?"

"What you were going to say. Please."

"I love you. You impossible, infuriating, secret-keeping—"

He cupped her face in both hands and kissed her. His fingers tangled in her hair, and she could feel him almost vibrating—or maybe that was her. She gripped his shoulders, pulling him closer, trying to memorize everything: the salt taste of his lips, the calluses on his palms against her cheeks, the soft sound he made when she bit his lower lip.

They broke apart only when breathing became necessary, foreheads pressed together, both gasping.

"Annie," he breathed against her mouth.

She kissed him again, softer this time but no less desperate. Three days. They had three days, and she wanted to spend every second of them like this, pretending the war didn't exist, that U-boats weren't hunting off their coast, that he wasn't about to sail away into danger.

When they pulled apart again, she realized she was crying. He wiped her tears with his thumbs. His eyes were the gray-green of a deep-sea squall.

"Don't you dare," she whispered. "Don't you dare not come back to me."

"I'll fight the whole Japanese navy if I have to."

"That's not funny."

"I'm not joking." He pressed his lips to her forehead, her temple, the corner of her eye where tears still gathered. "Everything I do over there, every day I survive, it will always be so I can come back to you."

A pelican dove into the river nearby, the splash startling them both. Annie laughed, suddenly aware they were on a boat in broad daylight where anyone could see.

"We should probably go."

"Yeah." But neither of them moved.

He grinned, and there was the boy she'd grown up with, the one who dared her to dive off the end of the pier, who taught her to change a bicycle tire. "You love me, and I have witnesses," he said.

"What witnesses?"

He gestured past the empty boat at the quiet river. "The pelicans. Very reliable, pelicans."

She laughed, and kissed him again just because she could.

They sat in silence for a while, shoulders touching, watching the light change on the water. The dock lights flickered on, casting long shadows across the deck. At last, Finn stood, offering his hand.

"I should walk you home. It's getting late." She took his hand and they walked home like that, sometimes talking, but not having to.

The streets of Fort Lauderdale had emptied as dusk settled over the town.

"Will you take Bean fishing while I'm gone?" Finn asked.

"Any time she wants," Annie promised. "And I'll teach her to navigate by the stars."

"She'd like that."

The Jeeves house appeared ahead, warm light spilling from the windows. Annie slowed her steps, reluctant for their walk to end. As they approached the porch, her father's voice drifted through the open window.

"...should never have happened!" Skeeter's voice carried through the screen door. "I told them we needed better security, but did they listen? Did they? Hell no!"

Then they heard her mother's garbled voice, and though they couldn't understand the words, her tone conveyed that she was trying to get him to calm down.

"Hilda, I tell you, they should have listened. It started in the east wing right after quitting time. Two men hurt, one pretty bad. He may never work again." Her father's voice was grim. "Security guard said he saw someone suspicious earlier, but lost track of him."

"You think it was deliberate?" Her mother's voice was barely audible.

"Fire chief says they found some kind of device where it started. Navy's sending investigators tomorrow."

The shipyard. Will. The suspicious behavior she'd witnessed earlier that day. She felt a rush of cold spreading through her limbs. Her fingers trembled against Finn's sleeve.

"Annie? What's wrong?"

"I need to talk to someone," she said.

"You can talk to me."

She shook her head.

Finn studied her face. "Now, what aren't you telling me?"

Annie glanced at the house, where her parents' conversation had moved on to other topics. She thought of Frank Chandler's card, tucked in her sketchbook. Of Will's cold eyes when he'd pinned her against the shed.

"There's something wrong. Believe me, Finn, I'd tell you if I could, but I gave my word. I have to find out what it is before anyone else gets hurt."

# CHAPTER THIRTY-SEVEN

*Fort Lauderdale*
*April 22, 1942*

Sleep eluded her that night. Over and over, her mind repeated her father's words: *Two men hurt, one pretty bad. He may never work again.* She'd had the chance to speak up, to tell that guard about Will, about her suspicions. She might have been able to stop him. But she had stayed quiet. She might have prevented the fire, but she had kept quiet. Now, these men were hurt. And it was her fault.

All this time she had been keeping Will's secret. Why? Yes, at first he was this intriguing handsome stranger. And she had rescued him. She wanted to protect him. He seemed so lost. And she had made a promise. Then, as her suspicions grew, it became something else. She didn't want to believe it. Didn't want to have to confess to Chandler. But she had to do something now. Something to make certain Will didn't hurt anyone else.

Annie climbed out of bed, sat at her desk, and switched

on the lamp. She opened her sketchbook to a fresh page and began to draw.

She squinted, trying to capture Will's face from memory: sharp cheekbones, straight nose, those changeable eyes that had shown her too many versions of himself. Which one was real?

After more than an hour, she sat back to study her work. It was good, maybe even her best.

Light filtered through the curtains telling her that morning had arrived at last. She clicked off her desk lamp and stood up to stretch. Time to get ready.

For this occasion, Annie chose her best dress and braided her hair with care. She examined herself in the mirror on the back of her bedroom door. Today, she wanted to be taken seriously. She nodded to her reflection, then ripped the page from her sketchbook and folded it into her pocket. The small white cardboard card followed.

In the kitchen, her mother stood at the stove stirring oatmeal and staring off into the distance.

"Morning, Mama."

Her mother blinked, shaking her head as if surfacing from deep water. "Are you ready for breakfast?"

"I'm not hungry." Annie reached for her hat on a peg next to the kitchen door. "I'm going for a walk."

"You look nice for a change. It's good to see you dressing like a young lady."

Annie shook her head and opened the screen door. Halfway through the door, she paused and turned back to her mother.

"Ma? Did you ever do something you knew might hurt someone, but you did it because you thought it was right?"

Hilda looked up, her eyes sharp. "What have you done, Annie?"

"Nothing...yet." Annie twisted Chandler's card in her pocket. "See you later, Ma."

Outside, the morning heat already pressed down like a wet, wool blanket. Annie pedaled through the streets, her dress whipping around her knees. Sweat trickled down her back by the time she reached The Deck. The restaurant wouldn't open for lunch for several hours, but the door was already unlocked. The dining room stood empty, chairs still upturned on tables.

"We're closed," Beck's voice barked from behind the bar where he counted bottles. "Come back at eleven."

"It's Annie Jeeves, Mr. Beck," she said. "I need to use your telephone."

Beck straightened, his captain's hat askew. "Phone's for business. Not for girls to call their boyfriends."

"It's important." Annie met his gaze. "Family business."

Something in her tone must have convinced him. He jerked his thumb toward the office. "Five minutes. And don't touch anything else."

"Thank you." Annie slipped behind the bar and into the small office. The telephone sat on a cluttered desk beside stacks of invoices. She pulled Chandler's card from her pocket and dialed with shaking fingers.

A clipped male voice answered on the third ring. "Office of Coordinator of Intelligence. How may I direct your call?"

"May I speak to Mr. Drake, please?" Annie said. "It's Annie Jeeves calling. It's urgent."

A pause. "Hold the line."

Annie waited, twisting the telephone cord around her finger. Through the thin walls, she could hear Beck shouting something at the kitchen staff. As usual, no one answered him. She imagined Miss Cora standing tall, her hair wrapped in a colorful scarf, eyes lowered.

"Mr. Drake is unavailable." The voice on the phone startled her.

"Please," Annie insisted. "This is urgent."

"I said he's unavailable."

"When will he be back? I need to speak with him."

"Mr. Drake is a very important man, miss." Annie could hear the smirk in his voice. "He can't be taking calls from young women every day. I will tell him you called when he returns."

"This is not a frivolous matter."

"Miss, perhaps you should discuss this with your father first. Mr. Drake is occupied with matters of national security."

Annie sighed. "Please tell Mr. Drake I called."

"If you have information, you can report it to the local authorities."

"But—"

"Good day, miss."

The line went dead. Annie stared at the receiver, her chest tight with frustration.

Local authorities? Her mind flashed to Sheriff Walter Clark's face, his contemptuous sneer when she used to take his lunch order. The way he spoke to her as though she were a half-brained three-year-old. Going to him was the last thing she wanted to do.

But what choice did she have? The shipyard fire wasn't a coincidence. Two men hurt. Evidence of sabotage. She couldn't wait for Chandler to decide she was important enough to talk to.

Annie replaced the receiver and strode from the office, ignoring Beck's questions as she pushed through the front door.

The first place she tried was Fuller Mansfield's office down near the waterfront. Annie found the office and rapped on the door. No answer. She leaned her bike against the building, then walked down and searched the docks. Most of the boats were out for the day, and only a handful of laborers were there unloading crates of conch and lobster from a small Bahamian freight boat.

The man on the phone had told her to go to the local authorities. Annie wondered if he would have said that if he had known the Clark brothers.

She shrugged. It was worth a try. There wasn't much other choice.

The sheriff's station occupied a squat brick building with barred windows. Inside, the air hung heavy with odors of cigarette smoke and sweat. A wooden counter separated the public area from the deputies' desks. Behind it, a heavyset deputy raised bloodshot eyes from his newspaper.

"Help you, miss?"

"I need to see Sheriff Clark," Annie said. "It's important."

The deputy snorted. "Ain't it always?" He jerked his thumb toward a bench along the wall. "Take a seat. He's busy."

Annie perched on the edge of the bench, clutching her arms tight against her stomach. A drunk dozed in the corner, snoring. Next to him, a dark-haired man sat erect, his arms resting on a briefcase upright on his knees. The wall clock ticked, each second stretching into eternity.

Nearly an hour passed before the inner door opened. Sheriff Walter Clark emerged, adjusting his tie, the large gem on his pinky ring shining even under the dim lights. His thinning blond hair was slicked back with pomade, his face flushed from the heat.

With a sharp lift of his chin, the Sheriff indicated the black-haired man.

The man rose and carried what looked like a very heavy case into the office. Sheriff Clark closed the door, and Annie went back to listening to the clock. The next time the door opened, the visitor departed without the case.

Clark fixed his gaze on her. "Whaddya want?" he asked, not bothering to invite her into his office.

Annie rose, smoothing her skirt. She glanced at the drunk man sleeping in the corner. "Could we go inside?"

Something flickered in Clark's eyes, amusement, annoyance, she couldn't tell. "Nope."

"I need to report suspicious activity. Possible sabotage out at Dooley's."

The sheriff leaned against the door frame and pulled a cigar out of his inside coat pocket. "That right?"

"There's a man in town," Annie continued, lowering her voice. "I believe he might be a German spy."

"A spy? Here in Fort Lauderdale?" He chuckled, turning to the deputy. "Hear that, Bob? We got spies here in town now."

The deputy grinned. "Better call J. Edgar Hoover."

Sheriff Clark lit a match and held the flame to the tip of the cigar. He puffed smoke as he spun the cigar.

Heat rose to Annie's cheeks. "I'm serious. He was at Dooley's Shipyard yesterday, acting suspicious. Then there was a fire."

The sheriff pulled the cigar from his mouth and tossed the burnt match to the floor. "I know about the fire."

"Then you should know that two men were seriously injured."

Clark shrugged. "One of them was colored. Did your daddy put you up to this?"

Annie pulled the sketch from her pocket and unfolded it. "This man. He calls himself Will Hersey. Claims he's from Indiana, but I think he's lying. Yesterday, I caught him sneaking around the restricted area at Dooley's, a few hours before the fire started."

Clark took the drawing, his expression bored. "Looks like every other Yankee tourist who comes through here."

"He's not a tourist." Annie's frustration mounted. "He had something hidden under his jacket. He fought with me when I caught him—"

"Fought with you, huh?" Clark's gaze traveled up and down her body. "Sure he wasn't just trying to get friendly?"

Deputy Bob chuckled.

Annie squeezed her fists at her sides. "No. He threatened me."

"So, what are we really talking about here?" Clark walked over and leaned against the counter. "Ernie told me about you. You been stepping out with this fella, and now you're sore because he's sweet on someone else?"

"That's not—"

"Because I got actual police business to take care of." Clark's voice took on a nasty edge. "Can't be wasting time on some girl's boyfriend troubles."

"He's not my boyfriend," Annie said through clenched teeth. "And this isn't personal."

Clark studied her face, something calculating in his gaze. "You're just another trouble-makin' Jeeves girl, ain't you? The one whose brother made one bad decision after another, like cozying up to a colored girl, then got himself killed playing hero?"

The words hit like a physical blow. "My brother died serving his country."

"Did he now?" Clark's mouth twisted. "Just like all those boys shipping out now." He waved the cigar in the air. "Like that Taggart boy. Heard he enlisted. Good riddance."

Annie struggled to control her breathing. "This has nothing to do with Finn or Jack. This is about Will Hersey and the danger he poses. He's not going to stop trying to damage that shipyard."

"Looky, girl." Clark tossed the sketch onto the counter. "We don't need you stirring up trouble. This town's got enough to worry about without hysterical women seeing spies behind every palm tree."

"I'm not being hysterical!" Annie's voice rose. "There's a fire chief's report. Evidence of sabotage."

"You'd do well to mind your own business." Clark cut her off, stepping closer. His voice dropped to a menacing whisper. "And tell that colored girl you run around with to watch herself. Emma, isn't it? Pretty name. Be a shame if something were to happen to her."

Annie felt a cold calm descend on her. "Are you threatening my friend?"

"Just making conversation." Clark smiled, revealing tobacco-stained teeth. "Funny thing about colored folks. They have all sorts of accidents. Fall down stairs. Drown in canals. Nobody asks too many questions."

Annie fought against the fury, keeping her voice steady. "You're supposed to uphold the law."

"I am the law in this county." Clark's voice was soft, enunciating each word. "And the law says you don't mix with coloreds, and you don't go around accusing respectable young white men of being spies without evidence."

"I have evidence."

"You have a drawing and a grudge." Clark straightened, adjusting his belt. "Now get on home before I decide you need a night in the lockup to cool that temper. And I'd hate to see what might happen to a pretty girl like you in my cells."

Annie backed toward the door, bile rising in her throat. Clark's eyes followed her, amusement dancing in their pale depths. He was enjoying this.

"Have a nice day now," he called as she pushed through the door. "And remember what I said about your friends."

Outside, Annie gulped the fresh air, fighting the urge to

vomit. Her legs felt unsteady as she moved away from the building. Clark wasn't just dismissing her; he was threatening Emma, perhaps others.

No one in authority would help her. Not Chandler, not Mansfield, not Clark. She was on her own against Will, against the sheriff, against whatever darkness was spreading through her town.

Annie walked northwest across Broward Boulevard. Her heart hammered against her ribs, from exertion in part but mostly from the sheriff's threats against Emma.

A group of men playing checkers under a tree paused their game to watch her pass, their expressions guarded. Children playing hopscotch scattered like startled birds at the sight of a white woman walking down their street.

The door opened almost immediately, as if Emma had been waiting. With one look at Annie's face Emma pulled her inside, glancing up and down the street before closing the door.

"Annie. Come inside."

The familiar scents of the Albury household, cinnamon and chicory coffee washed over Annie. The small front room was spotless, worn furniture polished to a soft glow. Elzo sat in his chair by the window, a book open on his lap.

"Lord have mercy," he said. "What is it, child? What's got you so riled up?"

Annie's knees felt weak. Emma guided her to the sofa, one arm around her shoulders.

"Will," she said, her voice no more than a whisper. "The man I rescued. I think he's a German spy."

Emma's eyes widened, her hand going to her mouth. "What? How do you know?"

"I saw him," Annie said, the words coming faster now. "Saw him at the shipyard. Right before the fire."

"We heard about that fire," Elzo said.

Annie nodded and turned to Emma. "I believe that was Will. He's not going to stop. Woody saw it in him the first day. He said he's a man with nothing to lose. And Clark—" Annie stared into Emma's eyes. "Sheriff Clark said he'd make you pay if I keep talking."

Elzo closed his book and leaned forward, his weathered face grave.

"Tell us everything," he said.

The story poured out of Annie, at least what she felt she could tell, of finding Will in the water months ago, his suspicious behavior around town and at the shipyard, and the fire.

"At Whiskey Creek, when we found that midget submarine—"

Emma's eyes grew large, and she glanced at Elzo.

Annie continued. "I know. We promised the naval officer we wouldn't talk about it. But I think your Gramps knows more about war than either of us, and I have to trust somebody right now. That day at Whiskey Creek, Will knew things. Things he shouldn't have known about German equipment."

Elzo studied her. "You learn to recognize evil in a man's heart when you've lived as long as Woody and I have," he said. "This Will. You say he looks like an American, talks like an American?"

Annie nodded. "Perfect English."

"The devil wears many faces," Elzo said. "During the Great War, I served with men who could tell a German spy by the way he held his cigarette. Small things betray us."

Emma disappeared into the kitchen, returning moments later with a tray of steaming cups. She offered one to Annie. The tea smelled of mint.

"Drink," she instructed. "This will settle your nerves."

Annie took a sip, the warmth spreading through her chest. "Nobody will listen."

"I'm listening," Emma said with a shy smile.

"The sheriff, he mentioned you by name." Annie reached over and touched her friend's forearm. "Said colored folks have 'accidents.' That nobody asks questions."

Emma's face remained calm. "Clark's been threatening colored folks since before we were born, Annie."

"He knows we're friends," Annie insisted.

Elzo's deep voice filled the small room. "Men like Clark feed on fear."

"So what can I do?" Annie set down her cup, tea sloshing over the rim. "Clark won't help. I can't reach anyone else. Two men have already been hurt. It could be my Pa next."

"And you think this young man will act again?" Elzo's eyes were sharp.

"I'm sure of it. Will isn't here by accident. I can't explain what he was doing in the water that night I found him. That's what made me struggle so long at believing he could be trouble. But the man I saw at Dooley's is desperate. And I'm sure he's not done making trouble."

"You can't go to Clark again," Elzo said. "Not after he threatened Emma. He won't forget."

"I know."

Emma spoke up, her voice quiet but determined. "Then we have to stop Will ourselves."

"Emma!" Elzo's voice was sharp.

"No, Gramps. If Annie's right, people could die." Emma turned to Annie. "Did you ever find out where he's staying?"

Annie shook her head. "We found an empty house up around Pompano. Pretty sure it was his place. But he was gone by the time we got there. He just disappears. Shows up when I least expect it, then vanishes again."

"We need to find him," Emma said. "Figure out what he's planning."

"It's too dangerous," Elzo interrupted. "This isn't some schoolyard bully. If he's really what Annie thinks—"

"Then he's dangerous," Emma said,

"Too dangerous for you girls to handle alone."

Annie felt a flash of frustration. "But who else can help? Clark is threatening Emma. My father would just go to Clark making things worse."

A heavy silence filled the room. Outside, the light was changing, afternoon sliding toward evening.

"I should go," she said. "Before it gets dark."

Elzo reached out to her and squeezed Annie's hand. "Be careful, child. Come in the back door next time. Fewer eyes that way."

At the door, Emma looked back at her grandpa, then slipped out the door with Annie. "Follow me."

The two young women walked around to the shed and squatted down where no one could see or hear them. "I think we're on our own on this one, Annie. Not even Gramps will help."

"I don't want to get you in trouble, Em."

"Sounds like we've got to be as courageous as the boys going overseas. What do you say we take the bus tomorrow up to Pompano, and we go check out that place where you think Will used to stay? Maybe we can lure him out."

"Okay, Em. But this is just a look-see. Seriously, I don't want to cause any trouble for you and your family."

"Don't worry. That old sheriff is only interested in money. He's too busy with his gambling interests and arresting black boys for loitering so he can fine them. He won't bother us for going on an outing together."

"Yeah. I have a nasty feeling I saw a fella from one of those gambling clubs take a briefcase full of cash into Clark's office today," Annie said.

"We can't change the Clark brothers' enterprise, but maybe we can stop Will Hersey."

The girls stood. Emma hugged Annie. "We'll figure something out," she whispered. "We'll meet on the boat tomorrow? Noon time be okay? I got chores."

Annie nodded. "See you tomorrow." Then she walked away, eager to reach home before full darkness fell.

A dog barked nearby, making her jump. Two sailors passed on the opposite sidewalk, their laughter too loud in the quiet street. Annie pressed her hand against her pocket, where the sketch remained folded.

Will was out there somewhere in the darkness, planning his next move, possibly even watching her at this very moment. But Annie was not alone. Emma also recognized the danger he posed. Together, they were the only ones who could stop him now.

# CHAPTER THIRTY-EIGHT

*Fort Lauderdale*
*April 23, 1942*

Two hours of scrubbing salt residue off every surface had left her arms aching, but the boat looked proper again. She wasn't good at waiting. Emma had her chores, and Annie's were on the boat. Finn was busy moving Bean into her new room at their house and packing up his own things. He had to turn over the keys to the cottage he and his sister had shared today.

Tomorrow. Finn was leaving in one day. She hoped they would have time tonight. Time to be alone.

She tossed the rag into the bucket and stretched her back, wincing at the tightness. The denim fabric of her overalls bunched up under her hands. Her clothes were fitting more loosely these days. Her mother was always telling her she needed to eat, but food had become the least of her worries.

The dock stood empty this Thursday morning. Most boats were either out with charters or tied up elsewhere waiting for weekend tourists. Only Cap's decrepit skiff bobbed three slips down.

She had spent half the morning splicing line and greasing winches, then scrubbing up. Her fingers were raw, grit settled under her nails, but she wasn't about to complain. Work meant purpose. Annie just needed to keep moving, or she'd have to think about Finn leaving and Will, a German spy. It still seemed so unreal even to think about it.

An anhinga perched on top of a piling across the river, its wings spread out to dry. Annie reached for her sketchbook and settled cross-legged onto the cockpit's wooden bench. She downed the last dregs of her glass of tea. Then she reached for the stub of pencil tucked behind her ear and flipped to a clean page.

The world narrowed to the snake-like curve of the bird's neck, the white feathered chevrons on her wings. Annie's hand moved across the paper, capturing the stillness and tension in the bird's posture. She'd drawn this bird a hundred times before, but each moment was different, each sketch a fresh challenge.

"You're good at that."

The pencil skidded across the page, leaving an ugly mark through the anhinga's wing. Annie's head snapped up. Will stood not three feet away, one hand resting on the lifelines. She hadn't heard him come down the dock.

"Will." Her voice sounded steadier than she felt.

He looked thinner, harder. Dark circles shadowed his eyes, and a week's worth of stubble covered his jaw. His hair was slick with sweat, and Jack's old blue-checked shirt hung loose on his frame, stained with sweat at the collar. Had it only been two days since she had seen him at the shipyard?

"Don't look so surprised." He seemed to examine her as if she were a bug pinned to a board.

Annie closed her sketchbook. "I wasn't expecting company."

"No?" He stepped closer, and the fabric of his shirt shifted. She saw the black pistol tucked snug at his belt. "Not even after visiting the sheriff?"

Annie's mouth went dry. She'd never seen a gun up close other than her father's hunting rifle.

"I had concerns." She held his gaze, refusing to look away first.

Will's laugh was bitter. "Concerns. That's one way to put it."

"So you're a Nazi." She stated it as a matter of fact.

"No, never. I despise Hitler."

The look on his face. She believed him. "Then I don't understand."

"You never will." He gestured toward the wooden launch tied alongside the *Tequesta*. "Stand up. We're leaving." His voice sounded brittle. "No shouting. Not if you want to stay alive."

She stood. The bird took flight, wings wide, vanishing into the river's glare. A scrap of pencil lead snapped under her shoe.

"Where?"

"Upriver. Somewhere we can talk without prying eyes." His hand moved to rest on the gun's grip under his shirt. Not pointing it, but the threat was clear. "Now."

Annie's thoughts tumbled into a blur. Emma was coming, but not soon enough. In an hour? Maybe less. No one knew Will was here. How was she going to get out of this?

"I said now!"

"All right, all right." She held up her empty glass. "Let me put this away and close up the cabin." She kept her voice calm, reasonable. "It would look suspicious if I left things unsecured."

Will hesitated, then nodded. "Make it quick."

Annie tucked the sketchbook under her arm and descended the three steps into the cabin. Inside, it was cooler, shadowed. She placed the glass in the tiny sink, forcing herself to breathe slowly. Move, idiot. Think. Think.

She looked around the familiar cabin. Was there anything here she could use as a weapon? No, not against a gun. The only serious knife on the boat was in a sheath next to the main mast, ready to cut away the rigging if necessary.

"Don't try anything stupid, Annie."

He was right. It would be stupid to go up against him with a knife. "I'm just going to grab my jacket," she said.

She placed the sketchbook on the table, and then opened the locker for her foul-weather jacket. As she pulled her arm through the sleeve, her eyes lit on the sketchbook.

That's it! She snapped open the book to an old page, a rough drawing she'd done years ago, just for Jack, of the Seminole chickee hidden out in the mangroves. Jack's hideout. It was on the North Fork. He said *upriver*. If he was looking for isolation, that was the direction they would go. She drew a crude arrow pointing to the drawing. Then she spelled out his name. Will.

"What's taking so long?" Will called from above.

"Just tidying up," she answered. Emma would be expecting her to be here. Annie placed the open sketchbook face down on the small table where her friend would see it. Emma knew the hideout well.

When Annie emerged from the cabin, Will had already climbed down into the launch. He looked up at her, impatience written across his features.

"I could run."

"And if you did, I could shoot you. Or one of your precious friends."

"Would you?"

"Don't try my patience any longer. Untie us and get down here," he ordered.

Annie worked, unwinding the painter from the cleat, climbing down into the smaller boat. The outboard motor started on the second pull.

"Head upriver," Will instructed, settling in the bow, facing her. The gun lay across his lap now, accessible and hidden under his shirttail. "Past the Andrews Avenue Bridge, then into the North Fork."

The launch struggled against the current. They passed beneath the railroad trestle, the shadow momentarily cooling Annie's face.

Not long after they entered the North Fork of the river, the mangroves closed in around them. The air grew thick with the smell of mud and decaying vegetation.

A mullet jumped, slapping the water. Birds called from the twisted branches overhead. The sounds and smells of the city fell away behind them as they proceeded upriver. No more houses with curious faces at the windows to notice their passing.

Will pointed at the outboard. "Can't you go any faster?"

Her only chance was to delay. Hope someone would notice her missing. "Don't want to damage the prop by hitting something. Not many boats go up this fork of the river."

The channel narrowed further, forcing Annie to slow the motor to navigate around submerged branches and roots. Ahead, the river bent to the right, and Annie knew what waited around that curve. The small clearing. The chickee hut left behind by an old Seminole trapper. The hut that Jack had reclaimed.

As they rounded the bend, the clearing came into view, along with the pitched roof of palm fronds now weathered and sagging in spots. The sight of it pierced Annie's heart.

How many afternoons had she spent here, listening to Jack's wild plans for the future? How many storms had they weathered under that roof, laughing as rain pounded the thatch?

Will gestured toward the muddy bank. "Pull in there."

Annie steered the launch to shore, cutting the engine as they glided the last few feet. Fresh footprints marked the mud. Will's coming and going. A corner of the canvas tarp fluttered free from the ropes behind a cypress knee, partially concealing what looked like wooden crates.

Will had taken Jack's sacred place and made it his own. A spy's hideout. A base for enemy operations.

She climbed up the bank and stepped onto the wooden platform, the weathered planks springing slightly under her weight. Will motioned with the gun toward the doorway. Once inside the hut, she saw that Jack's childhood sanctuary had been transformed into something alien: a war room in miniature. Maps tacked to support poles. A radio of some kind connected to a large battery nestled beside a bedroll. Notebooks filled with tiny, precise handwriting in German. Annie's eyes darted from object to object, cataloging each new betrayal.

"Move over there." Will gestured with the gun toward the far side of the platform.

Annie stepped around a stack of food cans. American brands, she noted, and a canteen. Her gaze fixed on Jack's fishing spear still hanging on the central post. He'd carved it from cypress, spent weeks getting the balance just right. Will had left it untouched, like a museum piece.

"Did you know this place was my brother's?" Her voice sounded strange to her own ears.

"Not at first." Will kept the gun trained on her as he moved to stand between her and the entrance. "I found an old journal. He was in love with your colored friend. That is something I do not understand."

"So, you are a Nazi," she whispered.

"Shut up. I told you, I despise the Nazis. But the Americans aren't so different. I see how most white Americans treat the colored. Even my American father used to call them animals."

"That's not the same as sending them to camps."

"Your country is sending the Japanese Americans to camps. Germans to camps. You're no better than Germans. One day this country will have a Hitler. You'll see."

Will moved to the radio. With his free hand, he adjusted a dial, producing only static. His movements were jerky, uncertain. Sweat beaded on his forehead despite the shade.

"I should have disappeared after the incident at Whiskey Creek. The submarine." His accent had shifted, the German undertones noticeable now. "That was the protocol. Move if compromised."

The full reality of her situation washed over Annie. She stood in a remote hideout with an armed Nazi spy. No one knew where she was except perhaps Emma, but Annie had no idea if she would find the sketchbook or even understand the message. Will had nothing left to lose.

"But you didn't disappear," she said.

Will paced the dirt floor, gun still pointed in her direction. "No. And do you know why?" His laugh was bitter. "Because of you."

"The fire at the shipyard. That was you, wasn't it?"

He didn't look at her, didn't answer.

"Two men were hurt. One of them still might die."

"You don't understand."

"Will, look at me. What happened to the kind man I kissed on the beach?"

"Stop it." He hit the side of his head with his free hand. "I can't get you out of my head. I'm supposed to leave, go join Max and Jorg. But here I am." He stood staring out the door of the hut for the longest time, not saying a word. At last, he shook his head and turned to face her. "It doesn't matter. I'm a dead man either way."

"Why?"

"That fool Erich."

She knew she had to keep him talking.

"Tell me about Erich."

He inhaled, then blew the air out through rounded lips. "I felt sorry for him at first. He was so inept. I didn't think he would ever make the cut to be part of the team."

"Team?"

"There were four of us. We were chosen because we were fluent in English. My father really was American, you know. I was born in this country. My mother was German. She wanted to go back to Germany in '31 after my father was killed." He stopped again and seemed lost in his memories.

Annie waited. She calculated the distance between them. Six feet. Too far with the gun in play. She needed him closer, or distracted. "So tell me what happened to Erich."

He sighed. "They called it Operation Pastorius. The four of us were sent on a U-boat. When we were at sea, they read us our orders."

"And what were they, Will?"

He stared at her, conflict raging behind his eyes. "We were supposed to report ship movements and sabotage military installations. I started with light signals. But you know that." He gestured to the radio. "Then I found this radio on a boat and stole it. Got back in contact with U-123, Kapitän Hardegen. Had to take it down to the beach to make contact, though."

His breathing was growing more rapid. Talking about it all was making him angry, but she needed to kill time.

"My orders were to radio coordinates at night, supply ships, troop movements." He broke off, shaking his head.

"So what does that have to do with Erich?"

"On the U-boat, I learned my primary mission was to protect the bumbling fool, to bring him back alive. His uncle is a vicious SS-Obergruppenführer. The submarine captain told me if I failed, Erich's uncle would kill me and my family. But Erich died before we even made it to shore."

His unfocused eyes appeared to be looking inward at some painful memory. "I realized I was the only one who knew what happened. If I wanted to live, I had to make them think Erich and I were ashore working together."

"So, you've been helping the U-boats find targets." Annie thought of all the men who had been killed by torpedoes off the Florida shore. The burnt bodies that had been washing up on their beaches.

"Annie, no. I am not what you think. I started leaving things out." His face contorted into a plea for understanding. "Delaying reports. After the submarine incident, Berlin ordered me to eliminate any witnesses." He swallowed hard. "Especially you."

Annie fought to keep her expression neutral, though her heart hammered.

"But you didn't."

His eyes locked with hers. "I couldn't. Don't you understand? I betrayed my mission. I told them I had done it. I was lying to them. For you."

Will's pacing grew more agitated. The gun wavered in his grip as he moved back and forth across the dirt. "Why did you do this to me?" The question burst from him, ragged and desperate.

He trailed off, searching for words. Annie saw her opportunity in his distraction. She shifted her weight, preparing.

"I was just following orders," Will continued, his voice rising. "I didn't want to join this mission, but they gave me no choice. Then you pulled me from the water and everything changed." He paused, staring at her with something like wonder. "Why did you have to be so..."

"I didn't do anything, Will." Annie softened her voice. It was too late to keep hoping for a rescue. She was on her own. Jack had taught her once, go for the gun hand first, strike hard at the wrist or forearm. "I just saved a drowning man."

"You should have let me drown!" The words exploded from him. "Now I'm trapped. I can't go back—I'll be shot for failing my mission. I can't stay here—I'll be executed as a spy." He stepped closer, his free hand reaching toward her, pleading.

Five feet now. Not ideal, but his guard was dropping.

"I'm sorry," she said, meaning it despite everything.

His shoulders slumped. Four feet between them now.

Will hung his head, unable to look at her. "So am I."

# CHAPTER THIRTY-NINE

*Fort Lauderdale*
*April 23, 1942*

Annie lunged forward, driving her right fist up toward his face just as her father and Jack had taught her. Her knuckles connected with his jaw with surprising force. The pain in her hand exploded.

Will's head flew up, and he staggered backward out the door of the hut, stunned. Annie pivoted and followed him, bringing her left forearm down hard across his right wrist.

The gun flew into the underbrush.

For one suspended moment, they both stared at the weapon. Then both dove toward it.

Will's fingers reached it first, but Annie brought her knee up hard into his side. He grunted, the gun slipping from his grasp again. Annie scrambled for it, fingers brushing the metal grip.

Will recovered faster than she expected. His elbow caught her in the ribs, knocking the wind from her lungs. He shoved her aside with brutal force.

Annie felt herself falling. Her back struck a large cypress root, pain shooting up her spine. She gasped, struggling to draw breath as black spots danced in her vision.

When her sight cleared, Will stood over her, gun in hand again. His lip was bleeding where she'd struck him. His eyes had gone cold.

"Don't move." He pointed the gun at her chest.

Annie remained still, her lungs drawing in air in painful gulps.

"I could have killed you already," Will said. "If that's what I wanted."

"What do you want?"

Something flickered in Will's eyes. Uncertainty? Regret? She couldn't tell. He reached down and grabbed her arm, hauling her to her feet.

"You shouldn't have gone to the sheriff," he said. "Now I have no choice."

"You brought me here to kill me, didn't you?"

He jabbed the gun toward Annie, the tremors in his hand visible now. "We need to move. They'll be looking for you soon." Annie rose from the log, pain radiating from her ribs where he'd struck her. Will's eyes had taken on a frantic quality, darting between her and the entrance to the chickee hut. Whatever internal battle he'd been fighting seemed to be over. The trained soldier, the desperate man with nothing left to lose, was taking over.

"Where are we going?" Annie asked. The afternoon light was fading. Soon darkness would swallow the narrow waters, making navigation treacherous. Staying here was her best chance.

Will grabbed her arm, his fingers digging into her skin. "Doesn't matter. Just move."

He dragged her toward the hut entrance, the gun pressed against her back. He pushed her through the door. Annie stumbled on the uneven planks, her mind racing for options. The launch was their only way out. If she could delay, create distance between them and the boat...

"Will, please," she began. "You don't have to do this."

He handed her a burlap sack. "Collect the food."

Annie picked up the cans and shoved them into the bag.

He gestured toward a blanket. "That, too. Now let's go." He prodded her spine with the gun.

Annie exited the hut first.

"Will, don't do this."

He grabbed her braid. "Why did you go to the sheriff?" He yanked her closer, his breath hot against her ear. "Don't make me hurt you!"

"No, stop! Annie!"

The voice—female, terrified, familiar—cut through the humid air. Emma stood at the edge of the clearing, her dark skin glistening with sweat, chest heaving from exertion.

Will reacted with military precision. He locked one arm across Annie's chest while the other pressed the gun to her temple. The cold metal against her skin made her shiver.

"Emma, run!" Annie shouted. "Get help!"

"Too late." Will's voice sounded calm, but she felt the tremor from the hand that held the gun. "Who else is with you?"

Emma's eyes were wide with fear, but she stood her ground. "Nobody. I came alone."

"Liar." Will backed up, dragging Annie with him into the partial shelter of the chickee hut's entrance. "Call them out, or I swear I'll shoot her."

"Please," Emma begged, a single tear sliding down her face. "Don't hurt her."

The sound of splashing water and breaking branches answered Will's question. Two figures emerged from the undergrowth on the opposite side of the clearing. Finn in his work clothes, and beside him, Fuller Mansfield still wearing his tweed jacket..

"Annie!" Finn's voice broke on her name.

Will's arm tightened around her throat. "One step closer and I swear I'll pull this trigger."

Annie couldn't see Will's face, but she felt his racing heartbeat against her back, the fine tremors running through his body. He was terrified.

"Everyone stay back," Mansfield called, his voice calm but carrying. He held Finn by the arm, preventing him from rushing forward.

"Let her go, you Nazi bastard!" Finn shouted, struggling against Mansfield's grip. "I swear to God if you hurt her—"

"Shut up!" Will's shout was edged with panic. "All of you, shut up!"

"Finn, please," Annie managed, though Will's arm restricted her breathing. "Don't."

Mansfield pushed Finn behind him and took a single step forward, empty hands raised. "Son, let's talk about this."

"Stay back!" Will pressed the gun harder against Annie's temple. "I'll kill her. I will."

"No, you won't." Mansfield's voice remained steady. "I don't see a Nazi here. I see an American boy caught on the wrong side of a bad situation."

Will's breathing quickened. "You know nothing about me."

"I know your father was American," Mansfield said. "That means something in the eyes of the law."

Annie felt Will stiffen against her.

"How did you—"

"We can help with your family in Germany too," Mansfield continued. "But only if you put the gun down now."

Finn had gone still, his face pale beneath his freckles. Emma stood frozen at the opposite edge of the clearing.

Annie took a risk. "Will, I know you've been holding back information, protecting people," she said. "Those aren't the actions of someone who believes in what they're doing."

"Shut up." Will's voice cracked.

"My brother said there's always a choice," Annie continued. "Even when it feels like there isn't."

"I said shut up!" Will's arm tightened around her throat.

"You're not a killer, Will." Annie reached up, placing her hand over his on the gun. The metal was slick with his sweat. "I know you're not."

Time seemed to stretch. Annie felt every heartbeat, every breath. Will's hand trembled beneath hers.

Then, slowly, the pressure of the gun against her temple eased.

"I can't go back," Will said, his voice weak. "Not after what I've done."

"You don't have to," Mansfield promised.

With excruciating slowness, Will lowered the gun from Annie's head. His arm fell away from her throat. She stepped forward, out of his grasp, legs shaking so hard she almost fell.

Will looked at the gun in his hand as if seeing it for the first time. With deliberate movements, he placed it on the ground and slid it toward Mansfield.

"I'm sorry," he said, looking at Annie. "I'm sorry I couldn't be the man you thought I was."

Mansfield moved then, retrieving the gun. He pointed it at Will and told him to sit on the ground. Then he looked at Annie. "Are you all right?"

She nodded. "There's a radio in the hut."

Annie went to take a step forward, and her legs buckled beneath her. Finn caught her, wrapping his arms around her.

Emma appeared with rope from the tarps at the side of the hut and held the gun while Mansfield bound Will's wrists.

Annie pressed her face against Finn's shoulder, inhaling the familiar scent of him.

"My God," he whispered into her hair. "I thought I'd lost you."

"You're here. You're real." Her voice broke. "For a moment, I thought I'd never—"

"Shh," Finn whispered. "I'm here."

Emma joined them, her arms encircling them both. "Finn walked me to the boat, and we found your sketchbook," she said, her voice shaking. "I saw the drawing, the arrow. I knew where you'd be."

Annie looked from one to the other. "I only knew the direction, upriver. I didn't know it would actually be here."

"We got lucky for sure," Finn said. "Mansfield was in his office, and his car was right there."

Over Finn's shoulder, Annie watched as Mansfield led Will toward the trail that would take them out to the main highway. Will glanced back once, his expression unreadable in the fading light.

Finn's arms tightened around her, and she buried her face against his neck. "I can't believe you're leaving in the morning. I don't want to let go of you."

"My sweet Annie. You almost got killed, and that's what you're thinking?"

"I was so afraid I wouldn't have a chance to say goodbye."

# CHAPTER FORTY

*Fort Lauderdale*
*August 25, 1942*

Rain hammered against the tin roof, while Annie stood at her bedroom window, watching fat droplets splatter against the glass. The sheen of water made everything outside blur and shimmer, turning her own front yard into something alien.

She tugged at the white collar of her new navy blue dress, the crisp fabric scratching against her neck. The matching shoes pinched her toes. The girl reflected in the window glass looked like a stranger—hair neatly pinned, lips pressed together in concentration.

Three months had passed since that day at the old trapper's chickee hut when Will had pressed a gun barrel to her head. First, it was weeks of answering questions from stern men in suits, of nightmares that left her gasping in the dark. Then, just when she was back to work on the *Tequesta*, Chandler came by with his offer.

"This is ridiculous," she muttered, pressing a damp palm against her forehead. She had showered just twenty minutes ago, but already the oppressive August humidity was making her hair stick to the back of her neck.

Thunder rolled across the sky as she turned away from the window. Her open suitcase lay on the bed, half-filled. Tess's tail twitched under the bed where she was hiding from the thunder.

There was still time for her to change her mind. Why did she let Chandler talk her into this crazy idea of going off to study at a college in Tallahassee? This house was where she belonged, here with her family, running charters on the *Tequesta*. The war had taken everything from her. Jack gone forever. Finn had gone to the Pacific front. She hated this war and the way it was changing everything. The *Tequesta* was fully booked for charters, and now she was giving it all up to get gussied up and go off to college?

She'd accepted Chandler's proposal when she remembered Finn's words from the day they'd kissed for the first time. Finn said he was going to fight to preserve the life they had here.

Annie glanced at the nautical chart of Florida taped to the wall above her suitcase. The southern part was covered with annotations of every inlet, every sandbar, every treacherous shoal she'd ever navigated.

What do you pack when you're leaving everything and everyone behind?

She pulled the chart down and studied the blank expanses, tracing the Big Bend coastline with her finger. Then she folded the paper with care and placed it inside her suitcase.

A photograph of Jack in his uniform sat on her bedside table. Annie picked it up, rubbing her thumb across the glass. In the picture, he was grinning, his captain's hat at a jaunty angle, so full of life she couldn't believe he was gone.

"I'm doing this, Jack," she whispered.

After wrapping the frame in a cardigan, she nestled it between her clothes.

Annie turned her attention to the other items she'd laid out on the bed: her most-worn clothes, her old shoes, her father's brass compass, and a single sweater for the chill she knew was coming. She placed it all inside, and it didn't even fill the case.

On her desk lay two books. Her most recent sketchbook, the one containing drawings of the *Tequesta*, of Emma at the helm, of Finn laughing in the afternoon sun, as well as Jack's copy of Weems' *Air Navigation*, its margins filled with his scribbled notes. He had been studying that book ever since he first started flying lessons. Annie had avoided opening it after his death, but now she could smile when she touched his illegible scrawl.

Both books went into her canvas shoulder bag, along with a tin of pencils of varying hardnesses, her wallet containing twenty-seven dollars and forty-three cents, and three sticks of Wrigley's Spearmint gum. The bag had accompanied her on countless excursions aboard the *Tequesta*, had been splashed with saltwater and dried in the sun more times than she could count. Now it would accompany her on a different journey.

Outside, lightning flashed, turning her bedroom brilliant white. Annie counted—one, two, three—before thunder crashed overhead. The storm was above them now.

Annie looked around her room one last time. She had expected to feel more sorrow at leaving, but she found a curious blend of nerves and anticipation coursing through her.

"Tess, come out and say goodbye." The dog's head poked out from under the bed. Annie knelt down and kissed her wet nose. "You take care of the rest of them. You hear?"

Another thunderclap shook the house, and the dog disappeared back under the bed.

Annie closed the suitcase and set it on the floor. The room felt smaller, as if it had already shed her presence.

The bedroom door flew open with a dramatic bang. Bean stood in the doorway, her red braids askew, green eyes narrowed. Without waiting for an invitation, she marched across the room, spun around and flopped down backwards onto Annie's made bed, arms spread wide like a bird shot from the sky.

"So you're leaving me here as an only child," Bean announced, staring up at the ceiling. Her voice carried the peculiar blend of accusation and resignation that only a ten-year-old could perfect.

Bean had been living with them since Finn shipped out with the Navy three months ago. In that short time, she had entrenched herself in the Jeeves household.

Annie smiled. "You'll hardly be alone. You've got Ma and Pa."

Bean rolled onto her stomach and propped her chin on a pair of fists. "They're not the same as having a sister." She stuck her lower lip out in a pout.

"Well, someone has to make sure the old folks don't worry too much about me and Finn." Annie sat on the bed beside her. "And you're just the girl for the job."

Bean considered this, then sat up and nodded. "I can do that."

She reached into the front pocket of her overalls and pulled out a folded paper. "I made you something." She unfolded a crayon drawing of a house with four figures standing beside it, labeled "Pa," "Ma," "Bean," and off to the side, "Annie" with an arrow pointing away.

"It's us. So you don't forget."

Annie swallowed hard. "I could never forget you, Bean. Not any of you."

"Finn said he wouldn't forget us either. But now his letters don't come so often." Bean wrinkled her nose, a gesture so like her brother, it made Annie's chest ache.

"I'll write you every week, and I won't be so far away."

"Promise?"

"I promise." Annie folded the drawing and tucked it into her canvas bag, next to Jack's book. "And I'll be back for Christmas if I can."

Bean nodded. "If you see Finn before I do, tell him I'm taking good care of his fishing knife."

"I will," Annie promised, though she knew it was unlikely she'd see Finn before Bean did. His last letter had mentioned deployment to the Pacific, though the censors had blacked out where.

"You're not coming to the station?"

"In this rain?" Then Bean threw her arms around Annie's neck in a fierce hug that nearly toppled them both backward onto the bed. Just as fast, she released her and stood up.

"Pa says you need to leave in less than an hour, and Ma says it's going to take that long just to get you and your bags to the car in this weather."

Annie felt a peculiar twisting in her chest. Bean wasn't one for prolonged goodbyes or excessive sentimentality. Another trait she shared with her brother. This abrupt shift to practicality was her way of coping.

"Tell them I'm almost ready," Annie said, matching Bean's casual tone.

Bean nodded and headed for the door, but paused with her hand on the knob. "Annie?"

"Yes?"

"I'm glad you're going to college. Finn says girls should be able to do anything boys can. Even if it means leaving."

Before Annie could respond, Bean slipped out of the room.

"Annie!" Her mother's voice carried down the hallway. "There's someone here to see you."

Annie slung her canvas bag onto her shoulder and picked up her suitcase. The living room came into view as she emerged from the hallway, and there, standing near the sofa, was Frank Chandler, his thin-rimmed glasses speckled with raindrops and his immaculate suit damp at the shoulders.

"Mr. Chandler," Annie said, setting her suitcase by the door. "I wasn't expecting you."

Chandler offered a slight bow of his head. His hair was slicked back, and a small puddle had formed beneath his polished shoes. Despite his disheveled appearance, his posture remained as formal as ever.

"Miss Jeeves. I hope I'm not intruding on your departure preparations."

"No, sir."

"Not at all," her mother added, fussing with the sleeve of Chandler's jacket. "I was just about to fix some iced tea. You look like you could use something cool."

"That would be most kind, Mrs. Jeeves."

As her mother dashed toward the kitchen, Annie settled into the armchair across from Chandler. His presence was unexpected. Since the incident with Will, she had seen Chandler only twice, once for her formal debriefing, and once when he had presented her with the opportunity to attend the special four-month map-making program at Florida State College for Women.

Chandler waited until her mother had left the room. Then he leaned forward and spoke. "I thought you might want to know about Hersey."

That was not what Annie had expected him to say. A flash of memory swept through her: Will's shaking hand, the cold metal of the gun, the tightness of his arm around her throat.

"What's happened?" Her voice sounded steadier than she felt.

Chandler removed his glasses, wiping them with a creased handkerchief he produced from his breast pocket. "His trial concluded last week. Given the circumstances of his surrender and his subsequent cooperation in helping us capture the other members of his network, he was spared the death penalty."

Annie nodded, relief washing through her. She had testified at the closed military hearing, describing both Will's actions at the shipyard and how he had surrendered rather than harm her. She had spoken the truth, neither condemning nor defending him.

"They sentenced Hersey to twenty years at Fort Leavenworth. However, the other members of Operation Pastorius will not be as fortunate." Chandler replaced his glasses adjusting the fit with both hands. "It's not certain he will have to serve the entire sentence. After the war, he will likely be repatriated to Germany as part of a prisoner exchange program." Chandler shrugged. "His information was quite valuable."

Annie looked down at her intertwined fingers, knuckles white. "Thank you. For telling me."

"You deserve to know. Your actions saved many lives." Chandler straightened, his tone shifting to something more formal. "Which brings me to the second reason for my visit. Your special program begins next week, yes?"

Annie nodded. "I'm going to the train station in a few minutes."

"Excellent. I'm glad I caught you. I wanted to express how pleased we are that you accepted our offer." His thin lips curved into what might have been a smile. "Few young women would have shown your resourcefulness during the Hersey incident. Or your observational skills."

Annie fussed with her hair, uncomfortable with the praise. "I just did what anyone would do."

"Not anyone," Chandler corrected.

Hilda returned, carrying a tray with glasses of iced tea. Chandler accepted his with a nod of thanks before continuing.

"Mrs. Jeeves, you should be very proud of your daughter. She'll be joining other young women from throughout the country in the Military Mapmaking training program in Tallahassee. All were selected for their special aptitudes in navigation, geography, and visual-spatial reasoning."

Her mother smiled, her fingers fiddling with the hem of her apron.

Annie took a sip of her tea. "It's my first time leaving home. Being away from my family. I can't say I'm not scared by it all."

Chandler waved a hand. "After Christmas, if you are as successful as I think you will be in your studies, you will go on to work in Washington, DC. You'll do fine, Annie."

She bit her lower lip. He'd never called her Annie before. "I hope you're right."

Chandler set his glass on the side table. "The war has created the realization that we Americans don't have detailed maps of these far-flung places where we're sending our men off to fight. The ability to visualize terrain from limited data and render it accurately is..." he paused, searching for the word, "in this moment, invaluable."

"I'm grateful for everything you've done, Mr. Chandler," she said. "For this opportunity. And for keeping me informed about Will. I'll try not to let you down."

Chandler nodded, satisfied with her response. "Your country needs sharp minds, Miss Jeeves. Especially now." He glanced at his wristwatch. "I won't keep you any longer. I understand you have a train to catch."

# CHAPTER FORTY-ONE

*Fort Lauderdale*
*August 25, 1942*

As if on cue, the front door opened with a gust of wind and rain. Emma stepped inside, folding her black umbrella. Water beaded on her dark skin and dampened the hem of her coral-colored cotton dress.

"This rain is coming down like Judgment Day," she announced, then stopped short at the sight of Chandler. "Oh, I'm sorry. I didn't realize you had company."

"Come in, come in." Hilda crossed from the kitchen and took Emma's umbrella, propping it in the corner to dry. "You're just in time to see Annie off."

Annie jumped up and embraced her friend briefly. "Emma, this is Mr. Chandler." She turned to Chandler and completed the introductions.

Chandler rose and gave a perfunctory nod. "Miss Albury." His expression remained neutral, but Annie noticed how his eyes assessed Emma with detachment before returning to his iced tea.

Emma nodded, maintaining a careful distance.

"Emma has been my first mate on most all our Mosquito Fleet patrols," Annie said, a note of pride entering her voice. "We've spent countless nights on the *Tequesta*, watching for U-boats off the coast."

"Is that so?" Chandler's tone was polite but disinterested.

"Will you be able to continue your patrols while Miss Jeeves is away?"

"No, sir." Emma turned to face her with a big smile. "That's what I came to tell you, Annie. I'm going to college. I've been accepted at FAMC."

Annie squealed and threw her arms around her friend again. "Oh, Em. I'm so proud of you!"

"I had help. Mr. Walker, my high school principal, he called some of his friends up there, and they looked at my work. Mr. Walker says they were impressed."

"Excuse me, ladies," Chandler said, interrupting. "Can you explain what this FAMC is?"

Annie laughed. "That's what folks call the Florida Agricultural and Mechanical College for Negroes. It's up in Tallahassee, right near where I'll be."

Chandler nodded. "I see. Well, congratulations are in order then."

"Em, this is the best news ever!"

Chandler cleared his throat. "So, what happens to your boat now, Annie?"

"My pa had already hired Emma's grandpa Elzo to run the boat. He has more experience than just about any captain in Fort Lauderdale." Annie reached out and squeezed her friend's arm. "Emma should have been captain, but fishing charter guests aren't always..." She paused, searching for a diplomatic phrase.

"Enlightened?" Emma suggested with a subtle arch of her eyebrow.

"Exactly. They're not crazy about having a woman at the wheel, let alone a—" she caught herself, glancing at Chandler.

"A Negro woman," Emma finished for her, her voice matter-of-fact. "Most tourists come to Florida expecting certain arrangements. They get uncomfortable when those arrangements change."

Chandler had been watching this exchange with mild curiosity, but something in his expression shifted.

"You can navigate using celestial readings, Miss Albury?"

Annie laughed.

Emma straightened. "Yes, sir. My grandfather taught me the constellations, and Annie showed me how to use a sextant. Grampa served on merchant vessels throughout the Caribbean before settling here."

"And you're familiar with nautical charts? With plotting courses?"

"I've been helping Annie annotate charts of the coastline since we were sixteen," Emma replied. "I can calculate drift corrections for Gulf Stream currents in my head."

Chandler's head tilted slightly, the way it did when he encountered unexpected information.

"So what will you be studying, Miss Albury?"

Emma's face glowed with excitement. She turned to Annie when she said, "Math," and her smile was dazzling.

"You did it, Em." According to Emma, they tried to steer all the young women into education, nursing or home economics.

"Mathematics," Chandler said, the word seeming to trigger some internal calculation. "Do you enjoy solving puzzles, Miss Albury?"

"Yes, sir," Emma answered. "Crosswords, numbers, patterns, they've always made sense to me."

Chandler's eyebrows rose slightly. Annie suppressed a smile.

"And I don't suppose you are engaged to be married?"

Emma glanced at Annie with a quizzical look, then looked Chandler in the eye and answered, "No, sir."

"Well then." Chandler reached into his inside pocket and produced a small white card with only a telephone number printed in the center.

"I've never met anyone quite like you, Miss Albury. These days, our country must be ready to accept anyone with special skills, such as yours." He pointed to the card in Emma's hand. "Call that number tomorrow. Tell them Frank Chandler recommended you."

"I beg your pardon?" Emma studied the card for a moment, her expression guarded despite the courtesy in her voice.

"There may be an opportunity for you to serve your country," Chandler said. "For someone with your particular aptitudes."

"Thank you, sir."

Chandler turned to Annie. "Your train leaves soon, correct? I won't keep you any longer." He nodded to Hilda. "Thank you for the tea, Mrs. Jeeves."

As he reached the door, he paused, looking back at Emma with a thoughtful expression. "Nine o'clock tomorrow, Miss Albury. Be precise about who told you to call."

With that, he stepped out into the rain, unfurling a black umbrella against the downpour.

Emma stared at the card in her hand, then at Annie, her eyes wide with unspoken questions.

"What just happened?" she whispered.

Annie squeezed her friend's arm. "I think you just got noticed by the same people who noticed me."

Emma turned the white card over several times, as if expecting additional information to materialize on its blank reverse side.

"Do you think it's real?" Emma asked. "Or is he just being polite?"

Annie shook her head. "Chandler doesn't know how to be *just polite*. That man has a war to win. He wouldn't have given you that card if he didn't mean it."

Emma tucked the card carefully into her pocket. "Your Mr. Chandler doesn't strike me as a man who believes in equality of the races."

"He believes in useful skills," Annie said. "And you have those in abundance."

They moved back to the sofa, sitting close enough that their shoulders touched. Outside, the rain continued its assault, drumming against the windows.

"I still can't believe you're really leaving," Emma said. "First Jack, then Finn, now you."

Annie threaded her fingers through Emma's, an intimacy they rarely displayed even in private. "It's just for a few months. And I might see you in Tallahassee now. It's not like I'm going to become some new person."

"That's what they all say." Emma's smile couldn't quite mask the sadness in her eyes. "But places like Washington. They have a way of keeping people."

A flash of lightning illuminated the room, followed immediately by a crash of thunder directly overhead. Both women started, then laughed at their shared nervousness.

"I've got something for you," Emma said, reaching into her handbag. She pulled out a small package wrapped in brown paper and tied with twine. "It's not much, but I wanted you to have it."

Annie unwrapped the package. Inside was a silver compass rose pendant on a delicate chain. The eight points of the compass had been intricately engraved, catching the light as Annie lifted it.

"Emma," she breathed. "It's beautiful."

"Grandpa helped me make it," Emma explained. "So you'll remember where home is," Emma said softly. "No matter which direction you're heading."

Annie felt tears well in her eyes as she fastened the chain around her neck. The pendant rested cool against her skin, just below her collarbone.

"I'll never take it off," she promised, her voice thick with emotion. "And I'll write every week."

Emma squeezed her hand. "Just be brilliant, Annie Jeeves. Show those government men what a Fort Lauderdale girl can do."

"You too," Annie replied. "When you make that call tomorrow."

Emma stood, smoothing her dress with practiced care. "I should get going. Let you finish getting ready." She glanced toward the window, where the rain showed no signs of abating. "Besides, it's a long walk back home in this weather."

"Stay until Pa brings the car around," Annie suggested. "He can drop you at home on the way to the station."

Emma shook her head. "You'll need all the space in that old Chevy." She retrieved her umbrella from the corner. "Besides, I've walked through worse storms than this."

Just as Emma turned to leave, the front door burst open again, admitting Skeeter Jeeves in a gust of wind and rain. He was soaked, his flat cap plastered to his head, an anxious frown creasing his forehead.

"Annie! Thank goodness! We gotta go! Now!" He gestured wildly towards the street. "This squall's turning into a real frog-strangler. This is the worst I've seen in years. If the Ol Fumblebee stalls in high water, we're sunk."

Emma gave a final wave from the doorway, her expression a mix of hope and concern. Then, the black umbrella disappeared into the downpour.

Annie's father thrust a damp stack of mail at her. "Postman just came. Figured you'd want these."

Her fingers, clumsy with haste, sorted through the envelopes. Bills, an advertisement for war bonds, and then a familiar, looping script. A letter from Finn.

Hilda hurried in from the kitchen, a wax-paper-wrapped sandwich in one hand and a small thermos in the other. "Your lunch, dear. Don't want you getting hungry on that long ride."

"Thanks, Ma." Annie dropped the rest of the mail on the end table and stuffed Finn's letter inside her canvas bag along with the lunch. There was no time. No time for anything but the rush.

"Got your suitcase?"

"It's right there, Pa."

Skeeter was already halfway out the door, peering anxiously at the sky. "Hilda, grab her raincoat! Lord, listen to that thunder!"

Her mother grabbed the yellow slicker from the hall tree, practically shoving Annie's arms into it.

Everything was a blur of anxious faces, shouted instructions, the roar of the wind. Skeeter pulled Annie by the arm out onto the porch and into the teeth of the storm.

A deafening crack of thunder split the sky, so close the boards vibrated under Annie's feet. Simultaneously, a brilliant flash of lightning illuminated the yard in stark, ghostly white, then plunged it back into grey deluge.

"Go, go, go!" Skeeter yelled, already halfway to the car, shielding his head with one arm.

Annie ran, head down, the rain stinging her face, soaking through her new dress even under the slicker. She fumbled with the car door, yanked it open, and tumbled inside, the suitcase scraping her shin. Her mother scrambled into the front seat. Skeeter slammed his door, and the old engine coughed, sputtered, then caught.

The world outside became a watery blur. Skeeter gripped the wheel, peering through the frantic sweep of the windshield wipers as they battled sheets of rain. Water already pooled on Coontie Court, turning the street into a shallow river.

"Now remember to write if you need anything, anything at all," Hilda was saying, her voice tight with unshed tears. "And don't you go walking around strange cities by yourself after dark, you hear me? And make sure you eat three square meals, not just coffee and cigarettes like some of those college girls..."

Annie nodded, barely hearing the words. Her gaze was fixed on the rain-lashed window, the familiar landmarks of Fort Lauderdale. The shops, the movie theater, the curve of the New River were slipping past, distorted and fading.

The train station was a flurry of damp bodies and shouted announcements. Goodbyes became a rushed, clumsy affair on the covered platform, the roar of the storm nearly drowning out their words. Her father's hug was unexpectedly fierce, smelling of rain and Old Spice. Her mother pressed a tear-soaked handkerchief into her hand.

"Be brave, my girl," Pa's voice was gruff.

"We love you," Ma whispered.

Then she was climbing the steep metal steps into the train car, her canvas bag heavy on her shoulder, the suitcase bumping against her legs. She found a seat by a window, streaks of rain already obscuring the view. The train lurched, gave a metallic groan and then began to move.

A powerful wave of doubt washed over her. *What am I doing? Leaving everything, my family, Emma, the sea, the sky I knew. For what?*

Tears pricked her eyes, hot and unwelcome. She blinked them back, fumbling in her bag for Finn's letter. Her fingers tore open the envelope.

The train picked up speed, wheels clicking a rhythm against the tracks. Outside, Florida dissolved into a grey, weeping landscape. Inside, Annie unfolded the single sheet of paper, Finn's familiar handwriting filling the page.

*Dearest Annie,*

*I don't have much time, and the censors will probably black half this out, anyway. We're on a ship somewhere off Hawaii. Getting ready to head out, but they won't tell us where. Just west. Toward the Japs. It's strange, Annie. One minute you're home, fixing an engine, thinking about taking your girl fishing. The next... well, the next you're here, on a grey boat in a grey ocean, wondering if you'll ever see home again.*

*Don't you worry about me, though. I'm a good sailor, remember? And I've got something worth fighting for. Someone to come back to.*

*This war... it changes everything. But it can't change how I feel about you. Never that.*

*They won't even tell us where we're going. Just that it's important.*

*I'll write when I can. Stay safe, Annie. Be brave.*

*Love you forever,*
*Finn*

# CHAPTER FORTY-TWO

*Tallahassee, FL*
*December 22, 1942*

"Time's up, ladies! Pencils down!"

Professor Winters smacked her ruler on the oak lectern. The sudden crack ricocheted through the drafting room.

Annie straightened her back, blowing the tufts of loose hair out of her eyes. She heard the tiny click as she nervously pressed the end of her Eversharp mechanical pencil.

Around her, the other young women sat up. Then the room filled with the sound of creaking chair legs and rustling paper. Annie glimpsed Cat Donovan at the next table, already gathering her drawing tools. Her ash-blonde victory rolls remained intact despite four hours spent hunched over her drafting table.

"Still at it, Jeeves?" Cat asked. Her own map rested on her drafting table already rolled and secured with a rubber band. "You'll miss the spiked punch if you don't hurry."

Annie made a face at her roommate, certain that Cat was

looking forward to the farewell party much more than she was. "Quality, Donovan. Not speed."

Cat opened her mouth and placed the back of her hand against her forehead. "Impugning my accuracy? After I beat you by a solid three minutes? And who aced the aerial photo interpretation quiz last month, remind me?"

Annie folded her T-square with a snap. "We'll see who's sloppy when the grades post."

"Line up alphabetically, please." Professor Winters adjusted her half-glasses.

A ripple of excited chatter spread through the room as the young women lined up, maps in hand.

"Think Professor Winters will smile today?" one girl whispered.

"Mary-Louise said her brother sent an entire box of Hershey bars from his PX..."

A sharp rap of wood on wood. Winters' ruler. The room stilled.

"Ladies, less chatter, please." The room grew quiet. "In Washington, they'll want maps in half the time, with twice the accuracy. Lives will depend on your steadiness." She paused, her fingers touching a small gold star pin on her lapel.

Heads bowed. Annie's stomach did the same small twist it had done every lecture since September.

The line inched forward. At the front, Winters unfurled each map. She tapped a note here, scribbled a correction there. No one dared breathe until their linen was re-rolled and shelved in the oak cabinet marked FINAL PROJECTS.

Closer. Third in line. Annie traced the grain in the maple floorboards with the toe of her shoe.

Ahead, Winters paused over Eliza's sheet. "Excellent hill shading, Miss Hunter." Eliza glowed, stepped aside.

Annie's turn.

She put her roll on the desk. Winters pinned the corners with brass weights, then leaned down. Her lenses glinted.

Silence lengthened.

When she had first arrived in Tallahassee, Annie was miserable, homesick and certain that she had taken on something she shouldn't have. Her roommate was like a creature from another planet, and the work required hours of study. Several times she wanted to give up, to go back home. Only the best of young women would go to work in Washington, DC, and Annie didn't believe she would make the cut. In fact, she wasn't sure she even wanted to leave her home state. But around Thanksgiving, something changed. Now, she wanted more than anything to be in that top group to move on.

Professor Winters looked up. "Jeeves." She tapped a sharpened pencil at a section depicting the treacherous shoals off the Dry Tortugas. "Your understanding of bathymetry is exceptional. And the delineation of coastal depths on the St. Johns River system is commendable." A pause. "Your time spent on the water, I presume?"

Annie felt a flush creep onto her cheeks. "Yes, Professor. My family runs a charter boat."

"It's quite clear." Professor Winters' gaze met hers, a twinkle in her usually stern eyes. "This ability to translate practical experience into precise cartographic representation will be invaluable."

Annie nodded, backed away. "Thank you, Professor."

Cat's foot slid out, nearly tripping Annie as she returned to her seat.

A buzz of relief and anticipation filled the room. Annie began packing up her drafting set: the compass, T-square, French curves, dividers, technical pens, and rulers that had become extensions of her hands these past months.

When the last map slid into the cabinet, Winters stood

and addressed them. "You should all be proud of your accomplishments. When you arrived in August, most of you couldn't draw a straight line without a ruler. Now you're producing maps that military commanders could use to plan strategic operations. Your final grades will be posted later this evening." She paused as rain rattled against the casement windows. "I understand you have organized a farewell gathering at Gilchrist Hall? Attempt to stay dry and enjoy your party, ladies. Dismissed."

Voices exploded again, the volume lower this time, as if the ruler still hovered over their heads. Cat hooked an arm through Annie's as they exited the classroom and headed down the hall.

"Knew she'd swoon over your precious sandbars, Jeeves."

"Jealousy isn't flattering, Donovan."

They got to the exit door and looked out across the campus. Once they'd donned their raincoats, Cat bumped Annie's shoulder. "Race you to Gilchrist?"

"Don't trip over your own ego."

They ran anyway, saddle shoes splashing in the puddles, screaming with laughter, sticking their tongues out to taste the raindrops.

The pressure was over. Now it was just a wait for Winters to post their grades.

~

The dorm room in Gilchrist Hall looked like a cyclone had spun through it, tossing clothes, books, and four months of accumulated college life into chaotic piles. Open suitcases gaped on both narrow beds.

Cat's portable Victrola spun Bing Crosby's *White Christmas*, the needle crackling through the strings' high notes. Stockings, Christmas cards, and half-eaten Necco wafers littered the quilt between them.

Cat yanked a crumpled sheet of cardboard from beneath a stack of undershirts. "Behold—Annie Jeeves' very first relief map abomination." The September map was a lumpy smear of green and brown mud.

Annie lunged, swiping. "Give me that disaster."

"Uh-uh." Cat held it overhead. "Proof of evolution. Darwin would be proud." She tossed it onto the discard pile and whistled. "Look at you now. Miss Perfect Depth Contour."

"I wouldn't say perfect," Annie corrected, rolling her French curves inside a ragged tea towel. The brass compass nestled beside them like a precious egg.

Cat lifted a fat bundle tied with a blue ribbon. "And a perfect romance to match." She riffled envelopes. "South Pacific postmarks. How many? Twenty-six?"

"More like a dozen." Annie snatched them back.

"Your sailor boy's quite devoted." Cat loved to tease while exaggerating her South Carolina accent. "Let's see, that's almost one per week."

Annie caressed the top envelope, postmarked three weeks earlier from *Somewhere in the Pacific* with Navy censors' black marks obscuring key details. "He keeps me up to date. At least, when they're not cut to ribbons by censors."

Cat arranged her tortoiseshell combs in a neat row before packing them. "Must be nice, having a fella so crazy about you he writes novels from a battleship."

"Destroyer," Annie corrected. "And he's not on a ship anymore. He's... somewhere else now. Maybe the Solomons." Finn's last letter had hinted at jungle combat without saying exactly where.

"You're lucky," Cat said, her voice softening. "My brother

writes maybe once a month, and it's always the same three sentences: *Weather's fine. Food's terrible. Don't worry about me.*"

Annie felt something in her rise at the mention of brothers, but she pushed it back down. Tonight would be a happy time. She tucked the letters into an inside pocket of her suitcase, nestling them beside Jack's Air Navigation book.

Cat flopped onto her pillow and batted her eyelashes. "Tell me again how this Finn kisses."

"Oh hush. You have to settle on one fella to get letters."

Cat pressed the back of her hand to her forehead again. "I suppose I'm destined to die an old maid, then."

"Shocking, given your dance-card," Annie said, nodding to a wilted carnation pinned above Cat's mirror, a souvenir of an awkward fox-trot with a second lieutenant who'd stepped on Cat's toes all night.

"Low blow."

"You started it."

Cat walked over to the window and leaned against the frame, watching the dripping Spanish moss sway in the oak trees. "Your Fort Lauderdale can't be more than two stoplights and a shrimp shack."

"Try deep-water port, twenty charter boats lining the river docks, and a bridge that ties up traffic for half the county." Annie tossed a sticky candy cane at her roommate. "Plus ocean sunsets you couldn't paint if you had all Matisse's paint."

Cat grinned. "Defensive. I like it."

The door banged open. Eliza Hunter burst in, cheeks flushed, still wearing her lab coat. "Top marks! Winters gave perfect scores to only three projects." She twirled her finger in a large circle. "The three of us."

Cat squealed. Annie felt her knees go weak. She perched on the edge of her bed, dizziness making the room blur.

"No time to breathe," Eliza said. "Party at seven." She disappeared back down the hall.

"Let the good times roll. Wake up, Jeeves. It's party time."

Wardrobe chaos erupted. Cat chose fire-engine rayon, and Annie wriggled into a simple sky-colored dress her mother had mailed from Sears Roebuck for her twenty-first birthday.

They painted seams down their bare calves, no silk hose left on campus. A quick brush of face powder, a swipe of Victory-red lipstick. Cat pinned Annie's braid into a neat roll. "You look almost civilized."

The Gilchrist Hall common room had undergone quite a makeover. Someone had swiped a USO banner from the gym and strung it over the mantel. Red and green crepe paper streamers drooped from the ceiling beams, and colored lights twinkled on a tall Christmas tree in a corner. Near to the tree, a branch of mistletoe dangled from a beam.

On a table covered with a linen cloth, a large punchbowl sat next to plates and a sheet-cake iced with a map grid in green frosting. Someone had put on a Benny Goodman record, and the clarinet notes competed with the chatter.

Annie scanned the crowd, recognizing faces from their mapping classes mingled with young men in uniform, Army and Navy lieutenants from nearby training facilities who'd received coveted passes for the evening. The dormitory matron, her eyes missing nothing, leaned against the wall, arms crossed like a ranch hand trying to figure out how to wrangle this herd.

After an hour of sipping punch and chatting while watching Cat dance with every man in the room, Annie decided parties were not all the fun her roommate made them out to be. She was about to leave when Professor Winters arrived, not in her usual severe suit, but wearing a slightly softer dress of dark wool. She carried a cloth-covered basket. The music quieted as she stepped to the center of the room.

"Ladies," she began, her voice carrying over the remaining whispers. "Before the punch disappears, and Miss Donovan attempts to teach us all her unique version of the Lindy Hop..." A ripple of laughter went through the room. "I have a small token for those of you who will advance to positions of national service in Washington."

Professor Winters held up a slim, velvet-lined box. Inside, nestled on satin, was a gleaming Pelikan Graphos drafting pen, its interchangeable nib set fanned out beside it.

A collective gasp went around the room.

"These," Professor Winters said, her gaze sweeping over them, "are tools of exacting precision. Their origin serves as a reminder of the enemy's capabilities, and the standards we must not only meet but surpass. Use them with skill, with dedication. The maps you create will guide our forces, protect our ships, and bring our men home." One by one, she called the names of the selected graduates.

She then picked up a glass of punch. "A toast." Her voice held a note of uncharacteristic warmth. "To the Florida State College for Women, Advanced Geography and Mapping Program, graduating class of December 1942. You are without exception the finest, most dedicated group of young women I have had the privilege to teach. Merry Christmas to you all."

As the professor moved away, Cat nudged Annie's arm. "Look at you. The girl from the 'hardly a backwater' off to help win the war."

Annie smiled, tucking the precious pen into her borrowed purse. "We all are."

"Doesn't seem real, does it?" Eliza mused, watching couples dance to *In the Mood* as the music changed. "Four months ago, I was helping in my father's grocery store. Now I'll be mapping invasion routes."

"Four months ago I was navigating mangrove channels and waiting tables," Annie said. "Life changes fast in wartime."

Cat raised her punch cup again. "Merry Christmas, ladies. Enjoy your time at home. Here's to seeing you in Washington in the new year. To us!"

"To us!" Annie and Eliza said in unison as they raised their cups.

# CHAPTER FORTY-THREE

*Tallahassee, FL*
*December 24, 1942*

The train whistle gave a long blast as it pulled into Fort Lauderdale station. Annie pressed her cheek against the window, her breath fogging the glass. She scanned the crowd in the waning daylight. She was both excited to be home and exhausted after the hours spent waiting for a seat on a southbound train at the Jacksonville station.

Annie spotted her family the moment she stepped down from the train, her father's worn flat cap visible above the crowd. They stood beside the old Chevrolet at the far end of the platform. Her mother, arms crossed in her good blue dress, her father shifting his weight from one foot to the other like he always did when forced to stand still.

Four months had transformed Annie in ways she couldn't articulate; yet her parents looked the same, right down to the way her mother lifted her chin as she scanned the disembarking passengers.

"Annie!" Her mother's voice carried across the platform.

She raised one hand in a wave, hefting her suitcase with the other and pushing through the holiday crowd. There were servicemen in uniform, families clutching gift parcels wrapped in newsprint. The train station platform teemed with Christmas travelers, all of them looking tired but determined to celebrate despite the war.

"Look at you!" Skeeter caught Annie mid-stride, lifting her clear off the ground. He set her down but kept both hands on her shoulders, grinning like a new father. "You're all citified!"

Hilda nudged him aside and tugged the lapels of Annie's wool coat, a smile on her lips, but worry creasing her brow. "You've lost weight. I knew the cafeteria portions were lousy. And your hair—" She touched Annie's styled waves with hesitant fingers. "It's so... sophisticated."

"Nice to see you too, Ma."

They both laughed, tears sneaking out anyway.

Skeeter hoisted her suitcase into the worn back seat of the Chevy that looked even more battered than she remembered.

"Old Fumblebee's still running okay?" she asked.

"More or less," Skeeter replied, cranking the engine to life. "Parts are scarce these days. Had to trade a pound of smoked fish to Leroy just for a fan belt last month."

Questions came in bursts as Skeeter negotiated the holiday traffic.

"So, these fancy classes. Professors treatin' you right?"

"Fine."

"Roommate still messier than a bait shack?"

"Absolutely."

As they neared downtown, Annie noticed the changes.

"The Coast Guard took over the old basin," her father explained, following her gaze. "Got patrol boats coming and going up and down the river at all hours now."

"The Champ-Carr Hotel's been requisitioned for officer housing," her mother added. "And they've started building new barracks at the Naval Air Station."

"The whole town's changed," Annie murmured.

They turned onto the familiar streets of their neighborhood, where Christmas decorations were simpler this year. Painted windows instead of electric lights, palm wreaths without ribbons, and homemade ornaments replacing store-bought ones.

Inside, warmth and the odor of her mother's rosemary-stuffed mullet roasting alongside sweet potatoes; no turkey this year. Before she could even set her suitcase down, a red-headed missile launched from the kitchen, nearly knocking Annie off her feet.

"Annie! You're really here!" Bean squealed, arms locked around Annie's waist. "I've got so much to tell you! About the boat, and school, and how I caught a snapper bigger than Pa's head last week."

"Whoa, let her get in the door first." Skeeter laughed.

Annie hugged Bean tight, surprised at how much she'd missed the girl's exuberance. "I want to hear everything," she promised. "And I've got a present for you in my bag."

"Is it a compass?" Bean asked. "Emma says every navigator needs her own compass."

"Not exactly, but close," Annie replied, thinking of the miniature sextant she'd found in a Tallahassee antique shop. "How is Emma?"

"Home for Christmas," Bean reported. "I saw her and Elzo yesterday. When she heard you were coming home, said she'd visit tomorrow."

Dinner was a lively affair. Bean chattered non-stop. "Pa's been letting me help on the *Tequesta*! I can tie a bowline and a cleat hitch now! And before Emma left, she was teaching me all the stars. I can find Polaris and the Big Dipper, and I know which way is east even when the sun's not up!" Her small face glowed with pride.

Skeeter grinned. "She's got your sea legs, Annie. Spends every spare minute down at the dock, pestering the old salts for stories."

A familiar pang, a mix of pride and something akin to displacement, tightened in Annie's chest. Life here hadn't stood still after all. Bean was charting her own course, and Emma... Emma had been here, sharing her knowledge of the stars, before heading off not to Tallahassee, but to Washington. Howard University was what her letters claimed.

Her mother talked of victory gardens, soldiers injured during training filling the hospital beds, of scrap metal drives, and the biggest surprise of all: Ernie Finch now a tail gunner somewhere over Europe.

Supper clattered along. Skeeter told how Bean spotted a new unlit daybeacon and saved the *Tequesta*'s propeller. Hilda passed mustard greens, and complained about ration stamps. Annie answered what she could, skirted what she couldn't.

Later, dishes washed, she stepped onto the back porch alone. Cool air carried the mud and mangrove scent from the river. She guessed the tide was low, exposing the barnacles on the docks, where her old friend, the *Tequesta,* was waiting to welcome her home.

She pressed the compass rose pendant Emma had given her against her sternum. Somewhere west of the dateline, Finn scanned different stars. She mouthed silent words: *Come home safe.*

Behind her, she heard a curtain rustle, and saw Ma's silhouette. "Cold out there."

"Feels warm after Tallahassee. I just need a breather."

"Don't stay too long. Tomorrow, Emma's coming by."

Annie nodded, eyes still on the starry sky. Home looked the same; she wasn't sure she was.

The next morning, Annie was drying dishes when a light tap came at the back screen door. Emma Albury stood on the porch, a tentative smile on her face. She looked different, Annie thought. Taller, perhaps, or maybe it was the new way she held herself, a quiet confidence that hadn't been there before she left for Washington. Her dress, a simple but smart green cotton, and her hair styled with a new sophistication.

"Emma! Merry Christmas! Come in, come in." Annie pushed the screen door open.

Their initial greetings held a slight reserve, the months of separate lives and guarded secrets. They talked of their respective studies: Emma of mathematics at Howard, Annie of "advanced geography" at Florida State. The conversation felt stilted.

Annie longed for the easy camaraderie they once shared, the shorthand of unspoken understanding. She looked out the kitchen window. The sky was a brilliant, cloudless blue, a light breeze ruffling the hibiscus bushes.

"It's a perfect day for it," Annie said suddenly, an idea taking root. "The tide's just right. What do you say we take the *Tequesta* out? Just like old times?"

Emma's dark eyes lit up, the reserve melting away. A genuine, delighted smile spread across her face. "Oh, Annie," she said, her voice soft. "I'd like that. I'd like that very much indeed."

The *Tequesta*'s diesel engine rumbled a familiar beat beneath Annie's feet as she steered them down the New River. Her fingers gripping the wooden wheel felt as if they'd never left. Emma took to the deck, coiling the dock lines, stowing fenders, her movements practical but also elegant. Annie felt the accumulated tension of train travel and homecoming dissipate.

The air had that cold winter clarity that made the sun burn brighter and the sea sparkle with diamonds as every soft puff of wind ruffled the surface. Tallahassee, with its drafting tables and coordinate systems, seemed to belong to another world.

Once they cleared the jetties at Port Everglades, and the wide expanse of the Atlantic opened before them, they fell into the old routine. Annie raised the mainsail. Emma pulled the halyard to raise the jib and tied it off. Annie cut the engine. The sudden silence was broken only by the creak of the rigging, the gentle slap of waves against the hull.

Emma came to stand beside her at the helm, leaning against the cabin side, her face tilted up to the December sun. "Oh, Annie." She breathed a soft sigh of contentment. "I have missed this more than words can say. The smell of it. The feel of it." She spread her arms wide, as if to embrace the endless blue. "Howard University is a fine place, full of brilliant minds, but there's not a single sailboat on campus. Not even a rowboat."

Annie laughed. "Tallahassee has a few lakes. Good for practicing celestial navigation on a clear night, but not much for sailing." She nudged the wheel, heading the *Tequesta* more southeast, following the coast. "Not that I had the time."

They sailed in comfortable silence for a while, the boat rising and falling with the rhythm of the ocean.

"Your letters from Howard." Annie made her voice casual. "They've been... discreet. Lots about the architecture of the Library of Congress, not so much about what kind of 'advanced mathematics' has you burning the midnight oil."

Emma's lips curved into a wry smile. "And your dispatches from the 'Florida State College for Women Special Geography Program' have been masterpieces of evasion, Miss Jeeves. All those 'fascinating topographical studies' and 'challenging aerial photo analyses.' Sounded like you were preparing to re-map the Everglades single-handedly."

Their eyes met, a shared understanding passing between them. Out here, with nothing but miles of ocean and an empty sky, the weight of secrets eased.

"No prying ears out here, Emma," Annie said. "Just us and the fish."

Emma nodded, her playful expression fading into something more serious. She took a deep breath. "That Mr. Chandler, Annie. The man who gave me his card at your house, just before you left for Tallahassee?"

Annie nodded, her gaze steady on her friend.

"He did not offer me a scholarship to Howard, not really."

Annie glanced at her friend. "I figured as much. Your letters were a bit too vague about what you're actually studying there."

Emma's smile turned wry. "About as vague as yours about Florida State."

They exchanged knowing looks. Their letters had been exercises in deliberate omission, filled with dormitory anecdotes and weather reports while empty of details about their actual work.

Emma looked around them, then lowered her voice despite their isolation. "I'm not actually at Howard, Annie."

Annie leaned forward, elbows on knees. "I figured as much."

"They promised me a scholarship when the war's over. But for now, I'm working for the Army's Signal Intelligence Service," Emma confessed. "I'm in a special unit of Negro women encoding and decoding military communications."

"Chandler?"

Emma nodded. "The morning after you left, I called that

number. Two weeks later, I was on a train to Arlington Hall. It's a former girls' school they've converted into headquarters for the code-breaking operation." She watched as they passed a small motorboat, the driver staring at the two women on deck. "We're not supposed to talk about it. Not even to family. I signed an oath."

Annie smiled. "I know. Me too."

"I guess this talk between us is okay then?"

Annie winked at her friend. "I think it's best if after today, we pretend this never happened."

Emma took a deep breath and looked out at the horizon.

"So what's it like, Em?"

"We work with everything from looking through banking communications to find Americans who are sending money to the Nazis, to taking enemy intercepts—Japanese fleet mostly—breaking them to five-digit code groups, re-enciphering, and forwarding to the officers."

"That's... incredible."

"It's necessary," Emma said. "But it's not something you can write home about."

"I understand that," Annie said. "Now that I've finished my training at Tallahassee, I'll be going to Washington, too, working for the Army Map Service. The Military Mapping Course was just preparation. In Washington, we'll be creating detailed tactical maps from secret aerial reconnaissance photographs."

Emma let out a low whistle. "So we're both in intelligence work."

"Different branches, same war." Annie grinned. "Who'd a thought that would happen from the two girls who worked at The Deck."

Annie checked the sails and eased off the headsail sheet. She didn't want to get too far offshore and into the north-bound current.

"How do they treat you there? In Arlington?"

Emma shrugged. "It's okay. We're all colored folk. Even our supervisor, Mr. Coffee. He's an excellent instructor, very respectful. But the work itself..." Her eyes lit up. "Annie, it's the most challenging, exhilarating puzzle-solving I've ever done. We're breaking Japanese naval codes, tracking ship movements, saving American lives."

"I can tell you love it."

"Mr. Coffee says I have an exceptional mind for pattern recognition," Emma said, a hint of pride breaking through her usual reserve. "After proving myself on simpler tasks, I've been assigned to advanced cryptanalysis."

Annie's throat went tight. She reached across and gripped Emma's hand. "The world finally sees it," she said. "What I've always known." She had to blink back the sting in her eyes. "*Cryptanalysis*, Em." Annie threw back her head and looked at the main sail. "Hell, I'm not even sure I know what that is. But what I do know is you've earned this."

They sat in companionable silence for a while, the boat rocking beneath them, the vast Atlantic stretching to the horizon. Annie thought about the strange symmetry of their situations—both using their natural abilities in service to a country that still imposed strict limitations on them.

She turned the wheel hard over and brought the bow through the wind and onto a northbound tack.

The *Tequesta* sailed northward, riding the Gulf Stream, approaching the beach outside Whiskey Creek, the narrow inlet where, just a year ago, they had all been together.

Annie pointed to the stretch of white sand on shore. "Remember last Christmas? Jack and Finn laughing and splashing just over there? How could that have been only a year ago?"

Emma's gaze drifted to the shoreline. "I still think about Jack every day. Something will remind me, a song on the radio, a particular shade of blue that matches his eyes, the way someone laughs, and suddenly it's like losing him all over again."

Annie struggled to swallow before saying, "Me too."

"He's why I need to do this."

Annie nodded. "I get that."

"The work helps," Emma continued. "Knowing that every code I break might save someone else's brother or son or..."

"Or someone's Finn," Annie finished.

Emma nodded. "Have you heard from him recently?"

"Last letter came just before I left Tallahassee," Annie said. "I'm guessing he's in the Solomon Islands. I think he might be on a patrol boat now. The censors blacked out most of the details, but reading between the lines, I think they're preparing for a major naval operation." She reached for the familiar necklace, which hadn't left her neck since August. "I scan the newspaper reports every day, looking for battles in the South Pacific."

"That's the hardest part, isn't it?" Emma said. "The not knowing."

The sun had begun its descent toward the Everglades. Annie started the engine again, turning the boat's bow toward home.

"Will you be able to contact me in Washington?" Annie asked as they picked up speed. "I know things are... complicated there."

Emma massaged her forehead with her fingertips. "It's more segregated than here in some ways, less in others. At least there's no Sheriff Clark or the like. But the government buildings still have separate facilities. I suppose we might meet somewhere neutral." She sat up straight and touched one finger to her lips before she spoke. "There is a small cafe near Howard that serves everyone."

"I'd like that," Annie said. "Maybe once a month? To keep each other sane amid all this secrecy. When do you leave?"

"My train's on the 29th."

"Mine's on the 27th. I've got to find housing. Get settled. My new position starts January 2nd, and I don't even know the location. It's going to take time to get used to all these secrets."

Emma smiled and placed her hand on her heart. "You'll be fine, Annie."

"It's settled then," Annie said, turning the key. The engine rumbled to life. "Two Florida girls taking on Washington together."

They lifted their arms in unison, palms meeting with a slap before their fingers wove together: their old Mosquito Fleet pact.

Emma laughed. "Lord help Washington."

# CHAPTER FORTY-FOUR

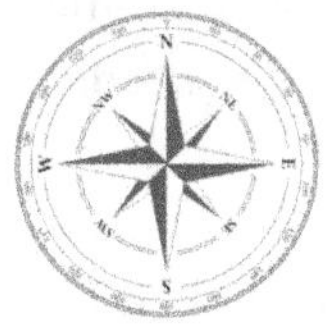

*Washington, DC*
*December 17, 1943*

"Move it, Jeeves! It's six twenty-eight!"

Their shoes pounded the wooden stairs as the two young women raced down from the third floor of their McLean Gardens government housing building.

Cat's fingernails stabbed her in the back. "If we miss this trolley, we'll be hoofing it three miles to work in the dark!"

Annie grabbed the banister and took the steps two at a time, her canvas messenger bag bouncing against her hip. She wanted to get out of reach of those bright red fingernails.

Just as they reached the lobby, Mrs. Brodigan, the house matron, stepped out from behind her door, blocking their path. Her gray hair was already pinned into its regulation bun. Her stern expression conveyed the authority that came from managing dozens of young women working around the clock for the war effort.

"Miss Jeeves." Mrs. Brodigan held up a dirt-smeared envelope. "Letter for you. Came yesterday evening."

Annie screeched to a halt on the linoleum floor. She snatched the envelope, recognizing Finn's ragged script across the front.

"Annie!" Cat careened around her and opened the front door. Her voice carried a note of panic. "The trolley's at the corner!"

Through the glass doors, Annie saw the yellow streetcar approaching their stop, its headlights cutting through the pre-dawn darkness. Cat was already outside, waving frantically at the conductor.

"Go!" Mrs. Brodigan shooed her toward the door. "Miss Donovan won't let them leave without you."

Annie stuffed the letter into her coat pocket and sprinted out the door. Cat had positioned herself in front of the trolley, arms spread wide like she was stopping a runaway horse. The conductor, a middle-aged man accustomed to the urgency of the government girls, shook his head with weary amusement.

"Every morning's a drama with you ladies." He shook his head as Annie hauled herself up the steps. "Like the building's on fire."

"Sorry!" Cat called out as she swung aboard behind Annie. "Can't be late for Uncle Sam!"

The trolley lurched forward, and Annie grabbed a leather strap for balance as she made her way to an empty pair of seats. Around them, the familiar faces of women heading to their shifts: typists bound for the Civil Engineering Building, file clerks for the War Department, and dozens of Annie's fellow mapmakers greeted them. The air buzzed with conversation and the rustle of brown paper lunch bags.

"Hey Cat! Did you hear about the game?" A girl from the photogrammetry section shouted. "The Contours beat the War Department stenographers 12-8 yesterday. Helen hit two home runs!"

"Speaking of entertainment," piped up another voice, "who's going to the USO Christmas dance at Fort Belvoir Saturday night? I heard they're bringing in a real orchestra from Richmond."

Cat's eyes lit up. "Oh, Annie, we should go!"

Annie ignored her. She'd pulled Finn's letter from her pocket and was studying the return address and postmark. Three weeks to reach her. Longer than usual. Her fingers trembled as she unfolded the thin overseas paper.

*My dearest Annie,*

*Can't tell you much about what we're doing, but I think you can guess from the newspapers. We're on one of those little plywood boats, fast as lightning. The skipper, he's a good man, from Maine. Lets me take the helm sometimes. We go places the big ships can't. The crew's good, though we lost Jimmy De Luca last month. Not sure if the censors will let me say that, but his folks ought to know he was brave.*

*The water here is the most beautiful blue-green you've ever seen... Sometimes, when we're running at dawn with the spray hitting my face, I can almost forget where we are. Almost.*

*Weather remains hot and wet, and I can't remember what dry clothes feel like. They call it the rainy season. I call it the mud season. The medic says I've got jungle rot on my feet. Nothing serious, he tells me, but it won't heal in this climate. I've lost about fifteen pounds since my last letter, which puts me at 140 soaking wet. Don't worry, lots of the guys are dealing with the same thing. We spend a lot of time in the latrine.*

*Worst part is the stink. It's everywhere. It hangs in the air, in the mud, gets in your clothes, your hair. Never thought a smell could haunt a man, but this one does.*

*The stars are different here, Annie. Makes me homesick for those nights we spent learning navigation with you pointing out the constellations. Sometimes I pretend you're here with me, and this time I can show you the Southern Cross like you showed me the Big Dipper.*

*I think about our first kiss on the boat every single day. It's what keeps me going when everything else goes to hell.*

*All my love,*

*Finn*

Annie read the letter twice, savoring every detail. A fast plywood boat? Obviously, a PT boat. Of course. Fast, agile, deadly. It was so like Finn to find solace on the water, even in the midst of hell. That minor detail—his hand on the helm—was a pinprick of light in the darkness. She was certain now. The small, fast boats that ran dangerous night missions in the island chains of the Pacific.

"—so I told him I'd only go if he promised not to step on my feet again," Cat was saying. "Annie, are you listening?"

"Sorry." Annie refolded the letter. "Just news from overseas."

"Good news, I hope?" Cat's voice carried genuine concern.

"Finn's still alive." That was as optimistic as she could manage.

Cat wrapped her arm around Annie's shoulders. "Your sailor boy is going to be fine, honey."

That was a promise no one could make.

The trolley rounded a curve, and the first hint of dawn was touching the tops of the bare trees. Residential Washington fell behind them as the trolley headed northwest toward the Maryland border, where the Army Map Service had relocated. Their unit had outgrown its original downtown offices.

"Next stop, Brookmount!" Mr. Patterson called out. "All you map girls better have your IDs ready."

Annie patted her pocket, feeling for the badge. Around her, two dozen other women were doing the same thing, the morning ritual of preparing to enter one of the war's most closely guarded buildings.

Building Number 1 appeared through the trees. Three stories of red brick, it might have looked like any other government office building except for the enormous cargo nets draped across its entire facade. Artificial foliage had been woven through the mesh, creating a patchwork of browns and greens designed to fool enemy reconnaissance planes. From the air, the building would appear to be nothing more than a wooded hillside.

"Still gives me the shivers," Cat said. "Like we're walking into a fairy tale where the castle's been hidden by magic."

Two armed guards flanked the steel doors. Annie presented her identification badge to the corporal on the left, waited while he compared her face to the photograph, then she passed through into the lobby where another checkpoint awaited.

"Morning, Miss Jeeves," said Lieutenant Morrison, the officer who supervised the morning shift change. "Building C, Level 2, Pacific Theater Operations. Same as yesterday."

"Yes, sir." Annie clipped her badge to her collar and headed for the stairs.

The interior of the building hummed with constant activity. Even at that hour of the morning, the night shift was still hard at work, bent over drafting tables and light boxes, their technical pens scratching precise lines across sheets of linen paper. The air smelled of developing chemicals, cigarette smoke, and the peculiar odor of hot metal from the printing presses running in the basement.

The drafting room occupied most of the second floor, a vast space filled with angled tables arranged in precise rows. Annie's workstation was a five-foot wide table positioned beneath a bank of fluorescent lights that turned everyone's skin a sickly shade of green. She would have preferred natural light, but there wasn't a window in the building.

She hung her coat on the back of her chair and settled into the familiar routine of preparation.

Her toolkit came out first: the precious Pelikan Graphos pen Professor Winters had given her, its interchangeable nibs arranged in a small velvet-lined case. Each nib served a specific purpose: fine lines for elevation contours, medium for roads and boundaries, broad for area features like forests or water bodies.

Next came the India ink. One small bottle lasted weeks if used with care, but a single spill could ruin hours of work.

She arranged her French curves in order of radius, their plastic edges worn smooth from constant use. The T-square came next, its metal edge straight. Finally, her compass set: one for large circles, one for small, and a proportional divider for scaling measurements.

The morning's assignment lay waiting in her inbox:

Marshall Group 1: Kwajalein, Roi-Namur, Ebeye. Structure detail mandatory: schools, mission houses, village huts, dispensaries. Deadline zero-six-hundred tomorrow. Accompanying the print-out was a stack of aerial reconnaissance photographs of the Marshall Islands, taken by Navy pilots flying dangerous missions over Japanese-held territory.

She spread out the latest batch of black and white photographs, images taken from 20,000 feet that revealed the atolls scattered across the Pacific. Somewhere in that ocean, Finn was navigating between similar islands aboard a PT boat.

"Rough night?" asked Dorothy Lee, the young woman at the adjacent table. Dorothy had been recruited from UC Berkeley's geography program and possessed an almost supernatural ability to interpret aerial photographs.

"Didn't sleep much," Annie admitted.

Dorothy nodded. They all had brothers or boyfriends or husbands somewhere overseas. The maps they created weren't abstract exercises; they were blueprints for survival.

For the next five hours, Annie lost herself in the meticulous work of mapmaking. Each reef required careful measurement and placement. Each potential obstacle, whether natural or man-made, needed to be marked. The maps they produced would be reproduced by the thousands and distributed to every ship, every aircraft, every combat unit that might need them.

At noon, the lunch whistle echoed through the building. Annie straightened, wincing at the stiffness that came from hunching over a drafting table all morning. Around her, the other women were capping their pens and covering their work with cloth sheets to protect it from dust.

Annie set down her pen and stretched her fingers, working out the cramps that came from gripping drawing instruments for hours. Her neck ached from bending over the drafting table, and her eyes felt dry from squinting.

Cat appeared within minutes, brown paper lunch bag in hand. "Come on, let's get some fresh air before I go crazy from the smell of ink and developer chemicals."

They bundled back into their coats and headed outside, joining the stream of government workers. The December air was sharp but clean, a welcome change from the chemical atmosphere of the Map Service building.

Cat led the way to a picnic table beside Dalecarlia Reservoir, its wooden surface dusted with sparkling frost. They brushed off the bench and sat down, unwrapping sandwiches and thermoses while Canada geese honked somewhere across the water.

"God, it feels good to see the sky," Cat said, tilting her face toward the sun. "I swear, those fluorescent lights are going to turn us all into moles."

Annie opened her thermos, releasing wisps of steam that carried the smell of coffee. "At least you get to see the printing floor. All I see are photographs of beaches I'll never visit."

They ate in comfortable silence for a few minutes, watching the water lap against the concrete dam. A few ducks paddled near the shore, oblivious to the war that had transformed the peaceful Maryland countryside into a center of military intelligence.

"You don't get out enough, Jeeves." Cat took a sip of her coffee.

"I sometimes meet my friend Emma at the cafe over near Howard University, but it's been a while now. She can't get away. I miss her."

Cat nodded. "Poor girl. The colored units work harder than we do, if that's imaginable."

"She's at Arlington Hall." Annie took a sip of coffee from

her thermos. "Sometimes I think about how much simpler things were back home. Emma and I could just hop on the boat and sail off whenever we wanted to talk."

"Which reminds me," Cat said, "you still haven't given me an answer about Saturday night. The Christmas dance at Fort Belvoir?"

Annie sighed. "Cat, you're something else. I appreciate what you're trying to do, but I'm not interested. I'm exhausted from these twelve-hour shifts, and when I'm not working, I want to read a book, take a bath, or write to Finn. Not make small talk with some homesick soldier."

"But Annie—"

"No buts." Annie's voice was firmer than she'd intended. "I know you mean well, but I'm not looking for anyone new. I've got Finn, assuming he makes it through this war."

Cat's expression softened. "Of course. I'm sorry. I just thought maybe you'd want to have a little innocent fun."

"I know." Annie reached over and squeezed her friend's hand. "You're a good friend for trying."

As if summoned by their conversation, two young men in uniform approached their table. Annie recognized Jim Bradley, Cat's latest beau. Jim was a Navy pilot, and beside him stood a tall, sandy-haired Army lieutenant she'd never seen before.

"Ladies!" Jim nodded at each of them. "Perfect day for lunch alfresco, isn't it?"

Cat's face lit up like an electric spark. "Jim! What are you doing here?"

"Met someone about the new airfield construction in Maryland," he said, settling beside Cat on the bench. "And I brought Eddie along to meet the famous Annie Jeeves I've been telling him so much about."

Eddie stepped forward with a shy smile, his hands clasped behind his back. "Miss Jeeves? Jim tells me you're from Florida. I spent some time at Fort Myers before my assignment here."

Annie managed a polite smile. "It's nice to meet you, Lieutenant...?"

"Henderson. Eddie Henderson." He gestured toward the empty space on the bench. "Mind if I sit?"

"Actually," Annie stood and began gathering her lunch things, "I need to get back inside. We've got a deadline on the Marshall Islands project."

She saw the disappointment flicker across Eddie's face, followed by Cat's embarrassed flush. Jim cleared his throat.

"Of course," Eddie said. "Perhaps another time?"

"Perhaps," Annie replied, though her tone made it clear she had no intention of there being another time.

She walked back toward the building alone, leaving Cat to smooth over the social damage. She felt bad about her abruptness, but she couldn't summon any interest in Eddie Henderson, no matter how nice he seemed. Her heart was somewhere in the Pacific, aboard a PT boat with a young man whose feet were rotting in his boots.

The afternoon shift stretched longer than usual. She drew each small building onto her map with meticulous care. The church's outline took shape, a simple rectangle with a smaller square attached, representing the bell tower that cast such a distinctive shadow in the photograph. She added the abbreviation "CHU" in neat block letters. American bombardiers would know to avoid it.

As she worked, her mind drifted to the maps she'd completed in September, detailed charts of Bougainville and the Solomon Islands that had seemed like abstract geography exercises at the time. Two weeks after she'd finished those drawings, newspaper headlines had screamed about American landings in those locations.

The connection between her desk work and combat operations never stopped feeling surreal. She would spend days mapping enemy territory in the sterile environment of the drafting room, then read about battles fought on that same ground over her morning coffee. Her maps became instruments of war.

By six-thirty that evening, when the night shift arrived to take over, Annie's eyes burned from staring at tiny numbers and her right hand cramped. She and Cat made the journey back to McLean Gardens in relative silence, both of them too tired for chatter.

They climbed the stairs, their legs heavy, bodies aching. On each floor, a large sign was posted stating that there would be a blackout drill that night at 9:00 p.m. The building's other residents were settling in for the night, and muffled conversations drifted through thin walls. The sound of radios playing dance music competed with the clatter of dish washing.

They reached their room on the third floor, and Cat kicked off her shoes with a groan of relief. The space was small but comfortable, with two narrow beds, a shared dresser, and a window that looked out over the building's courtyard, now covered with a blackout shade. Annie had hung her Florida chart on the wall above her bed. On Cat's wall were many photos of the Donovan family.

"I'm going to soak my feet in the bathroom sink." Cat clutched her robe and slippers to her chest. "Then I'm going to sleep for ten hours before we do this all over again."

Annie smiled despite her exhaustion. Cat's dramatic complaints were as much a part of their evening routine as brushing their teeth. She pulled her pajamas from under her pillow and began changing out of her work clothes, hanging her skirt on the bathroom door to avoid wrinkles.

The door opened, and Eliza handed her two warm bowls of baked beans.

"This is it for tonight." The friends took turns in the communal kitchen downstairs.

Annie took the bowls. "Thanks. We've got some crackers." She closed the door. "Dinner is served, Cat."

The building's hallways were unheated, and cold air seeped under their door despite the towel Cat had stuffed against the gap. As the two of them perched on their beds eating their lukewarm beans, Annie told herself, for the hundredth time, she was not in Florida anymore. She was taking her bowl to the bathroom sink when a sharp knock interrupted the quiet.

Cat groaned and buried her face in her pillow, but Annie padded over in her stocking feet to answer it.

Mrs. Brodigan stood in the hallway, her expression more serious than usual. "Miss Jeeves? There's a telephone call for you downstairs. They said it was urgent."

Annie's stomach dropped. She had never received a phone call before. An urgent call at this hour never brought good news. She grabbed her overcoat from the hook behind the door and threw it on over her pajamas. Slipping her feet into slippers, she hurried toward the stairs.

The telephone booth was in the lobby, a cramped wooden box with a single bare bulb hanging overhead. Annie slid inside and picked up the dangling black receiver.

"Hello?"

"Annie?" Her father's voice sounded thin and distant. "Annie, sweetheart, are you there?"

"I'm here, Pa." She pressed the receiver closer to her ear, trying to read the tone of his voice. "What's wrong?"

A long pause. "We had a visitor today. Navy man. Came to the door around three o'clock."

Annie's legs suddenly felt unsteady. A picture flashed in her mind of the uniformed officer who had delivered the news about Jack. She braced herself against the wall of the phone booth. "Pa?"

"It's about Finn, honey." Skeeter's voice cracked. "He's... they say he's missing in action. His PT boat went down during an engagement near some islands I can't pronounce. Happened a couple of weeks ago. They searched, found some bodies, but Finn..." He took a shaky breath. "Finn wasn't one of them."

The words hit Annie like a physical blow. *Missing in action.* Not dead, not yet, but lost somewhere in the South Pacific, injured or captured or worse. She slumped against the wall, the cold seeping through her overcoat.

"Annie? You still there?"

"I'm here," she whispered.

"The Navy man said Finn had listed me and your mother as his next of kin. Since he didn't have other family." Skeeter's voice trailed off, but she could still hear his breathing. "They'll let us know if they hear anything more."

Annie closed her eyes, trying to process what she'd just heard. Finn was gone. Maybe forever. The boy who'd taught her to tie knots and splice line, the man who had kissed her on the dock before shipping out, and promised to come home to her. He was lost somewhere on the other side of the world.

"Annie? Sweetheart?"

"I have to go, Pa." The pain in her chest made it difficult to speak, to breathe. "I have to... I need to..."

"I know, honey. I'm sorry. I'm so damn sorry."

Annie hung up the phone and stood in the booth for a long time, dizzy, trying to catch her breath, her hand still gripping the receiver.

Outside across the city, the sirens started. The blackout drill.

Annie pushed open the phone booth door and staggered

through the lobby. Mrs. Brodigan looked up from her desk with concern. Annie knew the woman was speaking to her, but the words didn't register.

Finn. Missing.

Only one person could understand.

Outside, the December night was a dry, bitter cold. The sky above the blacked-out city was full of millions of stars. Annie's breath formed clouds as she stumbled down the sidewalk, her bedroom slippers providing little protection against the frozen pavement. She was crying now, tears streaming down her cheeks and freezing in the wind.

She had to see Emma. Blackout or not.

Arlington was five or six miles away, but Annie knew the route. She was no stranger to walking. At least she would have the streets to herself. But at this hour, with her vision blurred by tears and her mind reeling from the news, the dark streets of Washington took on an alien quality.

She picked up her pace, her overcoat billowing around her, her flannel pajama pants doing little to keep out the cold. The sirens stopped, and the city grew eerily quiet. Past the government buildings, past the sleeping residential neighborhoods, toward the bridge that would take her into Virginia.

A blackout warden's whistle shrilled somewhere behind her. "Miss! You need to take shelter!"

"On my way home now!" Annie kept walking, faster now. The warden's reply was incomprehensible over the noise of her own breathing. Feet numb with cold, she kept moving, driven by the desperate need to reach the one person who might help her make sense of this nightmare. Nothing else mattered.

She was halfway across the Memorial Bridge when she heard them—male voices, loud and slurred with alcohol, echoing off the water below. Annie looked up and saw a group of sailors walking toward her on the other side of the road, their uniforms disheveled, their gait unsteady.

As they neared, one of them spotted her and pointed. “Hey! What’s a dame doing out here all alone?”

“Where you going, sweetheart?” another voice called out. “We could keep you company!”

Annie broke into a run, her slippers sliding on the icy pavement, her breath coming in sharp gasps. Behind her, she heard the sailors laughing and giving chase, their heavy boots pounding against the bridge deck.

# CHAPTER FORTY-FIVE

*Washington, DC*
*December 17, 1943*

"Hey sweetheart, slow down!"

Behind her, another man whooped. The blackout had turned the Potomac into a single sheet of ink. No moon tonight, just stars smeared across the sky, millions of them, each one reminding her how alone she was.

A year of twelve-hour days hunched over drafting tables hadn't prepared Annie for a midnight sprint across Washington. Her calf muscles cramped. A stitch stabbed under her ribs. She was done with running.

She stumbled to a halt, bent double, gripping her knees, gasping for air. No traffic, no streetcar bells. Washington had tucked itself in for the night. All she could hear was the wind-driven water slapping the bridge pilings and the ragged breathing of her pursuers closing in.

Three, maybe four of them, looming shapes in the oppressive dark.

"Well, well. Tired already, doll?" The voice carried more alcohol than malice, but Annie's heart hammered, regardless.

Their footsteps slowed as they approached.

The all-clear siren sounded across the city. Streetlights flickered back to life, casting everything in harsh yellow pools. Annie straightened, then turned to face them.

Four sailors stood ten feet away, their white caps askew, regulation pea coats rumpled from whatever bar had closed them out. The nearest one, a kid who couldn't be older than nineteen, swayed slightly on his feet.

"Stop it." She straightened, feeling the terror drain away. "Just stop right there. You're Navy men."

The kid snickered. "What gave it away, sweetheart?"

"Shut up, Kramer." An older sailor, a petty officer, stepped forward. "Miss, are you okay?"

Annie pulled her overcoat tighter around her shoulders. She ran the back of her hand across her wet nose. "Do I look okay?"

"Sorry, Miss," the older man said.

"Look, just leave me alone."

"These guys. They been drinking. Didn't mean to scare you." The three younger sailors were holding each other upright and grinning at her.

"You did a good job of it, for not trying." She put one hand on her waist and rubbed at the stitch in her side.

"Whatcha' doing out here all alone?"

Annie drew a big breath and exhaled. "I'm going to see my best friend. See, I just heard my fella, Finn Taggart, Petty Officer Second Class. His PT boat went down somewhere in the Pacific two weeks ago. Don't know if he's alive or dead. And now I've got a bunch of dumb yahoos chasing me in a blackout."

The laughter died. The swaying stopped.

"Aw, hell." The petty officer removed his white cap, ran his fingers through dark hair slicked back with Brilliantine. “Miss, I’m sorry. We didn’t know.”

“PT boats,” the tall one said. “Those boys got brass, running night missions in those plywood coffins.”

“They ain’t coffins,” the kid named Kramer snapped. “My cousin Danny’s on a PT boat. They’re fast as lightning.”

“When did it happen?” The petty officer shuffled his feet, hat in hand.

“I don’t know the exact date yet. I just heard about it from my pa.” Annie’s voice cracked. “They found some of the crew but not him.”

The sailors exchanged glances. The tallest of them cleared his throat.

“We ship outta Norfolk day after tomorrow,” he said. “Heading across the Atlantic with a convoy. Guess we’re all a little spooked about it.”

“I’m scared as hell,” Kramer admitted. “They say them U-boats hunt the convoys like sharks.”

Annie studied his face, round cheeks still soft with baby fat, eyes wide with fear. “They do. Anybody with a brain should be scared. The Germans aren’t messing around. I used to run U-boat patrols with the Mosquito Fleet off Florida with my family’s boat.”

The petty officer blew out a long breath. “That must’ve taken guts.”

“You ever seen a U-boat?” Kramer asked.

“I’ve heard them and seen them at the surface at night. Also seen a tanker torpedoed and watched it burn. Only two men survived. I rescued one of them. Just doing my job. Same as you’ll soon be doing yours.”

“You want us to walk you wherever you’re going?” the tall sailor offered. “Ain’t safe for a lady out here alone.”

Annie laughed as she shook her head. “No kidding.”

The petty officer cleared his throat. “Ma’am... Miss...” He

stumbled over the words, his earlier confidence gone. "We... uh... we're sorry. Real sorry. We were out of line. Too much shore leave, too much whiskey." He looked up, his eyes earnest. "Didn't mean no harm. Just being knuckleheads."

The four of them looked down at the bridge pavement, up at the sky, anywhere but at her.

"Apology accepted. Look, I'm headed to Johnson's Hill to deliver the news to my best friend. She loves Finn just about as much as I do." Annie stopped to get control of her tightening throat. She swallowed and continued. "You boys showing up there would cause more trouble than help."

The petty officer nodded. "Miss, you got more courage than most men I know. Hope your sailor makes it home."

Annie nodded, but she didn't trust herself to speak.

They melted back into the darkness, their voices fading as they headed toward whatever liberty they could find before shipping out.

Johnson's Hill rose from the Virginia flats like a bruise against the night sky. Even in the December cold, the smell hit her first: human waste, rotting garbage and wood smoke. Open sewers ran between the shacks, frozen over but still reeking. Outhouses leaned at dangerous angles, their doors hanging loose on rusted hinges.

Annie picked her way down the rutted dirt road. Some houses, if you could call them that, were little more than tar paper and scrap wood nailed together against the elements. Windows glowed behind gaps in the blackout curtains sewn by hand. Through the thin walls she heard babies crying, men coughing, and the crooning of The Ink Spots' song *Don't Get Around Much Anymore* playing on a radio. It was the noise of families crowded into small spaces, but not so different from what she often heard on the streets of her Sailboat Bend neighborhood back home.

These were the people who kept Arlington Hall Station

running. They were the janitors, the cooks, the trolley drivers, and some, like Emma, broke enemy codes twelve hours a day. As more people crowded into Washington to fill all the jobs the war created, the city couldn't keep up with the housing demands. The colored folks got the leftovers and were making do with a bad deal.

Emma's boarding house squatted at the end of the street, a weathered clapboard that listed to one side like a ship taking on water. Annie had met Emma there once before, so she counted windows until she found the right one. She tapped her knuckles against the glass.

As the blackout curtain slid open, Emma's face appeared, eyes wide with shock.

The window slid up with a groan. "Annie? What in God's name?"

Emma reached out, grabbed Annie's coat, and helped her climb through the opening. They tumbled together onto the narrow bed, Emma's feet tangling in the hem of her flannel nightgown.

"Lord have mercy," Emma whispered, pulling the window shut. "You're frozen solid."

The room was barely larger than a closet. The single bed piled high with blankets was pushed against one wall, beneath a half dozen pegs where her clothes hung. Atop the wooden crate that served as her nightstand was the photo of Jack on board the *Tequesta*. The room was so cold Annie could see her breath, and ice crystals had formed on the inside of the window.

Emma struck a match, lit a candle stub that sat in a saucer on the crate. The flame wavered, casting dancing shadows across the walls.

"I got a telephone call from Pa tonight." Annie's voice broke. "Finn's gone missing."

Emma's hand flew to her mouth. "Oh, honey. No."

"His PT boat sank. They can't find him. They searched and found some bodies, but not his." The words came out in a rush. "Navy said he's officially missing in action. That could mean anything. Captured, wounded, dead."

"Aw, Finn. Not Finn." Emma sucked her lips in over her teeth, and her eyes shone with tears.

"I hate this war, Em. It's ruining everything that's good in this world."

"Stop it." Emma wiped her eyes. "Don't you give up on him."

"I just can't lose him, too."

Annie collapsed against her friend's shoulder, letting the tears flow. Emma held her tight, one hand stroking her hair while whispering comfort.

"We're going to figure this out," Emma said at last. "When did it happen?"

"Pa said it was about two weeks ago."

"Okay. That's a start."

Annie pushed back and looked into Emma's eyes.

"Start of what?"

"Our investigation."

"Oh, Em, what can we do? We're thousands of miles away."

"We don't give up; that's what we do."

"But..."

"Listen. Between the two of us, we can do this."

"How?"

"I can try to get access to the traffic from that theater around the time his boat sank. The girls in my unit process Japanese communications. If I ask the right questions, mention I'm looking for patterns in a specific grid..."

"Do you really think you can do that?"

"Maybe." Emma bounced her tented fingers against her

lips. “It’s worth a try. But we’d also need to know the date and time.”

“I could contact Chandler. He’s connected. Maybe he could access classified reports, get us the exact date when and where Finn’s boat went down.”

“You think he’d help?”

“For me? He always says he owes me for catching Will and bringing down the rest of the Germans in his network. Can’t hurt to ask.” Annie wiped her eyes and wet nose. “But even if we find out where it happened, what then?”

“Then we calculate his chances. Look at different scenarios.” Emma voice was firm.

“Once we know where it was, I can pull the charts of that area. The Pacific theater’s all I’ve been mapping for six months. I’ll know the reefs, the current patterns, the prevailing winds. If I can calculate where he went in, I can project drift patterns, swimming distance to land.”

“Finn’s always been the strongest swimmer of all of us, Annie. It used to drive Jack crazy that Finn was better than him at something.”

“And he’d been doing patrols there for a while, so he was familiar with the local conditions. Once we know the area, I can calculate the tides and get inside Finn’s head. Figure out which direction he would have headed.”

Annie felt a flicker of hope, small but real. “You honestly think we can do this?”

“I think Finn Taggart is too stubborn to die in some godforsaken ocean without saying goodbye to you first.”

They talked for several hours putting together their plan.

“I should get back,” Annie said at last. “I have to be at work today.”

“You can’t cross town alone again. It’s still dark, and you’re likely to freeze to death in those pajamas.”

“I’ll manage. I made it here, didn’t I?”

"No, you are not walking." Emma spoke with newfound authority. "I'm taking you to see my supervisor, Mr. Coffee. He lives just a few blocks from here, and he's got a car."

Annie hesitated. She'd heard Emma mention him before, always with respect, sometimes exasperation. A Negro man running an all-female code-breaking unit was rare enough; one who'd risk his position to help a white woman was rarer still.

"I hope you're right about him. I'm losing valuable time if he says no."

"Trust me."

They bundled up in every piece of clothing Emma owned, wool stockings, an extra sweater, a coat that smelled like government-issue soap. The cold hit them like a slap as they slipped out the window, their breath forming white clouds that hung in the still air.

William Coffee's house stood three blocks away, a neat frame cottage that looked like a mansion compared to the surrounding shacks. Emma knocked on the front door.

"Emma?" Coffee appeared in the doorway, a distinguished man in his forties wearing a wool bathrobe over flannel pajamas. "What's wrong?"

"Mr. Coffee, I'm sorry to bother you this early, but this is my friend Annie Jeeves. She works at the Army Map Service. She needs to get back to McLean Gardens, and it's too dangerous for her to walk alone."

Coffee's eyes moved from Emma to Annie, taking in her obvious distress, the incongruity of the situation. His expression grew cautious.

"Miss Jeeves. Emma's mentioned your friendship before." He stepped aside to let them into a small front room warmed by a coal stove. "What brings you to Johnson's Hill at this hour?"

"Annie just learned that a dear friend of ours, her sweetheart, has been reported missing in action," Emma said. "Navy PT boat in the Solomons."

Coffee turned, and his face softened. "You have my deepest sympathy, Miss Jeeves. Though missing doesn't mean dead."

"That's what I've been telling her," Emma said. "But sir, she was so shook up when she heard, she walked all the way across town to tell me."

"Mr. Coffee, I know this is an unusual request," Annie began, "but Emma said you have a car, and I need to get back before my shift starts."

Coffee nodded. "I'm familiar with AMS. Important work." He glanced toward the window, where dawn was lightening the sky. "It's risky, you know, me driving a white woman through the city at this hour. If we're stopped—"

"I'll say I'm a colleague from work," Annie interrupted. "We were working late on a classified project and missed the last trolley."

Coffee considered this, then nodded. "All right. Give me a few minutes to get dressed. Don't you leave, Emma. You're coming with us."

Twenty minutes later, Coffee's well-maintained 1938 Buick pulled up in front of McLean Gardens. Annie climbed out of the back seat, then leaned down to the passenger's side window.

Emma smiled and entwined her fingers in Annie's.

Annie shifted her eyes to the driver. "Thank you, Mr. Coffee. I owe you a debt."

"Just find your young man," he said. "And be careful who you trust. You know what they say about loose lips."

Annie said goodbye, then turned and raced into her

building and up the stairs two at a time, her heart pounding with more than exertion. She burst into her room to find Cat sitting on the edge of her bed, already dressed for work, her face tight with worry.

"Annie! Where the hell have you been? I woke up, and you were gone. Your bed's still made."

"Emma and I have a plan," Annie said, stripping off her coat. "Help me get dressed."

"A plan for what?" Cat pulled Annie's work skirt down from the hangar on the bathroom door while Annie struggled into a clean blouse.

"Finn's missing in action. His PT boat went down in the Solomons." Annie's fingers fumbled with the buttons.

"Oh no, sugar. This goddamn war."

"I'm going to call Chandler today. He can access classified reports about where it happened."

"Annie, you can't be serious. You can't just find a sailor in the middle of the Pacific Ocean."

"I'm going to try, Cat. I've got to." Annie grabbed her shoes, hopping on one foot while she put them on. "I'm going to find Finn and bring him home."

# CHAPTER FORTY-SIX

*Washington, DC*
*September 14, 1944*

The whistle shrilled at 0630, and all around Annie the Army Map Service night shift scrambled for coats and lunch pails. Another twelve hours wrestling shadows into contour lines, islands into coordinates. Annie's lower back ached as she waited for Cat to finish her customary bout of hair-combing in the entryway mirror.

"My kingdom for a hot bath and ten hours of oblivion." Cat caught her eye in the reflection and raised one perfectly plucked eyebrow. "You look like death, doll."

"Just need more coffee." For the last nine months, Annie had lived on coffee, maps, and wishful thinking.

"I mean it." Cat yawned, eyes blinking with fatigue. "If you keel over, you're deadweight. I'll leave you for the crows and let the day shift pick over your bones."

"Let's get out of here before that happens."

They pushed through the front door and hustled toward the trolley stop with the other women who were now known around Washington as the Military Mapping Maidens or the 3M's. The familiar faces blurred together in the dim light: cartographers, photogrammetrists, intelligence analysts, all of them part of the vast machine now churning out maps for the European advance.

The trolley was already at the curb. Annie and Cat wedged into their usual seat, shoulders pressed close together. Cat dug in her purse and pulled out a slender velvet box. She snapped it open and thrust it under Annie's nose.

"You ever seen a ring like that?"

Annie had seen it. Twice already. And it had only been two days. Two days since Lieutenant Richard T. Harrelson III, of the Charleston Harrelsons, had slipped it onto her finger before flying back to England and the wild blue yonder of B-17 bombing raids. The engagement ring caught what little light filtered through the trolley windows, a modest diamond surrounded by tiny pearls, old-fashioned but elegant.

"It's lovely, Cat. Really."

"Richard's great-grandmother's ring," Cat continued, her South Carolina accent thickening with emotion. "Can you imagine? His family's had it for three generations. When I think about all the women who've worn it before me..." She paused, catching Annie's expression. "Lord, here I am going on about weddings when you don't even know if Finn's alive. I'm sorry, sugar."

"It's okay, Cat. At least one of us gets her happy ending."

Annie's attention drifted to the canvas bag at her feet. Inside lay nine months of accumulated documents: maps of the Solomon Islands marked with ocean currents, letters from naval officers, reports from Emma's contacts in signals intelligence.

"Richard said when he gets back, we'll have the biggest wedding Charleston has ever seen." Cat prattled on, and

Annie tried to listen. "Mama is already beside herself, planning the guest list. Daddy says he'll spare no expense. We'll live at the plantation, of course, until Richard builds us our own house on Meeting Street. Can you imagine, Annie? Me, a Harrelson!"

Annie managed a weak smile. "Sounds like a fairy tale."

She knew her roommate was over the moon with happiness, and she didn't want to ruin her joy. Her own fairy tale involved a ginger-haired boy and a fish camp in Florida, a dream now lost in the murky waters of the Pacific. She pressed her fingertips against her burning eyes and took a deep breath. Too much coffee, not enough sleep.

The trolley lurched to a stop at Connecticut Avenue. Through the window, Annie could see the familiar outline of McLean Gardens, their government housing complex, silhouetted against the lightening sky.

"This is my stop," Cat said, gathering her purse and lunch pail. "You sure you don't want to come back and get some sleep? You look like you're about to collapse."

Annie shook her head. "I'm meeting Emma first. I'll be back in the afternoon."

Cat's expression softened with concern. "Honey, maybe it's time to—"

"I'll see you tonight."

Cat shrugged, then blew her a kiss and disappeared into the throng exiting at the McLean Gardens stop.

Downtown Washington was just beginning to stir when the trolley hissed to a stop at the corner of Pennsylvania Avenue and 21st. Annie navigated the West End without thinking, walking past shuttered shop fronts and government buildings where early workers were just beginning to arrive. Somewhere, a newspaper boy hollered headlines. The September morning carried the first hint of autumn, a crispness that reminded her of Florida's brief winter season.

The Gunderson Coffee Shop sat wedged between a barbershop and a small bookstore, its painted sign faded but the windows glowing warm against the gray morning. Over the past nine months, Annie had made this stop part of her routine. A bell chimed as she pushed through the door.

Mrs. Gunderson looked up from behind the counter and smiled. "Annie, honey!" The Norwegian woman had to be past sixty, her gray hair tucked into a neat bun beneath a hair-net. "You look tired, dear."

"Long night," Annie said, rubbing her eyes. "Longer day ahead."

"Sit." Mrs. Gunderson pointed to a table. "When was the last time you ate?"

Annie ignored the question. She held out her thermos. "Can you top this off?"

Mrs. Gunderson sighed, but took it. "You girls, always living on coffee and air. When I was your age, I could eat a loaf of pumpernickel and still be hungry."

"Things were different then," Annie said. She fished some coins from her skirt pocket and slid them across the counter. "And two of the cinnamon rolls."

Mrs. Gunderson selected two plump rolls from the glass case, then, with a pointed look at Annie, added a third, misshapen one to the small paper bag. "This one's on the house. Extra sugar. You need it."

Annie mumbled thanks and headed for the door, paper bag clutched in one hand and the thermos in the other. Mrs. Gunderson called after her.

"You can't save anyone if you don't save yourself first, honey!"

~

Emma was already there, looking small and alone in her cardigan sweater and skirt in front of the Lincoln Memorial. She'd spread an old army blanket on the dew-covered grass near the edge of the Reflecting Pool, and she looked up when Annie approached.

"You look like death warmed over." Emma's voice was gentle, but her gaze was direct as Annie sank onto the blanket. No preamble, no false cheer. That was Emma.

"That's what everybody's telling me." Annie dropped her canvas bag with a thud. Then she sat down, knees popping. The dew seeped through her skirt. "You get here early?"

"I actually have a whole day off. I slept most of the night. Couldn't help waking up early, though." She unscrewed the lid of Annie's thermos and poured for both of them.

They didn't hug. They hadn't in months.

Annie took out the bag of pastries, set it on the blanket, and then started pulling out the paperwork from her own bag and Emma's. Within a minute, they had transformed their patch of grass into a war room. Charts of the Solomon Islands, naval intelligence bulletins, coded message intercepts, and the ever-present stack of Finn's old letters, many so blurred with rain or tears they were barely legible.

Emma spread the documents out, flattening them on the blanket.

She held out a cinnamon roll to Annie.

"No, thanks. Everything turns to sawdust in my mouth."

"Suit yourself." Emma took a big bite of the still-warm pastry. "I found something last week," she said between bites. "There was a PT boat out of Tulagi. Same class, same area, same month as Finn's."

Annie blinked, fighting to pay attention. "And?"

"Two survivors washed up in a raft on a reef on Buka. Navy said there was no way anyone could make it that far, but they did." Emma slid the sheet to Annie. "Tulagi to Buka is four hundred miles. With the right current? What do you think?"

Annie looked at the numbers. They meant nothing. The squiggles and arrows on the chart danced and wobbled.

Emma watched her, then tried again. "You see what I'm saying? If the currents were running hard, maybe he could have made it that far, too."

Annie's vision blurred as she stared at the page. "Why are you talking about someone else's boat?"

Emma hesitated, then said, "Because it's the closest we've come to a genuine lead in months. I want to believe it, but you have to help me make sense of it."

Annie's head dropped. "I can't," she said. "Nothing makes sense anymore. It's all noise."

Emma squeezed her arm. "It's not noise. You always see the patterns. Even back in Lauderdale, you were the one who made sense out of the shadows on the water."

"Not anymore." Annie's voice cracked. "My brain is sludge. I can't read, I can't sleep. I think about him and it's like..." She trailed off.

Emma reached over and pried the pencil from Annie's hand. "You need to sleep, Annie. You need to stop this before it eats you whole."

Annie wiped her cracked lips, angry and hurt. "How can you say that?" She knew that her blouse hung loose where it had once fit snugly. The bones in her wrists seemed too prominent, like a bird's.

"Because you're my best friend and you're wasting away," Emma said. "You're down to nothing. You keep going, and you won't make it to Christmas."

They stared at each other in silence.

Finally, Annie spoke. "I just need to know if he's alive."

Emma waited until their eyes met. "Look at me."

Annie met her friend's eyes.

"I know you think you cannot live without him. I, of all people, understand that feeling." Emma's words came out careful. "When Jack died, I wanted to die. I stopped eating. Stopped sleeping. Mama found me one night with all his letters spread out, trying to find some sign I'd missed, some clue that would bring him back." Emma's voice caught. "You can't bring him back by destroying yourself, Annie. I know that now. If Finn does come home and finds you like this—wasting away, half alive—what does he come home to?"

"You don't know what Finn wants!" The words exploded from Annie with surprising vehemence. "You think I should just give up? Just accept that he's gone and move on like nothing happened? Like we never grew up together, went fishing, sailed, laughed, and loved each other?"

"I think you should accept that you've done everything possible." Emma's voice remained steady. "We've contacted every naval intelligence officer on both coasts and analyzed tide charts and current patterns for hundreds of miles. We've tracked down survivors from a dozen PT boat incidents. What more can we do?"

Annie stared at the reflecting pool, its surface mirror-smooth in the still air. A duck paddled across, leaving a V-shaped wake that spread outward.

"I can still feel him," she whispered. "Somewhere out there. I know he's alive."

"Annie, living your life is not the same as giving up."

"I can't just stop looking. If I stop, then he really is gone." She reached for one document on the blanket. "I can't. Not after Jack."

Emma reached out, grasped her arm and held tight.

Annie wanted to fight back with the fury that had sustained her for months. Instead, she felt something inside her crumble. She knew it wasn't right to yell at Emma. She had suffered enough. Besides, Annie discovered the tears she'd been holding back for weeks wouldn't come.

"I can't even cry anymore." She didn't recognize her weak voice. "I used to be able to cry."

"Then maybe it's time to take a break. Get some sleep. Eat a proper meal. Take care of yourself." Emma reached for her, but Annie collapsed onto the blanket. She crawled over and rested her head in Emma's lap, curling her body into a fetal position. Her friend pushed some strands of hair off her face and began to sing.

*All night, all day. Angels watching over me, my Lord.*

Annie closed her eyes. Time ceased to matter. The sun climbed higher, warming their faces. Around them, the noises of Washington waking up, of government workers hurrying to their offices and tourists beginning their pilgrimages to the monuments served as the accompaniment to Emma's hymn.

When Emma stopped singing, Annie sat up. She looked down at the scattered papers and maps that represented nine months of her life. The evidence of her obsession spread across the blanket. "What if he comes back, and I've stopped looking?"

"If he comes back, we'll know. The Navy will notify next of kin. That's Bean and your folks." Emma began gathering the papers into neat piles. "Taking care of yourself isn't giving up on him, Annie. It's making sure you're strong enough to be there for him if he does come home."

"If?"

"Back when we first hatched our plan to find Finn, we both always knew there was a chance we wouldn't find him alive."

"Don't say that." Annie held out her hand, palm out, like she was trying to deflect a physical blow. Then slowly, she lowered the hand into her lap. Somewhere in the distance she heard a lawn mower, and she could smell the fresh cut grass.

"Don't you ever wish you could just go back in time to how it was before this damn war changed everything?"

Emma exhaled. "Sure. Annie, when Jack died, I thought my life had ended. Now, two years on, I'm proud of the work I'm doing here in Arlington. Back when you and I were working at The Deck, I never dreamed that I'd be doing this kind of work. And when this war is done," she patted her chest. "*I'm going to college.* Change hurts, and losing Jack almost broke me, but I survived. At the lowest moments of your life, it's difficult to believe it, but good can come out of it."

"I'm just not ready to give up on him yet."

"That's fair. You're strong, you're smart. You'll figure this out. But honey, right now, your country needs you to get some sleep and get to work."

Annie looked across the reflecting pool. She watched a mother and a toddler passing by. The child's tiny hand was wrapped around her mother's pinkie finger.

Stopping the search felt like stepping off a cliff. The search had become her life, her purpose, the thing that got her out of bed every morning. Without it, she wasn't sure who she was anymore.

Emma had packed both their bags. She stood up and stretched. "I'm meeting some girls from work for lunch. Want to join us?"

"I should go home." Annie stood and helped Emma fold the Army blanket.

"Promise me you'll try to eat something and then go straight to sleep?"

"I promise. But you know I'm not giving up, right?"

Emma laughed. "See you next week," she said.

# CHAPTER FORTY-SEVEN

*Washington, DC*
*September 14, 1944*

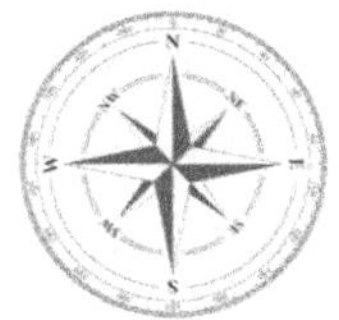

Annie almost nodded off on the trolley ride back from downtown to McLean Gardens. When she stepped inside the lobby of her apartment building, she found Chandler sitting on a bench, hat in hand, having a chat with Mrs. Brodigan.

"Good afternoon, Annie. I've just been having a very nice chat with this fine lady." Annie could have sworn Mrs. Brodigan blushed. "I've come to ask you a few questions. Do you have a moment?"

"Of course."

Chandler said his goodbyes to the house matron, then asked, "Shall we take a walk?"

Annie knew that meant what he wanted to discuss was for her ears only. She nodded and followed him out the door.

When they reached the street, Chandler pointed toward the Newark Park playground. Annie walked, waiting for him to say whatever was on his mind.

"You look tired, Annie."

"Too many night shifts. And you are keeping me from my bed this very moment. Why don't you just tell me why you're here so I can go back and try to get some sleep?"

"Tired *and* out of sorts," Chandler observed.

Annie rubbed her eyes and massaged her temples. "I'm sorry, Mr. Chandler. I've just not had a good day today."

"Still no word about your friend Finn Taggart?"

"Vanished without a trace."

They arrived at the park, and Chandler pointed to a bench. "Take a seat. I want to talk to you about an opportunity. You look like you need a distraction."

"You sound like Emma."

He cocked his head and looked at her, eyebrows raised.

"I spent the morning with her. She says I need to give this search a rest. Says it's going to be the death of me."

"Your friend is a very intelligent young woman. I suggest you heed her advice."

Annie crossed her arms and made a noise. "*Hmmph.*"

"Hear me out, Annie. I have an offer for you."

Annie sighed. "Again?"

Chandler nodded. "You know better than most that the success of our push into Europe depends on our knowledge of the terrain and accurate maps. You helped to create some of those 3,000 maps AMS produced for the Normandy invasion, and you know we have barely covered France. As we transition from air drops to ground artillery, we need more data, especially elevation. This war is going to be won by whichever side has the best data and intel."

"What does this have to do with me?"

"The OSS, working together with the OCE, that's the Office of the Chief Engineers, is putting together a special military intelligence team to collect the German geodetic data as our troops advance."

"I'm still not following why you're telling me this."

"This team will be small, no more than 20 people, and they need two clerks. Major Floyd Hough, the team leader, has asked for the names of two women from the WACs. He wants one who speaks French and German and another with mapping skills."

Annie was trying to follow what he was saying, but his words tumbled together. Her exhaustion made it difficult to concentrate. "But I'm a civilian specialist, and I don't want to be a clerk."

"Yes, you would have to enlist in the Women's Army Corps, but that can be done with the stroke of a pen. Annie, this team is going to London, perhaps in a matter of weeks, and then they will follow just behind the front line as the Allies move across Europe. The mission is to find, seize and catalogue Nazi map data. The young woman who brought down Operation Pastorius would be a perfect fit for this unit."

"Are you asking me to go to Europe?"

Chandler nodded. "Yes. All this is moving fast. They want my recommendations by the end of day tomorrow."

"I appreciate the offer. Truly. But *I can't.* I need to stay here. In case they find Finn. In case there's news."

Chandler removed his glasses and began cleaning them with his handkerchief. "Annie, it's been nine months."

"I know how long it's been." The words came out louder than she had intended. "But if I go to Europe, I'll be even farther away. What if they find him and I'm not here?"

"What if you're using this search as an excuse to avoid living? Do you think your young man would want that?" Chandler's voice was clinical, almost cruel.

Annie flinched. "That's not..."

"The success of this mission is critical, and I wouldn't be asking you if I didn't think you were the best person for the job."

"I won't change my mind." Annie picked up her bag, fingers white on the canvas strap. "Thank you for thinking of me."

She stopped when Chandler spoke. "Your friend, Petty Officer Taggart. If he could see you now, wasting away, not sleeping, destroying yourself. What do you think he'd want you to do?"

Annie didn't turn around. "He'd want me to keep looking."

"No." Chandler's voice dropped. "He'd want you to live."

Annie walked away without responding.

~

The walk back to McLean Gardens took ten minutes, but Annie barely noticed. She'd done the right thing. She had to believe that. Staying in Washington meant being here when they found Finn. Because they would find him. They had to.

And the work she was doing here with AMS was just as important. No one could say she wasn't doing her part.

She climbed the stairs to the third floor, already planning what she'd tell Emma next week. How she'd explain that she couldn't just abandon the search, couldn't run off to Europe chasing Nazi maps while Finn was still missing.

The door to her room stood open. Cat was pulling dresses from the closet, laying them across her bed in neat rows. Her trunk—the same one she'd brought from South Carolina two years ago—sat open on the floor.

"Cat? What's going on? Why aren't you asleep?"

Cat looked up, her expression a blend of joy and guilt. "Annie. I was hoping to talk to you before all this." She waved her crimson fingernails over the trunk. "I got a telegram from Richard this morning. His mother wants us married before Christmas." The words tumbled out. "Of course I called home. My parents are over the moon. They've already contacted the church in Charleston and want me home. Now."

"That's swell, Cat." Annie tried to sound enthusiastic.

"I'm catching the train tomorrow afternoon."

"Tomorrow? But that's..."

"I know it's sudden. Believe me, I know." Cat held up a blue dress, studying it. "But Richard's father arranged for him to get leave. His mother wants the wedding done properly, and that takes time. The dress fittings alone—" She caught herself. "Annie, I'm sorry. This is awful timing, I know."

Annie sank onto her own bed, the one she'd barely slept in for months. Cat was leaving. Tomorrow.

"That's so soon."

"I know." Cat folded the dress. "But the war doesn't wait, does it? If there's one thing this war has taught us, it's that life is short. Every day is precious. If we wait until everything is perfect, he..." She didn't finish the sentence.

A knock at the door. Eliza Hunter poked her head in, holding several envelopes. "Mail call, ladies. Cat, you've got a letter from your brother. Annie, nothing today."

*Nothing today*. The words had become so familiar they barely stung anymore. Annie stood and took off her overcoat. She remembered her promise to Emma to eat and sleep.

Cat was still staring at the envelope, glancing at the return address. "I just heard from my brother." Surprise tinged her voice. "He never writes this close to his last letter."

Cat sat on her bed and tore open the envelope. As she read, her expression shifted from curiosity to something harder.

"What is it?" Annie asked as she kicked off her shoes and unbuttoned her skirt.

Cat's voice was quiet. "He's writing about what happened

in St-Lô, France during that offensive in Normandy last month."

Cat scanned the page. "He says, *they called in bombers to clear the way for the ground advance. The weather was bad, smoke, confusion. The pilots didn't know exactly where the Allied front line was and the bombs fell short.*" Her hand went to her mouth. "Oh God. Annie, he says '*The pilots couldn't see the ground markers. The intel they had was wrong. That carpet bombing that they did, it killed General McNair and a whole lot of the 30th American Division... I watched it happen, Cat. Good men torn apart by American bombs because somebody somewhere didn't have the right coordinates for the target box. We're supposed to be the most advanced military in the world, but we can't even keep our own damn maps straight. Sorry for the language. But those men should still be alive. We need to do better.*"

Annie stared at Cat, but she was seeing something else. Her brother Jack, shot down at the start of his career because intelligence hadn't known about the German flak positions. Finn, missing in the Pacific, where the charts show the last surveys of some islands were done in the 1800's.

"Bobby's right," Annie whispered. "The maps. They matter."

Cat looked up from the letter. "What?"

"Chandler offered me a position today. With a team going to Europe." The words felt strange in her mouth. "I said no."

Cat set the letter down. "Why?"

"Because I'm scared." The admission surprised her.

"Annie—"

"Going to Europe means accepting that Finn might really be gone. I'm so tired of this war, Cat. I'm so tired of losing people."

She thought of Finn, somewhere in the Pacific. Dead or alive, she might never know. She'd spent nine months thinking that if she just looked hard enough, she could bring him home.

But Finn was gone. And she couldn't help him.

"What are you going to do?"

"I don't know." She was tired, so tired. "But I promised Emma I'd sleep."

"Then sleep. I'll be quiet as a mouse."

Annie nodded, too exhausted to argue. She pulled off her blouse, changed into her nightgown, and climbed under the covers while Cat continued packing. The room was warm, her bed soft. Her body ached for rest.

She closed her eyes.

Behind her eyelids, she saw Finn's face the day he left for the Navy. Saw Jack waving from the train. Saw the maps spread across the Lincoln Memorial grass.

Bobby's words kept intruding. *Those men should still be alive.*

She opened her eyes and stared at the ceiling.

Across the room, Cat had stopped packing and was sitting on her own bed, Bobby's letter still in her grip. She looked up from the pages. "You can't sleep?"

"Can't turn my brain off." Annie sat up, drawing her knees to her chest. "I feel like my whole body is buzzing."

Her roommate nodded and returned to rereading her brother's letter.

"Cat, can I ask you something?"

"Of course."

"Are you scared? About marrying Richard? About him going back to the war?"

Cat bit her lower lip and took a deep breath before she spoke. "Terrified. Every day he's in that B-17, I'm just seconds short of a full panic attack. But I'm more scared of not having this time with him." She looked down and straightened the engagement ring on her finger. "When he proposed, I almost said no."

"Hard to believe."

When Cat raised her head again, the lines in her forehead and the pain in her eyes revealed a woman Annie had never seen. "But what if he dies?" She paused after each word. "What if I'm a widow at twenty-three?" She stopped and looked at the ceiling, blinking back tears.

"Yeah. The '*what if*' that's always hanging over us."

"I love him, Jeeves. And I realized I'd rather have whatever time we get—than have nothing at all because I was too afraid to take that risk."

Annie climbed out from under her covers and crossed to Cat's bed. She sat next to her roommate and pulled her into a hug. "I'm gonna miss you, Donovan."

Cat hugged her tighter and swayed from side to side. "Gonna miss you too, Jeeves."

They sat that way for a while. At last, Cat inhaled and pushed against Annie's shoulders, holding her at arm's length. Makeup streaked her cheeks, but she wore a big grin. "You've got to come to the wedding! You'll love Charleston. You could be one of my bridesmaids! It's going to be fabulous."

Annie tried to imagine herself in a fancy dress at a wedding like something out of the movie *Gone with the Wind*. Instead, her mind conjured up images from the newsreels at the movie house. Young soldiers by the thousands advancing their way into France as artillery shells explode around them.

"Sorry, Cat. I can't do that." Annie stood and pulled off her nightgown, then reached for the blouse and skirt she had only just hung up.

"*Pshaw*. Don't you worry. I'll have folks who can do your hair, and measure you for your dress. And don't you worry about work. They'll give you the time off for a wedding. Daddy will pay for your train ticket, and we've got plenty of room at the house."

"It's not about you or the wedding, Cat. I have to go out," Annie said.

"Get back in bed, you fool. You need your sleep."

Annie slipped on her shoes and reached for her coat. "I need to talk to Chandler before I lose my nerve."

The walk from the trolley stop to the E Street Complex only took fifteen minutes, but by the time Annie reached the door she felt like she'd been dragging herself across hot sand for days. She was approaching twenty hours with no sleep. The city was loud now. All the quiet from the morning burned away by truck horns and the cars driven by workers starting to head home. She stepped around two men in navy-colored overalls arguing over a length of steel pipe, then up the stone steps to the glass doors.

The OSS building looked like every other government facility: limestone facade, blacked-out windows, a flagpole.

Inside, a beefy guard in Army green stood by the check-in desk, fingers laced over his gut. He looked her up and down, then pointed to the clipboard. "Name and badge," he said, not bothering to look up.

She fished her government-issue badge from her purse, clipped it to her collar, and scrawled her name on the sign-in sheet.

"I need to see Frank Chandler. Third floor."

The guard glanced at the clock on the wall. "Mr. Chandler's usually gone by now. Let me check." He picked up the phone and dialed. "Yes sir. Got a young lady here asking for you, sir... says it's urgent." A pause. He rested the handset on his shoulder and turned to her. "Name?"

"Annie Jeeves. Army Map Service."

The guard repeated this on the phone, then nodded. "He

says you can go on up. Write his name and the time here first." He pointed to the lines on the sign-in sheet.

The elevator seemed to take forever.

Third floor. The doors opened. Her footsteps echoed on the polished floor. The building was quieter at this hour, most offices already dark.

She rapped against the door before fear could stop her.

"Come in."

Chandler looked up from his desk as she entered, his expression unreadable behind his wire-rimmed glasses. The office was small and sparse—a desk, two chairs, a filing cabinet, a map of Europe pinned to the wall with colored pins marking the Allied advance.

"Miss Jeeves." He set down his pen. "I didn't expect to see you again today."

"I didn't think I'd be here either, sir."

Chandler leaned back in his chair, studying her. "So?"

"I've thought it over, and if you're still willing to recommend me, I'd like to join Major Hough's team."

"That's excellent news, Annie." Chandler's expression didn't change, but something shifted in his eyes. "What changed your mind?"

Annie thought about all the reasons—Emma's words, Bobby's letter, the maps that mattered, the men who'd died because of bad intelligence. But when she opened her mouth, what came out was simpler.

"I realized that staying was killing me. And Finn wouldn't want that. Neither would Jack." She met Chandler's eyes. "You were right. They'd want me to live. So, I'm choosing to live."

Chandler nodded. "Are you frightened?"

She smiled. "Terrified."

"Good. That means you understand the stakes. And you're going to be in the heat of it." He pulled a folder from his desk drawer. "The team ships out in three weeks. You'll need to settle your affairs, complete your security clearances, and attend several days of briefings starting Monday. The address where you'll report for training is in the folder. I'll call your superiors at the AMS and explain that you've been reassigned. Then we will get you officially enlist in the U.S. Army. Can you manage the rest?"

"Yes, sir."

"You'll be operating close to the front lines, Miss Jeeves. There's a very real possibility you might not come home."

Annie thought about the past nine months, the sleepless nights, the obsessive searching, the slow fade into nothing. "With respect, sir, if I stay here, there's a possibility I won't survive either. At least in Europe, I might die doing something that matters."

For the first time since she'd met him, Chandler smiled wide enough to show teeth. "That's the spirit that wins wars, Miss Jeeves." He extended his hand across the desk. "Welcome to the team."

# CHAPTER FORTY-EIGHT

*Paris, France*
*November 8, 1944*

The chill autumn wind bit at Annie's cheeks as she crossed the Place de l'Étoile. The Arc de Triomphe loomed against the pewter sky, its stone face pocked with shrapnel scars. Six weeks after Liberation and the City of Light still looked bruised, but Paris was learning to breathe again.

This early morning walk, a habit she'd picked up to get her bearings and orient herself to the strange new city, had become a joy more than a necessity. The brisk stride, the sting of the cold, it cleared the fog from her brain, settled the jumpiness in her gut.

The streets belonged to the military at this hour. Jeeps darted through the heavier traffic, their American drivers hunched over wheels, cigarettes clamped between their lips. A convoy of what Major Hough called deuce-and-a-half trucks rumbled past, loaded with young and loud GIs heading east. Several waved and whistled at her, but Annie kept walking, hands deep in her overcoat pockets. After two weeks in

Paris, she'd grown used to the attention her WAC uniform attracted. What she couldn't get used to was the hunger in Parisian faces; not just for food, but for things the war had stolen.

This wasn't Washington, where the war was headlines, ration books and gold stars in windows. Here, war was etched in the faces of the people and the chipped facades of buildings. Washington had its shortages, but nothing like this. There, you might miss your nylons or complain about no meat or coffee. Here, you might freeze or starve to death.

Annie remembered the burning tankers off Florida, the greasy smoke, the dead men on the beach. Few back home had seen that. Here, everyone knew war intimately.

The Hôtel Majestic rose before her, its facade dominating Avenue Kléber. The Swastika flag was gone, replaced by the Tricolore, but the shadow of Hitler's crooked cross remained. Now, American MPs flanked the hotel entrance, checking papers with their flat mid-Western accents. Annie flashed her ID and pushed through the heavy doors.

The lobby still smelled of the Wehrmacht: boot polish and Turkish tobacco embedded so deep that no amount of scrubbing could erase it. The French staff moved through these spaces, their faces blank. What compromises had they made to survive?

If Parisians could survive for four years, wasn't it possible Finn could survive for one? In a little over two weeks, it would be the one-year anniversary of the day his PT boat sank. Annie could not shake the feeling that she would know if he were dead. *Hold on, Finn. We're doing everything we can to end this war.*

She followed the corridor to what had once been the hotel's grand ballroom. She stepped into a cavernous room with high, ornate ceilings. The parquet floor bore the outlines of where heavy furniture had once stood.

She remembered Jack's first letter from England, where he wrote about how cold it was on this side of the Atlantic, about seeing snow for the first time. Winter was returning to Europe, and it would soon be her turn to see the white stuff for the first time.

The grand ballroom now served as a military mess hall, long tables and metal chairs replacing whatever elegance had existed before. Joelle Leclerq, the other WAC on their team, slipped in through a side entrance. Her hair, cropped in a tidy bob, stuck up on one side. She had not inherited style from her French mother, but she had a sharp mind, and her fluency in French was already proving invaluable.

"*Bonjour*, Annie. How was your walk?"

"Cold." Annie grabbed a tin cup, and they joined the queue at the serving station.

"Thought you might have run away," Joelle said, her accent half-Virginia, half-Parisian. "Or gotten lost."

"Just needed some air."

"Everyone's going a little crazy just waiting here in Paris. I overheard the men at table six say they are trying to brew whiskey in a radiator."

The coffee was chicory, bitter with an ashen aftertaste, but at least it was hot. They collected their rations, a piece of the stale bread that passed for toast and a small chunk of hard cheese.

The two women wove their way through the crowded room to the table their team had claimed. HOUGHTEAM was comprised of three Army officers, four civilian specialists, eleven enlisted men and the two WACs.

"Gentlemen." Annie nodded to the handful of men already seated at their table. Martin Shallenberger sat ramrod straight, his civilian suit well-pressed, a dark blue tie knotted at his throat. He was stirring his coffee with a bored expression. Annie found his air of superiority grating.

"Miss Jeeves." Shallenberger inclined his head. "Trust you slept well?"

"Like a baby." Of course, she'd been awake since 0400, staring at the water-stained ceiling, but better to agree than invite conversation.

Annie took a careful sip of the hot liquid, then chased it with a bite of the coarse bread.

"Paris isn't what it was, of course." Shallenberger dabbed his lips with a linen handkerchief. "The rationing, the general drabness... Vienna, even in '38, had more élan." He sighed. "Still, the architecture endures."

Major Hough sat at the head of the table, hunched over his plate, working through a stack of papers while he chewed. Their leader was the shortest man on the team, and with his prominent forehead, thinning red hair, and wire-rimmed glasses, he looked more like a meek professor than the leader of a military intelligence mission. Hough had returned from Aachen the day before, and he appeared pleased.

"*Guten Morgen, Fräulein.*" Bertold Friedl slid into the seat across from her. The Austrian linguist had a gift for appearing wherever conversation might prove interesting. "I've been thinking about your book dealers along the Seine."

"Oh?" Annie balanced a morsel of cheese on her bread, keeping her expression neutral.

"The Bouquinistes survived the Occupation by knowing what to show and what to hide." He leaned forward, dropping his voice. "If you're hunting German maps, consider what else they're not showing."

Before Annie could respond, Major Hough stood. The scrape of his chair killed all conversation.

"War room. Five minutes." He gathered his papers and strode out.

The war room was another ghost of the Majestic's opulent past. Ballroom Two was even larger than the dining hall, its towering windows still draped in heavy blackout curtains that plunged the space into perpetual twilight. Three scarred trestle tables and a dozen mismatched chairs occupied the center of the vast parquet floor. Every spare surface held books, stacks of linen maps, slide rules, protractors, brown-stained drinking glasses, half-smoked cigarettes.

Annie walked around the room's perimeter. They'd arrived in Paris with a mountain of gear. Heavy, tripod-mounted cameras stood like metallic insects, their lenses aimed at nothing. Boxes overflowed with unfamiliar devices, things with cranks and spools that she guessed were for microfilm. She walked past the boxes of what Hough had told them was 11,000 neatly typed index cards – representing the entire holdings of the Army Map Service, a portable library of American geographic knowledge.

This was the hunt. Not for a lost boy in the Pacific, but for the enemy's secrets, hidden in paper and ink.

Hough stood before a map of northeastern France, hands clasped behind his back. The others filed in, including the captain and first lieutenant who served as the team's military liaisons, Shallenberger with his perfect posture, and Friedl humming Maurice Chevalier's *Ça sent si bon la France*.

"I've just returned from Aachen," Hough began. "First German city to fall, and it proves that this mission is worth every second of our time."

He spread an ash-stained map on the table. "The Technische Hochschule, their technical university, took a pounding from our bombers. The library's a wreck, but thousands of volumes, survey records and research papers remain in the basement under the rubble. What caught my eye, though, wasn't inside."

He tapped a point on the map outside the main library building. "The Germans, in their haste to evacuate, had bundled up files, roped together, stacked right out in the open. Ready for trucks that never made it. Geodetic survey tables. Triangulation data covering vast swaths of German territory that our boys haven't even reached yet." He smiled. "Gold."

Shallenberger let out a low whistle.

"The immediate priority is to microfilm every single page of the Aachen data. We need to get it to the front. *Now*. Allied artillery units are desperate for accurate targeting information for western Germany. This data will save lives, shorten the war."

Annie felt the excitement, the thrill of the hunt. This was what she'd been recruited for. Not just her cartographic skills.

"Sir?" She raised her hand. "What about Paris? There must be more material here."

Hough's thin lips curved. "Precisely why you and Leclerq will start your reconnaissance today. The enlisted men can handle microfilming the Aachen data as it comes in."

He pulled a paper from his stack. "Libraries, map shops, anywhere German officers might have frequented. They were here four years, and they surely left traces."

"We'll find them, sir," Joelle said.

"I know you will." This time Hough smiled. "Take the bicycles. You can cover more ground that way."

Annie felt a flutter in her chest. After two weeks of unpacking, cataloging and filing, at last some real fieldwork.

The meeting broke up, everyone scattering to their assignments. Annie caught Joelle's arm in the corridor. "The Bouquinistes first?"

"*Mais oui*. The booksellers see everything." Joelle's eyes sparkled. "And they gossip worse than concierges."

They climbed the narrow stairs to their shared room on the third floor. Like everything else in the Majestic, the room had been stripped to essentials: two narrow beds, a dresser, hooks for their uniforms. Annie's sketches of Florida tidal charts pinned above her bed, were a reminder of another life.

They would wear civilian clothes today, simple wool trousers, blouses, and cardigans. Nothing to mark them as military. Just two American girls exploring Paris.

The bicycles waited in the hotel's rear courtyard. Sturdy French models that somehow had survived the Occupation and they'd bought from the Parisians. Annie swung her leg over, grateful for the freedom of movement her trousers provided. She'd never go back to skirts if she could help it.

They pedaled out onto the Rue Jean Giraudoux, joining the stream of morning traffic. Bicycle bells chimed on all sides as Parisians navigated around military vehicles and the occasional horse cart. Annie had to swerve to avoid a woman balancing a basket of turnips on her handlebars.

"This way," Joelle called, leading them southeast toward the river.

The city unfolded around them, elegant buildings with their wrought-iron balconies, shops with their windows still half-empty, cafés where ersatz coffee cost a day's wages. Annie admired how Parisians had adapted to scarcity: women's dresses showed ingenious repairs, men's shoes had wooden soles to replace worn leather.

They reached the Seine at the Pont de l'Alma, where the first Bouquiniste stalls were already open. The sellers huddled in their green metal boxes while books, postcards, and prints spilled across the pavement.

"Let me lead." Joelle propped her bicycle against the embankment wall. This was not the first time Joelle had visited Paris, and Annie was eager to learn, happy to assume her role as the naïve American.

They worked their way along the quai, Joelle chatting with each seller while Annie browsed through boxes of prints. Most offerings were tourist fare, views of Notre-Dame, reproductions of Impressionist paintings, battered copies of Hugo and Balzac. But Annie knew what they were looking for. She checked bindings, peered into portfolios, hunting for the telltale precision of German cartography.

At the fifth stall, she found something. Not German, but interesting. A pre-war Michelin map of the Ardennes, the kind Wehrmacht officers might have acquired for planning. She held it up, catching Joelle's eye.

"How much?" Joelle asked the seller, a wizened man with nicotine-stained fingers.

He named a price. Joelle haggled, asking for any other German maps, but the seller simply shrugged.

They were halfway down the line of stalls when Joelle, who appeared engrossed in a tray of old postcards, nudged Annie's arm. Annie glanced over. Joelle's eyes were fixed on a nearby bookseller, a stooped man with a Vandyke beard, who was deep in a hushed conversation with a younger fellow with slicked-back dark hair.

Joelle tilted her head, listening. Annie continued to flip through a stack of engravings, straining to catch any familiar words. Then she heard it. "*Kartographie*" and then, "*Oberkommando.*" German terms.

Joelle moved closer, pretending to admire a dusty globe. After a moment, she drifted back to Annie's side.

"He's talking about a collection." Joelle leaned closer, pretending to be interested in the book Annie held. "Belonged to a 'Generalmajor Werner.'"

"Werner?" Annie frowned. The name wasn't on any of their target lists, but a Generalmajor. That was significant.

"The younger man, he says this Werner had an extensive collection of military maps. Some are being offered for sale, discreetly." Joelle's eyes gleamed. "By a woman. A Madame Joubert. She has a shop in the Marché aux Puces, on Rue Jules Vallès."

"The flea market?" Annie had heard of it from Edward Espenshade, the geography professor on their team. He had tried to shock her with his tales of searching the flea market for his collection of rare, lewd literature.

"Yes. And the crucial part." Joelle's voice dropped, "Is that the Bouquiniste is planning to go see Madame Joubert himself. Later today, when his stall closes."

"So we're done here then?"

"*Absolument.*" Joelle glanced at her watch. "The Bouquiniste said his shop closes at four."

"So, we have to get there before him. Let's go."

They were already moving toward their bicycles. Annie felt the familiar rush. It reminded her of those nights off the coast of Florida searching for U-boats. The hunt was on.

They pedaled away from the Seine, the image of the stooped Bouquiniste spurring them on. Annie, with her innate sense of direction, navigated the streets, the borrowed bicycle's chain rattling in protest.

The ride to Saint-Ouen took them through a different Paris. North of the grand boulevards, the streets narrowed and darkened. Annie hadn't ever visited this quarter, but she had studied a map of the city and she could recall the layout of the streets.

Bomb damage showed more clearly here, buildings with their faces torn off, exposing wallpaper and staircases to the sky. This was working-class Paris, where the Resistance had been strongest and German reprisals harshest.

*Marché aux Puces de Paris Saint-Ouen* was an assault on the senses. Since Liberation, it had become a clearing house for the detritus of war. Family heirlooms sold for food. German equipment that had 'disappeared,' now offered for sale. Hawkers shouted, accordions wheezed, and a thousand conversations in a variety of languages melded into an overpowering hum.

"Rue Jules Vallès," Joelle panted, skidding to a halt at an intersection crowded with carts piled high with chipped crockery and tarnished silverware. "It should be this way."

They pushed their bicycles through the throng, their eyes scanning the faded street signs and jumbled shopfronts. Rue Jules Vallès was quieter, a narrow alley of antique shops and bric-a-brac stores, their windows crammed with dubious treasures.

"There," Annie said, pointing to a small, unassuming shop with a faded green awning: *Joubert – Antiquités*.

They leaned their bicycles against a wall, took a deep breath, and composed their faces into expressions of wide-eyed, American naiveté.

Madame Joubert's shop occupied a narrow storefront squeezed between a café and a dealer in broken furniture. The window display was artfully arranged: antique books, a large brass binnacle compass, some nautical charts that might have been valuable if they weren't water-stained.

"Remember," Joelle whispered. "We're silly Americans with too much money."

Annie nodded, arranging her face into the eager expression she'd perfected. They pushed through the door, setting off a bell.

The shop's interior was cramped and dim, shelves reaching to the ceiling. It smelled of dust and mildew.

A woman emerged from the back room.

"*Mademoiselles?*"

Madame Joubert had the faded beauty of someone who'd once moved in better circles. Her dress was of good quality but poorly mended, her hair dyed black so long ago the white roots dominated. But it was her hands, soft, manicured fingers that had never known real work that told the story of how she had spent her years of occupation.

"*Bonjour, Madame.*" Joelle spoke in American-accented French. "We are looking for maps. Old maps. Foreign maps."

"*Oui, oui.*" The woman switched into English. "Over here I have some exquisite maps of the village of Civray during the reign of *Louis Quatorze.*" She held up a map—an obvious forgery.

Annie smiled. "Not that old."

Joelle examined a map of Europe. "German maps, *peut-être?*"

Something flickered in Joubert's eyes.

"You are Americans searching for German maps?" She forced a laugh. "Why would anyone want such things? The *Boche* are gone, thank God."

"Oh, but they're so precise!" Annie gushed, playing her part. "My father collects military maps back in Delaware. See, he fought in the Great War, and he is just crazy for any authentic German maps or charts or documents. He's got this library at our house out at the lake. Whole room filled with these big old drawers that he keeps all his maps in. I'd pay very well to bring him back some little thing."

"Even better for lots of little things!" Joelle hooked her arm into Annie's. "I am Miss DuPont's secretary, and her father is my employer."

"I'd like so much to make dear Papa happy." Annie watched Joubert's face, saw the moment greed won over caution.

"Perhaps... I might have something." Joubert moved to lock the shop door, flipping the sign to *Fermé*. "But such things are not cheap. And there are risks, you understand?"

"Money is no problem," Joelle assured her. "And I assure you we can be very discreet. May we see what you have?"

Madame swiveled her head back and forth, examining both of them. "*Bien sûr.* This way."

Just as she turned, a knock at the door made them all freeze. Joubert's face went pale.

"Madame Joubert?" A man's voice outside, French but cautious.

Annie's pulse quickened. Joubert's eyes darted between them and the door, weighing her options. Finally, she called out: "*Fermé aujourd'hui*!"

The footsteps retreated. Joubert exhaled, then turned back to them, forcing a smile that resembled a grimace. "You see? Even now, one must be careful. Come. This way."

She led them to a back room, even more cluttered than the shop. She moved aside a stack of paintings. German officers on horseback, Bavarian farms with robust young men working in the fields. The type of thing that could get you arrested in Paris now. She opened a wooden cabinet.

Annie fought her natural reaction. Maps. Dozens of them. Not just standard Wehrmacht issue, but specialized charts, coastal defenses, V-1 launch sites, detailed surveys of the Pas-de-Calais. Intelligence documents that should have been destroyed or evacuated.

"Generalmajor Werner was a friend."

With the way Madame Joubert's voice quavered, Annie wondered if he had been more than a friend.

"He needed money for personal debts. I helped him. Before...he left."

Annie picked up one map, recognizing the meticulous German notation.

"How much for all of them?" she asked, keeping her voice steady.

Joubert named a figure that would have bought a small apartment before the war. Annie pretended to consider while her mind raced. They needed to secure these maps without alerting Joubert that they knew their true value.

"*C'est beaucoup*," Joelle said, playing up the hesitation.

Annie added, "We would need to visit the bank."

"Of course." Joubert was already wrapping the maps back up, her movements quick and nervous. "But please, you must be cautious. There are those who would misunderstand my friendship with the General."

They agreed to return soon with the cash. Joubert walked them out, her smile brittle as glass. As soon as they were around the corner, Annie grabbed Joelle's arm.

"DuPont. That was genius."

"*Oui*. But we need to get back. Fast!"

They pedaled hard through the afternoon traffic, not speaking until they reached the Majestic. Annie's legs burned as they ran through the hallways to the war room.

Major Hough looked up from a stack of microfilm cards as they burst in. His expression sharpened as he took in their flushed faces.

"Sir," Annie gasped, still catching her breath. "We found something. German tactical maps, including V-1 sites and coastal defenses. A collaborator in Saint-Ouen has them."

She gave him the details. Hough listened without interrupting, his face revealing nothing. When she finished, he was already reaching for the telephone.

"Lieutenant Morrison? I need a recovery team. Quiet but official." He gave the address and brief instructions. "No, I want the woman detained for questioning. Gently. She may have more material."

He hung up and turned back to Annie and Joelle. "Outstanding work. What made you suspect these weren't ordinary maps?"

Annie thought about it. "The precision of the notations. The way she handled them, like she knew they were dangerous. And one of them had coordinates I recognized from our target list."

"Good work." Coming from Hough, it was high praise. "Write up everything while it's fresh. I want a full report."

"Yes, sir." Annie felt a flush of pride. This was what she was meant to do. Not mourning the dead, but saving the living.

As they left the war room, Joelle bumped her shoulder. "Not bad for our first real hunt, ***non***?"

Annie grinned, feeling more alive than she had in months. "Not bad at all."

They spent the rest of the afternoon documenting their discovery, typing up reports in triplicate while they waited for news. Just before dinner, Lieutenant Morrison appeared with a satisfied expression.

"Got them all. Plus some bonus material. Seems Madame Joubert was quite the social butterfly during the Occupation. Her apartment was full of interesting souvenirs."

Annie felt a twist of something, not quite sympathy, for the woman who had bartered with the enemy for her survival. But that was the nature of war. Everyone made choices. Some just chose wrong.

That evening, as she lay in her narrow bed listening to Joelle's soft breathing, Annie thought about the maps they'd found. Somewhere, an Allied artillery unit would use those coordinates to destroy a V-1 site before it could rain more death on London. Lives would be saved because two women had played dumb and listened.

She pressed her hand against the compass rose pendant at her throat, the one Emma had given her. For the first time in months, she didn't think about Finn before falling asleep.

She thought about tomorrow's hunt.

# CHAPTER FORTY-NINE

*Frankfurt am Main, Germany*
*March 29, 1945*

The convoy of mud-splattered trucks groaned to a halt on what had once been a street in Frankfurt am Main. Annie gripped the wooden slat of the truck bed as she stood, her legs stiff from the bone-rattling journey through France and into Germany.

The two women climbed out of the truck and stood with the rest of the team, staring down at the ruins between them and the river.

"*Mon Dieu*," Joelle whispered.

Frankfurt was gone. In its place stood blackened rubble. Entire blocks had been reduced to brick dust and twisted metal. The cathedral spire stood alone against the sky.

"Move it!" Major Hough's voice cut through their shocked silence. "We're not tourists. Get the equipment unloaded."

Their headquarters occupied one of the few intact buildings in the *Bankenviertel*, the old business district. The four-story office block had somehow survived the bombing. The windows were blown out on the upper floors, but the structure stood solid. German civilians picking through nearby rubble stopped to watch as the Americans hauled crates of cameras, microfilm equipment, and boxes of documents into the building.

Annie grabbed a crate marked 'Triangulation Instruments,' her arms straining under the weight of the contents. Shallenberger supervised the delicate instruments while Espenshade directed the enlisted men with the heavier equipment. It took over two hours to unload everything.

Inside, the building still held traces of its former occupants—a calendar on the wall frozen at February 1945, a coffee cup on a desk with mold growing in the dregs, German memorandums scattered on the floor. Hough had claimed the largest office as his command center. He worked already spreading maps across a conference table that had survived the abandonment.

"Listen up," Hough said once they'd assembled in what had been a meeting room and would now serve as their dining hall. His overcoat was gray with dust, his glasses smudged, the stubble on his face nearly as long as his mustache. "I know you're exhausted. It's been a long three days on the road, and you've seen what's left of this country. But we're here to work, not to gawk."

He pointed to the map of the region taped to the wall. "Tomorrow is Saturday, March 31st. The clock is ticking. I want teams in Darmstadt and Wiesbaden by 0700. The damage is not as bad there, and the Germans evacuated in haste. We've received intelligence suggesting they had to leave materials behind. We need to find them before the Russians get here."

"How long do we have, sir?" Morrison asked.

"Weeks, maybe less. Every day counts." Hough looked at

each team member in turn. "Get some rest. Find your quarters. Be ready to move tomorrow morning."

A sergeant showed Annie and Joelle to a small second-floor office that would serve as their sleeping quarters. The window looked out onto a courtyard filled with rubble.

"Luxury accommodations," Joelle said, dropping her pack on a cot. "Still, better than that barn outside Metz."

"Or the back of the truck through the Ardennes." Annie tested her cot, which creaked but held. "At least we have walls and most of a roof."

"Home sweet home." Joelle pulled a chocolate bar out of her pack and broke it in half, offering a piece to Annie. "To our new château in Frankfurt."

They ate in companionable silence, too tired for much conversation. Annie unpacked her few belongings: a change of clothes, her mapping tools, letters from home wrapped in oilcloth. Her fingers lingered on the packet of letters. No new mail had reached them since leaving Paris.

That night, lying on the narrow cot with her army blanket pulled up to her chin, Annie stared at the ceiling, her thoughts preventing sleep.

Wiesbaden was only twenty miles away. Chandler once told her that Will's family was from Wiesbaden. His mother and grandfather still lived there or had when Will left for America.

She had read that prisoner exchanges had started in February. Would he move one day from an American prison to a German one? Was the family home still standing, or had it, like so many she had seen on their drive through Germany, been reduced to rubble and ash?

Saturday morning came too soon. Annie and Joelle were assigned to the Wiesbaden team along with two enlisted men, Corporal Davies and Private Chaikowski. The truck ride took them through a landscape of destruction. Burned forests, cratered fields, the occasional intact farmhouse. Twice, they had to stop at U.S. military checkpoints. The GIs who asked to see their papers appeared younger than her. Watching the devastated landscape made her *feel even* older.

Wiesbaden had fared much better than Frankfurt, though "better" was relative. The spa town's elegant nineteenth-century buildings were pockmarked with shell holes, and a few neighborhoods close to factories had been flattened, but the city center retained some of its former structure.

Their first stop was an address Hough had obtained from intelligence reports, and was supposed to be a Wehrmacht mapping office. At first they couldn't even find street signs. When they could, they were difficult to read. Joelle had been their guide as they had traversed Paris, then France and Belgium, but her knowledge of German not as good as her French.

Annie had collected old tourist maps during their searches in Paris, and she now consulted her tattered Michelin map of *Allemagne Ouest* that included an expanded map of the FrankfurtRheinMain region. But when they found the correct street location, they discovered only a crater filled with rainwater.

Joelle pantomimed swinging a baseball bat. "Strike one."

The second address led them to a building that still stood but had been looted. Empty filing cabinets gaped open, papers scattered on the floor, water-damaged beyond use. Anything that could be sold was gone.

By noon, Annie was tired and frustrated. Twice locals who claimed not to understand their questions had misdirected them, though she suspected they understood perfectly well.

The third address took them to a commercial district near what had been a printing company.

"Excuse me," Annie tried in her limited German with an elderly woman sweeping glass from her doorstep. "*Reichsamt für Landesaufnahme*?"

The woman shook her head, either not understanding or not wanting to understand.

Annie pulled out her map and pointed to various locations. "Office? *Büro*? Maps?"

The woman said something in German and gestured toward a building down the street. Annie thanked her and motioned for Davies and Chaikowski to follow her.

As they walked toward the building, she asked, "Chaikowski, how is it that a Polish guy like you doesn't speak German?"

The corporal was one of the three Richie Boys on their team, Europeans who had fled the Nazis to the US early on. They had been recruited to attend the secret Military Intelligence Training Center at Camp Ritchie, Maryland.

"I have other skills," Chaikowski said.

Annie nodded. So far, the Richie Boys had done most of the interrogations for the team, and she guessed that she didn't want to know more details about his skills.

The building's upper floors had collapsed inward, but the ground floor appeared intact. Through a broken window, Annie saw overturned desks and scattered papers. The door was locked.

"Want us to break it down, Private Jeeves?" Chaikowski asked.

Before Annie could answer, the elderly woman appeared again, shouting in German. She grabbed Annie's sleeve, tugging her back toward the street.

"Guess she's trying to tell us something," Davies said.

The woman kept repeating a word that sounded like

*Englisch* and pointing down another street. Then she put her fingers together and motioned putting food in her mouth.

"Hang on," Joelle started digging in her backpack. "I saved some M&Ms from my rations." She held out the small packet, and the old woman snatched it from her, turned on her heel and hurried away.

"I think you just got conned, Leclerq." Davies grinned. "I would have paid you good money for that candy."

"Have a little faith, Davies. Not all Germans are Nazis. Some of them think it's terrific we're here."

Minutes later, the woman emerged from a nearby alley with a younger man in tow.

Even gaunt and dirty, even with his hair shaggy, his face shadowed with stubble, Annie knew those eyes.

Will stared at her for a moment, his mouth open.

Then he bolted.

Annie's legs moved before her mind caught up. Three years. Three years since she'd watched military police load Will into a transport truck, his wrists in handcuffs, his eyes hollow with defeat. She'd testified at his trial, her voice steady as she described both his crimes and his surrender. She'd tried not to think about what prison would do to him.

Now she knew.

"Will, wait!"

Annie took off after him, dodging around a shell crater and nearly tripping over a pile of bricks. He was faster than he looked, fueled by panic, but she was stronger, better fed, and she'd spent months running between trolley stops in Washington. She gained ground as he turned down a side street.

"Damn it, Will, stop!"

She caught up to him in a dead-end courtyard where a bomb had sheared away half a building, leaving an apartment's rooms exposed like a dollhouse.

"Will, stop!" She grabbed his arm.

He sagged against a wall, chest heaving. "Annie."

"Why do you always have to disappear?"

He jerked his arm out of her grip, but he kept his head lowered, the shaggy hair obscuring his eyes. "Leave me alone." He looked like a cornered animal.

She could not believe this was the same man she had once kissed. "How are you even here?"

His attempt at a laugh sounded more like a cough. "You mean alive?"

"I mean here in Germany. Last I heard, you were in some prison in Arkansas."

"In January, they put me on a ship. No explanation. I thought maybe they were sending me back to stand trial here —let the Reich execute me as a traitor so they wouldn't have to feed me anymore."

"But you're here. You're alive."

"If you call this living. At Le Havre, they put us in trucks heading east." He rubbed a hand over his face. "Somewhere in Lorraine, we stopped at a farmhouse. The guards found wine in the cellar. By two in the morning, they were unconscious."

"You escaped?"

"Nothing dramatic. I just started walking. Three weeks, hiding in barns, stealing food when I could find any. I kept thinking if I could just get home, if I could see my mother..." His voice trailed off.

Annie waited. The curtains in the exposed rooms of the bombed building fluttered in the wind.

"She's dead." Will was quiet for a long moment. "Tuberculosis. Winter of '43. No food, not enough medicine."

"Will, I'm sorry."

"I was sitting in an American prison cell while she died alone." His jaw tightened.

Annie felt her anger at Will dissolve. From prisoner to fugitive to this.

"You're not safe here," she said. "You know that."

"I'm not safe anywhere." Will's eyes met hers. "I don't even know if Erik's uncle is alive or if he's been arrested." He laughed again, with the same bitter sound. "I'm an escaped prisoner to the Americans and a traitor and a failure to the Germans. If anyone figures out who I am, I'm dead either way."

Davies and Chaikowski caught up, hands on their sidearms. "We lost you back there," Chaikowski said.

Annie waved them back. "It's all right. This man might help us."

"You know this Kraut, Jeeves?" Davies asked.

She gave a single curt nod. "Met him stateside. He's American born, speaks English and German." Annie kept her voice steady, professional. "And he knows the city."

Will looked at the GIs and Joelle. "I'm not helping you loot what's left of Germany."

"We're not looting." Annie stepped between him and the others, lowering her voice. "Let me help you. Maybe we can help each other. I'm here with the Army Map Service. We're looking for maps. Geodetic surveys. The kind of things the *Reichsamt für Landesaufnahme* would have had."

Something flickered in his eyes. "Why would I help you?"

"Because right now, I'm the only person in Germany who knows who you are and isn't trying to kill you for it."

Annie heard Chaikowski clear his throat behind her. Over her shoulder she said, "Do you want to give us a minute?" *No patience, that man.*

"What about your grandfather?"

"Dead, too. Died a few weeks after I got back, just before you Americans arrived. Collapsed in the street when he heard the Reich had fallen." Will's voice held no grief. "He called me a traitor. Said I should have died with honor instead of surrendering."

"I'm sorry, Will."

"Jeeves," Davies said. "We need to get moving."

Annie held up her hand to silence the men behind her.

"Will, we need your help. The Russians are on their way, and we need an interpreter."

Will was quiet for a long moment. "My grandfather," Will said. "He worked as a clerk before the war. He still knew some guys. When the bombing started, they talked about moving things out of the government buildings. Hiding them."

"Where?"

"Basements. Always basements. The Germans thought they were safe from bombs there." Will met her eyes. "There's a building near the old print shop. My grandfather mentioned they'd moved important papers there from Berlin."

"The building we were just at? When you ran?"

Will shook his head. "No, behind it. Through the courtyard. The entrance is hidden by debris now, but I know where it is."

"Show me."

"Food first," Will said. "And not just for me. There are families on my street. We all need food."

Annie looked at Davies and Chaikowski. Davies shrugged. "We've got K-rations in the truck."

"All right," Annie said. "It's a fair trade. Food for the basement location."

Will led them back through the ruined streets, moving with more energy now that he had a purpose. The building Will led them to looked destroyed from the street. He showed them a path through the rubble to a steel door half-buried in debris.

It took all four of them to clear the entrance. Below, narrow stairs descended into darkness. Joelle produced a flashlight, handed it to Davies, and they descended into a basement that smelled of mildew and rat droppings.

"Holy smokes!" Davies moved the flashlight beam across shelves loaded with boxes, tubes, and flat packages wrapped in oilcloth.

Annie pulled on her gloves and opened the nearest box. Inside, perfectly preserved, were topographical sheets marked with the seal of the *Reichsamt für Landesaufnahme*.

"Geodetic data," she whispered, scanning the labels.

Joelle looked inside another box. "This covers all of Baden-Württemberg."

Davies was already counting. "There's got to be a dozen boxes here. Maybe more in the back."

Annie turned to Will. "Are there other basements like this?"

He hesitated, then shrugged. "More food?"

"I'll make sure of it." Annie meant it. "Will, this information could help end the war faster. It's for artillery coordination."

"There is nothing I want more than to see this war end."

They spent the rest of Saturday and into Sunday, searching at Will's direction. But it was not until late Sunday afternoon, hidden beneath a destroyed church, that they found what proved to be the real treasure.

"Eighteen bundles," Davies counted, awe in his voice. "All of them sealed, dated from just three months ago."

Annie examined the markings. These weren't just maps—they were the complete geodetic survey data for the region that would allow accurate artillery fire across hundreds of miles of German territory.

"We need to get Major Hough here," Joelle said. "He'll want to see this."

By Sunday evening, the entire HOUGHTEAM had converged on Wiesbaden. Hough himself came down into the church basement, his usual composure cracking as he saw the scope of the find.

"Outstanding work." He smiled. "This is exactly what the Third and Seventh Armies need. If I skip protocol, I can have this copied and in their hands within days."

As the enlisted men began loading the materials for transport back to Frankfurt, Hough pulled Annie aside.

"Your informant. He's reliable?"

Annie thought of Will, off sharing K-rations with hungry families in some bombed-out building. "He delivered what he promised, sir."

"Good. Make sure he gets adequate compensation. We may need him again."

That night, back in their makeshift quarters in Frankfurt, Joelle had her nose in a novel. Annie sat on her cot and wrote a letter home by candlelight.

*Dear Pa,*

*We've had a successful few days here in Germany. I can't tell you the details, but we found something important. Something that will help our artillery units and maybe save lives.*

*The destruction here is complete. Frankfurt is nothing but rubble and ash. These cities aren't wounded, they're dead. It's difficult to believe that these smoking ruins were once home to thousands of people. But we keep working, keep searching, because that's what we're here to do.*

*I think of Finn every day and pray his war is easier than this one.*

*All my love,*

*Annie*

She folded the letter, knowing she wouldn't be able to send it for days or maybe weeks. Outside, she could hear the rumble of trucks as they brought in more materials from Wiesbaden. According to the news on the radio, the war was almost over, but for many, like Will, the war would never end.

# CHAPTER FIFTY

*Frankfurt am Main, Germany*
*April 14, 1945*

The makeshift hospital occupied what had been a secondary school, its classrooms converted into wards. Annie followed Shallenberger through the corridors, stepping around stretchers holding men awaiting surgery or transport, men for whom the wards had no room. German wounded from the collapsing Western Front, most of them with smooth cheeks and bony wrists, children dressed as soldiers.

Major Hough had the team scouring the city and the countryside searching for what he called the "Mother Lode." In the last couple of weeks since arriving in Frankfurt, the team had made several remarkable finds in the surrounding countryside. Shallenberger got a tip from a captured officer of the *Reichsamt für Landesaufnahme*, or RfL, the German national survey agency, that the Germans had hidden something big in a region to the east called Thuringia. There hidden in doll factories, they had found the entire archive of civilian map data of

Germany's own territory. It had been their biggest score yet, but Hough was certain there was more. The Germans had occupied extensive areas of Russia, and the major was certain there was geodetic data from the east that had yet to be found.

"Remember," Shallenberger said, "we're looking for officers, anyone from supply or logistics units. They're the ones who would know where these materials are stashed."

Annie nodded, though her stomach turned at using wounded men as intelligence sources. Necessary, she told herself. The war with Germany was ending, but the race for intelligence had already begun. Russia wouldn't wait, and neither could they. Everything now was necessary.

They'd been at this for three hours, moving from bed to bed with a German nurse. Shallenberger and the nurse conversed in German, and though Annie had been picking up some German words since arriving in Europe, she understood little of their conversation. Most of the soldiers were too fevered or morphine-dulled to provide anything useful. One Wehrmacht captain had mumbled about document burning in Berlin before slipping back into unconsciousness.

"I'll take this ward," Shallenberger said, indicating a room full of officers. "You check the enlisted men's area. Sometimes they overhear things." He pointed towards the end of the corridor.

Annie pushed open the door to a large room that had been the gymnasium. She turned her head aside at the ammonia stench of urine and the sweet-rot smell of infected wounds. Cots stretched in rows, harsh sunlight streaming through high windows that had somehow survived the bombing. The men in that room had survived, but they were forever changed. Missing limbs, fingers, jaws, their eyes followed her slow walk down the aisle, as she tried her best to smile and nod at Germany's broken youth. Annie listened for conversation, but all she heard was labored breathing, coughing and moaning.

As she neared the back of the first row, she saw two soldiers who were talking in low voices. One had lost his left arm, the stump wrapped in brown-stained bandages. The other's head was bandaged, one eye covered.

She recognized the words *Geographie* and *Karten* in something the one-armed soldier was saying. He was talking about maps.

Annie slowed, pretending to check her notebook.

The other man's single eye grew wider. He responded in rapid-fire German, and she caught the words *militärlastwagen* and *Russland*.

"*Ruhe*!" The one-armed soldier made a sharp gesture. "*Die Amerikaner sind überall*."

Annie turned and began walking back to the door, her heart racing. She found Shallenberger in the corridor.

"I overheard something," she whispered. "Two enlisted men talking about geography. They mentioned maps. One used the word *Russland*. That's Russia, right?"

Shallenberger's eyes sharpened. "Which soldiers?"

She led him back, but the one-armed soldier was asleep or pretending to be. The other stared at the ceiling, unresponsive to Shallenberger's questions in German.

"I'll have Chaikowski work on them," Shallenberger said. "Good catch, Jeeves."

~

That afternoon, Annie volunteered to check additional locations in Wiesbaden. Shallenberger had given her a list of addresses, but she knew the real reason she was going back.

She spotted him sitting on a low stone wall in front of a building she assumed was his grandfather's house. Someone had converted the front garden into a makeshift shelter area. Families huddled together on blankets under tarpaulins hanging from ropes in the trees. A fire burned in the center of the yard, and the air smelled of unwashed bodies and boiled cabbage.

Will sat on the wooden steps, reading to three children from a water-damaged book. His voice was patient, gentle, nothing like the desperate spy who had held a gun to her head in Florida. When he saw Annie, he closed the book.

"*Später*," he told the children. Later.

They walked down the street in the pale April sunlight. Will's steps were slow, and Annie noticed how his clothes hung even looser than before.

"You're ill," she said.

"Just tired. And hungry. Like everyone." He leaned against a wall. "Did you find what you needed?"

"Yes. I came back to thank you. For helping us."

They stood in awkward silence.

"I once wanted to be a writer," Will announced. "Before all this. When I was young, in America, then here in Germany. It all seems so long ago now. I would write stories. Adventures, mysteries. I thought I'd publish novels one day."

Annie waited.

"I was nine when my mother brought me here after my father died. Nine years old, and within weeks I was in a country I didn't understand, with boys who hated me for being American. Later, my grandfather forced me into the Hitler Youth. Said it would make me German."

"What a time to return to Germany."

His laugh sounded more bitter than amused. "Hey, it worked, didn't it? By the time I was eighteen, I'd learned to keep my head down, to go along. When they burned books at my university, I stood in the crowd and said nothing. When they were rounding up Jews in Berlin, I watched and told myself there was nothing I could do."

"What could one person have done?" Annie asked, though she heard the echo of her own excuses in the question.

"That's what I told myself. Every day. What could one person do?" Will's voice was hollow. "So I took a job at the Propaganda Ministry to avoid military service. I translated their lies into English and told myself, at least I wasn't pulling a trigger. I became very good at not thinking about things."

His eyes met hers. "Do you know what it's like..." He paused, his breath wheezing. "To train yourself not to think?" He pressed a hand against the wall. "You see terrible things. And you look away. Again and again, until it becomes normal." He made a helpless gesture. "Until you're numb and you're just glad it isn't you."

Annie thought about the days she was so angry when her brother wanted to enlist. And again with Finn. How long had she practiced her own kind of not-thinking?

"When the Abwehr recruited me," Will continued, "I told myself I had no choice. But there's always a choice, isn't there? Even if it's between bad and worse. I chose to survive, to follow the path of least resistance. And look where it led me."

A cart rattled past in the street. Will watched it pass before continuing.

"This is what happens when we all tell ourselves there's nothing one person can do. I wonder if things might have been different if more Germans had realized there were always more of us than them."

Annie considered her own journey from the fish camp to here. She'd only acted when the war came to her home waters.

"In Florida," she said, "I didn't want to get involved either. I saw the preparation for war, knew it was coming, and I just wanted to go back to the fish camp and pretend it had nothing to do with me."

Will stared into the distance with glazed eyes. "I wanted to go back to the America of my childhood, but I wasn't that child anymore."

He reached into his pocket and pulled out a small, leather-bound book. "This was my mother's. Rilke's poems. She gave it to me when I still thought I'd be a writer." He pressed it into Annie's hands. "I want you to have it."

"Will, I can't even read German."

"Please. Keep it as an artifact. Something to remember me. Maybe you will learn a new language someday. Let something good come from our... acquaintance." He attempted a smile. "I used to think words could change the world. Now I know they can just as easily destroy it. Maybe giving away the last beautiful words I own is a kind of penance."

Annie took the book. The leather was soft, worn from handling. Inside the front cover, in faded ink: *Für meinen liebsten Wilhelm - Mutti, 1935*.

"Where will you go?" she asked.

He shrugged. "This is home, such as it is. I hope to teach the children when they're ready to learn again. Real literature this time, not propaganda." He looked back down the street at the families camped in his garden. "Maybe that's my destiny. To stay and help rebuild from what we all let happen through our silence."

"Take care of yourself, Will."

"*Auf Wiedersehen*, Annie. I think in another life, another world where people like me had more courage, things between us might have been different."

She wanted to say something comforting, but what comfort was there? She knew now she had loved Finn long before Will held a gun to her head.

Annie walked away, the book of poems weighing heavy in

her pocket, thinking about all the moments when good people chose to look away.

The convoy of trucks rumbled through the dawn mist toward Saalfeld. Hough rode in the lead vehicle, Annie in the second with Joelle, Friedl, and the Ritchie boys. Four days earlier, when she had returned from Weisbaden after saying goodbye to Will, she learned the U.S. 87th Infantry Division had captured the town, but they had kept on rolling east.

No one on the team was sure what they would find when they arrived. The intel from the wounded soldiers Annie had identified, combined with what Chaikowski had extracted through careful interrogation, had been specific enough: a warehouse on the southern edge of town.

"According to our informants," Hough had briefed them that morning, "the German military moved their entire geodetic archive here from Berlin. Everything they'd collected, including captured Russian materials."

Saalfeld itself was intact, a medieval town that had somehow escaped the worst of the bombing. The mayor appeared delighted to see the Americans and was eager to cooperate. Friedl translated for the Army driver as the mayor gave directions. The warehouse sat in an industrial area, unremarkable except for the fresh tire tracks in the mud outside.

The guards, such as they were, surrendered on the spot. Two old men and a boy who couldn't have been over fifteen, all of them looking relieved to be taken prisoner by Americans rather than Russians.

Hough used bolt cutters on the padlock. The doors swung open, and even he, their dispassionate leader, let out a low whistle.

The warehouse stretched back into shadows, shelf after shelf disappearing into the gloom. Filing cabinets lined one wall. The stacks of wooden crates reached to the ceiling. The smell of paper and ink was so thick she could taste it. Old documents, maps, the particular scent of German ink that she'd learned to recognize in Paris.

"*La vache*!" Joelle placed her palm on her chest. "It's a library. An entire geographic library."

Annie had imagined that the so-called Mother Lode would be boxes of survey data, perhaps some instruments. Like their other discoveries. But this? This was the accumulated geographic knowledge of an empire that had stretched from France to the Urals.

Hough stepped inside. He reached for the nearest crate, pulled back the lid, and lifted out a folder. Even from several feet away, Annie could see the precise German typography, the official seals.

"Find the lights," Hough said. "Everyone. Inside. We need to see what we have."

They moved in, flashlights cutting through the gloom until someone found the electrical panel. Under the harsh industrial lights, the scope became clear.

"Look at these markings," Annie said, examining the nearest crate. "Soviet geodetic surveys, Poland, Czechoslovakia, Hungary..."

"Here's France," Espenshade called out. "Belgium, Netherlands..."

Hough was already calculating. "Seventy-five truckloads, minimum. Maybe more." He turned to Davies. "Get on the radio. We need every truck the Army can spare. And men. At least a hundred. Tell them we have around ninety tons of materials to move."

"Ninety tons?" Davies' eyes widened.

"Maybe more from my estimate. And tell them time is critical. The Russians will be here within weeks."

Annie walked deeper into the warehouse, overwhelmed by the magnitude of what they'd found. Years of work, perhaps decades. The mathematical framework for an entire continent, all gathered in one place. She pulled out a folder at random. Detailed survey data for Ukraine, dated 1939. Another contained elevation charts for the Caucasus Mountains.

"Jeeves!" Hough called. "I need you to start cataloging. Priority goes to anything covering areas that will be in the Soviet zone."

"Yes, sir."

She set up at a makeshift desk near the entrance, beginning the monumental task of recording what they'd found. Box after box, folder after folder, each representing thousands of hours of surveying work.

By afternoon, the trucks had arrived from the 87th Infantry Division artillery unit. German POWs were brought in to load boxes under armed guard. The work was frantic, everyone aware that Russian forces were approaching from the east.

It was evening when Davies brought her an envelope. "Mail call, Jeeves. This one's been chasing you since Paris."

Annie smiled as she recognized her father's handwriting. Their letters to one another must have crossed tracks in mid-Atlantic. She stepped outside, where the setting sun painted the sky orange and pink, and leaned against the truck's fender in the last rays of sun.

For a moment, she just held the envelope running her fingers over the return address in her father's blocky handwriting, the stamped postmark. Letters from home always felt like time travel, news that was already old, reactions to events she'd moved past. What had she been doing on April 3? Searching basements in Wiesbaden. At last, she ripped open the envelope looking forward to the news about Bean's schoolwork, the crop of oranges from the fish camp, and how Ma's arthritis was doing.

The words blurred as she read, and her throat grew so tight she struggled to swallow.

*April 3, 1945*

*Dear Annie,*

*Hope this finds you well and keeping safe wherever you are. We know you can't tell us much about your work, but we pray for you every night.*

*I have news that I hope will bring you as much joy as it's brought us. Yesterday morning, a Navy officer came to the house. Not the kind of visit we've been dreading—this one brought good news.*

*They found Finn.*

The paper fluttered, blurring the familiar script. A loud sob erupted from somewhere deep inside her.

*He's alive, sweetheart! Alive and recovering in a Navy hospital in the Philippines. The officer said he was captured by the Japanese after his PT boat went down, spent over a year in a prisoner camp on some island I can't spell. He's lost a lot of weight and has some injuries, but the doctors say there's hope he'll make a full recovery.*

*They'll fly him to Pearl soon as he's well*

*enough, then on to San Francisco. When he's able, he'll be coming home. The officer said it might be another month, maybe two, before he's discharged, but Annie, he's coming home.*

She stared at the words she had been waiting for, reading them over and over, not sure it could be real. They'd found Finn. He's alive.

*Bean is beside herself with excitement. She's already planning a fishing trip for when he gets back. Your mother cried for an hour when we got the news, though she won't admit it.*

*We wanted to send you a telegram, but weren't sure where to reach you. I hope this letter finds you soon.*

*Come home safe, sweetheart.*

*All our love,*

*Pa*

She read it again, then again. Alive. Captured, imprisoned, but alive. In a hospital in the Philippines. Coming home.

"Annie?" Joelle had followed her outside. "What is it?"

"Finn's alive." The words came out as a whisper. "He's been in a Japanese prison camp. They found him. He's coming home."

Joelle pulled her into a tight embrace, and Annie let herself cry—for Finn, for Will, for all the boys broken by this war, for the maps they saved that just might stop the next war.

That night, Annie tried to sleep in the truck heading back

to Frankfurt. Her father's letter was tucked in her breast pocket, pressed against her heart. She held Will's book of Rilke poems, running her fingers over the worn leather.

She thought about Will's words, about her own reluctance to fight back against a changing world. She, too, had wanted to stay isolated in her beautiful corner of Florida while the world burned. Finn's courage had changed her.

And now Finn was coming home.

Will was staying to teach children who needed to learn how to think again.

And she? She was cataloging the wreckage, trying to understand how the world had come to this.

# CHAPTER FIFTY-ONE

*New Smyrna Beach, FL*
*May 18, 1945*

Annie pressed her forehead against the cool glass of the Greyhound bus window, watching the landscape change. South of St. Augustine, the live oaks draped with Spanish moss gave way to low palmetto scrub. They passed the occasional flock of white cattle egrets pecking the earth in a pasture, barefoot children laughing and running through the groves, brief glimpses of the deep blue Atlantic to the east.

The landscape outside her window was worlds away from the grey rubble of Frankfurt. Nothing like the bombed-out shells of buildings where families had once lived, where solemn children stood silent and staring from courtyards filled with ash. Here, the cattle grazed, the orange trees starting to fruit, and the only craters in the earth were the sinkholes that had always been there.

She tugged at the collar of her olive drab blouse, already dark with sweat. The WAC uniform had made sense in Europe—the tailored wool jacket, the long sleeves, the garrison cap perched to one side. In the spring chill of Germany and the cool crossing of the Atlantic, she'd been grateful for the layers. But here in the thick Florida heat, the uniform was suffocating in spite of the folks who had opened their windows ahead of her and the breeze that blew through the bus. Her wool jacket lay folded on the seat beside her, and even without it she felt like she was melting into the cracked vinyl.

"Excuse me, dear."

Annie turned to see a woman across the aisle leaning toward her. Middle-aged, wearing a faded cotton housedress, she stared at Annie with open curiosity.

"I hope you don't mind my asking, but what exactly are you wearing? Is that some kind of service uniform?"

Annie managed a polite smile. "Yes, ma'am. I'm in the Women's Army Corps. The WACs."

The woman's eyes widened. "Women's army? Well, I'll be. I didn't know there was such a thing. What do y'all do?"

"Clerical work, mostly. Maps and documents." Annie kept her answer vague, hoping the woman would lose interest.

"And they let you wear trousers and everything?"

"Just the skirt, ma'am." Annie gestured to her service skirt. "The trousers are for women mechanics and drivers."

"Women mechanics? My goodness. What will they think of next?" The woman shook her head, smiling. "My husband's cousin's boy is over in the Pacific. Terrible business, that. But I suppose it's almost over now, praise the Lord. That Hitler fellow being dead and all."

Annie nodded, not trusting herself to speak. Almost over. The fighting in Europe, maybe.

The woman continued chattering about her nephew and the war garden she was planting, but Annie's attention drifted.

How strange that this woman didn't even know the

WACs existed. She thought the war was "almost over" because Germany had surrendered. Annie had served alongside thousands of women in Europe. They'd driven trucks, operated switchboards, broke codes, analyzed intelligence, kept the whole massive operation running. And here was a woman who lived in the same country, who thought a woman in uniform was some novel curiosity.

Memories of the voyage home came back to her in fragments. She had boarded the USS Wakefield in LeHavre, France. The decks of the former cruise liner turned troop carrier were crowded with wounded soldiers and discharged personnel, all of them suspended between war and home. She'd been standing at the rail on May 8$^{th}$ when the captain's voice crackled over the loudspeaker: "*Germany has surrendered unconditionally. The war in Europe is over.*"

The ship had erupted around her. Men threw their caps in the air, nurses embraced, strangers wept with relief. Annie had only touched the compass rose pendant at her throat and thought about Finn.

The Pacific War raged on. Japan showed no sign of surrender. And after the news from her father that Finn was in a hospital in the Philippines, there had been no more news. While the Americans had taken Manila, the Battle of the Philippines was ongoing.

She'd spent most of the six-day crossing either watching the endless sea or below decks, helping the Red Cross nurses in the hospital ward. Amputees, burn victims, shrapnel wounds, boys with thousand-yard stares who flinched at sudden sounds. One young private from Ohio, missing his left arm, had asked her to write a letter to his girl back home. When Annie mentioned VE Day, he'd started crying. "I lost my arm three weeks ago," he'd said. "Three weeks before it ended." She'd held his remaining hand and hadn't known what to say.

The ship docked in New York on May 14th. The harbor had been chaos with hundreds of ships, thousands of people, everyone shouting, no one listening. She'd clutched her duffel bag and her discharge papers and followed the crowd to Penn Station, where she'd joined the masses of service members trying to get home. Two trains south, one to Washington, one to Jacksonville. Sleeping sitting up, eating stale sandwiches, watching America pass by the window. So much of it untouched by war. So many people had no idea what Europe looked like now.

"New Smyrna Beach!" the driver called out. "New Smyrna Beach, folks. End of the line."

Annie blinked, coming back to herself. The bus was slowing. Through the window, she could see the bus station—just a wooden bench under a narrow tin roof along the main highway.

And there they were. Pa, with his pipe gripped in his clenched smile. Ma, smoothing her faded cotton dress. Home.

The Greyhound bus slowed to a stop, and the driver pulled the lever that opened the door. Annie shrugged into the wool jacket despite the heat. She'd arrive home in proper uniform. Gathering her garrison cap and shoulder handbag, she stood and joined the line heading for the door.

The thick Florida heat hit Annie when she descended to the concrete. She stood breathing in the sea air mixed with the faint scent of orange trees and exhaust. New Smyrna Beach looked smaller than she remembered.

"Annie!" Pa ran through the crowd and wrapped her in a hug before she could set down her canvas duffel bag. His shoulders shook, and she realized he was crying.

"Easy, Pa." More than a year and a half. It had been too long since she'd felt these arms around her.

When Pa loosened his grip, Ma stepped forward. She

brushed a strand of hair from Annie's forehead. Not a hugger, her mother. "You're thin as a rail. We'll fix that."

Annie caught her mother's hands. "It's good to see you, Ma."

Behind her, a voice called, "Annie?"

She turned to see a girl, all coltish long limbs and fiery red hair pulled back in a messy braid.

"Bean?"

"It's Bethany now. I'm thirteen." And taller. Her chin at Annie's shoulder. Freckles, sun-kissed skin, the same stunning blue eyes as her brother.

"Look at you," Annie said, studying her.

"Haven't been Bean for ages." Bethany bounced on her toes. "Wait till you see what I can do on the boat now!"

"Let's get home before you tell her your whole life story." Pa hefted Annie's duffel bag. "Old Fumblebee's waiting."

The ancient Chevrolet Master looked like it had aged a decade in two years. Annie slid across the worn bench seat, her duffel on her lap, and Bethany squeezed in beside her.

"How's the Fish Camp?" Annie asked as they pulled out into traffic. She'd never seen so many cars on this road.

"Busier than ever," Skeeter said, navigating around a military convoy heading south. "Servicemen home, wanting to go fishing. Can't keep up. Smartest move we ever made moving back home."

Annie suspected it was Dooley's winding down the shipbuilding with the war coming to an end, but she didn't say as much.

"Your ma's picking up shifts at the New Smyrna Hospital, too. We're doing better than just keeping our heads above water."

The road south to Edgewater and the fish camp wound through orange groves and cattle ranches.

They turned down the sandy track, and there it was: the

weathered sign that read "Skeeter's Fish Camp - Bait, Ice, Boats for Hire."

"Woody!" Bethany hollered out the window before the car had even stopped. "She's here!"

The screen door of the bait shop slapped open, and Woody emerged, moving slower but still tall and straight. His hair had gone completely gray, but his grin was the same.

"Well, I'll be damned," he said, opening his arms.

Annie hugged him. The man was all bones now. "Hey, Woody. You keeping these people in line?"

"Somebody's got to."

"You're the man for the job."

"Well, it's good to have the smart one back. Your old man's gotten lazy."

She heard her father snort.

A flash of brown and white shot around the corner of the bait shop, and Annie barely had time to brace herself before Tess launched herself at her legs, front paws scrabbling against her skirt. The old Springer Spaniel's joints might be stiff with arthritis, but her enthusiasm hadn't dimmed. She bounced and whined, her whole body wiggling with joy.

"Hey, girl," Annie said, dropping to her knees to rub the dog's ears. "Did you miss me?"

Tess answered by covering Annie's face with wet, sloppy kisses.

"She's deaf as a post," Woody said, "but she's been waiting for you."

Annie buried her face in Tess's soft fur, feeling the last of her composure threaten to crack.

"Come on," Skeeter said, shouldering her duffel bag again. "Let's get you settled."

The air was cooler inside the house, smelling of Pine-Sol and cornbread. Annie walked past the kitchen table where she'd done homework, the mantelpiece where Pa displayed his fishing trophies, and the doorframe where her parents had marked her and Jack's heights as they grew.

Annie grabbed the back of Pa's chair as she felt the room start to sway around her. Was she really here, or was she going to wake up on a cot in a cold office in Frankfurt?

"Your room's just like you left it." Ma walked ahead of her down the narrow hallway to the stairs. "Well, mostly." Her mother turned around. "You coming?"

The bedroom door stood open, revealing the small space that had been hers for the first fifteen years of her life. The iron bedstead with its patchwork quilt and the rough pine dresser. But along one wall cardboard boxes tied with twine stood in two piles.

"Your books," Hilda explained. "And art supplies from the Lauderdale house. Some of your dresses, though I expect they won't fit anymore."

Annie moved to the window, pressing her palm against the familiar glass. And there, carved into the windowsill, were the initials: A.J. + F.T., surrounded by a heart. The work of a fourteen-year-old girl with a crush on her brother's best friend.

She was home.

Ma had outdone herself with the lunch spread: fried snapper caught that morning, collard greens, cornbread, and Ma's lemon cake that made Annie's mouth water just looking at it. After months of Army rations, the abundance was overwhelming.

"Ma, you have no idea how amazing this looks to me."

"Sit," Hilda commanded. "You look like a strong wind would blow you over."

"Too many meals of tinned meat and a couple of crackers." Annie settled into her old chair, the one with the wobbly leg Jack used to kick under the table during Sunday dinners.

"Tell us everything." Skeeter settled into his place at the head of the table. "What you can tell us, anyway."

"Not much to tell," Annie reached for the cornbread. "I drew maps. Lots of maps." She spread a pat of butter on the cornbread and sat watching it melt into the spongy bread. She felt the eyes of the whole family watching her.

"Oh, come on," Bethany said, bouncing in her chair like she was still ten years old. "You were in Paris! And London! Did you see the Eiffel Tower? Did you interrogate any spies?"

"Hush, child. Leave her to enjoy her meal." Ma piled a mound of greens onto Annie's plate.

Bean shoved an entire square of cornbread in her mouth and chewed, giving Annie her best version of puppy dog eyes.

"Okay, okay." Annie chose her words between bites, sharing what she could about Paris and the bomb damage in Germany. She described the *Bouquinistes* along the Seine, the cold winter in Washington, the strange experience of living in a Paris hotel where Nazis had slept just months before. She stopped short of talking about Germany.

"And you really found all those German maps?" Bethany's eyes were wide with admiration.

"I helped," Annie said. "It was a team effort."

"Did you see any Nazis?"

Annie thought of the wounded boys in the Frankfurt hospital, smooth-cheeked and hollow-eyed. The women and children picking through the rubble. And Will. "I saw Germans, Bean. They're people, just like us. Some good, some bad. Mostly, I saw what the war did to them."

Bethany frowned. She opened her mouth to continue questioning, but Hilda intervened.

"Bethany, let her eat."

She did stop asking questions, but the girl was unstoppable once she got talking. In the time it took Annie to take three bites of fish, Bethany had detailed her plans to help

Woody rebuild the boat slip and her opinion that the new Coast Guard station was full of 'prissy boys.'

"You should see her handle the *Tequesta* now," Skeeter said.

"I'm not surprised." Finn and his sister had always been fearless on the water. Bean cleared the dishes, and Ma rose to get the cake.

"Let me help, Mama."

Her father placed his hand over hers. "You're the guest of honor, Annie-girl. We're so happy to have you back home."

"Thanks, Pa. It's not feeling real just yet."

"So, what are your plans now that you're home?"

This was the question she'd been dreading. "I don't know yet, Pa. There might be an opportunity for peacetime work. But it would mean leaving again."

"What kind of opportunity?" her mother asked.

Annie thought of Major Hough's offer. "Geodesy. Surveying," she said. "It's mapping the world beyond just flat maps that show longitude and latitude. On land, you need to show elevation, too. You know, three dimensions instead of two."

Her parents exchanged a look, and Bethany said, "Sounds important."

"It is important. Most countries have their own systems for measuring the earth. Major Hough plans to get all of Europe on one system." Annie pushed the last of her greens around her plate. "But I can't decide until I know more."

Ma nodded. "You had any word from Finn?"

Annie shook her head. "Nothing." She heard the quaver in her own voice and paused to regain control. "Not that he'd have known where to find me to send a letter. But I worry, Mama. You know best that not everybody who goes into the hospital gets cured."

"Let's not borrow trouble now," Hilda said. "They got good doctors for our boys, and Finn is tough. Until we know different, we'll assume the best."

Annie agreed, though just talking about Finn gave her that panicky feeling. She pushed back her chair and stood. “I’m going to walk down to the dock. Check on the boat.”

The screen door slapped shut behind her. The afternoon sun slanted through the live oaks, dappling the sandy ground with shifting patterns of light and shadow. Fiddler crabs scuttled away from her footsteps, disappearing into their holes with tiny clicking sounds.

She stopped at the bait shack. Woody had left a *Closed for Lunch* sign on the door. It was all so normal, the everyday beauty of this place, so why was this ache in her chest making it hurt just to breathe? Reaching out to steady herself, her palm against the weathered wood, she closed her eyes against the memories. The smell of death in bombed-out ruins, the stench of gangrene wounds, the maimed soldiers and the blank-eyed children.

When she opened her eyes, she saw the *Tequesta* floating in turquoise water at the dock. Her white hull gleamed with fresh paint, her brass hardware polished to mirror brightness. Someone, probably Bethany, had coiled every line with Navy precision and scrubbed the pine deck until it glowed.

Why did she get to return to her family, her boat, all this? When so many others never would?

Annie kicked off her regulation shoes and stepped aboard, her bare feet feeling the slight give of the deck, the way the boat responded to her weight. This had been her classroom, her playground, her refuge. She’d spent the last three years on solid ground, but this, this was home.

“I’m back, old girl,” she whispered.

She ran her hand along the cockpit coaming. The wood was smooth and solid, well-maintained and loved. Bethany had done good work.

“Thought I might find you here.” Annie spun around. Emma stood at the end of the dock, her travel bag slung over her shoulder, wearing a simple, sleeveless blue dress that brought out the bronze in her skin. Her hair was shorter than Annie remembered, styled in smooth rolls on either side of her face. She looked older, more sophisticated.

"Emma! What are you doing here?" Annie jumped down onto the dock.

"Your father may have mentioned to my grandfather that you were coming home today," Emma said, dropping her bag and opening her arms. "Said you could use a friendly face."

Annie stepped into the hug, laughing through the tears. "He's a meddling old coot."

"The best kind."

They held each other tight, the months of separation dissolving.

"I can't believe you're here." Annie pulled back to look at Emma's face. "How long can you stay?"

"Just tonight. I'm catching a ride to Fort Lauderdale tomorrow to see Mama and Grandpa Elzo."

"Are you still at Arlington?"

"I'll tell you everything. But right now, I just want to hear about you. Paris! Germany! I got bits and pieces from your letters, but I want details."

Annie looked back at the house, and her folks were sitting on the porch, looking very pleased at the surprise they had arranged.

"I have an idea," Annie said.

~

"We taking her out?" Bethany appeared at the end of the dock, already dressed in canvas shorts and a sleeveless blouse, her red hair braided back from her face.

"If you're up for it," Annie said.

"Ha!" Bethany hopped aboard the *Tequesta* with simple

grace. "Am I ever!" She moved forward to inspect the jib sheets, quick and sure on her feet as she checked the rigging.

Emma raised an eyebrow at Annie. "She's gotten cocky."

"I've gotten good," the girl corrected. "There's a difference."

Tess appeared at the dock's edge, whining as she eyed the boat.

"Come on, girl," Annie said, patting the cockpit bench. Tess gathered herself and leaped, landing with a soft thud on the cushions. She settled into her favorite spot in the corner.

"Cast off the bow line," Bethany called, already at the stern cleat. "Annie, you want the helm?"

"All yours, Captain. Show us what you can do."

Bethany's grin could have powered the boat by itself.

They motored slowly through the marked channel, the girl's eyes moving between the mainsail and the water ahead.

They cleared Ponce Inlet forty minutes later, emerging from the protection of the land into the long, rolling swells of the Atlantic. The breeze was steady at twelve knots, perfect sailing weather, and Bethany eased the sheets to pick up speed.

"Your turn," she announced, gesturing for Annie to take the helm. "I want to check the jib trim."

But Annie shook her head. "You're doing fine. Emma and I are going forward for some girl time."

The young girl put her hand to her forehead in a mock salute.

Annie and Emma sat side by side on the lee rail, their legs dangling over the side, salt spray misting their faces. Tess shifted closer to them, content to have her people all in one place. The steady gurgle of water past the hull and the creak of rigging created a backdrop of familiar sounds.

"So," Annie said, "tell me what really happened in Washington."

Emma was quiet for a moment, staring at the distant horizon. "They shut down my section last month. Said they didn't need colored women breaking codes anymore, now that the white boys are coming home."

"They said it like that?"

"Just like that." Emma's voice held resignation but not bitterness. "Gave me a nice letter of commendation and a bus ticket home. Oh, and a recommendation to Howard University's mathematics department."

Annie felt a surge of anger. "That's rubbish. You were better at pattern recognition than anyone in that building."

"Maybe. But it wasn't just me." Emma shrugged. "Mr. Coffee and all the women in our unit were sent home after VE Day. I'm not even mad about it. I loved the work, but I was tired of running halfway across the compound to use the right bathroom, tired of having to prove myself every single day."

Annie wanted to say that it wasn't fair, but the war had beaten that argument out of her.

"What will you do now?"

"Howard accepted me for the fall semester. I got the G.I. Bill. I had to fight for it, but I got it. And Howard's offered a stipend for living expenses. So, I'm about to start college." Emma's face glowed with excitement. "I've got an apartment with another code girl near the school, and a job working in a restaurant over the summer."

"I know you'll do great."

"I want to study pure mathematics." Emma pointed her toes and dipped them into a swell. "Advanced calculus, number theory, maybe even work toward a doctoral degree some day. They're using mathematics in ways we never imagined, Annie. Electronic computing machines, statistical analysis... it's like magic, but with numbers."

Annie smiled at her friend's enthusiasm. Emma had

always been brilliant, but the war work had given her a newfound confidence.

"What about you? Major Hough must want you to stay on."

"He does. He's talking about creating a comprehensive geodetic survey, first of Europe, and then on to the entire planet. Mapping every mountain, every coastline, every island. Can you imagine? One mapping system for the entire world. He says the work we did in Germany is just the beginning."

"Sounds like the perfect job for you."

"It is. Or could be. I don't know anymore." Annie picked at a splinter on the deck rail. "Everything feels different now. The war, losing Jack, not knowing what's happened to Finn..."

Emma was quiet for a long moment. "You want to tell me about Europe? The real version, not the sanitized letters you sent home?"

So, Annie did. She told Emma about the dead-eyed Parisiens who had suffered years of occupation, bombed-out cities, the desperate German civilians who had allowed unspeakable evil to happen and had their homes and lives destroyed as a result.

She recounted the satisfaction of finding the cache in Saalfeld, but also the strange emptiness that had followed, the sense that all their careful work couldn't bring back the dead or heal the broken.

"And then there was Will," Annie said.

Emma's head snapped up. "Will? As in Wilhelm Hersey-Will?"

Annie nodded. "I found him in Frankfurt. Or he found me. I don't know." Annie described Will gaunt and desperate, scavenging in ruins. "He was broken, Emma. Ashamed for me to see him like that. Yet, he helped us track down intelligence that led to one of our biggest finds."

"That day on the river. He was so torn, trying to save himself, but in the end, he chose you."

Annie shrugged. "I hope he survives. It's going to be a long road back for Germany and for people like Will." She thought of the book of Rilke's poems in her duffel bag. Maybe someday she would be able to read them and make sense of it all. "When I last saw him, he said he wanted to become a teacher." Annie watched a pelican dive for fish off their port beam. "So many lives destroyed because of some crazy man who thought he was part of a superior race."

"It's not over yet," Emma said.

"Japan?"

"No, I mean in this country."

Annie rested her head on her friend's shoulder. "You're right. That's a whole other battle."

"Ready about!" Bethany called from the cockpit. The boat settled on the new tack, heading back toward the inlet.

# CHAPTER FIFTY-TWO

*Skeeter's Fish Camp, FL*
*May 18, 1945*

The sounds of celebration drifted down from the main house, Hilda's laughter mixing with Woody's harmonica and Skeeter's voice telling some story that had Bethany in stitches. Through the kitchen window, Annie could see them gathered around the table, probably working their way through the bottle of red wine Hilda had produced for the occasion.

"You don't want to go back in?" Emma asked as they settled into the boat's cockpit, a thermos of coffee between them and an old quilt wrapped around their shoulders.

"Not yet." Annie tipped her head back to study the stars beginning to appear in the darkening sky. "I've missed this. Just sitting on the water, watching the night."

The lagoon was mirror-still, reflecting the first stars like scattered diamonds. A fish jumped somewhere in the darkness.

“Remember our patrol nights?” Emma asked. “Sitting out here in the cockpit watching for German U-boats?”

“And arguing about everything.” Annie smiled at the memory. “Those nights when we’d see something on the horizon and couldn’t tell if it was a fishing boat or a periscope.”

“I still dream about those days. And before the war. About Jack.”

Annie’s chest tightened. Jack. “He would have made such a great pilot.”

“No would have. He was a good man. I was lucky to have him for the little time I did.” Emma’s voice carried the weight of old grief. “I loved him so much. Real deep down to the bone love.”

“I know you did.”

“Sometimes I wonder what would have happened if things had been different. If we’d been the same color, or lived somewhere else, or if the war had never come.” Emma sipped her coffee. “Stupid things to wonder about.”

“Not stupid. Human.”

Above them, the Milky Way spread across the night sky, and Annie picked out the constellations Emma had taught her.

“You ever think about getting married?” Emma asked.

“Hmm. Now there’s a question. I don’t know what I think about it.”

“I mean what about the idea of marriage? Kids, house with a white picket fence, all that. We’re taught that’s the dream.”

Annie considered the question. “Before the war, maybe. Teenage dreams. Now it seems naive. Like playing house when you’re five years old.”

“Maybe naive isn’t wrong. Maybe simple is what we need after all this complexity.”

"What about you, Em? Think you'll ever fall in love again and get married?"

"Me? Heavens, no. Jack was the one for me." She reached for her neckline and pulled out a silver chain. On it was the child's ring with a glass gem, the sort of thing one could buy at a five and dime. "Remember this ring? Jack gave it to me at the train station the day he left. We considered ourselves bound to one another." She chuckled.

Annie looked at her friend's face, her taut lips and dimpled chin, as she struggled against that laugh turning to tears.

"Now," Emma said, "math is my passion." She leaned back, resting her elbows on the cockpit combing. "Just look at that sky. I used to feel afraid thinking about what a tiny speck I am in this vast universe. Now math helps me to make sense of it, to see the beauty in it all."

From the house drifted the strains of Woody's harmonica playing something slow and mournful, one of those blues tunes he'd learned in his Army days. The music floated across the water, mixing with the gentle lap of waves against the hull.

"I should probably head to bed soon," Emma said. "Got to catch my ride early tomorrow."

They sat a while in comfortable silence. Annie felt the tension of the past months seeping out of her shoulders. This was what she'd missed most about home—not just the place, but the peace.

A sound made her lift her head. Footsteps on the wooden dock, with an odd rhythm that made the dock planks creak in an uneven pattern.

"Someone's coming," Emma whispered.

Annie peered around the cabin, trying to make out the approaching figure in the darkness. The figure was still in shadow. Medium height, shuffling, something wrong with his gait.

The footsteps stopped at the edge of the light. For a moment, he seemed to hesitate, as if gathering courage.

The man standing on the dock was a stranger and yet familiar. He stepped forward, favoring his left leg, leaning on a walking stick carved from driftwood.

"Finn?"

He stepped closer to the boat, moving into the full light. His eyes were the same, but set deeper in his skull, surrounded by lines that hadn't been there two years ago. He wore civilian clothes, jeans and a green shirt that hung loose on his slender frame. When he tried to smile, she could see the effort it cost him.

"Hello, Annie."

She froze, unable to speak. After imagining this moment so many times, she couldn't comprehend that it was real.

Emma jumped up. "Finn Taggart, you're a sight for sore eyes!" She stepped onto the dock and embraced him. "We've been so worried. Welcome home."

"Emma." He hugged her back, his movements stiff but genuine. "You look wonderful. Both of you do."

"I'll leave you two to catch up," Emma said. "I'm exhausted anyway, and I want to get an early start tomorrow." She reached back and squeezed Annie's hand. "Be gentle."

Emma's footsteps faded up the dock, leaving Annie and Finn alone. He stood at the boat's edge, wanting to come aboard but uncertain of his welcome.

"Permission to come aboard?" His voice still held the gentle humor she remembered.

Whatever had been holding her back broke, and she found her voice.

"Always."

Finn gripped the lifeline with his free hand, his walking

stick clutched in the other, calculating the step from dock to cockpit. What should have been a simple movement had become a complex problem of balance and timing. Annie rose to help him, but something in his expression stopped her.

He needed to do this himself.

Finn shifted his weight, testing his bad leg, then stepped over the toe rail onto the deck. His stick caught momentarily on the lifeline, and for a second Annie thought he might fall. But he recovered, settling onto the cockpit bench with a grimace of pain.

"Thanks," he said, though she hadn't done anything. He leaned the walking stick against the cabin side and looked around the familiar cockpit. "She looks good. Better than when I left."

"Bethany's been taking care of her. Your sister's become quite the sailor."

"I heard." Finn's smile seemed more natural now. "Your pa wrote to me a few times. Before..." He gestured at his leg. "Before this happened."

An uncomfortable silence stretched between them.

"You look..." Annie struggled for words. "Different. Older."

"And tired," he admitted. "Soul deep tired. But I'm here."

They sat in awkward silence again, two people who'd once known each other completely.

"You look different too," he said. "More grown-up, serious, maybe."

"I just feel old." Annie pulled the quilt around her shoulders. "Feels like I've aged a decade in two years."

"Want to tell me about it?"

"I wrote it all in letters."

"I want to hear you tell me."

So she did. Washington, the Map Service, the endless hours bent over drafting tables creating charts for battles she'd never see. Paris and the hunt for German intelligence. Frankfurt and the last discovery that had made the entire mission worthwhile.

"Sounds like hard work," Finn said when she finished.

"It was. Is. Major Hough wants me to join a peacetime project, now. Mapping the world."

She looked up at the stars. "And you?"

Finn was quiet for a long moment. When he spoke, his voice was careful, controlled. "I was captured three days after my last letter to you. We were running a night patrol near Bougainville, got surprised by a Japanese destroyer that had been hiding from our radar behind an island."

Annie listened without interrupting as he described the attack. The PT boat's desperate run for shallow water, the shells falling around them like deadly rain, the moment when a direct hit tore the boat apart and threw him into black water filled with burning gasoline.

"I woke up on a beach with my leg torn up and three Japanese soldiers standing over me. Two of the other guys from my boat were there too, but they died the first week in the camp. Infections." His voice remained matter of fact. "The Japanese wanted information about our patrols, our bases, radio codes. They were... persistent."

Annie gripped the quilt. She didn't need details to understand what "persistent" meant.

"They moved us around a lot. Different camps, different islands. Always hungry, always sick. Wondering if today was the day they'd decide we weren't worth the rice anymore." He flexed his left hand, and Annie noticed the irregular way his fingers moved. "The interrogation sessions were the worst. They had ways of making you think you were going to tell them everything, even when you knew you couldn't."

"And you didn't?"

"No. Funny thing about pain. After a while, it becomes

just another thing happening to someone else. You learn to go somewhere else in your head." He looked into her eyes for the first time since starting the story.

Annie felt tears threatening. The boy she'd fallen in love with had always been gentle, thoughtful, someone who worried about hurting fish when he removed hooks. What had they done to him to make his voice so cold when he talked about torture?

"How did you get out?"

"Dumb luck. They moved us to a new camp in the Philippines last fall, smaller place, fewer guards. One night during a cyclone, a tree fell on the fence. I crawled through and kept crawling for three days."

He described those three days: hiding in jungle so thick he couldn't see the sky, eating insects and drinking rainwater, his injured leg screaming with every movement. How he'd built a crude raft from bamboo and palm fronds, following the coast until he spotted American landing craft.

"The Marines who found me thought I was dead at first. Couldn't blame them. I looked like hell, couldn't talk after months of not speaking." He touched his throat self-consciously. "Took a while to convince them I was one of the good guys."

"When was this?"

"Late February. Spent over a month in a Navy hospital in Manila, another month in Hawaii. They wanted to keep me longer, but I told them I had somewhere I needed to be."

Annie studied his profile in the darkness. "Are you okay?"

Finn tilted his head to one side while he considered the question. "Some days are better than others. The leg will never be right—too much damage to the bone. I get nightmares sometimes. Wake up thinking I'm still in that camp. But I'm alive, and I'm home, and that's more than a lot of guys got."

His matter-of-fact acceptance reminded her of Emma.

"What will you do now?" Annie asked.

Finn was quiet for a long moment, staring out at the dark water. "Learn to be a civilian again, I guess. The Navy's offered me a disability pension. Not much, but enough to get by while I figure things out." He flexed his left hand. "Can't do much physical labor anymore, not the way I used to. But a fellow in the hospital in Hawaii told me about correspondence courses in naval architecture. Yacht design. Place called Westlawn."

"Naval architecture." Annie felt something shift in her chest. "You'd be designing boats?"

"Dreaming, more like. But I figure I could study while working in a shipyard somewhere. Drafting, maybe. Start small." He glanced at her. "What about you? This mapping project you mentioned?"

"It's with the Army Map Service. Peacetime project. The goal is to create a geodetic network, or datum covering Europe first, then the entire world. A standardized system for the entire globe using all the geodetic data we collected and more, creating accurate charts for aviation, shipping routes, to be ready if..." She trailed off, realizing she was talking too fast, saying too much. "Anyway, the work would be based in Washington, DC."

"Washington."

"For years. Maybe decades of work."

The silence stretched between them. A fish jumped. The notes from Woody's harmonica drifted across the water.

"You should do it," Finn said.

Annie turned to look at him. "What?"

"The mapping project. You should take the job, Annie." His voice was steady, certain. "That's what you're meant to do, isn't it? Not just making charts—making something that matters. Exploring the world, even if you're doing it from a drafting table in DC."

"Finn..." She wanted the job, but she wanted Finn, too.

"Annie, I spent a lot of time thinking in that camp. About what I wanted to say if I ever made it home." He shifted on the bench to face her more fully. "The old me would have told you to stay. Would have been scared you'd leave and forget about me. Would have tried to hold on so tight, I'd have crushed what we have."

His hand found hers in the darkness.

"But I'm not that boy anymore. And you're not that girl who wanted everything to go back to the way it was." He squeezed her fingers. "You know what kept me alive? Knowing you were out there becoming exactly who you were meant to be. Every day I thought: Annie's still fighting. Still finding her way. I can't give up if she hasn't."

Annie felt tears threatening. "I looked for you everywhere."

"I know. Your pa told me." Finn's thumb traced across her knuckles. "And now you found me. So here we are. Both of us different. Both of us with dreams that might take us somewhere other than Skeeter's Fish Camp."

"You're saying we should just... what? Go our separate ways?"

"No," he said. "God, no. I'm saying we should both go forward. You to Washington, me to... wherever makes sense for learning boat design. There are boatyards all up and down the Chesapeake. I could find work, take those courses, learn the trade."

"The Chesapeake." Annie's mind was already making connections. "That's close to Washington."

"Indeed it is." Finn smiled. "Might even be the same city, if I'm lucky. Lots of boats in DC."

"Lots of maps, too."

They sat with that for a moment, the possibility hanging between them.

"I can't make you promises right now." Finn reached out and smoothed a strand of hair back above her ear. "Can't promise I won't wake up screaming. Can't promise this leg will ever be right, or that I'll ever be the man I was before."

"I don't want the man you were before," Annie said. "I want the man you are now. The one who survived. The one who's brave enough to tell me to chase my dreams instead of asking me to give them up."

"And I want this woman who's sitting next to me right now. The one who hunted Nazi maps across Germany. The one who's going to map the whole damn world." He brought her hand to his lips, kissed her knuckles. "So here's what I'm thinking. We both go do what we need to do. Build our careers. Learn our trades. Figure out who we are in this new post-war world we've got."

"And?"

"And we write letters. Visit when we can. See if this thing between us is strong enough to survive time and distance and change."

"We've already survived years of war."

"Then maybe we can survive this too." Finn's voice grew softer. "Because I love you, Annie Jeeves. I loved you when we were kids racing through the palmetto scrub, and I loved you every day in that camp when remembering your face was the only thing that felt real. And I'll love you if it takes me five years to get my life together enough to ask you properly."

"Ask me what?"

He smiled. "You know what. But I'm not asking tonight. Not like this, when I've got nothing to offer but a broken body and big dreams."

"Finn—"

"Let me do this right." His hand cupped her face. "Let me

become someone worth asking. Let you become whoever you're meant to be. And then, if we still want this, if we still fit together after all that growing, then I'll ask you properly. With a ring and everything."

Annie felt tears slide down her cheeks. "You're an idiot if you think I need you to be anything other than exactly who you are."

"Maybe. But *I* need it." He brushed away her tears with his thumb. "I need to know I can stand on my own two feet. Well, one and a half feet—before I ask you to stand beside me."

"So we're doing this? Both chasing our dreams and seeing if we end up in the same place?"

"If you'll have me. On those terms."

Annie thought of the project with the Geodetic Division of the AMS, of the years of work ahead. Of the woman she'd become in Europe, who'd traced geodetic data across bombed-out cities. That woman didn't need to choose between love and ambition. She could have both. She could build both.

"I'll have you," she said. "On those terms and any others. But I'm not waiting five years for you to feel worthy enough. You hear me, Finn Taggart? You're already worthy."

"Then we have a deal." He smiled. "Partners. Building our lives. Seeing where they intersect."

"Partners," Annie agreed.

When he kissed her, it was different from their tentative goodbye before he went off to the Navy. This kiss held the weight of everything they'd survived, everything they'd lost, everything they might still find. It tasted of hope and uncertainty and the courage to face both.

When they broke apart, Finn rested his forehead against hers. "I'm home," he whispered. "Finally, home."

Annie reached for the compass rose pendant at her throat. "We both are."

They sat in comfortable silence, the lagoon stretching dark and quiet around them. Inside the house, Woody's harmonica played something slow and sweet. Tomorrow she'd wire Major Hough and accept the position.

Above them, the constellations wheeled across the sky. Cassiopeia, Ursa Minor, Orion. Emma had taught her those constellations years ago, on nights that felt like a lifetime past. Back then, Annie had thought navigation was about finding your way home.

Now she understood it was about finding your way forward.

THE END

# AUTHOR'S NOTE

*Whiskey Creek* is Book 1 of the *Florida Chronicles*, a trilogy tracing the stories of three generations of women. This first installment focuses on the generation born around the same time as my mother—those who came of age and entered their twenties during the tumultuous years of World War II.

Like most historical novels, *Whiskey Creek* is inspired by real events, though the primary characters are figments of my imagination. While I have tried to render the period as accurately as possible, I have occasionally taken liberties with the facts in service of the narrative.

Having spent much of my life sailing and living aboard boats, I sought a nautical angle for this history. I found it in the stories of American civilians who volunteered to patrol our coastlines immediately after Pearl Harbor. At that time, the Navy and Coast Guard lacked the vessels to meet the growing threat of German U-boats. These volunteers were known as the Picket Patrol, the "Hooligan's Navy," or, in Florida, the "Mosquito Fleet." While I never found a specific record of a female volunteer, I chose to exercise the novelist's prerogative to imagine one.

As I researched Fort Lauderdale in the late 1930s and early 1940s, it became clear that I could not tell Annie's story without acknowledging the lives of the city's Black residents. Once Emma's character was created, she took on a far more significant role than I had initially envisioned. Her journey was inspired by the real Black women code breakers at Arlington Hall, a segregated unit whose vital work helped win the war under the supervision of William Coffee.

Many of the settings in this book—The Deck Restaurant, Ivy Stranahan's home, Merl Fogg Airfield, and Whiskey Creek—are real Florida landmarks. Similarly, some of the figures are drawn from history. Sheriff Walter Clark, who held office almost continuously from 1931 to 1950, was a notoriously corrupt and racist individual involved in the gambling and liquor trades. Cap Knight was also a real, colorful character who transitioned from fisherman to rum runner to gambling house owner.

Once I decided that Annie's expertise would lie in navigation, I discovered the "3-Ms," or the **Military Mapping Maidens**. These young women, recruited from universities nationwide, produced tens of thousands of maps essential to the war effort. I have tried to present their history as faithfully as possible.

The area where I took the most artistic license is in the description of **Operation Pastorius**. This mission did occur: four German spies landed via U-boat at Ponte Vedra Beach on June 17, 1942, carrying explosives and incendiaries intended to sabotage American defense production. Four others landed on Long Island. One of the New York-based spies eventually surrendered and identified all the others, ending the mission within two weeks. Of the eight spies, six were executed, and two were imprisoned until their return to Germany in 1948.

The inclusion of midget submarines was inspired by

readers of my blog. Friends who lived in Florida at the time shared memories of seeing these "mini-subs" washing up or being towed to shore. Although the Germans did not develop the specific models described in this book until 1944, I found the imagery too compelling to omit, and I moved their arrival up to 1942 for the sake of the story.

Finally, my research into the importance of cartography led me to Greg Miller's article in the November 2019 issue of ***Smithsonian Magazine***, "The Untold Story of the Secret Mission to Seize Nazi Map Data." The article featured a photograph of the roster for Major Floyd Hough's team, with two WACs (Women's Army Corps) listed at the very bottom.

I decided my Annie would be one of them.

# THANK YOU!

Thank you for purchasing and reading ***WHISKEY CREEK.*** I hope you enjoyed it.

Reviews help other readers find books they might enjoy. If you feel like writing an honest review and posting it on Amazon, Goodreads, or on whatever platform you used to purchase the book, I would be most appreciative!

Would you like to know when my next book will be available? Sign up for my Sailingwriter newsletter to read about my adventures as a writer/digital nomad who is currently traveling around North America in a converted ambulance named LANCE. As thanks, I will send you a link to download a free copy of my short story collection, *Inklings*.

Newsletter: https://sailingwriter.com

# ALSO BY CHRISTINE KLING

The South Florida Adventures series:

Surface Tension

Cross Current

Bitter End

Wreckers' Key

Mourning Tide

The Shipwreck Adventures series:

Circle of Bones

Dragon's Triangle

Knight's Cross

# ACKNOWLEDGMENTS

I would like to thank the following people and or sources who helped me during the course of writing *Whiskey Creek*:

My developmental editor, The Gentlepen, https://www.thegentlepen.com/

My beta readers, copy editors, and proofreaders: Barbara Lichter, Mary Jastrzebski, Kathleen Ginestra, Cynthia Smith Park.

Joan Mickelson, author and historian from Hollywood, FL who also told me the story of seeing a German mini-sub washed up on Hollywood Beach during the war and was an enormous help with local history and editing.

Patricia Moss, of Miami who wrote me that her father found a German mini-sub while fishing and towed it onto Miami Beach where it was soon impounded by military security.

For more information on German midget subs: https://uboat.net/fates/midget.htm

Emmanuel A. George, Curator and Community Liaison at the Old Dillard Museum

Emily Calderon, Special Collections Librarian, African American Research Library and Cultural Center

Broward County Digital Archives: Oral History Interviews by Kitty Oliver

Sources about U-boats off the American coast:
*Operation Drumbeat*, by Michael Gannon
*The Seas That Mourn*, Patrick D. Smith

Sources about the lives of black residents in Florida in the 1940's:
*My Soul is a Witness: A History of Black Fort Lauderdale*, Deborah Work
*Pearl City, Florida: A Black Community Remembers*, Arthur S. Evans and David Lee

Source about the Black women cryptologists:
*The Invisible Crytologists: African-Americans, WWII to 1956*, Jeannette Williams with Yolande Dickerson

Fiction about the American Homefront in WWII:
*The Physicist's Daughter*, Mary Anna Evans
*The Last Thing You Surrender*, Leonard Pitts, Jr.
*December '41*, William Martin
*The Keeper's Son*, Homer Hickam
*Radar Girls*, Sara Ackerman (several more titles set in Hawaii)
*The Women of Arlington Hall*, Jane Healy

## ABOUT THE AUTHOR

Christine Kling has spent more than thirty years messing about with boats, and she now writes nautical fiction. As a full-time writer and nomad, she is traveling the world aboard planes, trains, boats and various recreational vehicles with her husband and two pups, Razz and Zoë. Find out how to follow her books and adventures at christinekling.com.

www.ingramcontent.com/pod-product-compliance
Lightning Source LLC
Chambersburg PA
CBHW071957110726
47910CB00005B/1559
*9780991050871*